REBECCA WEST was born Ci̲____ London in 1892. She adopted the n____ the strong-willed character of that____ drama, *Rosmersholm*. She began t____ journalist and political writer in London as early as 1911, in *The Freewoman*, and was soon deeply involved in the causes of feminism and social reform. Her only child, Anthony West (b. 1914), is the son of the novelist H. G. Wells. In 1930 she married Henry Maxwell Andrews, a banker, with whom, until his death in 1968, she shared a country estate in Buckinghamshire, social activities in London and extensive travels abroad. It was after their journey through Yugoslavia just before the war that she wrote perhaps her most famous work, *Black Lamb and Grey Falcon* (1937). She was created Dame Commander of the British Empire in 1959 and died in 1983.

Rebecca West wrote fiction, journalism, criticism, essays, biography, history, travel and satire. Her fiction includes *The Return of the Soldier* (1918), *The Judge* (1922), *Harriet Hume: A London Fantasy* (1929), *The Harsh Voice* (1935), *The Thinking Reed* (1936), *The Fountain Overflows* (1956), *The Birds Fall Down* (1966), *This Real Night* (1984) and *Sunflower* (1986). Other important works include *The Strange Necessity* (1928), *The Meaning of Treason* (1949) and *A Train of Powder* (1955). Some of her early writings (1911–1917) have been collected into one volume, *The Young Rebecca* (1983). All these fictional works and five works of non-fiction, including her memoir *Family Memories*, are published by Virago. In forthcoming years Virago will be editing and issuing Rebecca West's other unpublished writings.

REBECCA WEST

THE
STRANGE
NECESSITY

ESSAYS AND REVIEWS

WITH A NEW INTRODUCTION BY
G. EVELYN HUTCHINSON

Published by VIRAGO PRESS Limited 1987
41 William IV Street, London WC2N 4DB

First published in Great Britain by Jonathan Cape Ltd 1928

Introduction copyright © G. Evelyn Hutchinson 1987

British Library Cataloguing in Publication Data
West, Rebecca
  The strange necessity.
  1. English Literature — 20th century
  — History and criticism
  Rn: Cicely Fairfield Andrews   I. Title
  820.9'00912   PR471

ISBN 0-86068-507-4

Printed in Great Britain by
Anchor Brendon, Tiptree, Essex

TABLE OF CONTENTS

	INTRODUCTION	vii
I	THE STRANGE NECESSITY	13
II	UNCLE BENNETT	199
III	THE CLASSIC ARTIST	215
IV	GALLIONS REACH	229
V	TWO KINDS OF MEMORY	243
VI	THE LONG CHAIN OF CRITICISM	257
VII	SINCLAIR LEWIS INTRODUCES ELMER GANTRY	269
VIII	SHERWOOD ANDERSON, POET	281
IX	BATTLEFIELD AND SKY	291
X	WHAT IS THIS OTHER CONTINENT?	303
XI	THE TOSH HORSE	319
XII	TRIBUTE TO SOME MINOR ARTISTS	327

INTRODUCTION

The principal study, originally called *A Hypothesis*, which makes up rather over one half of this book, is an informal and very personal treatise on aesthetics. It illuminates everything else that Rebecca West has written and as her most intellectually challenging work aids greatly in any perspicacious and penetrating study of what she has done.

The essay is written contrapuntally, the two main themes being derived from James Joyce's *Ulysses* and from Ivan Petrovitch Pavlov's *Conditioned Reflexes*. The conjunction of these two books may seem odd to today's reader but would have appeared more natural in the middle 1920s when *The Strange Necessity* was being written and when both Joyce and Pavlov were very widely discussed in the intellectual world.

We first encounter the author in Paris, walking from the Odéon towards the Boulevard St Germain. She will soon be enjoying herself ordering three hats from a favourite milliner and buying a black lace dress. She has just closed the door of Sylvia Beach's bookshop, where she has acquired a copy of Joyce's *Pomes Penyeach*. She stops in the street to open the book and immediately starts wondering why the unmistakable badness of the poem she is reading should give her pleasure. She thinks of Joyce's major works, recognising the extraordinary power of his prose, and at times the curious sentimentality of his verse. The pleasure in this recognition appears to come from the good work of art telling us something valid about the world, while it is hinted that under some circumstances the bad works may do likewise, indirectly, by telling us about their author and his nature as part of existence.

In Joyce's case the overall verdict must be one of genius, though never entirely unflawed. She recalls various incidents in his prose writings and particularly dwells on the feeling of peace given her by the unpunctuated forty-two pages ending *Ulysses*, the rhapsodic monologue of Marion Bloom 'from meeting any of whose equivalents in the real world may the merciful Powers preserve me'. She now starts considering her plans for the next day, for a time her last in Paris, debating with herself whether she should go to Versailles or should stay in Paris with time to visit the Louvre to enjoy the peace that she would get from a picture of a young man wearing a snuff-coloured coat. She starts wondering why any things so utterly unlike as Marion Bloom and Ingre's picture could create comparable and very important effects in her mind. 'What is the meaning of this mystery of mysteries? Why does art matter? And why does it matter so much? What is this strange necessity?'

As the essay proceeds, she thinks of Pavlov. Quite significantly she had come across his book, so insistent on determinism in the neural physiology of learning, after an afternoon spent against her will in the Casino at Monte Carlo. Here she says she had been made to suffer by exposure to an environment from which she can learn nothing. She has a correct intuition that series of random numbers are useful in some kinds of scientific research, though she wrongly believes the roulette wheels to operate too slowly to produce anything of real value. She discusses a childhood confusion between the Casino at Monte Carlo and the Abbey of Monte Cassino, though the poignancy of the confusion would not be apparent for nearly a couple of decades. She reports no beautiful naked showgirls who in some such places may set a lovely living symmetry against the obsessional stochastic anxiety of the 'old ladies in funny hats . . . who sit and write figures in their little exercise books as if they were children who must do their lessons.' Relief rather is given to her by Pavlov's book, though she does not say exactly how the book came to her that evening at the right time and in the right circumstances. From it she concluded that Pavlov's whole approach provides not only a series of interesting facts related to the processes of learning by association but also a hint of a general theory of human understanding. In such a theory a system is built up partly as science and partly as art to fulfil a role comparable to that of the cerebral cortex, the outer layer of the brain that Pavlov believed, largely correctly, to be responsible for most of our higher learning, even though we know now that such activities depend also on the integrity of various deeper parts of the brain. The social result of this is the elaboration of a system in which art and science are carried on by innumerable individual human beings, each with its own learning mechanism selecting 'out of the whole complexity of the universe those units that are of significance to the organism'. Anything that is of value in living will tend to persist and be cultivated if it gives pleasure as art and science do. She is well aware that her hypothesis of our higher activities forming a sort of social supercortex requires much further examination. How it may apply to the plastic arts and music is less obvious than its application to literature and science. She believes that this application to painting and music is intuitively correct but only appreciated as a non-verbal experience.

Though her ideas hardly give a complete account of aesthetics, she felt strongly that they underlay her own activity as a literary artist. Twelve years later in *Black Lamb and Grey Falcon,* she describes her own aim in writing in the very terms of her theoretical point of view. 'I have never used my writing to make a continuous disclosure of my personality to others but to discover for my own edification what I knew about various subjects which I found to be of importance to me; and that in consequence I had written a novel about London to find out why I loved it, a life of St Augustine to find out why every phrase I read of his sounds in my ears like the sentence of my doom and

THE STRANGE NECESSITY

the doom of my age, and a novel about rich people to find out why they seemed to me to be as dangerous as wild boars and pythons.'

Since what she found to be of importance to herself is likely to be significant to other sensitive intelligent people, the exploratory aspects of art are likely to be of general importance, so that the whole process becomes social. She considers a number of situations in which these social aspects are paramount. In some of these the details are topical and may appear at best as merely picturesque, as in the treatment of the horse as a symbiont on society in early twentieth-century British India or Ireland. Perhaps the most interesting example that she gives concerns the role of popular religion as an art form in Italy, in which she sees a stabilising force that tends to disappear among immigrants in America. Though in retrospect this example may appear to tell but part of the story, her treatment of it is of great interest in relation to the rise and fall of Mussolini. This kind of interaction between art and life is broadly what all her writing considers, justifying the very low barrier that she sometimes uses in separating the fictional from the historic. In the end she sees in the whole production and appreciation of art a process that made her go on living. In this her conclusion is like Professor L. B. Slobodkin's description of evolution as an existential game, a game in which evolutionary change gives a continually renewed capacity for living in a constantly changing

xi

world. More life is the prize one receives for living wisely and imaginatively.

The other eleven essays of the volume are varied pieces of literary criticism. The first one, 'Uncle Bennett', is of some importance as a picture of certain aspects of the British literary scene in the first third of the century, containing a short but very interesting judgment on H. G. Wells. In other essays on English and American writers, Sacheverell Sitwell is ingeniously if a little harshly contrasted with Thomas Hardy, both coming out about equal but neither with top marks. Even more surprisingly but more truly, she contrasts Sinclair Lewis, to his great disadvantage, with the enchanting actress and pianist Yvonne Printemps, whose memory some of us have treasured for more than half a century. All the other essays contain other comparable delights. As we near the end, a study of Miss Ethel M. Dell introduces us to the 'thudding, thundering hooves of a certain steed at full gallop . . . the true Tosh-horse'. The book concludes with a rather puzzling but beautiful piece called a 'Tribute to Some Minor Artists.' Ever since my late wife introduced me to Rebecca West's works in the 1930s, this book has provided me with immense and continuous pleasure. I hope it can now start doing so, for another half century or more, to a new public.

G. Evelyn Hutchinson, New Haven, Connecticut, 1987

I

I SHUT the bookshop door behind me and walked slowly down the street that leads from the Odéon to the Boulevard St. Germain in the best of all cities, reading in the little volume which had there been sold to me, not exactly pretentiously, indeed with a matter-of-fact briskness, yet with a sense of there being something on hand different from an ordinary commercial transaction: as they sell pious whatnots in a cathedral porch. Presently I stopped. I said 'Ah!' and smiled up into the clean French light. My eye lit on a dove that was bridging the tall houses by its flight, and I felt that interior agreement with its grace, that delighted participation in its experience, which is only possible when one is in a state of pleasure.

I was pleased by a poem that I had just read; the following poem:

ALONE

The moon's grey-golden meshes make
  All night a veil,
The shore lamps on the sleeping lake
  Laburnum tendrils trail.

The shy reeds whisper to the night
A name — her name —
And all my soul is a delight,
  A swoon of shame.

It may seem inconceivable that this poem should

bring pleasure to any living creature, for as art is in part at least a matter of the communication to the audience of an emotion felt by an artist, this is plainly an exceedingly bad poem. 'And all my soul is a delight, a swoon of shame' are words as blank as the back of a spoon. Nevertheless this poem gave me great pleasure, because I had considered it in the light of its authorship. For it is not the words to a song, it is not by Mr. Fred E. Weatherley. It is not by Miss Helen Wills, whose sole poetical production (published, I think, in *Vanity Fair*) it very closely resembles. It is, on the contrary, as one might say, by Mr. James Joyce. It is one of the poems, and not noticeably the worst, included in the collection he has called *Pomes Penyeach*. And because he has written it I was pleased, though not at all as the mean are when they find that the mighty have fallen, for had he written three hundred poems as bad as this his prose works would still prove him beyond argument a writer of majestic genius. Indeed, the pleasure I was feeling was not at all dependent on what my conception of Mr. James Joyce is: it was derived from the fact that, very much more definitely than five minutes before I had a conception of Mr. James Joyce. Suspicions had been confirmed. What was cloudy was now solid. In those eight lines he had ceased to belong to that vast army of our enemies, the facts we do not comprehend; he had passed over and become one of our friends, one of those who have yielded up an account of their nature, who do not keep back a secret which one day may act like a bomb on such theory of the universe as we may have built for our defence.

For really, I reflected, as I went on my way down the Street of the Seine, this makes it quite plain that Mr. James Joyce is a great man who is entirely without taste. So much is proved by the preservation of this poem against considerable odds, for it was written at Zurich in 1916, and there was the removal to Paris, there were eleven years, there was space and there was time, in which to lose it. And lack of taste, when one comes to turn over the handicap he has laid on his genius, is the source of nearly all of them. It explains, for example, the gross sentimentality which is his most fundamental error. What do I mean by sentimentality? I had to think. There appeared before my eyes another part of France, the Provençal village where I spend my summers, the crook in the high street where the men sit at little tables with heads bent sideways and downwards as if they all had stiff necks, watching the game of *boules* that incredibly goes on, parting and reassembling as the automobiles fly past, in the puddle-pocked, wheel-harassed roads. It is not a likeable game. It brings two kinds of unpleasantness to the ear, for when the *boules* meet the spurting sound of their impact is like an exchange of rude remarks, and when they meet only with a little force, as must often happen in a game played on such a surface, that sound has the futile quality of feeble rudeness, of failure in an enterprise where even success would have meant nothing pleasant. And there comes from the onlookers never that tense yet languid cry, only a little more than a deep breath, which tells that a crowd is participating through attention in the deep peace of a beautiful movement: instead came

praising, blaming 'Ohs!' and 'Ahs!' which show that
they are not resting, that in this pastime there has not
been lifted from them the human burden of discrimination and calculation, that load of pricking
needles. It is, therefore, better as one passes to raise
one's eyes to the great umbrella pine which is the
steady roof to all the squint-sitting people, making
out of a hundred branches, a million twigs, a form as
single as a raindrop, casting a shadow as of an un-
divided substance. It had seemed to me that the men
squatting at their *boules* were like the sentimental
artist, that the pine-tree was like the non-sentimental
artist.

For the non-sentimental artist has an intention of
writing a book on a theme which is as determined
and exclusive as the tree's intention of becoming a
tree, and by passing all his material through his
imagination and there experiencing it, he achieves
the same identity with what he makes as the growing
tree does. Now neither tree nor artist has eyes, neither
has ears, neither is intelligent: simply they are becoming what they make. The writer puts out his force and
it becomes a phase of his story, as the tree puts out
its force and makes a branch. Both know how much
force to put out, and where next to reassert it, because having achieved this identification with their
creation they would feel a faulty distribution of
balance as one would a withered limb. Since that
which was made first wandered in the path of its
making, as things created from the real elements do,
like veins and rivers, the second exercise of force
cannot be arranged according to a mechanical symmetry, but must balance irregularity with irregular-

ity, and again the artist who has identified himself with his theme feels this as almost automatic an adjustment as a movement of his own body. In *La Princesse de Clèves*, in *Adolphe*, in the pages of Stendhal, there is established a perfect equilibrium, there are no patches or pages or chapters that are notably better or worse than the rest (though there are, of course, climaxes dictated by the theme); there is no character which is not displayed in the right extent of space with the right degree of emphasis, because each writer has passed the theme and its characters through the imagination and knows the value of each character as one knows the weight of an object one has held in one's hand; there is no part which rebels against the whole, there is the peace of unity.

But the sentimental artist is becoming nothing, he has ears, he has eyes, he is being intelligent, he is playing a game, he is moving certain objects according to certain rules in front of spectators. Those objects one may take as the isolated units of his material which he has passed through his imagination by an unfortunately discontinuous process. He sees that one of those objects occupies a certain position on the ground, and knows that he will score a point if he can remove it to another position; he therefore sends another of these objects rolling along to displace it. *Shock* . . . one hears that ugly sound. Often one hears it in the uglier form produced by weak impact, for this method presents more hazards than real creative writing. To communicate one's experience to an audience is no trouble to an artist, since in point of fact giving formal expression to a work of art is to interpret one's experience to oneself, so that one merely permits the audience to look over one's shoulder. But to condition the expression of one's experience out of regard for the effect on one's audience's mind is to bring into the artistic process a factor so little of a constant, since that mind is perpetually changing according to the social and intellectual movements of the time, and one's understanding of it is as unstable, that it is comparable to playing bowls on a highroad.

Now one hears that *shock* very often in modern literature, in the writings of persons who have practised some revolutionary austerity regarding the superficialities of writing and feel, therefore, having a streak of Puritan optimism in them, that they must thereby have bought salvation. Mr. Arnold Bennett feels he has ranked himself for ever as a dry wine by what he mixed with himself of Maupassant; nevertheless he has put on the market some grocer's Sauterne in the form of several novels that are highly sentimental so far as their fundamental balance of values is concerned. There is, for example, *The Pretty Lady*, in which there is an antithesis between a society woman and a prostitute, which is as wooden and made for a purpose as a clothes-horse. It is more than doubtful if a theme which presents itself to a writer in the form of a contrast can ever be the occasion of great art. To say 'I am going to write a book about the contrast between two characters,' instead of saying, 'I am going to write a book about two characters,' is like saying, 'I am going to write a beautiful book,' for both beauty and contrast lie in the eye of the beholder. If one writes to create these

effects, instead of to render an account of the values
these characters have in relation to one's theme, one
will be constantly tampering with one's imaginative
knowledge of them to prove one's point. Anyway, in
The Pretty Lady facts regarding the prostitute are
rolled into position; other facts regarding the prostitute are rolled along to impact with them. *Shock.*
In Katherine Mansfield's *Miss Brill* facts regarding
the old maid with her pink nose pinched by her
personal winter are rolled into position; towards
them are rolled facts regarding the young and their
brutal personal spring. *Shock.* Far too volitional the
impact to excite pity. We refuse to join in the game;
we suspect Katherine Mansfield as we do Charles
Dickens when Little Nell is dying, and we feel that
he relishes our tears as he would a kipper to his tea,
and realize that if the logic of the book's being suddenly demanded an eleventh-hour recovery he would
have hit the child on the head without the slightest
compunction. To these and other sentimentalities
Katherine Mansfield was decoyed by her knowledge
that her attempts at Tchekovian directness and
purity had been successful so far as an austerity of
diction and economy of material and means were
concerned. She could turn a coach-and-four in the
smallest attic, she could make the coach-and-four of
a pumpkin and white mice, of a disappointment and
dull people; and she took that partial victory for the
entire triumph, which was indeed hers in *Prelude*
and *At the Bay*, which are Tchekovian in spirit as
well as in ingredient. She could not believe that
though she had removed her sentence so far from
Charles Dickens she might remain quite close to him

in the matter of sentiment. Even so the young American expressionist dramatists push their methods so far past Toller that they cannot believe that their content nestles side by side with *East Lynne*. And even so James Joyce, confident in his own revolutionary quality, because his sentences wear the cap of liberty, weakens his masterpiece by executing it with hands made tremulous by the most reactionary sentimentality.

Shock. One hears the sound again and again in *Ulysses.* Seduced by his use of a heterodox technique into believing himself to be a wholly emancipated writer, James Joyce is not at all ahead of his times in his enslavement to the sentimental. That is manifest in isolated incidents. For example, the volitional character of Miss Brill is as nothing compared to that of Gerty MacDowell, the girl who sat on the beach to the detriment of Mr. Bloom's chastity. Her erotic reverie is built up with as much noisy sense of meeting a special occasion as a grand-stand for a royal procession, in order that we may be confounded by the fact of her lameness. *Shock.* But, more important still, his sentimentality deforms the conception of one of the two protagonists, and that the one which should have been presented with the most careful sincerity and grace: the young Stephen Dedalus, whose quarrel with the grossness of man's theory of living (as symbolized by the Roman Catholic Church) and the grossness of man's living (as symbolized by Leopold Bloom) is meaningless unless they are destroying in him a sincere and graceful spirit. But the young man is transparently a hero. His creator has given him eyelashes an inch long.

And how he comports himself! He rolls his eyes, he wobbles on his base with suffering, like a Guido Reni. This is partly, of course, a consequence of Mr. Joyce's habit of using his writing as a means of gratifying certain compulsions under which he labours without making the first effort towards lifting them over the threshold that divides life from art. An obvious example of this is his use of obscene words. This might be a perfectly justifiable artistic device. I would hesitate to say that some artist may not at some time find it necessary to use these Anglo-Saxon monosyllables which are in a sense so little used and in a sense so much, for the completion of some artistic pattern. But that Mr. Joyce is not this artist, that his use of obscene words is altogether outside the æsthetic process is proved by that spurt of satisfaction, more actual but also more feeble than authentic artistic emotion which marks the pages whenever he uses them. Simply he is gratifying in his maturity the desire to protest against the adult order of things by the closest possible verbal substitutes for the practical actions, originating in the zone against which adults seemed to have such a repressive prejudice, by which he could register such feelings in his infancy.

It would be odd if an infantile trait should exist in such pungency alone; and, of course, it does not. There is working here a narcissism, a compulsion to make a self-image and to make it with an eye to the approval of others, which turns Stephen Dedalus into a figure oddly familiar for the protagonist of a book supposed to be revolutionary and unique. In his monologues on æsthetics, in his unfolding of his

theory concerning Shakespeare, he enjoys the unnatural immunity from interruption that one might
encounter not in life but in a typical Freudian wish-
fulfilment dream. Buck Milligan the base, Lynch
the banal, Best and Eglinton, the vocational Dubliners, intervene not as arguers but as accompanists.
That is familiar. There is a sense of portentousness
in his dislike of his environment, as if the author
should turn his head to his audience and say in an
awe-stricken whisper, as of a curate noting that the
Bishop is not pleased, 'He does not like it'; there is a
sense of separation from the mob in all his desirable
qualities, of monopoly, of total lack of response from all
others. These too are familiar, and as features in fiction
of a not at all revolutionary sort. They are, in fact, the
constant ingredients in almost every novel in which
an Oxford or Cambridge graduate looks back on the
Oxford or Cambridge undergraduate that he was five
minutes previously and reverently commemorates
the chrysalis. Such novels are written by talent or
less, and *Ulysses* is written by genius, but there is in
both the same narcissistic inspiration, which inevitably deforms all its products with sentimentality,
since the self-image which it is the aim of narcissism to create is made not out of material that
has been imaginatively experienced but out of
material that has been selected as likely to please
others. *Shock*. Again the values have been externally
adjusted.

Now if a writer can juxtapose sentimental material
like this with material to which his imaginative
experience of it has given absolutely just values — like
the exquisitely pathetic picture of the visions of a

sweet and ordered life that sometimes come to the
squalid Dublin Jew Leopold Bloom, which is evoked
in the question-and-answer part of the book simply
by cataloguing the specifications of the little country
place of which the creature often dreams – he has
really remarkably little taste. It is as odd as if a man
who had inherited the finest diamonds in the world
should know nothing about gems and should constantly be buying worthless paste. One feels that if
he had not something more than a negative deficiency
in good taste, a real positive attribute of bad taste, he
would have learned better from his own possessions.
And it occurs to one that a person who has this
attribute is the very last person from whom one would
look for a new development in literary technique.
If he goes wrong in dealing with the content of his
work, in the emotional values, where the psychic
necessity which made him write the book is working
to make him say what he means, he is far more likely
to go wrong in dealing with its form, in which
matter the intellect, with its confounded freedom of
choice, can have its own way.

And James Joyce does go wrong. This is not to
say that he does not write beautiful prose. The description of the young man bathing in the first part of
Ulysses, blue seas engulfing clean white limbs which
because of their youth and beauty seem like the
waters, not as dense as earth, while from Buck
Milligan there come slow indolent shouts of lewdness, like the roaring of a bull far down under the
waters, far down under the earth, waiting for the
hour when it may hammer its hoofs up some high-
way into that foolish thing, so extravagantly much

less dense than earth, the light, and trample down to the earth all fair bloodless things like grass and flowers, and all things that having blood within them are disloyal to their corruptible content and seem ethereal, like these clean white limbs; the description of the Dublin summer afternoon, threaded with creeping bodies, with creeping minds, that do not know quite what they do, that do not do quite what they know, that are like ants, over which men express respectful wonder at the creative powers of nature, but on which they tread without compunction; the description of Marian Bloom, the great mother who needs not trouble to trace her descent from the primeval age whence all things come, who lies in a bed yeasty with her warmth and her sweat, and sends forth in a fountain from her strong, idealess mind thoughts of generation and recollection of sunshine, and the two are one, twisting and turning, the two are seen to be one: these are outside the sphere and beyond the power of any other writer alive or dead.

But that does not alter the fact that James Joyce is safe only when he stays within tradition: or one might say rather within a tradition, for the times when he is best able to give perfect form to his genius are when he is not trying to escape from the influence of his classical training. There are two stories in *Dubliners* which are among the most beautiful short stories that have been written in our time; and both of them guide their exquisite spirits to deliverance along a path prepared by Latin poetry. One of them is called 'A Sad Case': and it tells of an obscure middle-aged man, a cashier in a bank, a sub-intellectual, liking to be squeamish alone with his books, who some years before had made the acquaintance of a sea-captain's wife, herself not a young person either, and had broken it off because she disclosed a quiet, desperate passion for him, and such things were not in his line. On the night of which the story is written, as he takes his evening meal in an eating-house, he reads in a local newspaper a paragraph describing the woman's suicide at a level-crossing. He is stunned at first. He goes back to his little room and reads over again the report of the inquest. There is evidence that of late the dead woman had taken to intemperate habits, and at that he runs away into disgust at her. Her passion for him seems part of her looseness, he hates and repudiates her. But the room grows cold, he goes out and has a hot punch in a public-house. A feeling of loneliness comes on him. He goes out into the Park where he and she had walked four years before and is desolate. Then he hears the complaining drone of a goods train winding its way down in the valley. It seems to be saying her name. It goes on for a long time. Silence falls. The black and empty sky remains, and that is all. The human heart has achieved nothing to counter its emptiness. It is as logically impossible that an arrangement of such drab colours should be beautiful as that the sight of two sardine tins and an old boot lying on a railway embankment should make us glad, but the æsthetic process which is above logic makes them shine before us like one jewel; and the particular kind of process which organizes these colours to beauty, as the crystalline principle sees to it that the molecules of a jewel radiate colour and light instead of having the substance of bread or lead, is that which organizes the most enduring parts of Latin poetry. Through these pages, in which the suffering of the man and woman stand up in the night like the last columns of a ruined temple, exquisite and desolate integers of a final and irremediable incompleteness, there sound precisely those accents which in one's schooldays one groped for and could not find when one tried to translate the passages in the Æneid where people grieve, where they say, 'manibus date lilia plenis.' . . .

The sentences are austere in colour, they drive straight down, they bring the earth something not soothing yet a benefit, like the grey spears of rain, like the lines of Virgil.

And in the other and still more marvellous story, 'The Dead,' which is one of the few masterpieces of mysticism, it is Lucretius who is recalled. There is a fine upstanding young middle-aged man, good at slipping the right Christmas-box to Lily the caretaker's daughter as she helps him off with his coat at the old Miss Morkan's New Year dance, good at carving the goose at the sit-down supper, good at making a speech which pleases the old ladies and sets the guests singing, 'For they are jolly good fellows,' going through all these performances with just their right spice of contempt for those before whom he performs to guarantee that he should be right not only with this society but with the one above it. Throughout the evening he looks across the room at his wife, about whom there is a certain romantic distinction which marks her superior to the people about her, which makes him therefore still

more superior to them in possessing her, and rejoices
because he is going to spend the night with her, not in
their house in the Dublin suburbs, which is too well-
used by domesticity, but in an hotel near the old
ladies' house, in a strange bare room, which can be
furnished with a new and undimmed mood. It is
typical of his egotism that as he leads her along the
road he remembers tenderly passages not from the
love-letters she wrote to him, but from those he
wrote to her. But when he has her alone in the little
room she will not melt into his easy mood of voluptuousness. She turns her face away, and when he asks
her what is the matter she bursts into tears and says
that she is thinking of a song which one of the guests
had sung at the party. A boy whom she had known
in the West in her youth used to sing it to her . . . a
boy who had been in love with her . . . a boy, she
sighs at last, who is dead. He had died for love of
her, being in a decline and coming nevertheless
through the rain to a tryst in her garden. There can
be no love-making this night. Her husband lets her
sob herself to sleep, and lies awake beside her thinking with humiliation of the dead boy's love, passion
such as he had never known; and of the dead boy's
death, which also he feels to be an experience above
any that have come to his warm bustling organism.
Through the window-panes, in the light of a street
lamp, he sees the snowflakes falling. The snow will
be falling all over Ireland, on the graves of the dead,
on the houses of the living. We perceive that the
destiny of man is not comfortable, that he is born
naked and without a quilt, that his end, so far as the
farthest sight can see, is to lie in ground that is cold

enough to chill though not enough to check corruption, and we perceive also that what raises him to a dignity which enables him to return the stare of the stars without shame are precisely those discomfortable elements, and not the moments when he contrives to forget them.

These two stories by themselves should explain why we rank James Joyce as a major writer. But the uncertainty of his power over his medium is manifest when he makes use of the same tradition with equal vigour and the most fatuous results. There are two colossal finger-prints left by literary incompetence on *Ulysses* which show that a pedantic accuracy about the letter and an insensitivity about the spirit can lead him wildly astray even while he is still loyal to the classicism. It was M. Valéry Larbaud who first detected that the title of that great work was not just put in to make it more difficult, that there exists a close parallelism between the incidents of the Odyssey and *Ulysses*: that Leopold Bloom is Ulysses, Stephen Dedalus is Telemachus, Marion Bloom is Penelope, the newspaper office is the Cave of the Winds, the brothel the Place of the Dead, and so on. This recognition plunges Mr. Joyce's devotees into profound ecstasies from which they never recover sufficiently to ask what the devil is the purpose that is served by these analogies. The theme of *Ulysses* is essentially Manichæan: Leopold and Stephen are Ormuz and Ahriman, the dark force of matter that rots as well as blossoms and the spirit of light that emerges from it and contends with it. But surely there was nothing in the philosophical world more alien from the Greek genius than Manichæanism,

since the motive force which inspired it was its need
to prove that there was no conflict between nature
and beauty, and that whoso accepted the one begot
the other by the act of acceptance. When one looks
at the works of art recovered from the ruins of the
City of Khochu, which are our first intimations of
what Manichæanism functioning as orthodoxy produced other than what we have gleaned from the
reports of its enemies, one is amazed by the way that
though the externals of Greek art are faithfully
borrowed and respectfully superimposed on more
Oriental forms, the admission that there is a fundamental disharmony in nature causes it to create
effects that are totally different from anything which
one could possibly experience on account of Greek
Art. It is as if one met two beautiful sisters, much
alike, but one a happy wife and the other a tragic
widow. For Mr. Joyce to write his Manichæan
epic with a dove-tailing fidelity to a Greek
pattern is as sensible as it would be to write a
novel about Middle Western farm life in French
alexandrines.

The other finger-print he has left on his own
masterpiece springs from not so fundamental a confusion, but it is as ominous in its bearing on his fit-
ness to invent a valid new method. His devotees
never weary of pointing out as evidence of his
scholarship that the scene in the Lying-In Hospital
consists of a series of parodies of a large number of
great writers ranging from the Early English to the
Victorians: the theory being that the mind of Stephen
Dedalus picks up the bawdy conversation of Bloom
and the medical students and translated it into terms

of the literature in which he had been saturating himself. What they never pause to notice is that even as parodies, and perhaps the parody is the art-form which produces the largest percentage of execrable specimens, these are noticeably bad. The imitations of Bunyan and Sterne, even allowing for the increasing cloudiness of drunkenness, completely disprove all that is alleged concerning the quality of Stephen's mind.

It would be unlikely that a person so much in need of help from tradition, and so capable of going wrong even when he hasn't, should do anything but fall on the floor when he lets go of it: and the method he adopts when he does proves, if one examines without infatuation, to be a wild flounder. It is executed deliberately, but it is conceived in confusion. Its keystones are inclusiveness and incoherence: Mr. Joyce's admirers lay stress on the fact that *Ulysses* tells the whole story of twenty-four hours in the life of Leopold Bloom, and they admire enormously passages such as 'At four she. Winsomely she on Bloohimwhom smiled. Bloo smi qui go. Ternoon. Think you're the only pebble on the beach? Does that to all. For men.' But this is not a new æsthetic. For it is precisely that faith which inspired the well-known artist of the Victorian era, Mr. W. P. Frith, to commit his notorious paintings. It was his effort, which was surely crowned by success in a certain sense, to tell the whole story of what happened in an area a hundred yards square on the Derby course which resulted in 'Derby Day'; and it is true that 'Bronze by gold heard the hoofirons, steely-ringing,' and the ensuing passage vividly convey the effect of

a bronze-haired barmaid and her golden-haired col-
league standing behind the bar of the 'Ormonde,'
but consider how well done, how really awfully well
done, the cockade on the footman's top-hat in the
right-hand foreground of Mr. Frith's achievement,
and the so veritably pink lobster he is lifting from the
luncheon-basket. The brilliantly informative presentation of insufficiently related objects is no novelty
in any of the arts. Not only is this method old: it is
also logically unsound in both its foundations, since
inclusiveness and incoherence can be present in
works of art only as the result of interesting and rare
special cases. The problem of art is to communicate
to the beholder an emotion caused in the artist by a
certain object; and though it is possible that every
attribute of that object, all its relations in time and
space, are relevant to that emotion, it is not very
probable. It is far more likely that the object will
have a number of attributes which are merely cords
that secure it a place in the world of physical fact, in
the world of naïve realism, which is the world in
which it must be for the artist to catch sight of it, but
from which he must remove it in order to treat it; and
that it has yet other attributes of a sort which might
interest another artist but not this particular one. So
far from being a way of handling the literary medium,
inclusiveness is a condition which may or may not
legitimately exist in a work of art owing to factors
quite outside the conscious control of the artist; and
which does not legitimately exist in *Ulysses*, since
many of the excrementitious and sexual passages
have a non-æsthetic gusto about them which implies
that, in order to write them at all Mr. Joyce has

had to step out of his artistic process, even to the extent of losing touch with his characters. For every now and then Leopold Bloom, in whom there is no reticence, in whom there cannot be reticence since it is among the restrictions of life which he has forgone because he suspects them of being purposive, adopts towards sexual matters a coy titillating hesitancy. 'I wonder if she knew I.' In fact there are aspects of Leopold's life during the twenty-four hours which interest the artist in Mr. Joyce so little that it refuses to part with its knowledge to him while he insists on writing of them. Inclusiveness is therefore in these instances æsthetically fatal to Mr. Joyce.

Incoherence, that is to say the presentation of words in other than the order appointed by any logic of words not in sentence formation, is at least a real device and not just a condition, and while it also is suitable for the handling only of a special case, that special case is certainly contained in *Ulysses*. But unfortunately Mr. Joyce applies it to many things in *Ulysses* as well as that special case. To begin with, he writes down these strings of words as if they corresponded to the stream of one's consciousness; as if, should one resolve to describe one's impressions as they came, one would produce isolated words and phrases which would not cohere into sentences. Yet there is nothing more certain than that sentences were used by man before words and still come with the readiness of instinct to his lips. They, and not words, are the foundations of all language. Your dog has no words, but it barks and whines sentences at you. Your cat has no words, but it has a considerable feeling for the architecture of the sentence in relation

to the problem of expressing climax. Your baby has
no words, but it will use sentences for hours together,
sentences sometimes pausing for thought and adding
a pungent dependent clause, till it builds up a kind of
argument-like mass. Indeed, the chief difficulty of
teaching a child to talk is to persuade it to abandon
the wordless sentence, which perfectly conveys all
the emotional communications it wishes to make, and
to go through the labour of memorizing words for
the purpose of making the intellectual communications it will feel no need to make for some years to
come. A mother who points to a doll and repeats
'doll' over and over again to the child who for some
time has been perfectly well able to convey that she
wants the doll in her arms by saying 'Wa wa *wa* wa,'
must seem to the child to be positively unteaching it
to speak, to be cramping and deforming a faculty;
which probably adds to the dark suspicion of the
adult world held by the young.

Even an amazingly large part of adult life could be
carried on without words. One can perfectly well
open one's mouth and by simply letting the emotions
act on the larynx cause a series of sounds which
inform the hearer that one means, 'I love you more
than anything in the world,' or 'Everything was
peaceful and happy till you came and now you have
spoiled it all,' or 'How nice you are looking,' or
'This steak is burned.' A great many quite good
plays could be performed with rhythmic howls in the
place of dialogue and lose almost nothing by the
change. 'Tons of Money,' for example, would have
suffered very little. Even the entertaining effect of
Mr. Noel Coward's comedies, though verbal wit

33

contributes to it greatly, is very largely dependent on the amusing and entirely characteristic cadence of his sentences, which suggest that if one takes up almost any situation which the world pretends is sacred and solemn and of precious substance and examines it calmly, one will find that it can be snapped across and crumbled between the fingers like a biscuit. Except for the most complicated forms of human action and for those late human growths, literature and philosophy, words are not really necessary, and since they are only elaborations of sounds it is extremely unlikely that they occur to the mind except in the sentence form in which man has always handled sentences. The common conception of the sentence as something into which the higher faculties build a mess of words with which certain lower faculties present them, that it represents sense constructed out of nonsense, is as much an error as the old-fashioned idea that when a man saw a triangle his mind crawled round each of its three sides collecting the information that they were joined together and formed a triangle instead of receiving an impression of a triangle as instantaneous as an electrical discharge.

Both errors depend on a similar assumption which, on examination, it proves impossible to assume. The theoretical man who becomes aware of the triangle by synthesis of its lines instead of becoming aware of the lines by analysis of the triangle is supposed in some mysterious way to have grasped all the attributes of these lines except their relationship to one another (the sum of which is the triangle), though that may well have been their most salient points; the man who perceives phenomena in a way that can be conveyed by isolated words and phrases is supposed in some equally mysterious way to have grasped all the attributes of these phenomena except their relations to the universe (since the structure of the sentence is simply an arrangement to exhibit such relations), although those may quite possibly be to him by far the most important and most obvious of their attributes. And, indeed, if one puts one's friends to a test one will find that not only is the idea of nonsense as a primary state of language improbable theoretically, but it can be disproved practically by the fact that people invariably find it a painful effort and ultimately an impossibility not to talk sense. If one asks them to put away so far as possible all consciousness of a listener and to record what they see going on outside the window or what is passing in their own minds, and beg them to do this without using the sentence form, however anxious they may be to accede they presently stumble and stutter uncomfortably and finally are dumb. Against their will what they have to say coagulates into sentences: short, simple sentences, but nevertheless sentences. Hence I refuse to believe Mr. Joyce when he describes the 'Ormonde' Bar in verbal sneezes, or goes further in the successor to *Ulysses* and presents as a picture of the stream of consciousness: 'Liverpoor? Got a bit of it. His braynes coolt parritch, his pelt massy, his heart's adrone, his bluidstreams acrawl, his puff but a piff, his extremeties extremely so. Humph is in his doge. Words weigh no more to him than all the raindrops of Rethfernhim. Which we all like. Rain. When we sleep. Drops. But wait until our sleeping.

Drain. Sdops.' This is likely, like the incoherencies of Mr. Frith: but, like the incoherencies of Mr. Frith, it is not true.

Nevertheless nonsense does exist. It is the emblem of the martyrdom of certain of God's children, and has long been known as such. Where have we been familiar from our childhood with strings of words which suggested their successors by some other link than that of sense, by rhyme, by jingle, by following some path of assonance that leads into parody of learned language or the vocabulary of science, into dog-latin or chit-chat of *barbara* and *celarent*? Wherever we read of the Shakespearean fool: of the court jester. Now, the point about that kind of a fool is that he is no kind of a fool. He is some one who has perspicacity enough to see that through the developing genius of man life is leaving earth on a flight into the skies, and in a panic pulls it back and drags it to the marshy places, so that it may get stuck in the mud, pushing it down into the ooze to make sure it clogs whatever wings it may be growing, holding it down if need be till the filth covers its mouth and smothers it, because surely such a death is better than spinning downwards through nothingness and breaking one's body on the stones. The part of the fool was to circulate in palaces and gardens, foci of man's ambition, plague-spots where life was getting out of hand, and tweak romantic lovers by the sleeve and gibe at their passion in order that they should feel shame at loving differently from the beasts of the field and retreat to the safe underground burrow of lust: to sit at feasts where men wear crowns and women show their bosoms and to

36

remind them by lewd jokes that it is of no avail for men to gird their corruptible skulls with incorruptible jewels and for women to put their best curves foremost, the flesh is still subject to a thousand ridiculous contretemps, and that government and grace will not check putrefaction: to take language, the prime instrument by which man is moving life on this perilous journey away from its material bases, and to mock its highest uses, crying to priests and philosophers, 'Listen to what I am saying. It sounds exactly like what you are saying. What I am saying is gibberish. Are you quite sure of the nature of what you are saying?'

And this is what, in relation to modern life, is the function of Leopold Bloom. For a long time the court jester was a figure that English life could not tolerate, because a state of doubt about the destination to which human evolution led was so general that anybody who expressed anything but admiration for the higher faculties of man was as unpopular as a person who voices a general panic concerning which every one has up till then kept silence. The particular aspect of civilization which was appalling them was the political problem; and it is interesting to notice how as history brought them nearer and nearer to the crux of their problem in the French Revolution and left them sitting face to face with its consequences, as it did till the end of the Napoleonic Wars, coarseness in life and art were increasingly banished until the dawn rose chalk-white on the Victorian age. Then there set in another condition in which the court jester was equally unwelcome. For through the economic consequences of the industrial revolution and the expedients which had been devised to solve the political problem, there emerged into power a new class, the middle class. It was scared stiff by its position: it found itself unable to act with the self-assurance and candour of the aristocracy: it felt fear of the working class, from which it had only recently separated itself, partly because it was reminded of its origins, and partly because of the menace of organized labour. It had, therefore, no use at all for the artist who hinted that in this life some stories do not have a happy ending; or who exhibited that freedom of manners and morals which were characteristic of those hated classes above and below it. A precise parallel can be seen in the America of to-day where a similar class that is sure of itself only economically shows the same tendency to doctrinaire idealism, Puritanism and intolerance of tragedy and satire. This state of affairs leads, of course, to the non-appreciation and non-appearance of the repudiated type of artist. In England it even had a curious retroactive effect on the reputation of a very great man. It is habitually taught in school and handed about as current coin in criticism that the works of Dean Swift are primarily political allegories, and that he was first and foremost a controversialist; which is to say that so far from mocking the higher human activities, he was an active participant in them. But when one examines his works without prejudice one finds that, particularly considering he belonged to the nation which is more obsessed by politics than any other in the world, very little of his work has a political inspiration. It is not the affairs of Queen Anne's England that makes him bare his teeth with savage laughter;

it is because the beginning of man is *inter fæces et urinam* (as St. Augustine put it), and his end the digestion of worms. The free and shameless aristocracy had recognized his genius so that it could not be later denied, but at least its character could be disguised.

Under this Victorian suppression the impulse of man to be candid about the fundamental good sense of walking on all fours and wallowing in the agreeable smoothness of mud and the warmth of dung found no outlet except on the old-fashioned variety stage and the old-fashioned pulpit: the message of Marie Lloyd and Little Tich was that the ideal state of mind was to squeeze all possible enjoyment out of smacking behinds in basement kitchens and the inherent humour of cheese, kippers, and mothers-in-law, since seeking other aspects of life is to find danger; and the appeal of the most popular Roman Catholic preacher of modern times, who had a pronounced Cockney accent and a turn for exercising buffoonery within the confines of the sermon, was surely that he passed into the sphere where it is insisted that man should practise the decorum of ritual and ordered thought and ordered conduct and proved that the insistence was a sham, that one could go right up to the altar-rails and perform like the natural quadruped man and neither priest nor God would say a word. But of serious representation of the court jester there was nothing. That is why there is such tremendous force behind *Ulysses*: it is the liberation of a suppressed human tendency. And that is why James Joyce is treated by this age with a respect which is more than the due of his competence: why *Pomes Penyeach* had been sold to me in Sylvia Beach's Bookshop as if it had been a saint's medal on the porch of Westminster Cathedral.

The importance of Leopold Bloom, how deep a criticism of life he is, can be seen only if one considers the ground plan of *Ulysses*, which is much more important than its laboured parallels with the *Odyssey*. There appear to be six characters of the first importance in the book: four living, and two dead who are still in life because of their influence on the living: Stephen Dedalus, his father Simon Dedalus, and his dead mother, May Dedalus; Leopold Bloom, who takes charge of Stephen during his wanderings through nocturnal Dublin (and who might, considering a certain memory of May Dedalus' face seen in a shady wood, be more truly Stephen's father than Simon, but of that we are never sure), his wife Marion, and their dead son, Rudy. These are, however, incarnations of but three types designed to show their different phases. Simon Dedalus and Leopold Bloom are different phases of the Universal Father, that which begets, which spills life anywhere, without care for its fate: and May Dedalus and Marion Bloom are different phases of the Universal Mother, that which conceives, which cherishes any life that is given to it, without care for anything but its physical fate; and Stephen and Rudy are different phases of the Universal Son whose fate is Death. For Simon also is a buffoon, a court jester, a Shakespearean fool, one that loves to look on offal and claim kinship with it and laugh with it like a brother. But he is not presented in his completeness because a son dares not look on the nakedness of his father.

Merely he is left as an indication of the relations that exist between the Father and the Son in the world of fact. All his gross characteristics are isolated, and the dark meaning of him divulged, in the person of Leopold Bloom. That person grows before our eyes as hardly another person literature has created in our time. Here part, though not all, of Mr. Joyce's cloacal preoccupation, is appropriate to his work of art, for the court jester, desiring to recede from life, looks back with nostalgia on the dung which he regards as the parent substance of the universe; his mediæval prototype was wont to remind the rich and great as they sat in state at feasts of this base origin by japes very odd to modern minds, which they hailed with laughter, laughter which is the soul's sign of relief at some promise of surcease from its efforts. Every thought of that long day in which Leopold Bloom is exhibited, every action, has that peculiar squatting baseness which comes of a deliberate regression; for though he is entirely absorbed in the dingiest phases of his environment this is by a deliberate though unconscious choice, for he has ability above the average. One feels shame at him, as one does at a white dancer who tries to imitate negro movements, putting off the racial pride native to her without being able to acquire the racial pride of the African so that there is no pride at all but only shame, when he flies away from human love into a sweating infatuation for his wife which makes him willing at the end of the day to lie down by her on the imprint left by the coarse body of Blazes Boylan, which is not innocence like an animal nuzzling by its mate, but a defilement of a known glory. His lack of dignity has

the widest possible range, he travesties the whole
nature of man, the instinct for art he parodies by
his rootings in second-hand bookshops for the
works of Paul de Kock, the instinct for science he
parodies by pondering on unsavoury oddments of
knowledge, contemplating curious ways of meeting
emergencies, like a dog sniffing cracks and crannies
in a city pavement. He can match his power of
belittlement with the most tremendous experiences
life has to show, for at the funeral of Paddy Dignam
he crops the occasion with the beard-wagging lewdness and gravity of an old goat. Of course he has
power, for he is the father, the progenitor of all
humanity, the frustrator of all humanity, he sends it
out on its search for the goal, he eternally turns it
back from the goal. Jew he is, being like Judaism
which was the Father of Christianity, the dark and
massive materialistic religion that engendered the
ivory-white faith which was all spirit, the religion of
burnt offerings and vows of vengeance to which in
times of stress men and peoples return, letting the
new faith die. A tender father he is too; when he
guides Stephen through the filthy squalor of nocturnal Dublin he is loving to the boy, his arm is
round him in the brothel, he insinuates himself into
the young mind with all manner of gentleness in
Skin-the-Goat's cabman's-shelter, in the dirty kitchen
of his mean house he gives him of his gross and
greasy best, pouring into his cocoa the cream ordinarily reserved for the breakfast of his wife Molly.
It is true that the boy is in this vileness because of
him; that he is trying to plunge down into drunkenness and stupor because there is so much Leopold

42

Bloom in the world that he knows everything noble in himself to be defeated.

But that, too, is part of a fatherly plan. Leopold Bloom, the court jester, the Shakespearean fool, forbids the children of men to indulge in flight because he loves them. It is dangerous, they will die before their time. Let them keep near to earth and live out their days. Even his attitude is a sacrifice, for he too knows the desire to fly. Even he has risen from the earth at some time or other. For otherwise he would not be so wise about that desire and the delight of its gratification. He knows how his children are tempted, it breaks his heart to prevent them, but out of his great love he must. So when Leopold Bloom talks and thinks gurgling nonsense, when he translates the experiences that life is offering him into gibberish, as he does at Paddy Dignam's funeral, when he pulls away the substructure of sense on which language is supported, when he lets words fall about like fragments of a broken cup, finally disconnected, eternally useless, he is performing an act which beautifully expresses the essence of his being. So far as he is able he is saving his kind from the miseries of thought and the higher passions, like a man tearing up the death warrant that condemns his child to death. It is part of the martyrdom of his love that it must be done clownishly, with no upgrowth into dignity, squatting and snuffing.

I do most solemnly maintain that Leopold Bloom is one of the greatest creations of all time: that in him something true is said about man. Nothing happens to him at the end of *Ulysses*. Nothing is suggested in the course of the book which would reconcile him to the nobility of life. Simply he stands before us, convincing us that man wishes to fall back from humanity into the earth, and that in that wish is power, as the façade of Notre Dame stands above us, convincing us that man wishes to rise from humanity into the sky, and that in that wish is power. But it is when one considers the rest of the work in both these expression of man's desires, the part of *Ulysses* that is not Leopold Bloom, the part of Notre-Dame that is not the façade, that one is overcome by fury at Mr. James Joyce's extraordinary incompetence. In Notre-Dame there is the façade, there are the two towers, richly carved to suggest the elaboration of life which will inevitably co-exist with its elevation, sturdily proportioned to suggest that that elevation is mechanically possible, can endure in the real world where there is pull and stress; and behind the façade and under the towers are the naves and the transepts and the baptistery, and the whole body of the church, built reasonably high to show that when man worships he has already risen higher than when he sits by his fireside or in his little shop, but built lower than the towers, to show he has not yet risen very far. But behind Mr. Joyce's Leopold Bloom there are no such expositions by proportion. Instead it is as if behind the façade of Notre-Dame there were another couple of towers leaning over at an angle of sixty degrees and then behind them another couple lying almost flat with the ground. There are not adequate indications of the factors in man that are not Leopold Bloom. There are, as a matter of fact, some pretty bad holes in Mr. Joyce's façade, for again and again Leopold Bloom is represented as receiving impressions directly in the form of gibberish, without any translatory efforts on his part.

But worse still, the two other characters in the book are made to use gibberish, though that is so much outside their characters that it renders the book pointless. In *Ulysses* the figure of the Son is divided into two persons: Stephen Dedalus, who is alive, and Rudy Bloom, who is dead, in order to convey that the Son is perpetually alive and perpetually dead, that he is always being born and being killed, and that though it is the Father who kills him he mourns him after his death. Rudy Bloom, of course, was not killed by his father in any sense of having been murdered by him, but he died so near his birth that his life was still entirely in his parent's charge, and he was a delicate child of the sort to whom the sordid environment they had decreed for him would be dangerous; just as Stephen's soul was waking nothing but affection in Bloom, but nevertheless was dying of what Bloom and his kind had made of Dublin. The slim and fragile ghost of Rudy, appearing in the brothel scene where Leopold Bloom's mind vomits in delirium, perfectly serves its part, configures the delicacy which his father has utterly excluded from his life: which he has killed. It is Stephen's part to configure that delicacy as it was when it lived and invited its death. That he can do only by being order. He must be a white Ahriman that the dark Ormuzd may hate him, he must have form that that which is formless should be incensed and resolve to reabsorb him into its chaos.

But Stephen talks and thinks gibberish nearly as

much as Leopold Bloom. The very characteristic
which is most expressive of Leopold's difference
from Stephen and need to destroy him is constantly
manifested by Stephen himself. This robs the book
of much of its effect, and it is only to be explained
by supposing that Mr. James Joyce, when he found
himself attaching gibberish to the person of Leopold
Bloom, simply did not understand what he was doing
and imagined, as many of his followers have since
done, that he had discovered a new method of universal applicability. The filtration of darkness into
the child of light gives a great many readers a mistaken impression that this book, which is actually a
heartbroken lament because the Kingdom of Heaven
is not by any means at hand, is on the side of the
disorder which actually it resents as one did not know
modern literature could hold resentment. It can do
this more easily, of course, because Stephen Dedalus
is not quite a valid character, because he is conceived
and executed with a pervasive sentimentality that
makes the fastidious reader suspect the worst of him
and his author. Mr. Joyce's incompetence, though
it is present in his treatment of the Mother, inter-
feres not so much with the function she plays in
the book, because she is conceived and executed
with a magnificent integrity of feeling. She is
divided into two persons, into May Dedalus and
Marion Bloom, for the same reason that the Father
was bisected; since the Mother is seen in relation to
the Son, Stephen Dedalus, it is necessary that all the
sexual aspects of her which he could not bear to contemplate in his own mother, should be isolated in
some other woman. That is Marion Bloom: who for

the most part of the book is an over-ripeness frowst-
ing too long after wakening in tumbled blankets,
the rumour of a contralto whose coarse volume,
attractive, repulsive, one could swear by the end of
reading that one had heard with one's own ears, a
reported reagent on the physiological processes of
the grosser Dubliners; but who in the last forty-two
pages becomes one of the most tremendous summa-
tions of life that have ever been caught in the net of
art.

In the course of the Clark lectures Mr. E. M.
Forster delivered on ' Aspects of the Novel,' he discusses whether any but the simplest rhythms, those
that consist of repetition plus variation, have ever
been created in fiction. 'Is there any effect in novels,'
he asks, 'comparable to the effect of the Fifth Symphony as a whole, where, when the orchestra stops,
we hear something that has never actually been
played? The opening movement, the andante, and
the trio-scherzo-trio-finale-trio-finale that composes
the third block, all enter the mind at once and extend
one another into a common entity. This common
entity, this new thing, is the symphony as a whole,
and it has been achieved mainly (though not entirely)
by the relation between the three big blocks of sound
which the orchestra has been playing.' I should have
said that the monologue of Marion Bloom which is
the end of *Ulysses* perfectly achieved just such an
effect: just such a unified beauty. It is, of course,
Mr. James Joyce being the writer he is, badly
botched at points. There has always seemed to me
something mysterious in the prodigious sexual athleticism in the two middle-aged Blooms; and the

47

mysterious becomes the preposterous when a woman who is presented to us as above all a creature of healthy rhythms is shown immediately after she has had a thoroughly satisfactory sexual encounter as being immersed in frenzied and aggressive fantasies inexplicable save as the torments of abstinence. Also, though most of the wildness of the chapter is typographical cheating, a surface effect which is created by the lack of punctuation, and would instantly disappear and show a groundwork of ordinary ecstatic prose if a few commas and full stops and dashes and exclamation marks were inserted, there is some use of gibberish; and that is absurd in a speaker whose whole importance lies in the terrifying degree to which she is organized for purposefulness. But these confusions cannot blur the strong, tremendous pattern and rhythm of which his imagination has achieved in this presentation of the Mother.

There is that in her reverie which sets before one the image of a recumbent woman. The air above her, that is to say the air above our mother earth, seems to become full of men, whom she calls into existence by her desirousness. Men and men and men crowd the air of the universe, with vague faces, with defined bodies. Surely there is no air left to breathe, it is all full of men. One thinks of the art of many countries, of many ages, of times and spaces which have nothing in common but this business of engenderment: of Demeter, shaped like a ship built for cargo, moving on the earth as a ship moves on the waters; of a stone arch in India carved with more than computable figures emblematic of fertility, more figures than can ever have been carved, that must surely have multi-

plied by fission under the artist's fingers, surely now
multiplying so under the beholder's eyes, and surely
to be trusted to multiply still more when his back is
turned; of the Chinese goddess that is called of mercy
but has no particular interest in mercy, who looks
down on city squares where passers-by do not wait
long enough to watch the executioner's sword fall on
all the fourteen bared napes and on dark rivers where
the bodies of children float in tiny fleets, and is not
disturbed, knowing that however far death throws
the ball, she can throw it further; of Mayan houses,
where those live who have such a passion for life that
there is no plate or jug or spoon that is not moulded
like some form of life, vigorous and hideous, without
reference to dignity or beauty, for life is the point and
not those qualities, though they too can be produced,
produced so plentifully that the gods are never without worthy human sacrifices, a luxury that can be
allowed them because women can repair the losses;
of Raphael's Madonna, drooping her cheek to the
hapless child whom she has borne that He may be
crucified.

All these attitudes arising out of reproduction that
have ringed history and the globe are to be found in
this dingy little room in Dublin, in the innocent and
depraved, the tender and callous musings of Marion
Bloom. They move, these creations of her need to be
fertile: this one serves her youth and goes, that one
serves her maturity and goes, even she throws the
noose of desire round Stephen Dedalus and draws
him near to her. The Mother is going to draw the
Son back into her body, by his consent he will become the Father, who will beget a son. By observing

the rhythm of Marion Bloom we have been given knowledge, not otherwise stated, of the rhythms of Leopold Bloom and Stephen Dedalus. Surely it might be said that 'all enter the mind at once, and extend one another into a common entity.' It is not the philosophy which gives the book beauty. That eternally Leopold Bloom and Simon Dedalus will kill Rudy Bloom and Stephen Dedalus, but that that will be no victory, since eternally Marion Bloom and May Dedalus will raise up their enemies against them, is not a happy ending on the facts. Personally I would prefer man to draw a better design, even if it was drawn but once and was not repeated like the pattern on a wall-paper. But I claim that the interweaving rhythms of Leopold Bloom and Stephen Dedalus and Marion Bloom make beauty, beauty of the sort whose recognition is an experience as real as the most intense personal experiences we can have, which gives a sense of reassurance, of exultant confidence in the universe, which no personal experience can give.

I know, for I felt it there, on the Rue de Rivoli, down which I was walking when I arrived at this point in my consideration of *Ulysses*. Since my buying of *Pomes Penyeach* at Sylvia Beach's bookshop that morning I had done quite a number of things. I had been to my dressmaker and had bought a black lace dress underneath Pruna panels in which there plunged through blue-green waters nudes so enchanted by the marine moment that they had suffered a slight sea-change from humanity, that the whiteness they showed to one as they flashed downwards seemed a mere local bleaching as may be found

50

on the bellies of fish, and that one could conceive
their flesh to be solider than their bones which one
could imagine as tiny and flimsy and recondite, like
the bones of a herring. I had been to a milliner's
shop which the head *vendeuse* of a famous house had
just started as her own venture and had ordered three
hats, and had sat playing with the models, two on my
lap, one on my head, changing them about, little
dove-like things that laid wings of dark felt softly
against the face; I was amused by their contrast with
their maker, who leaned over me, trying to sell me
more, her protruding eyes and wide mouth becoming
negro-animated because of that commercial ambition
which in a Frenchwoman seems as honourably primitive, as much a part of the mechanism of human increase, as a breast swelling with milk. I had lunched
in a divine house that is at the end of the Ile St. Louis
like the prow of a ship, in rooms with walls golden as
the last leaves that fluttered down from the trees on
the quay, which are like smudges drawn with a sooty
finger down the grey view of the river by a naughty
child leaning from the window. My host, tawdry
with that spuriousness which comes of having been
for long a professional Latin among Anglo-Saxons,
was amusing as certain dogs are amusing because
though they are stupid they are so true to type
and what they do is so prognosticable. And at
our table was a crystal dish full of a certain kind
of preserved strawberry dredged in sugar; which is
better than any other sweet to eat, since it is like
holding the best days of summer in one's mouth. I
had called at a bank for letters from people whom I
really like, I had had half an hour with a lawyer dis-

cussing an investment. And all the time my mind had pounded away at this matter of *Ulysses*, had refused for more than a minute to relinquish James Joyce.

Yet I like dresses, and the wide light *salons* where one buys them. I like hats, I like rooms with walls the colour of autumn leaves, I derive pleasure from the recognition of character. I like strawberries; the people whom I like I love. If I do not do sensible things about investments I shall spend my old age in a workhouse, where nobody will understand my jokes; and I do not particularly like *Ulysses* or James Joyce. Except when the book is at its greatest I resent being rapt into the squalor of Dublin; I detest the sentimentality and the subjection to simple and groundless and unpleasing fantasies which are the special weakness of Mr. Joyce. Why could I not give the whole of my psychic energy to Paris, on which autumn was lying like very fine eighteenth-century gilt, to dresses and hats and the Ile St. Louis, to my amusing and spurious host and his strawberries, to love and money? Yet the soul knows best. There must have been something in *Ulysses*, something about James Joyce, the understanding of which was more essential to me than anything of these things. What could it conceivably have been? I got an inkling when, in throwing my mind back over the days, I perceived which components of it have best resisted the competition of *Ulysses* in my memory. There were the Pruna panels; they had established themselves in my mind. So too, but with less certainty, had the black lace dress. But the hats had gone; and the house in the Ile St. Louis, though it was pleasant, had left no image that would become

a part of me. Exquisite though the place at least may
be, it will inevitably fall out of my memory some day
because of a missing element of reality, as a necklace
with a faulty clasp is sure sooner or later to slide off
one's shoulders to the ground. Of course the letters
from the people that I really like were real enough;
but the visit to the lawyer had hardly happened.
The Pruna panels; a black lace dress; letters from
the people that I really like: if one could find out
what forces lie behind these experiences which have
apparently satisfied the soul that they like *Ulysses* are
necessary to it, one might come to understand its
conception of necessity. The Pruna panels are obviously an expression of art. The black lace dress . . .
that is not so easy . . . it is impossible to say that
that is the expression of anything of which my three
hats are not equally an expression, yet they have as
definitely remained on the outer rim of consciousness
as it has been caught into some inner circle of it. The
letters from the people that I really like are an expression of love. By love I mean all that which leads
through personal relationship to the perpetuation of
the agreeable in life, and the frustration of the harsh.
Art: a black lace dress, apparently irreducible to any
other terms; love. The list is perplexing. But now
I recall something about the black lace dress. Of
course, I chose it because it reminded me of that
plate in Goya's *Caprichos* which is called *Volaverunt*:
the dark woman with tired eyes, who rides through
the air away from some place where she can no longer
bear to be, on the back of three squatting witches
who hold their knees up under their chins with
crooked rheumatic arms, and spreads out her lace

shawl like wings so that she may travel faster where they take her, she wears a dress like that. The list runs then, art, art, love. The expressions of art are, of course, flimsy enough for that force. The Pruna panels are not profoundly serious: the black lace dress is an obscure cross-reference. The emotion my letter caused me was a thousand times more intense than that which the panels could give me. Their content was utterly different from the content of my letters. Even more strikingly different, praise be to the Lord, is the content of *Ulysses*. Yet there is a bridge built between the emotions which are caused in me by my letters, and the emotions which are caused in me by the Pruna panels, the dress, *Ulysses*. But there can be no such bridge. There is, however. I feel that there is a bridge: which is to say that in the world of my feelings that bridge exists. It must have been built by my soul because my soul felt the need of it. Now I begin to be reminded of something: of a realization that came to me once when I was reading in the mystical writings of St. Teresa of Avila. I had often wondered in reading her life, and the lives of other saints, how those who had been visited by Christ Himself and had had wisdom put into their hands like an open book could submit to the supervision of confessors and investigators and bishops and cardinals, and should show themselves such eager and humble suppliants for the approval of the Church. What could they gain from the Church? What need for anything but one's own cell and a subjugated priest to give one the sacraments, when one's own ecstasy had brought one the Godhead Itself? But this half-page of St. Teresa's writing gave me the clue, made me perceive that in the Church was such a confirmation of her individual experience as amounted to its infinite multiplication: that the visit of Christ, the presentation of wisdom, are beneficences directed to the highly personal part of the individual, but in the collective experiences of all the other children of the Church, there is proof that the tide of the Godhead can rise higher and higher till it swamps not only a saint's cell but all the life there is, that the universe is conquerable by delight, that delight is its destiny, that some day there will be no place for pain, and that the part of the individual which partakes of continuity with the rest of the universe rejoices in the salvation of its substance. For just this same purpose of obtaining confirmation of my personal experience I cross this bridge in my mind between the things that are factually related to me and the things that are factually unrelated to me. I recognize the emotion as certainly as one recognizes the colour green. But what possible confirmation of my personal experience can be contained in a picture of people whom blue-green waters had mysteriously introjected with the plasm of fish, a black lace dress not very closely resembling one worn in an etching of a woman about to cast herself away to magic, the squalor of Dublin as seen by a man with a cloacal obsession?

Whatever mechanism may be working works mysteriously. As I continued on my way along the Rue de Rivoli, still full of that sense of peace and satisfaction and reassurance which rested on me like a pencil of brightness, proceeding from the rhapsodic figure of Marion—from meeting any of whose equivalents in the real world may the merciful Powers preserve me!—I was conscious of another pencil of brightness searching for my breast, whose beneficence also I could receive if I would but stand in the way of it. It proceeded almost visibly from certain grey walls, garlanded with stone that has taken on the variegation of living matter, being pearly above, where the rain falls, and soot-black, black-cat-black, beneath, on the other side of the street; from the Museum of the Louvre. I said to myself, 'Ingres!' Greedily I promised myself another deep draught of just such peace, just such satisfaction, just such reassurance, as I had been receiving from James Joyce. Now, how could that be? How in the world could two artists so entirely unlike in every way as Ingres and James Joyce conceivably cause a like emotion? To begin with, there is no reason why objects so utterly different as a book and a picture, whose approach to the spectator is along such different sensory avenues, should have anything like the same effect. But there is even more reason why a mind furnished as Ingres' (in the manner of the drawing-room Empire style of a silly but beautiful and competent woman) should create the same impression as a mind furnished like James Joyce (which is furnished like a room in a Westland Row tenement in which there are a bedstead and a broken chair, on which there sits a great scholar and genius who falls over the bedstead whenever he gets up). Ingres must have been a perfect idiot. When he committed allegorical pictures of nude ladies being rescued from dragons, it is as if Time had turned over in his sleep and been vexed by a prevision of disinfectant advertisements; and in his representation of the harem having its Turkish bath he gets the effect of crowded merriment that has often rewarded the efforts of Mr. Fred Karno. One is certain that his taste in literature and music was all for the momentary and the worst of that. Only he knew how to handle a brush so that it was a part of his will; astoundingly his medium seemed a friend and not the enemy — which it is to nearly all artists. He had the innocence of the eye that all the rest of the world has lost long ago, so that he looks on flesh as Adam might have looked on Eve before lust rose in him, and lets its values be manifest in their purity, and on the Rivière family as if they were the first human beings ever created and his soul rushed forward on the tide of a new dispensation to greet them and apprehend all their qualities.

Hardly to be prognosticated as the fruit of the same earth is James Joyce, good Latinist, good Aquinist, master of tradition, who can pour his story into the mould of the *Odyssey* and do it with such scholarship that the ineptitude of the proceedings escapes notice, who pushes his pen about noisily and aimlessly as if it were a carpet-sweeper, whose technique is a tin can tied to the tail of the dog of his genius, who is constantly obscuring by the application of arbitrary values those vast and valid figures in which his titanic imagination incarnates phases of human destiny. It would not seem possible that two people of such different sorts, progressing along such divergent paths and arriving at the two points, surely as nearly unrelated as any two points in the universe, of painting a bright-eyed young man with dark hair curling damp on his forehead and a snuff-coloured

coat, and of writing the reveries of a slut between
blankets in a Dublin back bedroom and should thereby cause in a total stranger to the world of both, in
whose life there is nothing which either a young man
with dark damp curls and a snuff-coloured coat or a
Dublin slut recalls or symbolizes, the most intense
and happy emotion. And this emotion is not merely
an isolated incident, not merely a discharge of
psychic energy caused by an unusual stimulus. It is
part of a system; it refers to one of the rhythms of
which we are the syntheses. For I was saying to myself, 'If you go to Versailles to-morrow you will not
have time to see the Ingres,' and although Versailles
is one of the places in which of all the world I like
most to be, I decided to stay and see the Ingres: and
then I remembered that when I had been in Paris
four months before I had had to make the same choice
and that then I had chosen to go to Versailles, but
that the time before the choice had been as it was
now; and I recognized that in noting those altera-
tions of attitude I had detected my organism recognizing its necessities by the state of its appetite, as it
does when it feels hunger acutely half an hour before
dinner and not at all half an hour after it. But what
is the necessity that is served in me by the contemplation alike of a young man with damp dark curls
and a snuff-coloured coat and of a Dublin slut? What
is the meaning of this mystery of mysteries? Why
does art matter? And why does it matter so much?
What is this strange necessity?

II

It can easily be understood why an artist creates works of art. There is no difficulty about that. I take it that from man's earliest moments his most immediate necessity is to know what it is all about. He is not, as older philosophers used to insist, activated by the will to live as a single motive. If he were moved by one force which had no competition but inertia his mind would not be the complicated instrument it is; thinking could have become what Dr. John Watson, the apostle of Behaviourism, alleges it to be, a matter of 'tracing paths for action' in the crudest sense. Indeed in such a simplified state of existence man would have become the force itself, and on account of him would have no need for the conceptions of inertia or thought. But since it is a necessity for himself and for his species that he should accept the duty to live for some unspecified time and an equal necessity for himself and for his species that he should accept the duty to die at some unspecified time, it is useful and not inconsistent with reality to conceive him as the battleground of two opposing forces: the will to live and the will to die. It is not at all reasonable to suppose, as Metchnikov did, that these forces play a non-competitive part in the life of the organism, the will to live slowly but not too reluctantly giving up the stage to the will to die as the biological necessity, for the death of the individual makes itself felt. Naturally the will to live is intensest in the young and vigorous organisms whose most imminent problem is life; but there is so much continuity in the stuff of a species that an in-

stinct which has to be strongly present in one phase
of its existence usually sweeps through the others,
just as the sexual instinct, though intensest in mature
people, is by no means absent from people too undeveloped or too old to exercise it usefully.

Moreover, the individual needs a certain amount
of the will to die from his earliest days to reconcile
him and a world where he walks in constant danger,
and where it is constantly borne in on him by the
deaths of others that his end must be death. To discover what this conflict may mean, what forces are
engaged, how they should be organized, and what is
likely to be the outcome of it all, is the constant aim
of the individual, pursued with more or less effec-
tiveness according to his innate qualities and the luck
he has in his environment, from the first moment he
emerges into consciousness to the moment when he
leaves it. His will to live suggests that he should take
his milk like a man; his will to die suggests that he
should leave it. Wailing, he debates the matter with
himself and with external forces. His mind takes
elaborate notes of all such conflicts, on the behaviour
of himself and of the eternal forces, on the decisions
arrived at, on their outcome; and presently he con-
structs a working hypothesis of life. He says to himself, '*This* appears to be the pattern of life. It will be
safe to act as if this and that feature were going to
recur in this and that order.'

Needless to say, this hypothesis is so far from
achieving an accurate version of life that it is fair to
call it a fantasy. It is full of falsity, because the child
is at the mercy of the false logic with which external
appearances perpetually present us. A spoiled baby

may easily believe that it creates its bottle by its crying; an ill-treated baby will almost certainly form the
impression that a great many movements terminate
naturally in pain. Furthermore, it appears to be true
that a state of mind exists in the child at birth which
can be roughly suggested by saying that it has
shadowy intimations of the main phenomena of
primitive life. One may hail this as an inheritance of
racial knowledge: or one may simply whittle it down
to saying that just as the cellular memory makes an
embryo remember what its progenitors' ears were
like and construct two for itself out of its flesh and
blood, so it makes it remember what mental mechanisms its progenitors used for recognizing and responding to the more important facts of life and do
its best to make itself replicas in the more difficult
medium of mind-stuff, and that therefore when it is
faced with these essential facts it shows a capacity for
handling them which is comparable to the capacity
which comes in adult life from fore-knowledge. But
to inquire into the exact nature of the process is here
not relevant: what matters is that the human animal
is put in possession of material which inevitably pro-
vokes it to construct a hypothesis covering the whole
of existence at an age when it is bound to fall into
every sort of error about it.

This fantasy about life, therefore, stands not a
dog's chance of corresponding with reality. Nevertheless it will be cherished by the individual with
what intensity is in him, because the situation of
a new arrival in this universe is subjectively as desperate as that of any shipwrecked sailor, and he
has nothing else to which he can cling. It is estab-

lished in his mind with the fixity of something that has come into being to satisfy an urgent psychic necessity, at a time when no argument can reach it to modify it, because the channels of intellectual communication are not sufficiently developed. All subsequent mental structures are built on it as a foundation, so that anybody who consents to make modifications has to show audacity and self-sacrifice. Furthermore, the mind will be inspired by its sense of self-preservation to push the hypothesis down out of the conscious into the unconscious, where it is inaccessible to the criticism of its possessor's or other people's reason.

It acquires, therefore, this fantasy, a domination over the individual which could not be surpassed, and which is not normally ever broken. Throughout the whole of his life the individual does nothing but match his fantasy with reality and try to establish, either by affirmation or alteration, an exact correspondence between them. Behind this search, of course, deeper down in the soul, there rages the perpetual conflict between the will to live and the will to die; and the fortunes of that war determine the way in which the individual conducts this and all the more superficial activities, while they in their turn react on what determines them. But that conflict is so deeply hidden that it is not often particularly useful to inquire into it when one is searching for the springs of behaviour. If one is dealing practically with a chair it is better to remember that it is made of wood than that it is a mass of whirling molecules.

There are a great many ways in which human beings conduct this effect to establish a correspon-

dence between the fantasy and the reality. There is
a vast number of people who have so little force in
them that the fantasy is feebly conceived and reality
dimly apprehended, and the whole event as nearly
like nothing happening as makes no matter. There
is another vast number of people who in a passion of
self-love conduct the effect wholly by affirmation, by
turning their eyes inward, so that they will see
nothing which compels them to admit they may be
mistaken about the nature of reality, and sacrifice
nothing of their fantasy as they will sacrifice nothing
that is a part of themselves. There is a vast number
of people who use themselves to prove their case, who
work out their fantasies in the sphere of conduct.
These actionists form the largest class of human
beings. And there is a number of people, not vast
at all, who at some early age become infatuated with
the idea of playing with human products. They too,
of course, work out their fantasies in the sphere of
conduct to a certain extent; but the main force of this
experimental passion goes into taking the things
which human beings can produce and compelling
them into forms and patterns which are concentrated
arguments concerning reality and their opinion of it.
They take clay of which children make mud-pies, of
which grown-up actionists make plates and jugs, and
they simultaneously gratify the instinct to play that
was in the children and the instinct to work out a
fantasy that was in the actionists, by using it to make
statues. They take words, in which children sing
nursery-rhymes and the actionists quote prices of
cooking-stoves over the telephone, and promise to
love, honour and obey one another, and again they

simultanesously enjoy both such gratifications by
writing books.

Plainly they are in an enormously advantageous
position. Even they enjoy a kind of extension of life
over and above the normal. For if an actionist has a
fantasy which, owing to some twist of symbolism,
leaves him with a feeling that there is nothing in the
world so desirable as a red-haired woman between
the ages of twenty and twenty-five, he can do little
about it except achieve the closest possible contacts
with as many young women of this sort as possible;
and that opens the door to a multitude of dissatisfac-
tions, in view of the limited number of such contacts
made possible by the relative scarcity of red-haired
young women and the brevity of the human span,
and in view of the fact that when encountered the
red-haired young woman will be busily working out
her own fantasies and will most probably be quite
unwilling to perform the part for which he has cast
her in his fantasy. But an artist in the grip of a
similar fantasy is in much better case. He can, and
often does, work out his obsession in the sphere of
conduct. But also he can create in whatever his
medium may be innumerable red-haired women.
His art will permit him millions of the contacts with
his symbol which actuality concedes so grudgingly,
and since his red-haired women will be parts of his
fantasy and not be acting independently, he will
be able to judge from their behaviour what his
fantasy really is and thus be able the better to
hold it up to reality. For these reasons an artist's
life is incomparably more free and less bewildered
than an actionist's and naturally everybody who can

be an artist is one. There is no mystery about that.

Where the mystery comes in is the effects of the artist's activity on other people. It is easy to understand why it is fun for him; but why is it, if certain conditions are fulfilled, such fun for us? When one tries to enumerate the conditions that have to be fulfilled one is again impressed by the unique mysteriousness of the proceedings. When the result of the artist's activity is good art, then it is fun for us; when the result of the artist's activity is bad art then it is not fun for us. But is it as impossible when talking of any other commodity in the world to define what one means by good and bad as it is in this case? If one says that one likes meat if it is good and dislikes it if it is bad, one knows as one speaks that one means by good meat that which has been well fed when it walked this earth, has been killed in the right way, kept the right time after killing, and has been properly cooked so that it is tender and juicy and full of flavour, and by bad meat that which, not having been as justly dealt with, is stringy and dry and tasteless. But good art. . . . Well, what gives us fun is usually remarkable for its high horse-power. It is the product of a powerful nature that has been able to form an interesting and intricate fantasy or which is able to prosecute with spectacular vigour the effort to make the fantasy and reality match. The real impressiveness of a genius like Goethe lies not in the perfection of any individual piece of work he performed, but in the ubiquity which he displayed scouting on every frontier of the collective intelligence. There is nothing particularly rich or varied in the design of the

65

orgiastic fantasy of Burns and the necrophilic fantasy
of Poe, but they achieve greatness by the eagerness
they display in holding them up to reality so that the
parts which correspond show, as it were, a double
thickness and become more certainly the possession
of all collectors of the real. The supremely impressive
genius, of course, manifests power in both these ways,
and for that exacts respect even if there is little in him
which seduces affection. It is rarely possible to feel
liking for Dante, who has that air of taking local
politics seriously which makes the Minor Prophets
so unlovable. Even his bursts of joy have worry instead of tragedy as their contrast, as if he had come
out of the Town Hall to cool his head after a stormy
scene in the Council and found the fresh winds of
philosophy pleasant against the creased forehead;
though those winds seem to have passed through
woods close to the ground, where there were prim-
roses, they cannot blow away all the argumentative
confusion in the air. But that the first instinctive
movement of his imagination should have explored
so much of life and that his intellect should not have
tired and drawn back from any of the occupied terri-
tory (as Goethe's frequently did in the same situation) is manifestation of a strength which compels
homage, just as a mountain range, though its slopes
may be incomparably more bleak than the rolling
country at its foot, compels by its mass and form a
recognition that it is more prodigious than the rolling
country.

If such people, translating into the medium of one
or other of the arts the material towards which their
fantasies direct their attention, pass it through their

own emotional systems and sincerely set down the
values its integers assume in that process without
falsifying them to make an impression on the audience, then the products will be free from the sentimentality which prevents a performance from being
a work of art. If, in that state of authentic values,
they possess beauty, then they are works of art. But
'beauty,' as Hume wrote, 'is no quality in things
themselves; it exists merely in the mind which con-
templates them.' It is the name we give to a recurring element in work created under these conditions,
which invariably causes pleasure whenever it recurs.
But to add further confusion into the sphere of
elusive entities we give the same name to a recurring
element in life, which also causes pleasure whenever
it recurs, but which does-not give the same sort of
pleasure and is not even associated with the same
material objects.

It is no use pretending that the emotion one gets
from reading a beautiful poem or looking at a beautiful picture or listening to a beautiful symphony is
the same that one gets from enjoying contact with
a beautiful character or admiring a beautiful breaking wave. The pleasure derived from art is calmer
and more profound, less actual but more permanent.
Moreover, certain objects which are beautiful when
encountered in art would not be reckoned so by any
but artists searching for material when encountered
in life; much of the subject matter which Rembrandt
used exemplifies this. But it is no use going round
and making the discrepancy seem logical by saying
that what we call beauty in life is that which is
most useful to man in life. This is sometimes true:

for example, any sensitiveness of the nerves which makes colour delightful to man would be worth while encouraging because so much of the framework of his existence is coloured, and therefore certain harmonies of colour pleasing to sensitive optic nerves would be counted beautiful. Nor is it any use saying that what we call beauty in art is that which is most useful to man in art. Though that too is sometimes true; for example, the representation of objects unpleasing in reality — as in the case of a gross and clumsy woman painted because of the lights in her hair and skin — that the elements which made them unpleasing are eliminated or used as a basis for some new pleasantness, while the existing pleasing elements are perpetuated, so that the original black mark against creation on account of the object is cancelled. But the identity of nomenclature cannot be explained by a common property of usefulness, because that which we call beauty in art is very often not to be interpreted in any way as serving any useful purpose; music cannot be justified as useful by anything but the most far-fetched word-twisting. Also there happens to be another emotion derivable from art which is different in effect from that which is caused by beauty, and which seems to be much more veridically related to the idea of use.

Much more. . . . To turn back to *Ulysses*, the reverie of Marion Bloom gives one the deep glowing satisfaction which is derived from beauty, while other passages give one quite another sort of pleasure. There is, for example, a scene at the end of the funeral chapter in which Leopold Bloom intrudes himself on another mourner, a solicitor who has a proper contempt for the advertisement canvasser, with the information that the other's hat is crushed, and receives a snubbing for his pains. It is like a queer little end-piece in which an artist's pencil scrawls on the blank page some image that has been evoked by the preceding chapter. It leads nowhere, it is the climax of nothing, simply it evokes Bloom in his characteristic squatting pose, which is something like prayer but which offers his hind-quarters to be kicked. He has felt in his heart a genuine movement of courtesy, but the part of him which has determined that nothing good shall come to fruition, that everything good shall be turned back on itself, and uses lack of dignity as its instrument, takes it in charge and turns it into something which discredits warmth and gives coldness a near victory. This incident does not give the serenity which is born of the contemplation of beauty. In the emotion it causes there is far less profundity and a far more immediate energizing quality. Is it indeed the same sort of pleasure that I experienced when reading Mr. James Joyce's mediocre poem called 'Alone'? Now that particular sense of pleasure was obviously not derived from artistic qualities inherent in that poem, for there are none; it was derived from the light thrown on this poem on a certain system of relations, on the nexus of forces which is Mr. James Joyce. When I apprehended the particular facts concerning him which this poem reveals, which are his want of taste and the power of self-criticism, the facts I had previously known about him fell into place and formed a recognizable design. I would now, when dealing in any way with the works of James Joyce, have the same advantage over myself in my previous dealings with them that a person who goes to France a second time has over some one who goes there for the first time. I would know my way about. Even so, every one who has read this scene between Bloom and John Henry Menton would know their way about any situation which should be subsequently presented to them by a collision of similar forms. The thing has been done, the absolute truth about that situation has been set down, we are by that much more completely masters of reality than we were. If every such situation, every such collision of forces, were as truly described, we should be masters of all reality. . . . One is reminded of a certain book which suggests to one that some such ambition must be the inspiration of a part of literature; though curiously enough that book has nothing to do with literature, or any other kind of art.

I saw that book for the first time this summer, at the end of an afternoon I had spent drearily enough in the Casino at Monte Carlo. That is an establishment of which I shall retain till death a confused notion arising from one of these indelible misapprehensions with which one engraves one's mind in infancy; for having, when I was about four years old, heard my father and a friend talking of St. Thomas Aquinas and his education at Monte Cassino, and later on having heard the same friend describing a visit he had paid to the Casino at Monte Carlo, which he called Monte, I put two and two together and made five. I cannot think it was merely by chance that this feat of addition seemed to be corroborated many years later on my first visit to the Casino at Monte Carlo, as an excursion of the pious

from some village over the Italian border was being
conducted round the tables by a parish priest, who
was explaining to them the principles of roulette.
There must be a minor god of fantasy. I have, therefore, a feeling of wonder and expectation about the
place, as the point where life might at any moment
cast its routine like a skin and disclose itself as other
than it has always seemed to be. Also I adore the
mural decorations, which are surely one note in a
certain chord of which the other notes are the old
Madame Tussaud's Exhibition, Amelia Bingham's
house on Riverside Drive, and the furniture of the
modern Palace at Seville. Nevertheless, I suffered
horribly, then as every time that I am made to go to
that or any other casino and gamble. This was not
reluctance to lose my money, for my losses were not
my financial funeral, since our host had given each of
his guests a prodigious number of counters to lose.

Nor was it repugnance to the crowds. For it is
pleasantly in consonance with my infantile views of
the place that round the tables where the play is low
are all the old ladies in funny hats at which one's
Nana told one not to point, who sit and write figures
in little exercise books as if they now were children
and must do lessons or be punished; and pleasantly
in consonance with the desire that the primitive shall
be right, always a part of the infantile attitude, is the
evidence which clusters round the table where play
runs high that the savage is essentially right in his
objection to be photographed, since without doubt
those who are constantly subjected to the process
show it in a kind of thumbed look about the face, in
a coarsening of the skin and features as if a likeness

was constantly being sweated out through the pores.
No, the reason could be nothing but that wheel and
ball. And it was so. Every time it started in a fresh
cycle I felt the incredulity that the universe could be
so cruel as not to send some interruption, and this
of a compensatory deliciousness, and the subsequent
flat horizonless despair, which one feels when one
hears some one telling a not very funny anecdote for
the hundredth time, or when one listens to a husband
whom one no longer loves embarking on a rationaliza-
tion by grievance of a fundamental incompatibility:
when, in fact, one is exposed to an incident which is
not in itself pleasing and from which one can learn
nothing.

That is the point: from which one can learn
nothing. It is true that if one sat and watched the
wheel spin millions of times one might collect observations that would have a bearing on the laws of
chance; but by that time one would be too senile to
report them to the proper authorities. Hence the
only people who can endure gambling are those who
have a specific neurosis on the subject (like Tche-
khov, who liked putting his money, which is to say
the means of living, at the mercy of fate, which he
conceived as perpetually leading life in the direction
of futility, of release from purpose) or people who
have said 'No' to the Universe, who do not want to
find out about things. If one has said 'Yes' and
determined to possess it with one's mind, time spent
in a casino is time given to death, a foretaste of the
hour when one's flesh will be diverted to the purposes of the worm and not of the will. So it happened
that when, on returning to my home in the cool of

the evening, I found Professor Pavlov's *Conditioned
Reflexes*, it was as if I had made an escape from the
tomb into full sunlight, from a twilight place of wailing into an occasion of hilarity. For that now famous
book is as superb an attempt to learn something as
ever was made, as successful a victory of comprehension over the universe.

It is the book which tells us, as physiology has not
been able to tell us before, what use the cortex, which
is to say the brain, does for the body that contains it.
The specific point which is attacked is the brain
of the dog. For about twenty-five years Professor
Pavlov and his assistants carried on a series of experiments on dogs which were designed to study their
conditioned reflexes, that is to say, to study their
reactions to the same kind of confusion as life; for a
conditioned reflex is an acquired reaction of the
nervous system to the stimuli which the environment
thrusts on it. The basis of all behaviour is, of course,
the simple reflexes, the inborn instinctive reactions of
the nervous system, such as the salivation which happens in a dog's mouth after the introduction of food,
in which case it serves the purpose of beginning to
digest it, or after the introduction of acid or any other
distasteful substance, in which case it serves the purpose of diluting it and washing it away. Professor
Pavlov, following up a suggestion dropped by Herbert Spencer, identifies reflexes that do not concern
chiefly the activities of separate organs and tissues,
that have to do with reactions of the organism as a
whole, as the instincts. It appears that there are many
more instincts than used to be supposed; one might
think that the clamant consciousness which distin-

73

guishes organic from inorganic matter was the yeasty ferment caused by the working of so many responses to life. Professor Pavlov claims to have established the existence of a specific freedom reflex. 'It is clear that the freedom reflex is one of the most important reflexes, or, if we use a more general term, reactions, of living beings. This reflex has even yet to find its final recognition. In James's writings it is not even enumerated among the special human "instincts." But it is clear that if the animal were not provided with a reflex of protest against boundaries set to its freedom, the smallest obstacle in its path would interfere with the proper fulfilment of its natural functions.' One was right in one's conviction that liberty is not a luxury.

For these instincts are fundamental things. They persist in animals that have had their brains removed. They are demands ingrained in the flesh. And there is also another reflex which is enormously apposite to human life, to Professor Pavlov, to this question of why art matters, and that is the investigatory reflex. 'I call it the "What-is-it" reflex. It is this reflex which brings about the immediate response in man and animals to the slightest changes in the world around them, so that they immediately orientate their appropriate receptor organ in accordance with the perceptible quality in the agent bringing about the change, making full investigation of it. The biological significance of this reflex is obvious. If the animal were not provided with such a reflex its life would hang at every moment by a thread. . . .' One remembers stories which one has heard regarding the unpopularity of Professor Pavlov with the authori-

ties during the first years of privation under Bol-
shevism. He and his assistants continued their work
throughout these horrors; many of these experiments
were carried on by people who had never been not
quite hungry for years, who were cold because they
had no warm clothing. The Bolshevists realized
what an ornament Professor Pavlov was to Russia
and they had no complaints regarding the discretion
of his conduct. But they complained bitterly about
his levity. The old gentleman (he was then in his
seventies) would crack jokes regarding the situation.
He appeared to them to belong in spirit to the old
world of ballet-dancers and officers debauching the
clear day and sober night with revelry. He laughed
deeply, heartily, so that he could be heard, he made
full-bodied jokes that could be remembered, while
the Bolshevists drew down the corner of their
mouths. They, poor dears, were making extensive
attempts to inhibit at least the freedom and the investigatory reflex; whereas he was feeding his investigatory reflex like a king, filling it full of the good
factual cheer that it wanted. One is accustomed to
see this antithesis between those who deny their
instincts and those who satisfy them represented in
reference to another and more obvious instinct: to see
the celibate monk set by contrast against the happy
lover. But it appears that other instincts know how to
clap and cheer when fed, to mope when starved.

It occurs to one that the portentous emphasis laid
on sex by society, the tendency to regard as a constant source of danger an instinct which in the mass
of people exists in a quite mild and tractable form,
may be due in part to a desire of man that his destiny

should be easier than it is. The situations arising out of the sexual reflex must so plainly be simpler than those arising out of these subtler reflexes. They refer to a particular relationship between two kinds of people, man and woman, within certain ages. They would operate therefore on a field which would be narrow compared to that covered by the freedom reflex, by which the animal must protest against *any* boundaries set to its freedom or the investigatory reflex, by which the animal must inquire into *all* phenomena it encounters. The situation caused by the latter must be infinitely more difficult for the mind to cope with than these presented on the narrower field; and observe the proof in this situation that they are less important even emotionally, for although the emotions they cause may be more diffused and less catastrophic they are as effective in their influence on general behaviour. Though the Bolshevists are not what the Tory Press paints them, they have the short temper of celibates; and Professor Pavlov has the exaltation, the extravagance of a great lover. 'As the fundamental nervous reactions both of men and of animals,' he writes, 'are inborn in the form of definite reflexes, I must again emphasize how important it is to compile a complete list comprising all these reflexes with their adequate classification. For, as will be shown later on, all the remaining nervous functions of the animal organism are based upon these reflexes.' Amazing to any writer this blithe formulation of the duty of taking what is practically a complete inventory of life! Comparable to the superb folly of the bridegroom who promises to love his bride eternally! Comparable to the gorgeous and glowing insanity of Balzac, with his intention for accounting for the whole story of society in *La Comédie Humaine*, of shutting up all France in the planned three hundred volumes!

Yes, one is reminded of art, or, rather, of an art, of literature . . . and not for the last time in this volume. There is talk later on of the temperamental differences in the dogs on which experiments were made, of their characters. 'At a time when we were still quite unfamiliar with the subject of conditioned reflexes, we met in some of the experiments with considerable difficulties on account of a drowsiness, which developed from the use of certain conditioned stimuli and under certain conditions of experimentation, and which we were not able to overcome. We thought to get rid of this drowsiness by choosing for our experiments dogs which outside the experimental conditions were very lively. Animals were selected which were extremely vivacious, always sniffing at everything, gazing at everything intently, and reacting quickly to the minutest sounds. Such animals when they get acquainted with men, which they do very quickly and easily, often become annoying by their continuous demonstrativeness. They can never be made to keep quiet either by orders or by a mild physical punishment. It was, however, soon found that these animals, when placed in the stand and limited in their movements, and especially when left alone in the experimental room, were the quickest to become drowsy, so that their conditioned reflexes quickly diminished, or even disappeared altogether, in spite of frequent reinforcement by food or acid . . .' As one reads, a secondary image comes

77

out of the page, a synthesis of milk and roses, of gold, of colours at best in youth and utterly delible by age, which shapes itself into the likeness of the girl with whose girlish prettiness the hero falls in love, thus breaking his more real relationship with the wise, kind, but more broad-beamed heroine, yet ultimately becomes annoyed by her 'continuous demonstrativeness' and her aptitude to become drowsy when life became grave and noticeably continuous. One says to oneself, 'The kind of character Edith Wharton and Anne Douglas Sedgwick like to write about,' but that they write about not quite honestly. Always they are a little too much on the side of the broad-beamed heroine, always they represent her as putting the girl-wife to bed when she gets influenza, though in this world the influenza germ is no respecter of solid worth and it is as likely as not that the girl-wife puts the kind wise heroine to bed. They do not make that immense gesture of detachment which Professor Pavlov makes: 'It is an interesting point but one which cannot be pursued here, whether this type represents a higher or lower stage of nervous development. . . .' So with the determination of making no point that cannot be proved, writes Jane Austen.

Of character as the artist treats it the book makes us think then; of situation as the artist treats it we think later. 'A big flood which occurred in Petrograd on the 23rd September, 1924, afforded us an opportunity to observe in our dogs prolonged neuropathological disturbances which developed as a result of the extremely strong and unusual external stimuli consequent on the flood. The kennels of the animals which stood on the ground at about a quarter of a mile's distance from the main building of the laboratory were flooded with water. During the terrific storm, amid the breaking of the waves of the increasing water against the walls of the building and the noise of breaking and falling trees, the animals had to be quickly transferred by making them swim in little groups from the kennels into the laboratory, where they were kept on the first floor, all huddled together indiscriminately. All this produced a very strong and obvious inhibition in all the animals, since there was no fighting or quarrelling among them whatever, otherwise a usual occurrence when the dogs are kept together.' We remember, 'On the road to Siberia, Barin, we were all brothers.' Repeating those words, one perceives how thumb-marked the situation has become in Russian literature. The minor Russian novelists keep a rubber stamp moulded in the design of a large number of people huddled together in misery and claiming to attain thereby a mystical fusion which shall last in joy throughout all eternity, just as the minor English novelists keep a rubber stamp moulded in the design of a male and female clipped together in delight and claiming to attain thereby a mystical fusion that shall last throughout eternity. Both Russian and English should do penance on their knees, and should stay there for the same length of time, for the offence lies not in the design but in the use of a rubber stamp, since a novelist has no reason to inscribe his pages with any design but that resulting from the inter-lacing of his characters' idiosyncrasies. But when we read on and learn of the altered reactions which the dogs exhibited in the laboratories, their tragedy becomes real to us, we think of a higher kind of art: Mitya in *The Brothers Karamazov* and 'I've had a good dream, gentlemen. I've had a good dream.' It was the experiment also that, in the case of the girl-wife dog, shifted our mind from Edith Wharton and Anne Douglas Sedgwick to Jane Austen, it was the record of her behaviour in the laboratories.

These experiments are carried on by a number of people who must have a sort of creative imagination not at all unlike the artists', a prophetic sense that if out of the innumerable phenomena of the universe one makes a certain pattern, an agreeable consequence would follow. They take place, it seems, in a building that is isolated by a deep trench, in sound-proof rooms, and they all depend on the fact that an animal's mouth produces a copious salivary flow when food or a distasteful substance is introduced into it. First of all, the dogs are subjected to a preliminary minor operation which consists of the transplantation of the opening of the salivary duct from its natural place on the mucous membrane of the mouth to the outside skin, on the cheek or the chin. Then in the daily routine each dog mounts a wooden stand and is secured by loose loops, and to the new opening of the salivary duct there is fixed a device of glass funnels and tubes which run into another room where an experimenter is sitting quite isolated, lest his movement should distract the dog, watching an electric register that tells the amount of saliva which has been secreted. Food or distasteful substances are then administered to it, but never simply, never to evoke merely the inborn reflex on which the dog is capable even if its brain has been removed.

Always the administration is combined at varying intervals with that of other stimuli. Food is shown to the animal; and the saliva begins to flow as if food had been introduced into its mouth. That does not happen with a dog whose brain has been removed, which will die of starvation in the midst of plenty, because it will only start eating if food chances to come into contact with its mouth and its tongue. But the brain will do a lot more than that. If a metronome is sounded at 160 a minute before food is given to the dog, and this is repeated several times, the saliva will begin to flow at the sound of the metronome alone, so long as it beats at the same rate. It will respond similarly to all sorts of stimuli, auditory and visual and tactile, singly and in groups, applying to its own responses a certain logic. There is a kind of blind fumbling for the idea of causality in the refusal of all dogs to respond to a stimulus that comes after instead of before the administration of food or acid. One dog was given over four hundred snuffs of an odour just after he was given acid, and it never acquired any power to produce saliva at all; but when another odour was given him at the same interval of time before food it produced saliva almost immediately.

Other patterns of stimuli derived by the experimenters disclose how the dog's brain makes up its mind that it is being fooled, and refuses these reactions of salivation, and how it behaves similarly when it is being over-stimulated and has to protect itself from fatigue; how it reacts if one varies the strength and kind of its stimuli, and if one removes this part of its brain or that. And out of all

these patterns is formed a larger pattern, which portrays for us the mental life of the dog. It appears
that there is as perfect continuity between the mind
of the animal and the mind of man. So far as can
be seen there is no mystical element peculiar to the
cerebral activity of man. What one had always
feared were the specific weaknesses of man's mind,
the cracking of the human mind under the peculiar
human destiny, are there in the animal too. Dogs can
have neurasthenia, they can have true hysteria, the
most fantastic tropes and turns of suggestion are
theirs also: a dose of apomorphine produces in the
dog nausea, secretion of saliva, vomiting, and sleep,
and after five or six days the preliminaries of injec-
tion are in themselves enough to produce these symp-
toms. Evidently it is nothing new for this dark vein
to run through mind-stuff, it argues nothing against
its survival. Indestructible is the rich tissue of the
normal reactions here exposed, with their perpetual
battle to find the most valuable link between the
reflexes and the environment, to bring the individual
to a victorious relationship with reality, by innumerable tricks and feints and advances and
retreats, sometimes seeking refuge every now and
then in error and apathy, leaving such refuges
always before the falsity has had time to imperil the
organism.

And that is not all; there is another drama that is
played there and yet not there. 'These results' (of
certain experiments) 'will throw some light upon one
of the darkest points of our subjective self – namely,
upon the relations between the conscious and the unconscious. The experiments if confirmed will have

demonstrated that such an important cortical function as synthesis ("association") may take place even
in those cortical areas which are in a state of inhibition on account of the existence at that moment of a
predominant focus of strong excitation. Though the
actual synthesizing activity may not enter our field of
consciousness the synthesis may nevertheless take
place, and under favourable conditions it may enter
the field of consciousness as a link already formed,
seeming to originate spontaneously.' Mysterious
choices appear, manifested in differences of general
behaviour, or more subtly and with more amazing
significance, differences in sensitivity towards matters in which there is no logical ground for the
existence of any such discrimination. One dog will
have a marked preference for visual stimuli; another
of apparently identical physical characteristics is far
more willing to react to auditory stimuli. Fido and
Rover are partaking of a mystery of which, further
up the table, Cézanne and Beethoven are participants
also. This continuity of the animal and the human
mind is the best news we could have. If the higher
human achievements were the product of activities
peculiar to man they would form a pyramid standing
on its apex, incapable of not collapsing. If we are not
related to the apes and all the lesser beasts, we are the
loneliest of orphans and when we die our kind dies
with us. But if the higher human achievements are
the products of the same sort of activities that have
brought organic life up from the primeval ooze, then
they are a pyramid which has the earth for its base
and shall not perish before it, and if organic life en-
genders and is engendered by a force that has found

so many manifestations, should we fail our failure is of not such great moment, since no doubt it could find another instrument. This news makes one take life at once more seriously and more carelessly. The money that one has is good, one can buy things with it, but if one comes to an end of it no great harm is done.

Then it occurs to me . . . what other activities form small patterns before one, from the synthesis of which one gets a sense of a larger pattern, which portrays for us the mental life of . . . man? But this is the business of literature. The whole proceedings are extraordinarily reminiscent of literature. The experiments themselves form close parallels to imaginative works of art. There is first of all the observation of the dogs themselves: the preliminary phase in which the experimenter tries to form some conception of the type of nervous system which the particular dog he is going to use possesses, so that it can be judged how far its reactions to stimuli will be normal and can be taken as the basis for generalization. If the experiment stopped there, with the experimenter merely watching the general behaviour of the dog in uncontrolled conditions, the result would be like the formless novel of character which most living citizens of Great Britain and the United States can now write as easily as they can breathe: 'Portraits of Some People, who so far as the author tells us do not matter a damn,' might be the alternative title of all of them. If these experiments were not preceded by these observations and consisted simply of the administration of the stimuli and the record of their effect the result would be like the old-fashioned novel of plot.

| Time. | Stimulus applied during one minute. | Amount of Saliva in drops during one minute. | |
		From Submaxillary Gland.	From Parotid Gland
1.53 p.m.	Meat powder pre-	11	7
1.58	sented at a dis-	4	2
2.3	tance	0	0
2.8	Same plus tactile stimulation of skin	3	1
2.13	Same plus knocks under the table	2	1
2.18	Meat powder at a distance	0	0
2.20	Prof. Pavlov enters the room containing the dog, talks, and stays for two minutes		
2.23	Meat powder at a distance	5	2
2.28	Same	0	0

One would not lose much if this method had been used in nearly all detective and adventure stories, in most novels that were written before the nineties, and in certain novels of to-day which the idiosyncrasy of the author has preserved from participation in the current absorption in character. It would be entertaining to rewrite *The Green Hat* as a timed record of the administration of stimuli to a subject ('the subject submitted to the experiment willingly and gave powerful and repeated reflexes'). But there is still another element in the experiment. The preliminary observations of the character of a subject coupled with observations of its behaviour under stimuli is not enough. The stimuli must have been chosen by the prophetic sense of the experimenter as likely to trace out through the nervous reflexes of the subject a significant pattern. There must be a theme to the experiment. The theme to this particular experiment is that 'the extinguished alimentary conditioned reflex' (the animal was given no food so it ceased to produce saliva at the sight of meat-powder after the second disappointment) 'is restored both by the actual presence of the extra stimulus (tactile and auditory) and by its after-effect (after-effect of stimulus of Professor Pavlov entering the room).' There is now some point to the dog story. It is now an entity, it gives satisfaction, it gratifies the investigatory reflex.

Now, if we turn to literature we find that a condition very similar to that which changes a dog story to an experiment is necessary if a novel (or a play or a poem) is to become a work of art. It is not enough for the author to combine the novel of character and the novel of plot into a whole, though that is an advance on writing them singly. The combination may be extremely entertaining, and interesting, and moving, but it will remain a casual and inessential flower in the button-hole of the universe, unless the prophetic sense of the author invents a story which when enacted by these particular characters traces a significant pattern. The novel must have a theme. Its story must be a myth, in which bodies which are embodiments enact an event which is a type of event. Innumerable competent novels have been written

86

about odd-seeming country clergymen who were dis-
liked by their flocks more than their deserts; there
have been innumerable competent novels about
thefts that the investigation has proved no theft.
The second-hand bookshops are populated by such.
There have been several novels no doubt about both
clergymen and thefts. But in *The Last Chronicles of
Barset*, Anthony Trollope wrote a novel about a
clergyman and a theft which has a theme. The mean
anxiety of the countryside to believe that poor un-
attractive Mr. Crawley should have stolen the money
sent to him as a gift, and their oddly enough equally
sincere relief when it was proved that he did not,
illustrate the curious tendency among human beings
for the happy to hate the unhappy, as if they spread
their unhappiness as an infection, form a typical
pattern traced out by human reflexes; an interesting
pattern because it is so immensely at variance with
the way that humanity claims it behaves; an affecting
pattern because it was concerned with such funda-
mentals as the primitive belief that all misfortune is
the punishment for guilt and the pain wrung from
the victim of this unjust suspicion unalleviated by
any more than the superficial conscious sense of
innocence, since in him also there is this belief.
Anthony Trollope passed the whole of this material
through his imagination (probably not knowing
exactly what he was doing, or how he was doing it, or
how important it was that it should be done, since the
presentation of this knowledge to himself would have
absorbed energy and he could do the job just as well
without it), and having thus gained an accurate non-
sentimental view of it he told the truth about it so

helped him God. And at the end of it he has established just how certain kinds of people act in certain circumstances that uncover their attitudes to recurring and fundamental factors of life, just as Professor Pavlov has established how a certain kind of dog behaved when it was given meat powder under certain conditions. An experiment has been conducted, an observation has been made, bearing on a principle, it has been faithfully reported.

Such too was the case with the scene between Leopold Bloom and John Henry Menton. That reminded me of Professor Pavlov's book in the first place, because the kind of satisfying emotion it gives is the same that *Conditioned Reflexes* gave me so dramatically after the Casino at Monte Carlo had tormented me by wholly denying it. Now, when we turn to Professor Pavlov's book we see an identity not only in emotional effects but in structure between these physiological experiments and a certain kind of imaginative work. This identity of structure implies an identity of function. Now the physiological experimenters admit that their function is to satisfy the investigatory, the 'What-is-it?' reflex; and the novelist has nothing definite enough to put forward as the function of his work for us to be anything like sure that his answer should not be the same. It is possible that the novelist may claim that he writes to create beauty. But beauty is that other factor which creates that other emotion, that ecstacy which is surely different from this brisk consciousness of stimulation. Beauty may be present in a novel, but on the other hand it may not, and still the novel may be valuable, because of the presence of this first factor which seems to bear this close resemblance to Science. We have strong grounds for suspecting that art is at least in part a way of collecting information about the universe.

III

Such is the case of *Adolphe*. I do not know that the writing of Benjamin Constant has any great individual beauty. *Adolphe* was composed about the time of Waterloo and the eighteenth century had established a habit of expecting and creating grace: a far from original cabinet-maker would probably have made quite good furniture in those days. 'Charme de l'amour, qui pourrait vous peindre? Cette persuasion que nous avons trouvé l'être que la nature avait destiné pour nous, se jour subit repandu sur la vie, et qui nous semble en expliquer la mystère, cette valeur inconnue attachée aux moindre circonstances, ces heures rapides, dont tous les details échappent au souvenir par leur douceur même. . . .' Chateaubriand and Lamartine did it better. Yet *Adolphe* is a book of extreme importance, of great power to excite readers and build itself into the structure of their minds so much so that one is unable to believe that it will not be immortal. Its triumph lies in its telling of the truth. It is powerful because it, too, conducts an experiment, it observes accurately certain activities which have their bearing on a principle, it reports them as accurately, and at the end it is established how certain kinds of people act in certain circumstances that uncover their attitudes to recurring and fundamental factors in life. We perceive Adolphe, the motherless neurotic, delighting in his father's coldness, converting every episode in his existence, however much it might promise sunshine and fellowship, into a moonlit solitary moping walk in some scenery exquisite yet a proof of squeamish-

ness in those who choose to traverse it, being wild
enough to be a sign that those who like it reject
the human garden, yet no wilder than a park for
crude nature also is rejected. One is reminded of
a long white hand with bitten nails. One perceives
Ellénore, her manners disciplined to a greater soci-
ability by the agreeing sweetness of her heart, her
soul free of squeamishness and rejection, but her fine
eyes distraught. She belongs to the more creative
type of misery. It does not satisfy her might to con-
vert the episodes of her life into sources of tragedy by
regarding them in a melancholy way, by changing
them in her mind. She must change them in the real
world, so she precipitates herself from situation to
situation in which suffering was inevitable. Here it
is not the nails but the full, generous lips that are
bitten. 'On l'examinait avec interêt et curiosité
comme un bel orage.'

The experiment is superbly designed by the type
of prophetic imagination that makes the scientist or
artist to exhibit the workings of the common
principle of which both Adolphe and Ellénore are
exemplars: that there are beings in whom the will to
live is utterly defeated save only physically, in which
the will to die triumphs universally in all mental and
spiritual matters; by whom the pursuit of happiness
is abandoned, and the pursuit of unhappiness sub-
stituted with the frenzy of those lost in darkness who
feel because of the primitive sense of guilt that it is
right they should be lost, and that it should be in
darkness, and that their pain should be to its utter-
most. Ellénore has bought herself a magnificent
estate of misery in her youth, before the book begins,

by becoming, though a woman of good birth, the mistress of a nobleman, and bearing him two illegitimate children. Beside the obvious torments to her pride inherent in the situation, there was further opportunity of suffering in her lover's loss of fortune. But this has begun to pall. In those who pursue unhappiness there is a profound Don Juanism, there is an incapacity to live monogamously with one tragedy, one must go on seducing events and getting them with fresh births of agony. Besides, the situation with the Comte de P. has begun to alleviate itself. His social ascendancy compels most people to treat her with civility; and her own dignity and probity have made many of those feel a real liking and respect for her. Also, she could not hope that such embarrassments as persisted in her situation would keep their first power to hurt her. And the Comte de P. was about to recover his lost fortune. Comparative serenity was looming over her like a dark cloud, when she met Adolphe, who was drawn to her by the sense that here was some one who was seeking the same goal as himself.

For their purposes the match is superb. The fracture of the old relationship guarantees them much misery. Ellénore loses the close companion of all her adult life, that is to say a great part of herself, and her two children, another great part of herself; and she sinks back and further into the state of courtesanship from which her personality and the Comte de P.'s efforts had lifted her. Adolphe gains more of a favourite pleasure by alienating his father still further; and he is frowned on by his society as the thief of another man's mistress. Moreover, there is no danger that the new relationship can treasonably lead them into happiness, for above and over the social difficulties it has an inherent disadvantage of the gravest sort, since he is twenty-two and she is in her middle thirties. All this is exhibited together with the devices by which they were able to persuade themselves that they were behaving in accordance with the sane man's practice of pursuing happiness: Adolphe's consciousness that it was a fine thing for a gentleman to be a rake ('Ellénore me parut une conquête digne de moi'): Ellénore's consciousness that for a lady *dulce et decorum est* to be wearied of but not to weary ('Qu'exigez-vous? Que je vous quitte? Ne vous croyez pas que je n'en ai pas la force? Ah, c'est à vous, qui n'aimez pas, c'est à vous à la trouver, cette force dans ce coeur lassé de moi que tant d'amour ne saurait désarmer'); and the tremendous joy and excitement that must occur when two natures so fitted for expression set themselves to contrive delight for one another.

Point by point the movement of the affair in time and space is plotted, with the use that the two make of each new position to further their campaign towards unhappiness. When he leaves her to go for a sojourn in another town to satisfy his father he writes her letters that keep the thing alive, though while he writes them he wishes he were dead; when she goes to visit him there she comes flapping her passion at him like the great gaunt wings of a bird of prey; and always in her heart she is mourning over the vast sacrifices she has made for him, and in his he is frantic because he is wasting his youth and not getting on with his life and the career to which his talents should have predestined him. One can conceive the stretch of time and space through which they pass as a length of patterned stuff in which it is their mysterious duty to reappear at intervals, essential factors in the pattern, two strange, strained figures, not united and not separated, the man fleeing out of the woman's hands yet never choosing quite to escape, the woman not grasping him for her own yet never letting him go. One can conceive the threads that compose these figures, when once they are running at the back of the stuff, feeling an agony till they have thrust their way to the right side to play their part in the pattern; for what more imperative duty can lie on human beings than to play the part in the pattern which they think is theirs by destiny? But they must appear only for one instant, for an inch or two, lest their attitudes develop into finality and purpose, lest instead of tormenting indecision comes a decision and an end to torment, which is not as much desired as one might think.

That end to torment came, and was no prelude to happiness, when Ellénore, with her superior vehemence, that unwieldy abundance of power, raised the agony engendered by the situation to such a degree of intensity that she died. 'L'exemple d'Adolphe ne sera pas moins instructif,' says the epilogue, 'si vous ajoutez qu'après avoir repoussé l'être qui l'aimait, il n'a pas été moins inquiet, moins agité, moins mécontent; qu'il n'a fait aucun usage d'une liberté reconquise en prix de tant de douleurs et de tant de larmes. . . .' He had never been capable of having that career from which he had fancied that Ellénore debarred him, because he did not truly

94

desire it. What he desired was to feel debarred from
it by some one who could give him no compensation,
being too old and no longer loved. To be destitute
was his ambition, however much he might rationalize
his proceedings in sensible sounding phrases that
drop on the page like little hard round pebbles. . . .
'Je me demandais souvent pourquoi je restais dans
un état si penible: je me répondais que, si je m'eloig-
nais d'Ellénore, elle me suivrait, et que j'aurais pro-
voqué un nouveau sacrifice. . . .' How entirely con-
vinced we are that Adolphe would have thought
these thoughts and used these words! Indeed, it is
with a feeling of entire conviction that we close the
book. *This much we now know. . . .*

'*This much we now know. . . .*' Yes, we say it again
and again in literature. We say it when we read in
Proust:

. . . 'In this way I used to submit my impressions
of life to my grandmother, for I was never certain
what degree of respect was due to anyone until she
had informed me. Every evening I would come to
her with the mental sketches that I had made during
the day of all those non-existent people who were not
her. Once I said to her: "I shouldn't be able to live
without you!" "But you mustn't speak like that";
her voice was troubled. "We must harden our hearts
more than that, you know. Or what would become
of you if I went away on a journey? But I hope that
you would be sensible and quite happy."

' "I should manage to be sensible if you went away
for a few days, but I should count the hours."

' "But if I were to go away for months" (at the

bare suggestion of such a thing my heart was wrung)
". . . for years . . . for . . ."

'We both remained silent. We dare not look one
another in the face. And yet I was suffering more
keenly from her anguish than from my own. And
so I walked across to the window and said to her,
with a studied clearness of tone but with averted
eyes:

' "You know what a creature of habit I am. For
the first few days after I have been parted from the
people I love best, I am wretched. But though I go
on loving them just as much, I grow used to their
absence; life becomes calm, bearable, pleasant; I
could stand being parted from them for months, for
years. . . ."

'I was obliged to stop, and looked straight out of
the window. My grandmother went out of the room
for something. But next day I began to talk to her
about philosophy, and, speaking in a tone of complete indifference, but at the same time taking care
that my grandmother should pay attention to what I
was saying, I remarked what a curious thing it was
that, according to the latest scientific discoveries, the
materialist position appeared to be crumbling, and
the most likely thing to be, once again, the survival
of the soul and re-union in a life everlasting. . . .'

We say it too when a note is sounded at the other
end of the scale, when we read in Jane Austen the
passage concerning Mr. and Mrs. John Dashwood's
discussion of how much he should do to honour his
promise to his dead father to take care of his step-
mother and half-sisters:

'His wife hesitated a little, however, in giving her consent to this plan.

' "To be sure," said she, "it is better than parting with fifteen hundred pounds at once. But then if Mrs. Dashwood should live fifteen years, we shall be completely taken in."

' "Fifteen years! my dear Fanny; her life cannot be worth half that purchase."

' "Certainly not; but if you observe, people always live for ever when there is any annuity to be paid them; and she is very stout and healthy, and hardly forty. An annuity is a very serious business; it comes over and over every year and there is no getting rid of it. You are not aware of what you are doing. I have known a great deal of the trouble of annuities; for my mother was dogged with the payment of three to old superannuated servants by my father's will, and it is amazing how disagreeable she found it. Twice every year these annuities were to be paid; and then there was the trouble of getting it to them; and then one of them was said to have died, and afterwards it turned out to be no such thing. My mother was quite sick of it. Her income was not her own, she said, with such perpetual claims on it; and it was the more unkind in my father, because otherwise, the money would have been entirely at my mother's disposal, without any restriction whatever. It has given me such an abhorrence of annuities, that I am sure I would not pin myself down to the payment of one for all the world."

' "It is certainly an unpleasant thing," replied Mr. Dashwood, "to have those kind of yearly drains on one's income. One's fortune, as your mother justly says, is *not* one's own. To be tied down to the regular payment of such a sum, on every rent day, is by no means desirable: it takes away one's independence."

' "Undoubtedly; and after all you have no thanks for it. They think themselves secure, you do no more than what is expected, and it raises no gratitude at all. If I were you, whatever I did should be done at my own discretion entirely. I would not bind myself to allow them anything yearly. It may be very inconvenient some years to spare a hundred, or even fifty pounds from our own expenses."

' "I believe you are right, my love. . . ." '

And so on to Mrs. Dashwood's rhapsodic speech: 'Altogether they will have five hundred a year amongst them, and what on earth can four women want for more than that? They will live so cheap! Their housekeeping will be nothing at all. They will have no carriage, no horses, and hardly any servants; they will keep no company, and have no expenses of any kind. Only conceive how comfortable they will be!' – and the comfortable resolving chords of the decision between the happy married couple to do nothing for the widow and the orphans save 'send presents of fish and game.' Do not these passages and thousands like them make one suspect that there is a very close resemblance indeed between art and science, a resemblance so close that we might say that art is science, only more scientific? The precise parallel we have established is merely between the work of art and a particular kind of scientific experiment – a physiological experiment: but there is so precise a parallel between an experiment in a physiological laboratory and one in a laboratory used for research in physics or chemistry, so far as prophetic imagination on the part of the experimenter, the structure of the experiment, and the resultant establishment of a fact as true in the particular circumstances which have been manufactured, that we may safely take the parallel as between art and science. And one may say that art is more scientific than science because it has some technique for expressing the emotion of the subjects of its experiments, and science has none (except such rough quantitative methods as this registering of salivation and the recording of such bare facts as 'subject more excited,' or 'subject less excited,' although it must admit that emotion is as real as any of the other phenomena it investigates).

But it may be objected that there is this fundamental objection to any such parallel: that Professor Pavlov's dogs are real, and that Adolphe and Ellenore, the 'moi' of Proust and his grandmother, Mr. and Mrs. John Dashwood are not. They are fantasies. They are just what their authors chose to make them. They do just what the author chose they should. But is that true? Is not the choice of imaginary characters a new and completely justifiable technique which man has invented to deal with material that cannot be put into a test-tube or isolated in a laboratory and made to salivate, that suffers from self-consciousness and has learned to lie?

The basis of this new technique one can imagine to be of this nature. We all have a certain body-consciousness that packs away a great deal of latent information about how we feel when we move, and also gives us a working knowledge of what we can do

with our muscles and our nerves and all other physical possessions. A child may make a mistake about
its capacity before it has thoroughly tried it out; but
most adults can almost invariably recognize whether
they can or cannot perform a certain physical feat.
We can look at a dancer going through a dance of
progressive difficulty and know, 'I can do that,' 'I
can do that too.' 'And that too,' until there comes a
time when we know 'But I cannot do that.' When it
comes to those movements which are unlike those we
can make we can easily imagine what it is like to
make them, because the dancer has only the same
muscles that we have, though hers are in a different
state of development. On the foundation of our
experience we are able to penetrate imaginatively
into the experience of others. Even a fat and heavily
clad old gentleman can participate in the joy of
Suzanne Lenglen if he sees her springing across the
tennis-court and in the discomfort of a raw-boned
consumptive if he sees him sitting on an Embankment bench on a chilly night. Hence it happens that
if a drawing of realistic pretensions representing a
human body is shown to a person of ordinary powers
of observation, he immediately feels either a calm
sense of rightness which analysis will show to be the
result of the conviction that this particular body is
represented in an attitude within normal human
capacity; or he feels an unhappy sense of wrongness,
which analysis will show is due to a conviction that
this particular body is represented in an attitude outside normal human capacity. People with purely
verbal memories and those who have not used their
bodies much, will probably be wrong about it; and

people with keen sensory memories, athletes, or anatomists, are likely to be correct in their judgment.

Now it does not seem at all unlikely that we should have a mind-consciousness which tells us as fully about other people's minds as our body-consciousness tells us about other people's bodies. It may be objected that although such a mind-consciousness undoubtedly exists whatever the behaviourists may say (for otherwise we would have no knowledge of other people whatever) it acts less powerfully than the body consciousness because while the dancer and the spectator, the old gentleman and Suzanne Lenglen and the Embankment consumptive, have more or less the same nervous and muscular systems and the same skeletons, each human being has a psychical outfit quite different from every other human being's. But the difference in human beings is probably not so great as we suppose from the surfaces they offer us. It may be admitted that every human being is as unique psychically as physically; but that is the result partly of the inevitable unique circumstances of his life (nobody can occupy exactly the same position in the space-time system that he does, and even if he is one of twenty clerks working in a whitewashed room with a steel-framed window he must see the angle of the walls and the chimneys outside as nobody else does); and partly to that mysterious particle of the soul which dictates the fantasy and chooses what the soul shall do, which makes Fido and Cézanne respond to visual stimuli, Rover and Beethoven to auditory stimuli. It may be doubted if there is much else working for uniqueness. The inner material on which this particle works

seems to differ in degree rather than kind. The
fundamental groundwork of every human being's
character lies in its handling of its instincts (and
these are so purely the product of the relations between the body and the environment that it is not
conceivable that organisms having the same sort of
bodies should not have the same instincts). Now
though the mysterious particle may forbid us to
handle our instincts in certain ways we are nevertheless physically and mentally capable of handling
them in those ways. A bishop is physically capable of
going out on Saturday night and getting drunk on
gin and coming back and beating his wife; he is even
mentally capable of following the line of thought
which actuates people who do these things. All he
cannot do is to choose this course of action in real
life; though probably, such conduct being so much
the reverse of what is expected from a bishop, he
sometimes obeys the human tendency to run away
from reality in the form in which it is being experienced to the experience of some other form in
fantasy, and under suitably symbolic disguises follows that course of action. He is not therefore so
different from the man who does go out on Saturday
night and gets drunk and beats his wife that he has
not a pretty good idea of what he is like, and even
what it is to be him. That he may deny this knowledge for purposes of self-regard is of no importance.
He can, if he has the active power of empathy which
makes the creative artist, or the passive power of
empathy which makes the appreciator of art, imagine
that he has made the wifebeater's moral decision
about the kind of life he wants to lead, and imagine

also that the same environmental stimuli are being
applied to him; and he can then put into action the
psychical mechanism which he does not use and
which the wifebeater does. In fact, he can for the
time being become the wifebeater. If anyone asks
me how it is possible for imagined stimuli to have the
same effect as real ones, I answer candidly that I do
not know, but point to the phenomena of hypnotism,
which have proved under controlled conditions on innumerable occasions that imagined stimuli can have
precisely the same effect as real ones, and furthermore I will point out that no psychologist has ever
furnished an explanation of hypnotism for which one
would reward him with a drink.

The position of affairs and how it permits the
artistic process can be grasped if we consider the soul
as a house and two inhabitants. This house has innumerable rooms: one for each character-trait that
can be based on each possible reaction to the fundamental instincts that the soul's material surroundings
and the state of culture at the time produce. Of the
two inhabitants one is a mysterious being who acts
towards the other as Merlin to King Arthur, as
Virgil to Dante. He seems to have a far greater
knowledge than the other of what is in these rooms:
but he is very far from being all wise, and he not
infrequently works against the happiness which it is
the other's aim to achieve. But in any case he has an
ascendancy over the other which enables him to tell
him in what rooms he shall live. For the house is
cold. It is impossible to live in any of the rooms unless they are warmed and the house is heated by a
hot-water system of which one may take the furnace

and fuel as symbols of the innate gifts of the individual whose soul this is and the experience. It rests with Merlin to turn on the radiators, by which we may understand the conscious interest of the individual. Now, there is no sense anyway in turning on the radiators in too many rooms. No man can have the time to be both Napoleon and Shakespeare even if he combined in himself the capacity of the two. But also there is the paramount necessity felt by Merlin that his King Arthur should by his life work out the pattern that he feels a life ought to form. That ultimately decides what rooms are inhabited. These arrangements are never entirely to King Arthur's liking. Inevitably, since the fantasy does not correspond exactly with reality, living according to the fantasy brings him into painful conflict with reality.

Against this he rebels and goes into some of the other rooms and tries to turn on the radiators and settle down there; or he at least puts his head into the other doors and wonders what it would be like to live there. This exploration of different phases of one's own being involves an exploration of other people's beings also, since this identity of instinct and in most cases of all but the most immediate circumstances will mean that in the houses of most souls (particularly of those living at the same time or within the orbit of the same civilization) the rooms have certain close resemblances. Furthermore, as from the beginning of time every individual has had to watch all others to see that his safety was not threatened, there must be now a human habit of watching other people and trying to deduce their

inner lives from their behaviour which will enable the
extent of these resemblances to be inquired into and
recorded as fully as any phenomena we encounter.
Because of these things it may be judged that man
has as much capacity for psychical as he has for
physical empathy, that when he reads a novel or a
poem representing human beings enacting life the
feelings of satisfaction or dissatisfaction he has,
which on analysis will show is due to a conviction
that the representation is or is not parallel to what
occurs in real life, is as likely to be on the whole valid
as his feeling when shown a drawing of a human
figure that is or is not 'out of drawing.'

Now this makes it possible for authors to invent
characters whom we cannot dismiss as being just
what the author makes them, and whose proceedings
are not simply what the author chose they should do.
Let us try to understand how Benjamin Constant
came to write *Adolphe*. It is commonly said that it is
the story of his own relations with Madame de Staël,
but that is not accurate. It is true that he was having
an affair with Madame de Staël and that it was going
badly, that in Adolphe's father he exactly depicted
his own, and that he had in his youth frequented the
house of an elderly woman of witty and pessimistic
spirit, whose death made him melancholy, but there
the points of resemblance end. Madame de Staël
was no such superb storm as Ellénore; she was good
weather to go sailing by, if one was fond of the sport.
She was neither beautiful nor *déclassée*, there was no
Comte de P., there was not more than a year's difference in their ages, the liaison lasted fourteen years,
until his marriage, which was provoked by a series of

circumstances quite outside the sphere of Adolphe and Ellénore. M. de Staël had died and Benjamin Constant had asked her to marry him, and she had refused except on the condition that she need not change her name, a condition which betrayed her belief that she had made it more glorious than he had made his. In pique he rushed away and married in secret an aristocratic widow, Charlotte von Hardenberg, thus touching Madame de Staël in the point which is most vulnerable. It is regrettably true that while one cannot imagine a Somerville or Newnham don being fluttered at dancing with the Prince of Wales, few of their male colleagues could be trusted not to perceive a certain special glamour about a Duchess. So universal is this tendency among males, not sparing the most intelligent, that a woman of talent has perpetually to reconcile herself to the fact that though she may be as beautiful as Aphrodite and as amusing as Mercury, Lady Mary Binks has already been given the victory over her irrespective of her merits. This marriage made Madame de Staël refuse to relinquish her hold on Benjamin Constant, and for some years there was an agony of that love which insists on its dues and in effect is hate. One may conceive that Benjamin Constant wearied exceedingly of these circumstances and the parts that both of them played; and would very willingly have fled into a fantasy where life bore a different appearance; but that morbidity in him which made him accept Madame de Staël's wildest statement about what the world thought of him for his marriage and desertion of her, and say quite seriously to Madame Récamier that when he went to Paris he drew down the blinds of his carriage lest the crowd should see him whom they regarded as a monster, made him choose a fantasy in which sex still led to misery and disaster. He simply opened the door of another suite of rooms and looked in and said: 'If I lived there, this and that would happen,' and his empathy forbade him to invent a detail that was 'out of drawing.' His sensitiveness was so great that his empathy was practically infallible. Hence the power of its operation to convince the empathies of his readers that what he has written is true: a power so great that there has sprung up this curious legend that it is a literal account of his relationship with Madame de Staël in spite of the fact that it is impossible to know anything of the literary history of the period without seeing that such could not be the case.

So too with Proust, about whose work there is the same unfounded legend of fidelity to historic fact, though it would seem obvious that the keystone of the book, the quiet and self-possessed 'moi' who slips dapperly through the intricacies of Parisian Society, distinguished only by his ill-health, is not the same as the real eccentric whose ill-health was regarded by Parisian Society as only one diamond of his harlequin costume. His book is the celebration of a life-long love, the love of 'moi' for his grandmother. In his youth, when he was still her little child, the world seemed to be infinitely full of glorious objects that might be possessed, of superb avenues leading down to glamorous distances that visited would lose no glamour. From his home in the country there were those two long walks, the one which passed by the estate which belonged to

Swann, the other which passed by the estate of the
Duc de Guermantes, which were delicious not only
because of such things as hedges of hawthorns rococo
with prodigious blossom, or water-meadows half-
hidden under a shining veil of buttercups, but because the estates hidden behind the boundaries suggested two ways by which life might be plundered of
all those delights. One was Swann's way, the way
that is open to any person of intelligence and sensibility who trains his taste as if it were a sporting dog
to point and retrieve everything precious that the
world has to offer. The other was the Guermantes'
way, the way that is open to any person who dis-
misses his intelligence to a subordinate position and
places himself entirely at the disposal of a tradition
that ensures, at least for those who profess it, a
certain magnificence of life and the elimination of all
meanness from it.

The book is the record of his disillusionment. If
there had seemed an effulgence on the face of the
earth it had been only a reflection from the fount of
all light, the grandmother. Neither Swann's nor
Guermantes' way led to anything glamorous, there
appeared to be no objects glorious enough to be
even worth possessing, to one who had possessed
this supreme glory. To prove his point he conveys
what both men get out of life by making their wives
much more than women, by making them symbolic
figures of an immense significance, such as religion
rather than art has achieved, which, like those religious achievements, inspire by the weight of what
they signify, by the force it exercises in human
affairs, a worship that one would suppose to be

evoked only by qualities far other than those they represent, so that multitudes seem to feel an actual pleasure in bending the knee to Kali instead of fleeing from her. It is impossible not to sympathize with 'moi' for his childish infatuation with Swann's wife Odette, though she is really one of those 'women of no virtue,' who give the phrase a meaning more real than it usually has. For there is nothing she would feel she could not do, since her free use of her body has been due neither to generosity nor to passion, but to an inability to perceive that one should perhaps surrender oneself with greater reserve than one feels in taking small change out of one's bag and using it in brisk exchange for a needed article. Moreover (what is perhaps more important) she would use words with equal unchastity, so that she is a complete humbug. That taste has its aberrations, that after it has been trained to serve its master perfectly for a lifetime it may conceive a 'longing' as morbid as those old wives ascribe to pregnant women and saddle him with such a wife as this, such an inadequate companion for life and one's departure from it, is the condemnation of Swann's way; that the Guermantes' way leads no further is shown by the exposition of the Duchesse de Guermantes, who, when her life-long friend blurts out that he cannot join her party to Italy because by the time it starts he will for some months have been dead of an internal malady, does not lose her consciousness that if she fails to break off the conversation immediately she will be late for quite an important dinner in the Faubourg St. Germain, and says, 'Qu'est que vous me dites là? Vous voulez plaisanter.'

This exposition is as spectacular as anything in fiction because in Proust's desire to do the fullest honour to her beside whom they were dross he labours to show that regarded from any other point of view than comparison with this grandmother who was brighter than the sun and moon, they were precious enough. To that end he works to set before us, to deliver over to its senses with no diminution due to the indirectness of our apprehension, the delicious decorative quality of both women; of Odette, sitting in her warm drawing-room, in a dress white as the snow outside the window, the whiteness of the crêpe and the snow forming as it were the octave notes of an arpeggio, between which the rosy silk of the Louis XIV chairs, the purple of the Parma violets she kept always in a crystal bowl by her side, the flesh tints of the roses, the flames of her favourite giantesque chrysanthemums, were the intervening notes that made a more momentary claim on the attention; of Oriane, gliding across the polished floors of great rooms like a swan on a lake. Even so when in the affair of Albertine he sets out to demonstrate that sexual love is not to be named as love at all (if one takes as criterion that earliest love), that it can precipitate those who become involved in it down into the blackest pits of obscene misadventures, he makes the very figure he chose for demonstration irresistible with the supreme charm and persuasive exquisiteness which transforms into glowing beauty all its constituents, even if they include cruelty and vulgarity. And even so he builds up pictures as sensuously and intellectually rich as those of the performance of Berma, the hotel life at Balbec,

the personalities of Bergotte and Elstir, the loves of
Saint-Loup and Rachel, the parties of Marie-Gilbert,
so that he can represent them in his last volume as
robbed of all their richness by time, and prove it to
be the only wisdom to start this unprecedented use of
memory to run back and back and back into that
past and its holy and incorruptible inhabitant.

To establish this argument about life, to coerce
events into this pattern, was his passion, whether he
were living or writing. He was therefore at spiritual
ease when he wrote his masterpiece, his Merlin was
pleased with him, he allowed him free access to all
the rooms in the mansion, thus enabling him to
bridge over certain formidable difficulties. For actually, though this is a true story in its essence, there
are certain factual departures from the truth which
necessitate throughout the most delicate readjustments. Most important of these are the changes
which had to be made because in real life the love
that consumed Proust was not for his grandmother
but for his mother. He made this transposition, one
supposes, out of that curious impulse which comes on
those who love to conceal where concealment is of no
purpose, as a cocotte who is boasting to a companion
of a new and adorable client will say, 'He says he is a
manufacturer from Nottingham,' when actually he
has said he was a shipowner from Cardiff. The little
lie serves no purpose, since one way or another the
man's identity was kept a secret, and one can only
guess that by making it the speaker creates an illusion in herself of being engaged in a love affair such
as protected women have, who are so loaded by
society with proof of its regard — homes, reputations,

legal titles — that they hedge themselves round with the extremest secrecy. Even so one can imagine that Proust rebelled against the insipidity resulting from the universal tolerance of the love between himself and his mother, and, deciding that no kind of lovers should have any sort of advantage over him and her, went through the motions of one of those ruses which notoriously add to the excitement and prestige of the more romantic type of love affair.

At any rate, for whatever reason he did it, he raised stupendous problems for himself; to see with what infallible wisdom he solved them turn back to the scene between 'moi' and his grandmother I have already quoted. It is exquisitely designed to be appropriate to the particular relationship of grandmother and grandson: so much so that it would be grossly inappropriate to any other. For a mother would do wrong, unless she suffered from a menacing disorder (which would introduce a new element into the situation and start quite another story) to alarm a boy, particularly of so nervous a disposition, by talking of their impending separation by death, since it would be extremely unlikely that this would happen for some years to come. But a grandmother, yes. It would be in the character of a wise and loving old lady, however much she was averse from scene making, to warn the boy that he must not depend on her too much. Observe, too, the perfect suitability of the terminating incident. In a prosperous and cultured home like that of 'moi' where the mother would not be so absorbed in domestic duties as to abandon her intellectual life, she would not have appeared enough in the guise of receptive listener that the boy would talk of philosophy; but grand-mothers admit that time has been too much for them and that they cannot keep up, they do sit and listen when the boy talks of modern marvels and own themselves learners. Analysis can find no point at which Proust's invention of the relationship between the old lady and the boy does not run parallel with what, so far as human intelligence and emotion can diagnose, the reality of such a relationship would be. Nor can it find any point at which he fails in making those readjustments which were necessitated by his other important deviation from fact.

For it is established as definitely as anything can be that the person who played the part in Proust's life which he ascribes to Albertine differed from Albertine in the most essential points. Yet from the time she first appears on the beach at Balbec, leading her little band who all had 'that mastery over their limbs which comes from perfect bodily condition and a sincere contempt for the rest of humanity,' till her horse dashes her against a tree and she dies by that muscular violence by which she had lived, she is down to the smallest movement, to the attitude her head and hands assume when she is pushing her bicycle, to the most subtle turn of phrase when she is telling authority a sulky untruth or demonstrating by the use of some adult catchword that she is grown up, a perfect copy of the hoyden. When Proust wrote of her he exercised imaginatively those psycho-logical mechanisms which in life he did not use and hoydens do. This feat of empathy he performs over and over again, on each fresh character, for in the whole of *A la Recherche du Temps Perdu* there is not one character which utters one syllable or makes one gesture which is not uniquely appropriate and at once an inevitable growth of their destiny and a determinant of it, as syllables and gestures are in real life. Never does he fail: not with Françoise the old servant, with Saint-Loup the young aristocrat, with Bloch, with Elstir, with Bergotte, with old Madame de Villeparisis, with the Princesse de Luxembourg, with Jupien and Rachel, with Cottard. All these names mean living people.

Perhaps this is the secret of the extreme pleasure one derives from reading Proust. The pleasure one derives from seeing a greatly gifted dancer perform for a short time is intense; but if she dances for a long time with undiminished grace and invention that pleasure is reinforced by a delighted sense of the strength which must be the source of this power of continuance. And if the stage is covered with people dancing equally well and without fatigue provided their movements are not mutually destructive and form a harmonious composition, there is a still more enhanced sense of the delicious wealth of human vitality. That Proust performs this feat of empathy not in a poem, not in a short story, not in a novel, not in the case of a single character, but throughout a book as long as thirteen novels (far longer than *Ulysses*) in the case of a whole society, gives some such reinforcement of the purely æsthetic pleasure. It is for that reason that in spite of his intellectual findings about life, which leave Thomas Hardy's pessimism beaten at the post, it is invariably refreshing and exhilarating to read his work. That too is the secret of the tonic power of Jane Austen, whose

governing fantasy evidently coincided so nearly with
reality that it is not detectable in her books, so that
one does not know what they are 'up to' any more
than one knows what life is 'up to,' and could not
possibly construe them as a basis for optimism. Our
sense of well-being is derived from her protean liveli-
ness, which gave her the ability to run from character
to character, enjoying by empathy and causing us to
enjoy the light-heartedness of being wise and choosing circumstances that shall not strain our wisdom,
the safety of being a nice man with a reasonable
amount of intelligence and enough money, the delicious cosiness of being a fool. And it is because the
novel above all other forms of art can give this profound pleasure that the Puritan tendency has always
been to disapprove of the reading of fiction.

It may be objected: 'You have said nothing at all
except that some characters are well invented and
others are not. Well, we all knew that!' But what I
am suggesting is that our feelings when we encounter
in fiction characters which seem to us well invented
and others that are not so strong that they must proceed from something more than mere enjoyment the
pleasures of recognition and disappointment at not
receiving them: that here we are evidently participating in the exercise of some complicated mechanism
within the human organism, and I have suggested
how that mechanism works. It may be objected
again that if it does proceed from a certain mechanism it must be a rudimentary and unimportant one,
for it works all anyhow: since many people derive
this pleasure from characters that plainly have no
value under heaven, abortions mothered by print, in

which plainly no empathy has been performed, and others find the creations of the greatest artists repulsive and ridiculous. These aberrations do not, however, discredit the mechanism in the least. They only prove that like all other mechanisms it varies in efficiency with the individual. For the same people who derive pleasure from the characters of Jane Austen and Marcel Proust do not derive it from the turnip-ghosts of A. S. M. Hutchinson and Ethel Dell. It was Lady Oxford and not Vernon Lee or T. S. Eliot or Virginia Woolf who wrote to *The Times* registering ecstasy concerning the hero of *If Winter Comes*.

And when one asks why people who like bad novels have this strange preference one discovers that in them also this mechanism is working to fulfil a psychic need. Plainly their power of empathy is not working on real people: but it would be wasted if it were, since stupid and neurotic people live so much in the world of dreams that any exploration of the real world would be useless to them. It is far more important that they should have their neuroses formulated for them so that the healthy and progressive part of their minds can deal with them. Millions of narcissists have visualized themselves as Mark Sabres, as Messiahs whom the world is rejecting because of their holiness, in whom suffering is so precious and lovely that without doubt it must have power to save. It is well that the illusion which has been drifting through their heads as a hazy tiresomeness should be sharply defined so that even if they themselves greet it with self-loving enthusiasm the more developed members of the community can express their attitude towards it. Again and again in literature we have seen how the statement of a neurosis, though it may at first be hailed as a masterpiece, ultimately becomes discredited and leads to the at least partial disappearance of that neurosis. For example, the neurosis fostered by Benthamism in the first half of the nineteenth century, a form of Jehovahism which assured man that if he kept certain laws he would be happy and prosperous (in fact, that within his own universe he was God), withered away and died so far as literature was concerned once it had been objectified in Martin Tupper's *Proverbial Philosophy*. The writer of this kind of best seller should be reckoned as one who performs a repulsive but necessary function like Mr. Pierrepoint.

But on looking at the forms art takes among neurotics we are looking at something as different from its normal function as hysteria is from serenity; and to say that art is always nothing but the copy of dreams for ornamental and fulfilment purposes is like saying that all people whoop and yell in moments of excitement because some people do. If we transfer our attention to the proceedings of more developed types of humanity we have no excuse for denying that there is a process by which a man can use in fantasy psychological mechanisms which he does not use in real life, and since these are common to all other human beings he is thereby reconstructing the experience of other real people; so that the record by a person using this process, of the behaviour of imaginary people in a book is as sound a guide to the understanding of real people in the real world out-

side that book as the record of the behaviour of real
dogs in a laboratory is to the understanding of real
dogs outside a laboratory. In fact, art is out to collect
information about the phenomena of the universe,
just as science is; and its preference to do this by the
study of imaginary material shows its loyalty to the
scientific spirit. For it knows that most men if they
used in their writing the psychological mechanisms
they used in real life, would be tempted to falsify the
record of them in order to attain the values for the
self which were their objectives in real life; only by
transferring the operations of their empathy to fields
where they can reap no advantages or disadvantages
of this sort can they be trusted to make their records
truthfully.

It may seem that although I am writing now of
'art' I have, in fact, touched only on literature. But
I have chosen to base my argument on examples
drawn from literature for no reason except that I am
more familiar with that form of art than any other.
The painter and the musician use empathy in forms
different from that used by the writer; but their
dependence on it is probably as great. Perhaps the
painter uses it in a form more abstract than the
writer, and the musician in a form more concrete.
The other day I was standing in front of a very
charming picture by Bonnard, the subject of which
was something to do with the form impressed by a
hillside of a certain texture and contour on air made
a certain texture by light, and it occurred to me that
before the artist can have received his intuition of
this form he must have diverted his sight of the persistent quality of 'usefulness' that it had in the ordi-

nary person. He saw that hillside with a temporary
indifference to all its attributes that might affect
the well-being of creation (such as its suitability
as a site for a picnic which would have inspired
Mr. Leader, or its capacity for nourishing cows,
which would have inspired Mr. Sydney Cooper, or
its capacity for nourishing horses, which would have
inspired Mr. Munnings), as if he had been cut off
from such considerations by some limitations of experience; as if, say, he had been paralysed from birth,
was indifferent to food, and felt no affection for
animals. It occurred to me then that just as the
writer makes an effort to become a particular person,
just as Benjamin Constant became Adolphe and
Ellénore, and Proust becomes 'moi' and his grandmother, and Jane Austen becomes Mr. and Mrs.
John Dashwood, so the painter makes an effort to
become a generalized person, distinct from himself
not by being somebody else, but by not having certain
relationships to his environment which are hostile to
the innocence of the eye.

It occurred to me also that the musician, on the
other hand, goes in for a more particularized impersonation than the writer when I read that absorb-
ingly interesting study, *The Unconscious Beethoven*,
by Ernest Newman. I think there is no difficulty in
accepting the view of Beethoven's character held by
Mr. Newman; whom I count along with Roger Fry
and Virginia Woolf as Fortnum & Mason authors,
about whom one knows that they know all sorts of
things one would like to know just as certainly as one
knows that Fortnum & Mason sell all sorts of things
one would like to eat. It is utterly incredible that

Beethoven, who was a crawling snob, who cheated his publishers, was false to his friends and benefactors, and behaved like a petulant hysteric in his family affairs, should have built his music on the foundation of such an experience. But there is nothing mysterious in the situation if one grants that a man full of a passionate desire to live creatively, and unable to realize that desire through his relations with his kind owing to destructive compulsions arising out of an easily recognizable neurosis, stepped out of his unhappy circumstances by means of empathy into the experience of a person without such compulsions. He could not have become such a person altogether, because of his compulsion; but the part of him that wished to be such a person was strong enough to insist on being him in fantasy. It is perhaps because there is necessary for the making of a composer just such a thorough and prolonged impersonation that the greatest musicians have a mightiness about them which is certainly not transcended, and perhaps not equalled by the greatest painters or the greatest writers.

To doubt that painting and music are just as capable as literature of giving us information about the universe is to show ourselves hag-ridden by the intellect. It is true that literature alone presents us with information in a form on which the intellect can use her accomplishments of logic and the like; but painting presents us with material which does not wait for completion by the intellect, which rounds itself off in the present, which does not need to be treated as a premise because it is itself a complete syllogism, and music presents us with material on

which the intellect has already done all the work it
can, on the effects produced by a multitude of syllo-
gisms. When Michael Angelo carved the waking
woman on the Medici tomb he was recording the
behaviour of a certain mass at a certain instant which
was a complete event in itself. When Shakespeare
wrote the sonnet beginning, 'Let me not to the
marriage of true minds Admit impediments,' he was
recording a certain event of a much more complicated
kind (largely owing to the much more untidy position
it occupies in regard to time) which offers the intellect just the job it can do in its need for clarifica-
tion. When Beethoven wrote the Quartet in C
sharp minor he recorded an event of still greater
complication that was precipitated as the result of a
series of experiences of the simple kind that are the
subject of the plastic arts and those of the not so
simple kind that are the subject of literature: in
fact, he recorded what happens after a thing has
happened, what life amounts to after it has been
lived. It seems to be true that all the arts are on
a perfect equality regarding this necessity to collect information of one sort or another about the
universe.

IV

But why does humanity want to collect all this information?

That brings me back to Professor Pavlov's *Conditioned Reflexes*. In reading that book one feels again and again that one is lit up by a flash of pleasure, warmed by a glow of satisfaction, which obviously cannot proceed from any sensuous excitation arising from the beauty of the manner or matter ('With the help of injections of a suitable dose of caffeine the dog was brought back to its usual condition of wakefulness . . .'). When I was reading the book for the second time, on reflection I found that these emotional states persistently reviewed in my mind the memory of an incident which took place at some point in a period between seventeen and twenty-five years ago, when as a child I lived in Scotland. One afternoon I went the walk that runs alongside the Firth of Forth through Lord Rosebery's estate, Dalmeny, to Queensferry, where the estuary is spanned by the Forth Bridge; and as I passed one of the points towards the end of the walk where the bridge is in full view I felt great pleasure because of the attitude of a girl of sixteen or so who was playing with a child of about five. She had picked the child up in her arms, and it was trying to force her to put it down on the grass again, by putting its hands on her head and throwing its whole weight on them, and bouncing its laughing body up and down. The girl of sixteen, though strongly built, was short; and to withstand these assaults she had planted her feet wide apart and stiffened her neck. It happened to strike my eye that while she stood thus the line of her leg, and the line of her neck from the ear to the collarbone, was very like the line of the cantilevers which supported the Forth Bridge which was a tremendous black diagram across the western sky behind her. That matter in such different forms as this soft, rosy girl, and the vast and harsh assemblage of metals were adopting the same method of resisting strain caused me pleasure; and I have noticed since that most people feel some such pleasure when they see in one and the same composition (whether an artistic composition or merely a section of the real world which the senses can take in comfortably at one time) two or more objects using the same method to overcome some difficulty offered by the nature of the universe. That is the secret of many of the thrills offered by the acrobat. If one sees tumblers in an open space they seem less impressive than they do in a building, where architecture provides them with a kind of contrapuntal accompaniment, where one can look from a man who supports a pyramid of men upon his shoulders to slender pillars that hold up wide galleries. This pleasure proceeds, I suppose, from the recognition that as more than one object is showing itself able to surmount this difficulty by these means the chances are they are not a happy accident but an instrument which can be counted as one of the stable resources of the race.

Now Professor Pavlov's *Conditioned Reflexes* constantly caused in me a feeling which was evidently (since when I reflected on it these associations always came up) closely akin to this pleasure. Indeed, it seemed to be a powerful element in the creation of

the charm which invests that book to a degree quite
extraordinary in anything so technical. I could not
understand this until one day while I was reading
this book an electrician came into the room to attend
to the lamp-switches. He was a garrulous person and
bored me very much; and it happened to occur to me
that there was a comical contrast between my boredom and its grandiose ultimate cause. For the man
would not have been in my house on this occasion if
countless millions of years ago a species had not
developed in ways that made them avail themselves,
for the better prosecution of their function of living,
of certain vibrations of the atmosphere which they
discovered would impart certain spatial knowledge if
approached with the right tissues, thus adding the
eye in themselves and light in their environment.
This thought co-existed in my mind with the sentence I had just been reading: 'To present the final
conclusion of these experiments with the utmost
reserve, the cerebral cortex should be regarded as the
essential organ for the maintenance and establishment of conditioned reflexes, possessing in this
respect a function of nervous synthesis of a scope and
exactness which is not found in any other part of the
central nervous system'; and I felt this pleasure
which comes from simultaneous awareness of two
similar victories over the universe, in admiring the
eye for making itself, in admiring the brain for
making itself. Then I remembered I had felt that
particular pleasure in reading that particular sentence before the electrician had come into the room.
I could not have been comparing the eye with the
brain then. I was admiring the brain for making

itself, I was admiring . . . what else? Why . . . the
thing that Professor Pavlov was doing, or being, or
was being a part of, or was adding a part to, by his
experiments which led him to this conclusion . . .
which was somehow like the cortex, so like that the
correspondence between the processes of Professor
Pavlov's pages and the processes of the cortices he
described are as close as that of the swan and the
image of himself on which he rides. . . . Was it
perhaps that in conducting and describing his experiments he was functioning as part of an essential
organ for the maintenance and establishment of the
experiences which are the result of the conditioned
reflexes which are maintained and established by the
brain?

May it not be possible that the process of collecting information about the universe which we call
science when it can be most profitably extracted
through real material and art when it can be most
profitably extracted through imaginary material,
represents the activity of a collective and external
super-cortex which works on the material created by
the activities of the individual cortices? What the
physiologists make lay people like myself see is a
progressive resourcefulness of life. It makes itself a
substance that reacts to the external world: which, in
effect, means that it makes a substance that reacts to
the external world in ways profitable to itself; since a
substance that reacted in unprofitable ways would
cease to exist. On experiencing the extreme coyness
and impurity of the universe, on finding that perfect
forms of nourishment do not leap forward to offer
themselves to the organism, but, on the contrary,

may often maintain themselves (having themselves an instinct for survival) in as inaccessible positions as may be, and that reproduction is increasingly a need and a nuisance, and that even the negative blessing of repose cannot be enjoyed without shelter having been secured against organic and inorganic enemies, life so arranged matters that the brain made itself. And in the brain, Professor Pavlov says, 'The nervous system possesses on the one hand a definite analysing mechanism, by means of which it selects out of the whole complexity of the environment those units which are of significance, and, on the other hand, a synthesizing mechanism by means of which individual units can be integrated into an excitatory complex.'

But can it really be of the cortex he is speaking? For there never was a better statement of the duplex function that must be fulfilled by any work of art. Just as there never was a statement that threw more light on the apparently paradoxical combination of unalterable design and momentary inspiration which is characteristic of the work of art than Professor Pavlov's sentence: 'The extraordinary reactivity of the cortex on one hand, and the unbounded volume of stimuli pouring into it, on the other hand, are responsible for the two fundamental peculiarities of the cortical activity — namely, first, that it is determined in the minutest detail; and, second, that it is in a state of perpetual flux, changing so rapidly that it becomes practically impossible to observe any aspect of it in an entirely pure and uncontaminated form, and to appraise and control all the determining conditions.' That is exactly how it is, one says to oneself, if the artist is functioning correctly as an artist. The

minutest detail of his work is determined by the
strength of the stimulus which is making him write
or paint or compose, or whatever his job may be, and
the associations which this stimulus rouses in him.
But the minute he has recorded the reflex which is
aroused in him by this stimulus and these associations, this formulation of what before was not definitely thought, this realization of what was before only
vaguely apprehended, must alter his view of the
universe to a greater or less degree. The pattern may
be altered in some important respect, or that half-
millimetre of rosepink in the N.N.W. corner may be
one-millionth of a tone lighter, but in any case it
must make some difference. Hence, the reaction to
the next stimulus will be that of a totally different
self from that which reacted to the last one.

The process is as continuous as a straight line. It
is as discontinuous as the little packets of the quanta.
It abandons itself to the waters of time but is not
drowned, keeping in possession of the past without
losing hold of the present. It mirrors the nature of
life, which is orderly, so that some cry out because
they are confined as in prison bars; which is disorderly, so that some cry out because they wander in
a pathless jungle perpetually different with new
growths. So alike are art and the cortex, in their like
effort to select out of the whole complexity of the
universe these units which are of significance to the
organism, and to integrate those units into what
excites to further living. Surely the main differences
between them are that the cortex keeps its findings
within the head and art stores them outside; that the
cortex is an individual possession and that art, though

the product of individual effort, is virtually the property of as many people as are aware of it; and that art deals with experience from the point where the cortex finishes with it. 'The hostile sounds of any beast of prey serve as a conditioned stimulus to a defence reflex in the animals which it hunts.' Such negotiations between its host and the external world the cortex can undertake. But later, when it finds that itself is acting like an alchemy on what it perceived, that its conditioned reflexes are making and recording a pattern, whose loops and whorls confuse it and by causing that confusion threaten it, then it must let this other super-cortex, of which art and science are a part, make itself too.

This super-cortex would necessarily make itself external to man. Man's supremacy is due chiefly to his habit of keeping as much of himself as possible in an outhouse at the bottom of the garden. He makes a hammer and uses it when he wants it instead of going through life welded with its weight like the lobster and its claw. He makes an automobile when he wants to move more quickly through space instead of labouring through generations to develop his leg-muscles as was the tedious and less efficient method of the racehorse and the greyhound. He makes an aeroplane when he wants to fly, instead of embarking on the growth of wings that would be bound to disturb his balance at moments when he had no need of them. This habit is economical, for several people can use a hammer, an automobile, an aeroplane; and being detached from their makers they do not have to die with them. It also saves the organism from overcrowding. There would have been a severe conflict between the necessity of the human animal to keep itself small and mobile and its necessity to alter its diet when civilization altered its general conditions if we had not been able to externalize new parts of our stomachs in the forms of cooking-stoves.

In the case of a super-cortex for the analysis and synthesis of the more complicated forms of experience, all these considerations, speed, economy, the evasion of death, and the need to avoid overcrowding, would be especially urgent. To instal an organ in a man that made him individually able to undertake the problem would involve adaptations that would take thousands of years, while experience would not cease to press in upon him with more and more claims for elucidation. It would be necessary if he were to derive any benefit from the activities of any such organ that they should be pooled among those who shared his environment. To know better than one's neighbours is as often as not to be put at a considerable disadvantage. If, for example, all the great powers of Europe except one were converted to pacifism they would be forced to fight if that one power insisted on attacking them; and their troops would be very much less full of élan than those who attacked them in the joyous conviction that to fight is the done thing. The need to detach such super-cortical activity from the individual so that it should not partake of his death would be felt acutely in view of the fact that in these higher functions man matures with a slowness that is maddening in view of the short span of his life; and the inadvisability of housing it in the individual is demonstrated by the trouble that the cortex constantly inflicts on its host by the delicacy of its organization. No internal accident can put a jelly-fish out of commission as an accident in the cortex, say the formation of a clot of blood, can put a man or beast out of commission. The life of man, the life of the race, would hang on a thread if there was introduced into the body a system that would have to be still more delicate and involved.

This analysis and synthesis of the more complicated forms of experience would have to be carried on externally: by externally one means, of course, that though the initial reflex takes place in the individual and much of the paths traced by nervous impulse to which it gives rise lie within the individual, the final effect is outside him. The dancer, for instance, is moved by certain stimuli to pass from pose to pose: but the effect of these successive impulses is something outside him; it is the dance, the succession and the sum of the relationships between these poses and the poses of other dancers, if there are any, and in any case the background. And how the dance, of all arts, suggests by its beginning that we are right in this suspicion concerning the function of art! It is easy by rhythmic movements of the body to reinvoke the emotions felt in the two chief activities of savage life, war and sex. They can therefore be repeated over and over again, without consequences in the practical world, under controlled conditions; so that the community can find out at leisure what actually happens in these moments that encountered in reality flash by so quickly, can decide what are the most convenient ways to take these experiences, can educate its members by repetition to take them in these ways. In fact, the dancers are at once selecting out of the whole complexity of its environment the units which are of significance, and one synthesizing those individual units into an excitatory complex; they are carrying out what is at least an interesting parallel to cortical activity.

So too, we may gather, though less happily, because he lacked the active co-operation of the community, was the early man who drew on the wall of his cave. Mr. Clive Bell has somewhere expressed disapproval of these palæolithic artists for their preoccupation with exact representation, which, he says, makes them rank somewhere above Sir Edward Poynton and below Lord Leighton. Yet when I saw the remarkable collection of reproductions of such drawings in the Technological Museum at Madrid it seemed to me that though they limited themselves to such copying as would be done only by artists who would strike us as very poor, they did not by any means give the unpleasant impression which is given by bad art. We feel impatient with Royal Academy stuff of that sort because really the makers of it ought to have learned by this time that a copy of the universe is not what is required of art; one of the damned thing is ample. Only an extraordinarily massive stupidity could keep them in a position which the rest of humanity has left so far behind, so naturally their works have a disgusting quality as of a person too grossly fat to move. But these palæolithic drawings have, on the contrary, a certain tautness of quality. Indeed, they have the intensity of extreme exasperation: and I can imagine that they represent an early attempt at the analysis of experience, which, since it was unsuccessful, never led to the stage of synthesis. The artist had noticed that the sight of a charging bison on boys climbing a cliff for wild honey or a pregnant woman caused a certain emotion in him. It is possible that he even felt difficulty in localizing the emotion as something that was happening inside him, just as a baby of to-day with an inflammation in the ear cannot localize the pain and will be seen even to make motions with its hands as if it were beating off an external force. Probably his emotion may have seemed to him part of the scene, among those present.

At any rate, he wanted to clear up the whole business and therefore he took an inventory of the object responsible for the scene. What was it about a charging bison that caused this feeling? What was it about a pregnant woman that caused this feeling? He failed to find any answer for a variety of reasons: chiefly because he looked to discover by drawing the explanation not only of the emotion caused by observation through the eye, which alone could be adequately handled by drawing, but also the other co-existent kinds of emotion which alone could be adequately handled by literature and music: and because he had not yet discovered that the most important cause of the emotion might be that certain forms in the scene had reminded him of other forms, the imagination of which caused him extreme rapture, and that the only way he could analyse this phase of it would be to set down not the forms that actually existed but the other forms that were suggested. Still he made a good try: and if my hypothesis is not correct why did he try? Decoration may be dismissed as a motive. It would

have been far easier for the cave-man to grab a handful
of growing stuff or coloured rocks if he wanted to
brighten up the home. For amusement, he could
have wantoned with his wench. As for self-expression, many real artists are completely ignorant of any
conscious knowledge of this alleged factor in their
beings; frequently they have an aggrieved feeling
that their work has kept them from participation in
the world of action which would have enabled them
to get that pleasure from evacuation of the impulses
which must be meant by the word self-expression, so
be as it means anything. I have said elsewhere that it
is natural enough for people to be artistic, that it
gratifies such of them as have a disposition to play
with the human product, that it is an extension of
experience and power, that in every way it is fun.
But that relates to people availing themselves of the
condition of being an artist, once it is established. It
does not explain how that condition came to be
established among a species as indolent as ours.

Nor does it explain how such an indolent species
happened to keep on at it through the ages, amid all
manner of distracting circumstances. Indefatigably
they persist; as if what they were doing was to use
some essential organ that had been implanted in the
organism to supply some vital need. It may be objected that they do not persist nearly indefatigably
enough for this analogy to be sound, that there are centuries when little or no art of any validity is produced
over widely populated areas, whereas the human race
never slackens in its business of eating and reproduc-
ing and using its cortex on its conditioned reflexes.
But the intermittences of art are only such suspen-

sions of function owing to external or internal calamity that we are used to in the case of the individual, only writ as much larger and more impressive as would be bound to be the case with a vast, diffused, collective and external organ. The process of digestion changes so profoundly when for a long period there is no food in the stomach that it may be said to cease. An exhausted man is not sexually active, the brain hardly functions when an anæmic condition starves it of blood; and when a race is engaged in conflicts that absorb all its energies, whether these are wars, or attacks on the reluctance of earth to afford a man a living, or the practice of false religions dictated by political or economic opinionativeness (such as Roman and mid-Victorian materialism), they have none of the more complicated forms of experience and consequently provide the super-cortex with no material to make into art. It is true that there are intermittences which do not seem to be accounted for by this explanation, but most of these are exceptions only by a misuse of the word experience, or are the results of a handicap that lies heavily on one of the arts and forces it to discontinuity though with no ill-effects on the continuity of art as a whole.

The misuse of the word experience which is to blame is that singular one that applies the term 'a great experience' to any prodigious accident which absolutely debars from experience all those who become involved in it. To persons who indulge in this malapropism it must seem an unspeakable objection to my hypothesis that the Great War has not produced, nor seems likely to produce, any art that matters a halfpenny. But the truth is that the mass of people engaged in the war, particularly if they were of the type that is likely to produce art, were thereby tracing a pattern so unlike that which their Merlins would have chosen them to trace that they never directed on it any kind of absorbed attention. The men who sang, 'Nobody knows how bored we are, Bored we are, Bored we are, And nobody seems to care,' were actually having much less experience when they were present at the most tremendous battles that have taken place in history than when they were at home being bank clerks and school-masters and shop-assistants and what-not. Those to whom it was an experience, and who happened to be artists, did analyse and synthesize their impressions. *Revolt in the Desert*, though not great art, is a work of art. But the extremely unusual character of Colonel Lawrence's army career, and the extremely unusual character of his mind, show him to be the exception which proves the rule.

The art which labours under a handicap making for discontinuity is that which is based on the use of the eye. It commonly happens that at the beginning of each thickening and bubbling of experience which we call a civilization painting starts out to be a pretty good thing, once the painter realizes that his job is to play with lines and colours and does not undertake that of literature and music. But it also happens that one of the earliest ideas that most civilizations get into their heads is education; and the first thing that any educational system teaches its pupils is to read. This it does at their earliest possible age, so that usually the study has the prestige of the first step out of infancy, the first participation in the adult world,

as well as the awfulness of the first intellectual duty
demanded of one by authority. Nothing could be
conceived more certain to rob the eye of its innocence.
It is established that it is babyish to let the sight
wander about registering form and colour, it is postu-
lated that grown-ups find an activity in keeping with
their dignity and power in reading: and consequently the more directile members of society really
lose the power of using their eyes on anything but
print. Consequently the art of painting is more and
more the monopoly of people who try to induce
society to forgive them for their absorption in a
frivolous pastime by making their art as far as
possibly illustrative of the sacred art of literature, and
by making their pictures exact representations which
might conceivably be factually valuable like maps; or
of people who will not let society come it over them,
and are going to use their eyes if they like, and say be
damned to you all, like that disagreeable old party
Cézanne. In some civilizations, as in Africa, the
machine takes the place of print. (The Negro, placed
by the white man under an urgent necessity to
respect guns and tools, gets an eye for form that be-
tokens efficiency and loses his eye for purely decorative form.) Hence the history of art in any civilization always begins with a Milky Way of primitive
masterpieces followed by a long stretch of darkness
lit only by a few stars of great magnitude. But this
only means that the artistic impulse is side-tracked
into the other arts. That, of course, is regrettable not
only from the point of view of the pictorial arts, but
from the point of literature, which is naturally (in
these civilizations where print is the source of the

mischief) the art that receives such as are frightened away from the use of paint by timidity and a sense it is no use insisting on using that medium rather than any other, because they have not really anything of consequence to say. But it does not mean that anywhere, at any time, man has ever been without an artistic mechanism with which he treats what stimulus is given him by the higher forms of experience, any more than he goes about without his heart or his lungs or his brain.

V

And if against nature one separates man from this
mechanism, he suffers as if his heart or his lungs or
his brain had been cut out of him. Throughout the
works of Dostoevsky there is expressed a distrust of
the intellectual *émigrés* of Russia based on no other
fact than that they are *émigrés*; and what is evidently
the converse of the same theory is expressed in
various passages which dwell on the necessity for
every human being to remain embedded, physically
and mentally, in the life of the country in which he
was born. He alleges this theory to have a basis in
mystical reason. Shatov says, in *The Possessed*:

'Nations are built up and moved by another force
which sways and dominates them, the origin of which
is unknown and inexplicable. That force is the force
of an insatiable desire to go on to the end, though at
the same time it denies that end. It is the force of the
persistent assertion of one's own existence, and a
denial of death. It's the spirit of life, as the Scriptures
call it, "the river of living water," the drying up of
which is threatened in the Apocalypse. It's the
æsthetic principle, as the philosophers call it, the
ethical principle with which they identify it, "the
seeking of god," as I call it more simply . . . I
reduce God to the attribute of nationality? On the
contrary, I raise the people to God. And has it ever
been otherwise? The people is only a people so long
as it has its own god and excludes all other gods on
earth irreconcilably; so long as it believes that by its
God it will conquer and drive out of the world all
other gods. Such, from the beginning of time, has

been the belief of all great nations, all, anyway, who
have been specially remarkable, all who have been
leaders of humanity. There is no going against facts.
The Jews lived only to await the coming of the true
God and left the world the true God. The Greeks
defied nature and bequeathed the world their religion, that is, philosophy and art. Rome defied the
people in the State, and bequeathed the idea of the
State to the nation. France throughout her long
history was only the incarnation and development of
the Roman god, and if they have at last flung their
Roman god into the abyss and plunged into atheism,
which, for the time being, they call socialism, it is
solely because socialism is, anyway, healthier than
Roman Catholicism. If a great people does not believe that the truth is only to be found in itself alone
(in itself alone and in it exclusively); if it does not
believe that it alone is fit and destined to raise up and
save all the rest by its truth, it would at once sink
into being ethnographical material.'

And so on; as in many passages of not only Dostoevsky's novels but his letters. Now when one picks
oneself up after the wind of Dostoevsky's ecstasy has
blown over one and count the spoons there are never
any missing. The ecstasy has been an authentic translation of the senses which by sympathy has translated
one also to an intenser life. It has not been a chloro-
form mask clapped over one's face while a thief who
loves to filch from men what little they have of truth
goes through one's habitation. The only case one has
against Dostoevsky is that he does not invest his
work with the suave form that would count the
spoons for us as he went along, that would convince

us from the beginning that here is one of the white company that use the mind for righteous purposes. But at first this particular phase of his ecstasy seems an exception to the rule of authenticity. It so unfortunately resembles certain ululations concerning Cathleen ni Houlihan we have heard in our own time that we are prepared to put it down to his response to the Slavophil movement of his day, and feel the more sympathetic towards the intellectual *émigrés*, such as Turgeniev, in their attitude towards it. However, it occurs to me that one had better come off one's high horse about it, because there has been piling up all through the later nineteenth and the early twentieth centuries an immense body of evidence proving that it mattered nothing if Dostoevsky talked like seven Sinn Feiners distended with Gælery because his conclusions were as sound as Euclid. A man who goes out from his people cannot attain his full growth.

A considerable part of this evidence relates to the British Empire. That Empire, as all but the incurably naïve realize, is a political necessity, and a glorious one. The conditions of time and space being as they are, it was inevitable that the British Empire should exist; and on the whole it has been impossible to identify it, except for short periods and in certain small areas, as a degenerative process. But this need not blind us to the fact that the maintenance of the Empire involves a very heavy sacrifice in thrusting back certain of those who work for it into a state of being below the level of that enjoyed by their fellow-countrymen. The victims of this sacrifice are those who have to work far from the base or who have to

live in a country whose national life is made inco-
herent by the pressure of diverse races whom political
or economic reasons forbid to amalgamate. The
example nearest to hand is the Anglo-Irish Protestant Society. In Ireland life cannot (or could
not until Home Rule was gained) become coherent
because of the partition between the Protestant in-
vaders and the Roman Catholic native stock. Now
although this society was formed by a steady flow of
immigration during the Tudor and the Stuart dynas-
ties from the members of the most distinguished
families of England, it would be idle to pretend that
anybody desirous of visiting those places where culture and civilization have reached their high-water
mark would naturally find their way to Merrion
Square, since a narcissistic sense of their own charm
and a preoccupation altogether beyond reason with
the horse, are the distinguishing characteristics of its
inhabitants. It may be objected that those things are
not uncommon in the neighbourhood of Melton
Mowbray; but after all that is the cache of a particular set and does not absorb the activity of a whole
class. There are also the Cecils. The stock that has
left its base, we are therefore just in pronouncing,
has deteriorated compared with the stock that stayed
at home. In India the introduction of the English
into a country already predestined to confusion by
its vastness and its racial and religious enmities has
produced a whirlwind, at the heart of which (according to custom) there is a dead calm, in this case of an
intellectual nature, which is occupied by Anglo-
Indian Society. Of the gallantry of its members
there is no need to speak, of the sickening sacrifices

that are made by generation after generation of divided mothers and children it is too painful to speak. But it would be idle to pretend that anybody desirous of visiting those places where culture and civilization have reached their high-water mark would be likely to visit Simla any more than Merrion Square. Here, too, there is narcissism, though it takes the form of a sense of worth and correctness rather than charm, and a preoccupation beyond reason with the horse. One must regard polo as among the divinest sports, in which man looks and feels most like a god; but if one could meet a gentleman polo-player who seemed to have admitted to his soul that he and his friends could never play as pretty a game as their grooms and that the team which cannot be beaten belongs to a regiment of Southern Negroes stationed at a Missouri fort one would feel immensely easier in one's mind about that on which the sun never sets: not that one has any particular desire that full recognition should be given to the merits of grooms or Southern Negroes stationed in Missouri, but merely because the universe seems to have laid it down as a condition of survival that one must prefer reality. Though the Colonies have developed without such inflexible organization of fantasy (largely owing to the absence from those parts of a dominating military caste, which has the awful power of drill and discipline to impress its ideas on the community, as much when what it is thinking is nonsense as when it is sense), it yet remains true that the children of parents who have made good overseas usually long to go 'home' to England. I record these facts though mindful that my father was a member of an English family settled in the south of Ireland since the reign of Edward VI, that I am descended from one of the first governors of Madras, that one of my close relatives is counted as a maker of British Africa, and that the more I live in intellectual circles the less does this heredity displease me. In drawing attention to the psychic disadvantages of the situations they occupied or promoted, I am but counting the wounds my kin have suffered in the service of his country.

Another considerable part of this evidence relates to the United States. The United States, as all but the incurably naïve realize, is a political necessity, and a glorious one. The conditions of time and space being as they are, it was inevitable that the United States should exist; and on the whole it has been impossible to identify it, except for short periods and in certain small areas, as a degenerative process. But this need not blind us to the fact that the establishment of the United States involves a very heavy sacrifice in thrusting back certain of those who work for it into a state of being lower than that they would have enjoyed if they or their parents had stayed at home. I do not allude to the counterpart of Anglo-Irish and Anglo-Indian society which introduces into Boston and Philadelphia the elements of narcissism and fussiness about the horse (when the hounds meet in West Chester county it is apparent that that meeting was no accident) but to the immigrant population. Nothing is at first more surprising to the European than the attitude towards the immigrant which is expressed by the ordinary American. At first one is staggered when one hears 'the Wop' spoken of as a criminal, as an irreducible, incurably lawless and non-productive problem for the Eagle, and realize that a 'Wop' is an Italian, one of those heirs of the Cæsars, across whose lands one could, until the present régime, walk alone in safety all day long, meeting only courtesy, seeing nothing but perfection and that noble greed which wrings plenty from barrenness, which for years sells its labour to what inferno will buy it that it may own a shelf of earth, carries earth to it in baskets up five hundred feet of mountain path, and cozens wheat and olives to grow there; or does work not less magnificent than this pioneering in seeing that a Tuscan farm does not lose the character of a masterpiece which has been imprinted on it by a thousand priests of the plough. Reverence is so obviously the only apposite emotion one can feel for Italians as one knows them in Italy, that this 'wop' business suggests to one that the quality of insularity has nothing whatsoever to do with being on an island and that we have here a mere exhibition of race prejudice.

But in time it becomes borne in upon one that there is a difference between the Italian in Italy and the Italian in the United States. It is starkly true that Italians do not behave in Rome or in Florence or in Milan as they do in Chicago. There is notoriously far more political crime and misdemeanour than there ought to be in Italy, and in the rural districts there is a certain amount of secret society perniciousness; but all the same Italians do not, on their own soil, engage in vast illicit enterprises in the centre of great cities and chase their rivals round the town in automobiles, murdering them and the police and the general public. There is no equivalent in Italy of Scarface Capone. One's bewilderment increases when one learns that the Chinese immigrants also develop nefarious activities unknown to them in their native land. There they notoriously enjoy a horrific bit of revolution; but in the blood-thirsty struggle between secret societies which is known as 'tong warfare' they do not indulge except in the shadow of the Stars and Stripes. So, too, it appears that the Roman Catholic Irish, at home one of the most virtuous people save for political crime, have lost that good character here; and more astonishing still that the Jews, whom we in Europe know as almost pusillanimously law-abiding, provide here a quite considerable proportion of criminals. I am not for one minute suggesting that there are not millions of highly respectable citizens of Italian and Chinese and Irish and Jewish birth and extraction in the United States. What I am saying is that a certain number of persons of these origins show more anti-social characteristics than persons of these sorts would in their own countries.

One's first impulse is to say that the fault must be America's own: that she is evidently providing them with a corrupting social environment. But so far as this is true it merely means that the same deterioration has fallen on those stocks that in Europe contrive a reliable police-force and social order; and to a considerable extent it is not true at all. It is no use turning up one's eyes and suggesting that this horrid vulgar non-European thing called prosperity is to blame, because in point of fact a far larger proportion of immigrants than is commonly supposed is not much better off than it was in Europe and live in not more bean-fed societies. It is no use suggesting that the United States does not educate its citizens in social ethics, because I can hardly believe that in such education, direct or indirect, any real superiority can be claimed by two isolated Italian villages I know, which stand half a mile or so apart on a Mediter- ranean highroad and believe each other to be in- habited by the children of the devil (chiefly, I think, because one shows signs of being tinctured with more Arab and Semitic ancestry than the other), and meet to fight it out every half-year or so, and have no other relations with their fellow-men, yet never com- mit any grave offences of any sort; and I cannot think that any American Irishman has the confusing ethical upbringing in regard to the most serious crime of all that must have been the lot of every home-keeping Irishman till the present settlement of differences. No, what is happening to these people is happening inside their own selves. Dostoevsky was right.

Now why should anything disturbing have hap- pened to these people in their own selves? Dostoev- sky's account of it is a little too apocalyptic to be helpful: too much a mystical drawing in the Blake style, with the nations seen as naked men with muscles in torsion, like those used for illustrations in books of anatomy, and God as a bearded cloud pregnant with might. The trouble about Dostoevsky is that since the moments in which life seemed to him to have most meaning were those immediately pre- ceding epileptic attacks and were therefore not fol- lowed afterwards by any process of intellectual inquiry and elucidation, he is disposed to present his discoveries of life's meaning as if they were seen by a lightning flash and then veiled by darkness; except of course, when by successful empathy he enters into the feelings of other characters who have not this disposition. When one examines what he gives us as an explanation of his belief that man must maintain all his connections with his native country if he is to establish a connection with God, one is struck by the fact that he recommends the notions to practise an extraordinary arrogance. 'A people is only a people so long as it has its own god and excludes all other gods on earth irreconcilably; so long as it believes that by its god it will conquer and drive out of the world all other gods. If a great people does not believe that the truth is only to be found in itself alone (in itself alone and exclusively); if it does not believe that it alone is fit and destined to raise up and save all the rest by its truth, it should at once sink into being ethnographical material. . . .' No, we say, we know better. Dostoevsky may not have seen an elderly English Colonel alluding to 'those damned Frenchies' or a New York banker announcing that he has withdrawn his child from the Newfoundland School because it has accepted among its pupils the son of a Jewish millionaire, but we have, and we are perfectly certain that at no moment are such persons further from their gods. Reading over the passage again one comes on the sentence, 'Nations are built up and moved by another force which sways and dominates them. That force is the force of an insatiable desire to go on to the end, though at the same time it denies that end,' it occurs to one that that resembles the force which makes men artists. They have to go on writing, painting, making music, evidently proving something of immense importance to life, since they are willing to give their whole lives to it, yet refusing to alter their conclusions to make them serviceable to any current view which makes an attempt to explain life. They follow a purpose yet deny that purpose.

Then it occurs to one that the arrogance which Dostoevsky recommends to the nations is similar to that which is a necessity in the artist. The artist must exhibit what appears to the world as arrogance if he is a real artist, because he will know when he is going through the right mental movements of analysis and synthesis of the higher forms of experience just as one knows when one has achieved the right muscular movements of the Australian Crawl, and will claim to be an artist, which claim must seem conceit except to those able to judge of it, since they conceive him to make it because of his judgment of his work instead of his consciousness of an internal process. It is true that people who are not artists feel a certainty that they are; but that is no proof that people who are artists have not a specific feeling which tells them they are artists, any more than the fact that many lunatics believe themselves to be members of the Royal Family proves that there is not a Royal Family with a sense of its own position. Moreover, the artist must believe that what he is doing is of supreme importance, because otherwise his psyche would not give it all his forces. 'If the artist,' one might say, 'does not believe that he alone is fit and destined to light up the world with the beauty of his work he would at once sink into being . . . a mere crafts-man.'

The parallel is close. Art must have something to do with the situation as Dostoevsky envisaged it. And one remembers two touches from the part of the book where he spoke more clearly, since he described imagined characters, two touches which convince one utterly that Stavrogin is a man possessed by devils, who have led him far out into a desert, where he is lost. When (in the suppressed chapters of the book which the Soviet Government found in its archives and published some years ago) Stavrogin takes to the Bishop Tikhon his confession of the crime he once committed against a little child, which he intends to issue to the world in order that he may do penance and be cleansed, it appears that the document is full of mistakes in grammar and spelling. So too is the letter he writes when his devils have left him, and he is broken and without friends, and his one hope is that little Dasha, whom he has always treated with neglect and contempt, will take him to Switzerland. Languid this letter is, for he knows that since what he suggests is hopeful it cannot be part of his destiny, and indeed when Dasha received it he is already hanging in a hay-loft. Ill-written it is also, showing 'the defects in style,' says Dostoevsky ironically, 'of a Russian aristocrat who had never mastered the Russian grammar in spite of his European education.' These touches have almost an independent life of their own. They work on one's imagination after one has closed the book, and by their working they affect the image left by it as it would seem beyond the power of four or five lines out of seven hundred pages. When one is at the point of death, in soul or body, one could not cry out save in one's native tongue. Against impenetrable darkness one sees Stavrogin's beautiful head, that must be flesh because down the brows now meeting in agony there run drops of sweat, that must be marble because the lips will not part. Yet he knew enough Russian for the purposes of daily life: enough for ordering a meal, for making love, for courtesies to his hosts and guests, for talking to his mother. It was only the subtler use of language, such as makes art able to take it for a vestment, that he lacked. But when one repents or dies one would want to say the simplest things, one would want to say, 'Lord, have mercy on me, a miserable sinner,' or, 'Now let Thy servant depart in peace.' Surely he could say that? But perhaps it is necessary that by each word one should evoke an image which represents the deliberation of a people on the fact which is given in the dictionary as the meaning of that word: the knowledge of which deliberations one has absorbed through art.

Art, then, is involved in this matter. With that in mind one goes back and takes another look at the exiled societies which prove Dostoevsky's case. Whatever is wrong with them does not arise from any deterioration of their individual members. The Anglo-Irish and the Anglo-Indians have given us some of our finest soldiers; and soldiers resemble poets in that while mediocre soldiers are almost the silliest and most contemptible objects under the sun, a great soldier is one of the few human achievements which can make it conceivable that God will feel

sorrow at the cooling of the earth; and through the
Great War certain Colonials moved like Kings.
Rather the trouble with these societies seems to have
a negative origin, to proceed from the absence of certain realizations which have long been a part of the
atmosphere of the stock that stayed at home. It is
enlightening to read sometimes in the history of Irish
land legislation during the nineteenth century and
see how, although for obvious reasons the statement
of those differences would be minimized, the Tories
on this side of St. George's Channel were constantly
embarrassed in their championship of the Tories on
the other side by finding that ideas which were a
commonplace in England had not yet penetrated into
Ireland: in particular, that the modification of the
aristocratic attitude by which the English governing
class had adopted to check the effects of the French
Revolution had been envisaged neither as a necessity
nor a possibility by their Anglo-Irish equivalents.
The same conflict between parties theoretically in
agreement and socially identical is partially responsible for the eternal slight dissension between the
India Office and resident Anglo-Indians. The
Dominions are now so free from control by the Mother
Country and are so little dominated by a military
caste that they afford no grounds for any such comparison; but to the pro-Labour *geist* of Australian
politics and the anti-Labour *geist* of South African
politics life evidently seems far simpler than it has
done for generations at St. Stephen's. The outlines
have hardly been filled in at all.

But, it may be objected, this deficiency of ideas
must arise from the inferiority of the individuals

composing these exiled societies, because the books
in which these ideas are stated are sent in quantities
overseas for everybody who is capable of it to read
and digest. The evidence of our senses, however,
tells us incontrovertibly that these individuals are not
inferior. So far as natural equipment is concerned,
anyone would choose to be a Colonial rather than one
of the English-born. I can think of no happier fate
than to be born again a New Zealander with a touch
of the Maori to make one golden. But the matter
can be settled beyond all doubt by considering the
cases of these exiles whose superiority to the run of
men is indisputable but whose development has been
wrecked by no other cause than this deficiency of ideas,
though they had full run of all the books in the world.
Two are Anglo-Irish, the other is Anglo-Indian.

The Anglo-Irish who have found their way into
art in spite of the disadvantages of their environment — like Sheridan, Wilde, Synge and Shaw — have
usually been able to do so because they were revolutionary by temperament and wanted to create exactly
what their environment said should remain uncreated. They were therefore bound to be witty, since
wit is in its essence revolutionary, a readiness to show
that the foundations on which our assumptions stand
are rotten and might as well be kicked out of the way
with a phrase. Also their environment helps them to
be witty, for it is snobbish; and one of the few good
things about snobbery is that if within its nexus there
is born a man with brains it enables him to look the
universe in the face and say what he thinks of it.

They had another common attribute in their
attraction to the theatre, which again arose out of

their relationship with their environment. To an artist reared in a society which denies the truth known for a certainty to art by admitting the existence not of individuals but only of classes (in this case, it believes, of a Protestant class with all the higher virtues and a Roman Catholic class with the virtues that one would find in a good dog) an art that depends on the presentation of individual character has an irresistible charm. Moreover, the stage is such a vivid and concentrated art that a man with a dramatic turn of mind can pick up the drift of a movement after a few evenings at the theatre and see that his own imagination follows that course. Very soon after they left Ireland all these exiles affiliated themselves to some more or less lively tradition. Sheridan became a figure in the gay spectacle of English nineteenth-century comedy; Wilde with his light hand made an omelette of the society comedy which under Henry Arthur Jones's abominable handling appeared as a breakfast egg of the worst type; Synge apprenticed his mind to the French Symbolist School of design (compare *Riders of the Sea* and Maeterlinck's *Interior*, and the mocking spirit of *The Playboy of the Western World* with some of Villiers de l'Isle Adam's contrariwise short stories); Shaw caught hold of Ibsen for dramatic method, and for content the Fabian movement which was in the days of his youth attracting all the best young brains of England, falling easily into the conditions of art, through familiarity with his mother's life as a musician. It must be noted that never did any of them except Sheridan succeed in hiding the fact that their tie with the tradition they adorned was one of adoption rather than of birth. Their audiences felt something strange and foreign about them, and in fear of the unknown made false accusations against them. Wilde and Synge, writers of plays which one might not unjustly call sob-stuff, were called heartless; and the English public retreated before George Bernard Shaw's examination of their conduct and beliefs with nervous shrieks and giggles like a young woman at a native village at Wembley when a noble savage advances upon her eager to finger some of her trinkets. But even so each found a fairway for his spirit.

But there were two Anglo-Irish writers who could not use that particular pathway to liberation, not being revolutionaries; and it is interesting to see what happened to them. William Butler Yeats and George Moore are great artists of the kind that desires only to celebrate things as they are. They have done that with everlasting glory, but under a handicap which does not seem to press on native-born writers of the same sort. The handicap is hard to define. It seems as if they knew nothing of life except what they have found out for themselves. Their power of analysing and synthesizing their own experiences is unequalled, but they seem to be cloistered from the knowledge of anybody else's analyses and syntheses, and to be able to arrive at it only by leaving their cloisters and prosecuting a search for it, in which they seem to be aided by no clues whatsoever, and wander hither and thither. When Mr. Yeats, who is supremely wise about his own experience in his poems, looks around him (as in *The Trembling of the Veil* and several other of his prose works) at the world of which his experience is a part and a product, it is apparent from his

wild gestures, which are those of a man scrambling
to keep his foothold on the sharp tip of a steeple, that
he is so unaware of that world as to be practically
suspended in nothingness. Hence he has to resort
to the magical view of the universe, as those do who
for ignorance or whatever reason have to start again
where our savage forefathers did and try an empiri-
cist approach to the meaning of life. Woe inexpres-
sible is it to hear the greatest of poets talk like a
Regent Street clairvoyant, and tell strange stories of
(as it might be) seeing three crows fall dead in mid-
air with striking simultaneity on Good Friday,
reckoning by the old Erse calendar, and later hearing that three brothers named Crowe, close relatives
of Lady Gregory or A. E. or whoever were killed on
Easter Monday, reckoning by the old Erse calendar.
It may be true that God sometimes behaves like a
racing tipster of a certain sort, hanging about dark
places and offering passers-by to tell by whispers or
little slips of paper what is going to win the 3.30
to-morrow; but nice people do not discuss this possibility, any more than they do the peccadilloes of
dead great statesmen, for whether it is true or not
He has other claims upon our consideration.

George Moore took the problem differently because he is a moral genius. Among the works of
Samuel Smiles is one in praise of the thrift and industry of George Moore, and this has always seemed
to me exquisitely appropriate, although his subject
was actually a benevolent commercial traveller who
founded an orphanage in the northern environs of
London (the sight of whose gates, surmounted by a
bust with the words 'George Moore' carved large

beneath it and revealing some score of happy children playing in a garden, has made many an automobilist halt in interest and go home to read afresh *Memoirs of My Dead Life*). Here is a man who at the beginning of his life knew nothing whatsoever about art (not even what he liked) except that he was an artist, though of what kind he was not sure. He worried canvas like a dog to see if he was a painter; he wrote poetry that sounded like an angry woman working a sewing machine that was out of order; he multiplied incompetent novels that suggested roundhand crawling over the pages of an exercise book. He made himself the finest prose writer of his time. He has written page after page that have brought light into darkness, that have formulated what was not formulated, that have added immense tracts to the sum of reality controlled by comprehension. The discussion of the interview between Turgeniev and Dostoevsky in *Avowals* is one of those passages which make one see the author striking the black rock of the uncomprehended with the rod of his power so that there gushes forth the living water of meaning. That he knows nothing but what he has found out for himself is to say that he knows nearly everything, since the might that resides in this flaccid personality as the lightning in the heart of the wet soft cloud has made him advance on experience as Alexander advanced on armies. But just as astonishing is what he does not know: as, for example, that that piece of material, yes, that one, was meant by man to be used as a loin-cloth, not as a fancy cravat.

We can comprehend now the silence which has fallen on the genius of Mr. Rudyard Kipling for the last thirty years: that silence which however many books he may issue, he cannot break. No man has ever had more superb natural equipment for the career of an artist than this Anglo-Indian. Never has the instinct to play with the human product been exercised with such athleticism. He was astonished and delighted with the serviceability of words. He proved that they could be dark as night or bright as flowers, that they could be marshalled into funeral marches or set jiggety-wise as banjo solos, that they could be made into mirrors to reflect the ghats of Benares or the snows of Canada. There is no end to the appearances of the earth, and there are words to image them all, so a man need not be idle till the day he dies: thus he cheerily thought at the beginning of his career. But there was that in him which made the common folk feel not so cheerily about him, which made them feel that sense of changeling strangeness, not to be overcome by any admiration, which they have always felt towards Mr. Yeats and Mr. Moore. You will find an uneasy reference to it in an essay that Sir Edmund Gosse wrote on Mr. Kipling long before the falling of the silence. Concerning certain of the stories and the novels he complains that, in spite of the brilliant observation of the particular events and characters which form their subject, the author gives the impression of writing about them from the outside, as if he was separated from the society in which they took place by the wall of race, as if he were a clever Eurasian or Hindu.

Again here is some one who knows nothing of life except what he had found out for himself. On the high and isolated pinnacle of rock that is his personal experience he built himself a magnificent palace of many chambers; but it is not good for a man to open his windows and look down, down, down into empty space. He had too much horse-sense to try to fill in these surrounding chasms, which should have been filled in with man's experience and were not, with the tarradiddles about the universe which satisfied Mr. Yeats. He had not the sublime faith which made Mr. George Moore able to perform a miracle and merge his isolated pinnacle with the mountain of man's experience as if there had never been a division. All he could do was to shut the windows and pretend that his personal experience was identical with the universal. This is the motive of his constant sententious allegations that the morality of that relatively modern institution, the Indian Army, and the intellectual principles of the absolutely modern Disraeli-founded Tory Party, are the same as the morality and intellectual principles that upheld primitive tribes. This, fortunately for the efficiency of the Indian Army and the sanity of St. Stephen's, is not true, for as anthropology has told us with increasing positiveness during the last century the savage tribe is upheld not by truth but by myth that distorts the truth into forms acceptable to the complicated neuroses which, contrary to popular belief, civilization has diminished instead of increased. The artist in Mr. Kipling refuses to believe him on this point. It yearns to build its structures on ancient and universal wisdoms beyond a short-lived individual's acquiring, rather than on quick-eyed observation of such as Dick Heldar; and it is proud, because it knows that in the days when it still could build on such limited foundations it built better than other men, and is not willing to do work unworthy of his power. So it sulks and sits silent on his hearth.

What is this process which links the individual to the universal if he stay with his people, which leaves the individual solitary and desolate if he be an exile? I can conceive it most clearly when I think of Scarface Capone. There is a man who is superbly in possession of the present, who is destitute of the past. It must demand power amounting to genius to perform the analyses and syntheses of his own personal experience necessary to establish him as king of the Chicago bootlegging gangs. There must be perceptions concerning the qualities of friends and enemies that can proceed only from the most acute observation and the most prophetic imagination. There must be a capacity for seeing time and space as a canvas on which to place a valid design of crime which is like a considerable part of the process of art. But there was information as necessary to him as that given by his observation, his imagination, and his sense of design. Only the past could give it, and from him the past was obliged by lack of contact to withhold it. Expensively he and his friends have had to find it out for themselves. For there has come a halt to this gang warfare. Though the gangsters make their millions, they yet find experience of living by merciless murder in perpetual danger of being mercilessly murdered is not one that humanity can endure. Others may come and learn the lesson anew, but they have made peace, they have scattered, they sit in grotesque huge houses and in Florida hotels, as baroque in architecture as a decayed tooth, huddled in their great fortunes against their tired guilty nerves and the tedium that lawful living seems after the thrill of being killers, like old men huddled in their overcoats to defeat the cold wind and the coldness of their blood. They need not have needed to learn this for themselves if they had stayed in their own country. In a thousand million ways their country would have taught it to them, from the day they were born.

In Italy there would have been a religion for teacher. I do not mean to say that in Chicago there is no religion, for there is a great deal; but like Michigan Boulevard it is in the course of construction. That in Italy is the result of nearly two thousand years of revision by human needs. A shrine which the people do not find it useful to kneel before is untended, the glass breaks with the winter winds, the image falls forward on its face and is a little heap of rubble, the sun and rain scour the painting from the walls, there is presently a pedestal pitted in its upper half with a recess, which might as well be a thing not yet begun as a thing finished. It follows that a shrine in good condition may be taken as something not static, as something that is perform-. ing an active function towards the people, that stimulates them to perform an active function towards itself. The holy things in the churches, not less than the holy things by the wayside, are there because the mind of the people keeps them there: and in all countries the people do not keep idle mouths. It is a queer art-form this religion; diffuse and reluctant to explain its meaning in terms acceptable to the intellect, like all community art-forms; and in its mixture of ritual and dogma and didactics as impure as opera. In every age it throws up doctrines and figures objectifying the current neuroses: haggard masochistic ascetics, preachers who sadistically scourge sinners, weakly little saints who are as simple as infantilism can make them and die young, who all do miracles and turn the order of nature upside down. But in every age it continues to celebrate what within the area it covers is the order of nature, to represent it as worshipful.

It shows the Mother and the Child. It shows the Child grown to manhood, suffering, defeated, victorious. It shows the Father, Who is not presented as tangibly as these others, not as intimately offered to life and knowledge, which is as it is in life outside the Church, since a father is taken from his family by his need to labour on the terraces among his vines; but Who is obliquely indicated by beams of respect slanting up to the darkness where He fulfils the tasks of creation, even as the father in life outside the Church has to be invested with a special awfulness as the provider and defender, so that his absence may not let the mother overshadow him in power. These, say the community, are the elements of the experience that so far as it can see is the most important of all its experiences. Life seems to fall into the pattern made by these elements whenever it coheres solidly against death. Therefore the community celebrates this experience. In the dusk of a Church which typifies the darkness of the uncomprehended universe, images of those elements are set up very bright and visible, as befits those things which are generous and allow themselves to be comprehended.

That the character of the experience is predominantly pain is admitted by the lines between the Mother's brow which are a sign that she is sealed to agony, by the thorns on the Son's brow, by the appearance of the Father, which is that of a tired old man, who for all that the creeds say has not the look of one exempt from personal death. That the character of the experience is also predominantly pleasure (which is against reason, which is in accordance with fact) is admitted by the gilding of the Mother's robes, the fine substance given to the best affordable crafts-man for the covering of the Son's body, the silver and gold vessels maintained to keep up the absent Father's state, the burning of incense, the singing of music, the chanting of a language felt to be man's Sunday best because the learned read it and the sons of gentry study it, the ascription to all these Persons of a marvellous tenderness towards the world, which is a worthy symbol for man's capacity for love, and the power to reverse the order of nature and work miracles, which is a worthy symbol for his genius. Though religion may offer nothing what-soever to account for the universe it is unsurpassed as an analysis and synthesis of what is the core of a continent's experience, as a realistic work of art with the immensest conceivable subject and theme.

A child brought up within the zone dominated by this work of art, who therefore never hears or reads a word that is not the product of a mind equally dominated by it, must receive an impression of the excitatory complex which is the result of its analysis and synthesis. That must involve a sugges-tion of the profound undesirability of committing murder. In the presentation of our common destiny by the Christian religion there is a complete admission of the validity of the murderer's argument that the lot of an ordinary man is so tedious and toilsome and enslaved by necessity that if a man is ordinary it is doing no great injury to him and his fellows to curtail his tedium and his toil and his slavery, so it might as well be done if profit is to come of it : which it counters by as absolute a proof that the lot of the ordinary man is so extraordinary in its adventures and its ecstasies and its liberties of the will that to curtail his life is to steal from him and his fellows a treasure of wonder. The individual may be unable to receive that suggestion owing to his stupidity; or he may be unwilling to act on it because of a deep resistance to the community, making him wish to flout all its findings irrespective of what it costs him. But if he has the capacity of Scarface Capone, and has enough gregarious feeling to make him master not merely a handful of brigands but of large numbers of his fellow-creatures, and act not so much in defiance of the community as in creation of a new one within the old, he would be likely to avail himself of that other prophylactic against murder, the attitude which successive generations have taken up towards the murderer, which reveals itself in various forms, notably (in one country) in a rite, and (in all countries) in popular songs. If a man proclaims that he means to base his life on crime, that he is going to rob and kill because he finds working for money and respecting the right of others to live makes life too dreary, men and women alike give him their fascinated

attention, because they are always waiting for a
Prometheus to steal fire from heaven and get away
with it. They are heartily hoping that one of
human kind will at last break a path to a more violent
and coloured and easeful destiny; and because this
is a forbidden hope the excitement it causes arouses
by association the excitement caused by the hope of
forbidden sexual joys. Specially is this the case with
women, since to make this challenge to society the
criminal must have courage, which is a quality so
useful to the species that it is aphrodisiac.

But when Prometheus fails again, and the brigand
with the carabinieri's bullets through his head, the
revenge of the people in their thought is terrible.
They are enraged because the door of their disappointment has been clanged on them again. They
feel guilty because they have been hoping for something that was forbidden by what is evidently the
true God; and the specially hysteric and sobbing
sense of guilt that punishes sexual dreams rushes
forward from the darkness at the back of the mind.
There is much mean resentment against the dead
man for having led into sin those who surely were
innocent as babes till he tempted them; should he
not die at once up on that shelf of mountain where
the carabinieri got him, but lies coughing and asking
for water, there are those who would not give it to
him. There is also felt for him a just scorn: when
the silence closes in on him his life seems to have
caused just such a brief sharp report as the gun
that gave him his death and to have left as little
residue. Birds wheel above him, contemplating
descent to pick out his eyes. If he is to be saved

from that desecration it is because men who accept the obligation of performing tedious duties for no other reason than decorum, which he rejected, take the trouble to bury him who did not do that service to his victims. His end is dependence on the charity of those whom he despised for their conformity.

Hence, in Spain, the bull fight. That splendid show in which the experience of man in dealing with the criminal is analysed and synthesized, in which the bull, type of the Intractable, is received in a place that because of his coming is made to glow with fine costumes like the feathers of a bird in the mating season, is allowed to harry the weak obedient horse, and as many as he can reach of men who are made in God's image but nevertheless are under a necessity in this occasion to run as fast as their legs can carry them. But it is killed under the inverted cup of the audience's breathless, cruel attention, which if he tries the abandonment of force for mildness shivers not into kindness but into whistles and mocks at his cowardice, not to be stopped even by his dying. To the same end, in many countries, many songs and ballads. In England those ballads about highwaymen, which are flushed and loose-lipped at their thefts as if at lewdness, and turn merciless as Judge Jeffreys when they go to the scaffold. In Spain and Italy a hundred thousand folk songs, that by a slant in the time, a sliding of the voice as insolent as the wheel of a shoulder can be, tells what honest men think of the thief's corpse, how (basely) they threaten that perhaps they will leave him there to be made carrion by carrion, how (nobly) in their heart of hearts they wish they had been as those very honest men who not for a minute wished to rebel. Alas for Jane Addams and Hull House! It was not a settlement that Capone and his like needed, it was only a bar of music. That would have broken up the gang, before they were founded. On one condition: that the bar of music sung and heard by these whose thousand forefathers were used to sing and hear sequences of notes with that same meaning. Then, in a society interpenetrated with knowledge of this common worship and these folk-songs, no man would find himself anywhere which was not stamped with this conviction of the sacredness of life and the disagreeable mortality of the murdered. The imprint of this condition on his surroundings is of course no guarantee that he will act upon it, any more than the installation of a hot-water system in a man's house guarantees that he takes baths; but in both cases if the man is a normal person with the normal instinct for making use of what instrument for living life gives him he will take advantage of his opportunities like the rest of society.

There is actually no other way by which man can effectually be dissuaded from the act of murder when it seems to his advantage. A prohibition which is merely a prohibition, which is not a suggestion made by art, exerts no binding force, because he knows that the only reasons why it has not been suggested by art must be that it refers to a department of existence, like the parking of cars, too trivial to be submitted to the costly higher processes of analysis and synthesis — a supposition which, when applied to the taking of life, turns his scheme of values upside down and makes a madman of him;

or that it runs counter to the findings of the processes of analysis and synthesis, and is being put to him although it is untrue because it serves somebody else's material interests or prejudices, in which case he has a biologically quite sound instinct to resist it. Therefore you leave yourself with very little protection against murder except the actual physical presence of policemen, which it is wholly beyond the economic and moral resources of even a great city to provide in sufficient numbers and of incorruptible character, if one comes between a man and the art of his country (that is to say, the analysis and synthesis of the experiences that come to people of his type by themselves, so that the process is conducted in a way most comprehensible and serviceable to him).

That, of course, one could hardly do more effectively than by removing him to another continent, where even though his sense of self-protection may lead him to cling to such of his kind as have travelled there before him so as not to lose the benefit of this common fund of ascertained reality, he is still more strongly impelled to turn his back on them because the civilization of which he and they and it are parts is identified with economic conditions inferior to those he now sees around him; and because his tendency is to respect nothing which is not said in the language spoken by these who hold positions of authority in this new and superior economic dispensation. But from what he reads or hears in this new language he is likely to learn very little: partly because it is not probable that he (or even his children born on this foreign soil) will completely master it ; and partly because even if he does he will not be able to avail himself of the common fund of ascertained reality possessed by the people who speak it, since it will relate solely to experiences in the forms under which they presented themselves to that alien people, bound to be markedly different from the forms under which they present themselves to people living in another country under other conditions. Deprived thus of any real guidance as to the nature of experience, except what he himself can find out, the exile dashes about from experience to experience, trying to do, trying to make, but in a state of ignorance as to what doing or making are, and to what end they should lead. Hence Scarface Capone, symbol of the disaster of such exiles, engages in his disordered fantasies of conduct.

Hence Mr. Yeats, victim of another such transplantation, engaged in his disordered fantasias of philosophic speculation. Social forces, as inexorable as those which have sent Italians to the United States, sent certain English families to live in Ireland in conditions not those which the English genius uses for its development. In England art and science have in the main been carried on by a middle class which is unafraid to examine the nature of the universe and subject it to the change that comes of knowledge because it was a change in the nature of the universe which lifted their stock out of the working classes. The aristocracy was on the whole averse from the responsibility of conducting any such researches, because they were where they wanted to be, and change might put them somewhere else, though ultimately, of course, like everybody else, they are forced to accept the results of these researches by their deep instinct for self-preservation. Now, in pre-Home-Rule Ireland there was no middle-class which was prejudiced in favour of change by the thought of what change had done for it; since no access of wealth could raise a Roman Catholic Irishman of native stock to a position where he would not be treated as the inferior of a Protestant Anglo-Irishman. And the Anglo-Irish aristocracy was even more averse than the home-keeping variety from the practice of art and science, since both have an incorrigible tendency to lead to discussions of religious tolerance and political liberty, and are bound to create excitement, which always releases the repressions of those it fires, and in the case of a proud and conquered people causes a released repression known as rebellion. In consequence there was virtually no art and science in the Anglo-Irish community. That is to say, there were no analyses and syntheses of the experiences peculiar to that community.

Therefore a mystic like Mr. Yeats, when he sits down to consider what the parts of the universe that have not been illuminated by the clear moon-beam of his vision may be like, finds nothing to fill in the blanks except the primitive Irishman's world of Sidhe, which is the result of analyses and syntheses of experiences so much simpler than his own that they are as ridiculous as matter for his pen as a sailor-suit would be as apparel for his limbs. He thus produces a vision of the universe which is far madder in effect than that presented by William Blake, who was not nearly so sane as he is, who was prone to the disorder of hallucination, but who was embedded in England; who held in his hand an unbroken mystical tradition relevant to his circumstances to tell him what the other parts of the universe he had not time to look at with his seeing eye had seemed like when they were looked at by others who had that same eye. This tradition was not supported by the written word; it was (as happens in Protestant countries) barely recorded, but it passed from mouth to mouth of fervent preachers drawn from and maintained by this class that was willing to change the world. That it existed can be proved by such curious scraps of evidence as the trace left on modern science by that group of Quaker merchants who, at the time when William Blake was writing, had come to the conclusion that buying and selling and prospering gave a man not enough knowledge of God's works, and engaged in amateur scientific research in their evenings, and with luck adding this and that to optics and chemistry and botany. Isolated Anglo-Irishmen of great attainments there were; but there was no such seeping through the community of experience as the existence of this group indicates.

As much as Mr. Yeats was Mr. George Moore put at a disadvantage by his exile. Anglo-Ireland had had no *Tom Jones*. There has been no analysis and synthesis of the experiences which must be peculiar to a country where the native population, from which the imported aristocracy would naturally choose its mistresses and prostitutes, is inflexibly chaste, and the aristocracy therefore has to confine its sexual dealings to its own class, which has involved a great deal of sublimation and subterfuge. The attitude towards sex of the normal man who finds himself in these circumstances has not been depicted, because there has been no serious art running alongside Anglo-Irish life and reporting on it. When Mr. Moore attempts to supply this omission he repels his fellow-countrymen because he is breaking a silence that they wish observed, and affects his other readers in the same way because he constantly shows a superb mastery of such material as he himself has observed coupled with a complete unawareness of all the agreements to which humanity has come to regarding its feelings about sex, which reminds one of the mixture of knowledge and ignorance concerning the same subject which we find in the precocious child. In the child that mixture is dangerous, since it is likely to inspire him to become sexually active at a time when he is not ready physically or psychically for the experience, and may form unwholesome passions in the adult; therefore it excites loathing and abhorrence. This feeling many transfer for no other reason than association to Mr. Moore, though his occasional presentation of unnatural reactions to sexual fact should be counted as no more than tiny broideries of fantasy on the edge of an artistic fabric as well and truly woven as fine linen.

Infinitely less ominous are they so far as suggestion of the arrest of normal processes is concerned, than *Stalky & Co.* that twofold flight back to infantilism, back to school, which in order that the severance from the writer's present might be more complete was given the character of barbaric society to a degree that real schoolboys find comic. Those forces which prohibited the development of art in the Anglo-Irish community were present in a vastly exaggerated form in the Anglo-Indian community that, at first, in the new and glowing subject-matter it afforded his pen, seemed to have nourished the genius of Mr. Kipling; that in the last resort proved to have starved it. Useless was it for him to come home, to write with a desperate nostalgia stories that have the snug quality of wish-fulfilment fantasies about Americans who come to England and live in serenity for ever after because they chance on the house that cradled their ancestors. What the artist needs is to live in a world unified by common experience and a common art. Then he can serve himself by noting the postman's morning greeting, the first sentence in the newspaper leader, the type used for an advertisement on the hoardings, the way the flowers are planted in the cottage gardens – for all these phenomena are determined by the experiences of the human agents responsible for them and the effect on those agents of the analysis and synthesis of similar experiences of the artists and scientists who have operated within the same zone of civilization. A tradition is formed and offered him. But if his own experience relates to a distant and different civilization it will be of no use to him. It will not show him what the ultimate significance of that experience is; it will not show it to him in relation to the experiences of others that impinge on it. He is left isolated; it is no wonder he is panic-stricken.

Wild, wild, is the *émigré*, the *déraciné*. . . . Consider the increasing complication, the titanic efforts to spin cocoons out of themselves that would account for everything, which marked the works of those great exiles, Henry James and Joseph Conrad. In thinking of them and Mr. Yeats and Mr. Moore and Mr. Kipling we are thinking of men so strong in innate genius that under this as under any conceivable disadvantage they seem at an advantage compared with the rest of us. But look back at the wildness at the other end of the scale, at the arabesques described not among the stars but on the mud, at the immigrant gangsters. One is reminded of the description in Professor Pavlov's book of the proceedings of dogs that have been decorticated; that have had parts of their brains cut out. 'Sometimes the animal walked into obstacles, sometimes went round them. . . . If the hair on any part of the skin, especially of the neck and head, were touched however slightly by hand, other animals, mud, drops of rain, or any object with which the dog might come into contact, an extraordinary outburst of excitation followed, expressed by growling, barking, baring of the teeth and hostile movements generally. . . . The tendency of the nervous system to inhibition continued to increase, as did also the occurrence and severity of the attacks of convulsions, until on the 19th May, 1912, vigorous attacks continuing with only short intermissions during twelve hours, finally killed the animal. . . .' When the organism made the cortex make itself inside it, that making became an essential part of it. The organism cannot go back on its decision any more than it can go back into the past. When man made art make itself half-inside and half-outside him, that making became an essential part of him. He cannot go back on his decision if he is to

173

maintain himself as man, as part of a cohesive movement that is not swept away by time. It is possible for a man to carry on a sort of existence without art, of course, just as a decorticated dog need not die immediately. For it can be said in reference to the higher forms of experience, as Pavlov says of the lower forms of existence, that 'inferior analysing qualities are, of course, manifested by lower parts of the nervous system, and even by the crudely differentiated nervous substance in those animals which lack a nervous system proper.' A man to whom Henry Ford is a greater man than Shakespeare need not die of it. He can get along in the lap of a lucky economic dispensation exactly as a decorticated dog can get along in the shelter of a laboratory. But when he goes forth into the world he will be without a guide to see that he lives, instead of performing those disordered fantasies of conduct that in no way arrest death.

VI

To sum up:

Because of this train of thought it appears to me less of a maniacal delusion on my part to feel as I do that *Ulysses* and Ingres' portrait of a young man in a snuff-coloured coat are necessities to me, though I obviously cannot eat them, or use them for clothing, or shelter or fuel, and have absolutely no use for such information as they afford me concerning Dublin Jews and mid-nineteenth-century Frenchmen. I find it not hard to believe that the organism, having caused an organ to make itself within it, which is called the cortex, whose business it is to pick out of the whole complexity of the environment those units which are of significance, and to integrate those units into an excitatory complex that shall set its instinctive reflexes working, should find itself in consequence overburdened with experiences created by this organ, which in their crude state are as unprofitable to it as the whole complexity of its environment and its reflexes would be without this organ; and that the organism, being on the whole satisfied with the way the cortex works, causes another to make itself on much the same lines, to perform the same analytic and excitatory functions, which shall similarly make experience profitable to the individual.

This organ is collective and partially external. The conditioned reflexes maintained and established by an individual cortex sets up an experience which is objectified by him and communicated to other cortices, whose experiences are immediately modified by contact with it as well as by their own incessantly arriving experiences, so that they receive another and

new experience, which they also objectify and communicate with like effect on all within the same
sphere of communication. The individual may carry
through the business of analysis and synthesis and
communication himself, which is the way of the
creative artist; or he may lend his energy to the
business of communicating the excitatory complex
conducted by a creative artist, which is the way of
the interpretative artist; or he may simply accept
these communications, ignoring some and using
others as a guide for his behaviour, which is the way
of the non-artist.

The working of this organ is called Science when it
deals with man's experience of controllable material,
that does not tell lies to the observer; and it is called
Art when it deals with man's experience of uncon-
trollable material that can tell lies to the observer and
has to be circumvented in the exercise of this gift
before one can get the truth. This circumvention is
contrived by the use of empathy, which is our power
of projecting ourselves into the destiny of others by
fantasy, and which we employ in different ways to suit
the different arts. This power we enjoy because our
psychical uniqueness is due solely to the uniqueness
of our circumstances and of an element in ourselves
that chooses which of our psychical mechanisms we
shall use, and not to uniqueness in our outfit of
psychical mechanisms. By telling ourselves that a
stimulus is being applied to us which is not, in fact,
being applied to us, and that the element in us which
chooses which psychic mechanism we shall use has
chosen in a way that in fact it has not, we can describe
the psychic pattern that would be described by a

person to whom this stimulus has in fact been applied, and in whom the element which chooses has in fact made this choice.

The parts of James Joyce which created *Ulysses* and the parts of Ingres which created the portrait of the young man in the snuff-coloured coat, were parts of this collective and partially external super-cortex. They are analyses and syntheses into excitatory complexes of experiences apprehended by James Joyce and Ingres. The experience worked on by James Joyce is one arising out of the relationship of the Man, the Woman, and the Child; it is a re-analysis and a re-synthesis of a type of experience arising out of those relationships which recurs incessantly and has often been re-analysed and synthesized, notably on one occasion by the community art-form of religion in the form of the Manichæan heresy. What the experience which is the subject-matter of Ingres' portrait was I cannot say. I know what it was, and so does everybody know who has stood in front of it in a receptive state, but none of us can tell. For it cannot be put into words, since if it could it would not be a suitable subject for a painter. It would properly belong to the writer. We can be very sure that if it could have been put into words Ingres, whose confessions of fatuity in intellectual matters we have noted, would have made a mess of it. The function of the art critic is to write all round a work of art, but to leave a blank in the middle for it to express itself in its purely visual terms. He can describe the temperament that creates it, the emotion it causes, the historical influences that have affected it, but concerning the real subject (as apart from the actual one)

177

he cannot say a word. Mr. Roger Fry tries somewhere to explain the joy he had felt at seeing a picture
by Chardin, which was really a signboard painted to
hang outside a pharmacy, by attributing it to the
formal relations of the various bottles. Which is like
saying, 'We're here because we're here.' Even to
him, prince of critics, the subject refuses to state
itself. But there is no reason to suppose that these
visual experiences which have no statement to give to
the reporters are less valuable than those intellectual
ones which take kindly to being stated and restated
in words. So far as emotions can tell us – and in
these matters we have no other guide – they seem to
be equally good news to the organism.

Art is not a luxury, but a necessity. It is not
merely pleasant for me to read *Ulysses* and to see
Ingres' portrait of the young man in a snuff-coloured
jacket, it is necessary that I should do so. As a matter
of fact, it is not so extremely pleasant for me to read
Ulysses. It is full of mincing sentimentalities, it is
frequently incompetent, it is narcissistic, much of it
proceeds only too obviously from the workings of
one of the least pleasing fantasies conceived by man
concerning his birth. The type of which Leopold
Bloom is the modern incarnation, the court jester, is
familiar enough to our minds without this new exposition. As for this portrait by Ingres, there are
many pictures as agreeable. One has always many
calls on one's time in Paris, there seems no reason
why I should have allowed this picture to make
another. I would surely have had a sufficient range
of analyses and syntheses of visual experiences if I
had restricted myself to knowledge of such pictures

as hang in the galleries of London and New York, cities where I live for months on end. Nevertheless, my emotions warn me, with the poignancy which tells me that they are supporting and supported by the intellect, that I must know Ingres well; and warned me as urgently that I must read every word of *Ulysses*. Surely they issue this warning because art is not arbitrary, but is determined to the minutest details.

Ulysses is not as it is because James Joyce chose that it should be so; when Ingres faced the canvas to paint the young man in the snuff-coloured coat the canvas was already inscribed with the only portrait he would find it possible to paint. *Ulysses* is the product of the excitatory complexes of his time, whether derived from art and science or from straight unanalysed and unsynthesized experience, pressing on the individuality which is called James Joyce: the portrait of the young man in the snuff-coloured coat was a product of the excitatory complexes of his time, from the same dual source, pressing on the individuality which was called Ingres. Nobody has yet discovered (nor can we conceive how that discovery could be made) how far these individualities — and all others — are themselves the products of excitatory complexes, and to how much the residue that exists independently of them amounts. This imponderable residue is in a very important sense unique; but it is also very like all the imponderable residues, since it must in large part be a synthesis of the instincts.

The position is therefore this: I am a human being who cannot be very unlike James Joyce, because he also is a human being. I live in the same civilization, therefore I am exposed to practically the same excitatory complexes. Those which are derived from straight, unanalysed, unsynthesized experience may appear to be very different, but at least they will have a fundamental unity because they spring from the activity of our common human instincts. Those which are derived from art and science are more obviously the same. We both live in Europe, we have been exposed to the same philosophy, the same physics, the same pictures, the same books, the same music, and, what is fully as important, we have lived all our lives among people who were similarly children of Europe, who were imprinted by a like science and art. Now since we have such similar individualities, and are the subjects of so nearly identical a stream of excitatory complexes acting on our individualities, our experiences are bound to be very much the same.

It is therefore as certain as may be that I have among my experiences one that bears a strong resemblance to James Joyce's experience which made him write *Ulysses*. Either I have not analysed and synthesized it into an excitatory complex, in which case it roams about at the back of the mind, uncontrolled, unprofitable, and possibly mischievous; or I have analysed and synthesized it into an excitatory complex, in which case I can check up on the soundness of my process, and see what was peculiar to myself and what was universal in the form in which this common experience presented itself to me. In any event I have got to live in a world where a large number of people are to varying degrees conditioned by a knowledge of *Ulysses*. I shall not be able to analyse any experience of mine in which they take part unless I can fully comprehend their conditioning in this respect. Moreover, I shall find it easier to analyse my experiences with people who have not read *Ulysses* if I can put my finger on the differences in them which are due to this abstinence. Obviously it is imperative if I am to get on with my biological job of adapting myself to my environment that I should read *Ulysses*: as also that I should contemplate Ingres' portrait of a young man in a snuff-coloured coat, which is just as useful to me in control of those experiences dependent on the use of the eye. No wonder a human being that cuts itself off from art blunders round the world hitting against things as a decorticated dog blunders round in a laboratory.

But, it may be objected, surely this means that we ought to read all the books in the world, ought to see all pictures ever painted; for they too are the fruits of man's mind, they too make an impression on him. It means nothing of the sort. There are a million million manifestations of bad art, and on them one need not spend a second; because they do not represent processes of analysis and synthesis of experience terminating in the creation of excitatory complexes, but are attempts to make excitatory complexes out of the crude factual elements of experiences, which it is impossible to carry out with any but the most limited and momentary success. People who class *Ulysses* with pornographic literature, and demand pettishly why they should read it rather than any of the books that are sold in squalid little shops in Villiers Street, must, if they are honest, see that a considerable difference between the compared kinds of literature is indicated by the fact that contemporary writers of importance are riddled with allusions to James Joyce, they show few if any traces of the influence of Villiers Street. Even so, if Mr. A. S. M. Hutchinson's *If Winter Comes* were a better book than *Ulysses*, as many would maintain, misled by their approving sense that its action takes place with such admirable discretion in what house agents called 'the reception rooms,' while Mr. Joyce's characters use every room in the place down to the 'usual offices,' and that it urges us all to be kind to everybody, a course which Mr. Joyce neither recommends nor considers, it seems odd that it made no impression on critics and writers who cast their nets most widely for beauty in the sphere of art, and that few people except neurotics of the self-pitying type who identified themselves with Mark Sabre retain any recollection of it. The fact is that the Villiers Street authors set themselves to make an excitatory complex out of the crude facts of sex and succeed in making one that endures long enough to send some of their more undeveloped readers off for an evening of dingy adventure, and no longer; and Mr. Hutchinson set himself out to make an excitatory complex out of the crude facts of human suffering and benevolence and succeeded in making one that endures long enough to make another kind of undeveloped reader comfortably tearful throughout a lovely cosy afternoon in the company of China tea and crumpets, but no longer. Similarly, though the late Sydney Cooper's pictures of cows in a field are from the point of view of factual subject as worthy as Ingres' portraits of unimportant people (since cows in fields represent instances of things being where they ought to be, of square pegs not in round holes, which are only too rare in this disordered universe), it nevertheless remains true that neither Roger Fry nor any other critic of distinction writes impassioned books about him, and neither I nor (I am prepared to swear) any other of God's c.eatures ever hesitated between going on a delicious expedition and keeping a tryst in a gallery with 'that Sydney Cooper – you know, the one with the two Schleswig-Holsteins.'

The healthy human being automatically rejects excitatory complexes which are the results of statements about experiences instead of being the products of analyses and syntheses of experience, just as a sane business man rejects balance-sheets that are not the products of disinterested accountancy. Bad art is maintained by the neurotic, who is deadly afraid of authentic art because it inspires him to go on living, and he is terrified of life. When the wholesome non-neurotic artist and art-lover bursts in on him saying, 'You must have art!' meaning 'You must expose yourself to books, pictures, music, which will give you sound, strong, excitatory complexes,' it is a great refuge for him if he can point to books, pictures, music, which have no power to do anything to him at all, and say, 'I have art,' since the artistic process is so difficult to define that it is not easy to contradict him. Sometimes bad art, if executed with vitality and a free use of empathy in the imaginary instead of on the real, objectifies his neuroses and makes them more controllable, but ordinarily bad art is purely destructive. Criticism which applies certain standards to works of art, an atmosphere of

culture which develops a general sensitivity to the
quality of art, are therefore as necessary to a civilization as inspectors who tell the community whether
bridges are safe or not, and a system of education
which enables the community to grasp what they
mean and to act upon it.

Of course I felt as I did that day in Paris. It was
only logical that I should do so. I had passed through
a sun-gilded autumn day. I had walked on the Right
Bank below those edifices which have an air of having
been built from designs snatched by an architect
from a silversmith to whom they rightly belonged.
Being loyal to their first master in the way they
shine under light as stone does nowhere else in the
world, so that one feels like a nymph at the base of an
épergne. I had walked on the Left Bank, going down
the grey streets whose thousand shades of greyness
are as rich to the eye as any sunset, where one feels as
if one were a stone woman, a caryatid beside a door, a
mocking head under a gable, on whom a ray of light
had lit so brightly that it became a ray of life. As much
as that does one feel a part of the age that built these
streets, of which there can nevertheless be no human
survivors, so that if one is here at all it must be
through some magic art of packing life away in images,
such as they exercised over on the island, in Notre
Dame, in the saints on its façade, the deities on its
altars, the devils on its towers. The mere circumstance of being in these places at this time was exquisite; and I had preserved it from monotony by
withdrawing from them every now and then into
enclosed places, purposeful occasions that themselves
were also exquisite. I had gone into wide cool *salons*

184

to buy hats and dresses; I had gone into golden rooms
on the prow of the Ile St. Louis where golden leaves
fell slowly past the window-panes, turning and pausing in mid-air as if to find their footing down the in-
visible spiral stairways, and by a wood fire words that
mattered little as dead leaves because of silliness and
that because of grace were golden beautifully car-
peted one's inattention; I had gone into a lawyer's
office and had arranged to make money which I need;
I had gone into a bank and been handed letter upon
letter inscribed with the letters which to be sure are
those which form one's own name and address, yet
write in our minds the names and addresses of those
who have sent them to us so clearly that we immediately see the beloved faces, the houses where one is
welcome.

There was nothing here that did not delight me,
yet all the time I was plucked away by an urgent
necessity to think of James Joyce and the tedious
schoolboy Stephen Dedalus and the Dublin Jew
Leopold Bloom and his trollop; just as later I was to
be dissuaded by a picture by Ingres from going to
Versailles. When I looked back on the day nothing
seemed so real as this persistent, nagging preoccupation with *Ulysses*, or indeed the fact crying
to heaven for an explanation, to give me such
authentic pleasure; but there are certain curious
convolutions in the form taken by this pleasure, for
although it was interpenetrated with awe for James
Joyce, such as one must feel for one who performs
the miracle and clothes in the flesh of his living words
an Idea that man has conceived concerning himself,
it nevertheless permitted me, it even caused me to

feel glad when I picked up one of his poems and perceived that it was bad. At first sight fantastic, even as if that the only other elements of the day which in memory evoked the same kind of pleasure and partook of the same effect of reality, were the letters from my friends, a black lace dress that reminded me of a Goya etching, some agreeable but unimportant Pruna panels, surely unrelated phenomena.

But all this is logical. Perfectly logical. Never, I perceive, am I a more healthy, sane, non-neurotic animal than when I let art dictate my reactions. It was natural that the city of Paris should delight me with its variety of forms and colours; so large a part of man's knowledge and control of his environment is derived from the perception and handling of form and colour that any sensitiveness of the nerves which makes him take pleasure in them is of the greatest practical use to him and is bound to be highly developed. This delight was, of course, reinforced by the historical allusiveness of Paris, which brought up to my mind many other forms and colours, still further enriched by recollections of works of art which had analysed and synthesized experiences arising out of the disposition of these. But I was under a compulsion to turn my back utterly on all direct experience and to immerse myself so far as possible in art, for the reason that at that particular moment I was glutted with direct experience that had not been digested and was stored away in my mind in a crude state. For the past three months I had been living in a house in the south of France in a state which was more beautifully near pure living

than anything I had known for many years. I had
seen nearly nobody except my closest friends; I had
therefore wasted none of my energy on making
movements and speaking words that meant nothing
to me; I had therefore all my vitality left free for the
business of experience. When I swam there was no
sense that I ought to be doing something else to call
me out of the sea, so I was able to give a complete
spiritual loyalty to the water, to be blank to everything but apprehension of its qualities. When I sat
in the garden and looked up at the crossed weapons
of the palm-leaves the pattern their sharp edges
hacked out of the light-white sky was hacked also
out of the fundament of my attention. When the
villa cat, that plump, ginger-haired widow, came
down the path with her two young daughters, who
had the plaintive air which all pretty kittens have
of being helpless pawns in their mother's matrimonial
schemes, I could enter by comprehension into the
delicious ballet of their movements; I could participate in that good luck they have of being able to
engage in some frenzied pursuit with a passion
greater than that of the most passionate of human
beings, and to halt suddenly, setting the four paws
close together and closing almost completely the
eyes, colder than the coldest of human beings. How
they eat their cake and have it too, those cats! Every
minute seemed bursting with sensation as a ripe fig
is bursting with sweetness.

Now, that something has to be done with all these
experiences, that they cannot be carried about by the
individual in the form in which they were ingested, is
proven by the deplorable condition of all colonies of

expatriates who settle down in beautiful surroundings with nothing to do from year's end to year's end
but enjoy their sensations. Invariably such attempt
to mitigate the stream of experience that is constantly flowing towards them by clouds of alcohol,
and to organize life into some sort of pattern by the
invention of scandal. Individuals can handle the
burden no better than societies, as is witnessed by
the unending garrulity of explorers and big-game
hunters and old soldiers, about whose 'yarn-spinning
round the fire over a pipe' there is a neurotic and
unsatisfied quality, as there is too about the tedious
anecdotes that women of many loves tell in the
autumn of their days, that Proust makes Odette de
Crécy gabble in her old age. . . . 'One day I was in
the Champs Elysées. M. de Breauté, whom I had
only seen once in my life, started staring at me so hard
that I stopped and asked him how he dared look at
me like that. He answered, "I'm staring at you
because you're wearing such an absurd hat. . . ."'
And so on, until '*Nous eûmes deux années d'un amour
fou.*' But there is no profitable way of dealing with
one's experience except by analysis and synthesis
into an excitatory complex; that is why man has to
tolerate the maintenance of this monstrous organ
known as art, which is apparently so completely useless to all his other organs. So art it had to be for me
that day in Paris. No wonder I felt pleasure.

But why should I have chosen *Ulysses* as a point of
approach when I wanted to analyse my experiences
of the summer? What can there be in common
between that novel about Dublin dinginess and a
holiday spent in the Department of Var? Obviously

what brought *Ulysses* to my mind that day was a pure
accident, was my passing of Sylvia Beach's bookshop.
It would be a sufficient explanation of my willingness
to keep it in mind that I had to grow accustomed to
the movement of analysis and synthesis to which I
had for so long been a stranger, and that this book
was valuable to me because of the vigour with which
it performed that movement. It was like standing up
to dance the tango after one has not danced it for a
very long time, with one who dances it very well.
But also a novel about Dublin dinginess has everything in common with a holiday spent in the Department of Var. I do not think we can exaggerate the
fundamental unity of all art and all experience. In
both alike the individual is examining his environment to see what chances of survival it affords him.
This does not mean that he is looking for nuts to
gnaw or a cow to milk; it means that he seeks circumstances in which his soul can exercise certain
choices. There is, I believe, no experience which
falls outside this category and within sanity. I have
dug as deeply as I can into an emotion of my own
which seemed as light-hearted and arbitrary as any
one could know: a wild exhilaration such as one
might feel after whirling in a dance, that used to
come on me when I climbed to a certain low peak of
the Estorel Mountains; and at the end of my digging
I found that this emotion was as much concerned
with the place of man in the universe as if I had been
considering a religious creed. I was looking down on
the wide sea that was of a continuous substance yet
was of diverse colours, that sparkled with light (and
surely it is not possible for there to be light without

heat?) and yet was to my certain knowledge cool, that seemed flat as a field yet had a shifting edge of surf to show that waves were breaking; and I was looking on the black hills that mount in twisted cones of rock the colour of caked blood, that wear their forests as hermits wear the pelts of beasts, that are scarred by forest-fires as by wounds. As my eye passed from point to point of the landscape I realized the qualities of the contrasting substances presented, and my consciousness swung like a pendulum between the knowledge of the two states of matter that are called the land and the sea. I was back at the business of apprehending the qualities of substances with which I began my mental life – hardness, softness, roughness, dryness, wetness – I was considering the patterns I could make out of my relationship with those qualities, I was holding my attention to that curiously gabled cliff and bidding it accept that shape, I was hurling it down to spread itself over the flat field of the sea and bidding it cover the whole space with its acceptance, I was forcing it to keep in mind both cliff and water and seeing how it could balance them both and what a composition that made; and the game was enormously complicated by the associations I have formed during my life concerning these qualities, which make me feel terror of this one as for sterility, worship for this one as for fertility. By feeling such terror and such worship in those proportions I was finding a new and satisfactory equilibrium for my will to live and my will to die. And what else was James Joyce doing when he wrote *Ulysses*? Push back the superficial 'story' layer and you will come on the same process. It is the great human game. For that reason, as Santayana has put it, 'it might be said of every work of art and of every natural object, that it could be made the starting-point for a chain of inferences that should reveal the whole universe'; and it follows that all works of art are valuable to any human being who is part of the civilization that produced them. They will confirm his own researches into a common problem.

Nothing illogical, then, about my preoccupation with *Ulysses*. Nothing illogical, either, in my pleasure at finding that James Joyce has written a bad poem, nothing in that which is inconsistent with my great reverence for him. He is an artist, he has created a work of art, anything that helps me to understand that work of art, even if it be as intrinsically unpleasing an object as a bad poem, is welcome to me, because it helps me to establish myself in the universe. Nothing illogical, either, in the associations which linked in my mind at the end of the day, as sole survivors of that conviction that here was stuff not real or memorable which engulfed all my other experiences – a portrait by Ingres, a dress that recalled an etching by Goya, some panels by Pruna, letters from my friends. The portrait, the etching that lay as it were veiled in the folds of black lace, the panels by Pruna that were so marine that they seemed to fit the description 'wet paint' far better than much which has been labelled with those words, those were all works of art. It is true that the etching was rendered impure by the presence in Goya's intention of matter more suited to the medium of literature, and it is true that Pruna's work reminds one that his master Picasso lives in a villa not far from that debased little casino at Juan-les-Pins, and that one might go from one to the other; but they were works of art, they were attempts to analyse and synthesize experiences into excitatory complexes.

As for the letters from my friends, of course they rank in their effect on me with works of art, because love is a condition which makes one believe that life is presenting itself to one in the same assimilable state as art. One looks at a beloved object and says to oneself that at last a phenomenon has presented itself to one in such terms that it can be of the greatest possible use as an excitatory complex before it is subjected to analysis and synthesis, that it is of such a miraculous nature that it instantly delivers itself to one because of one's *beaux yeux* instead of reluctantly yielding to our laborious work on it. We protest that we know everything about it as if we had known it for a lifetime, that no knowledge has ever inspired us with such courage and power. In fact we are getting out of it exactly what art gives us, but without the effort of creation or perception, and we are travelling in a phase of experience where apple-dumplings grow on trees and rivers run ale, where life is no longer difficult to live. More joyful and intoxicating are the emotions we derive from love than those we derive from art, because they spring from a condition which promises an actual mitigation of the harsh intractability characteristic of the universe; whereas art never claims more than that it has a method of handling that intractability which is satisfactory if one knows how to use it. But both alike make me go on living. In a sense, of course, it is my

physical nature that makes me do that; but it might
drag my soul squealing at its heels, howling as the
neurotic does for the lost peace of the womb. Since
crude experience is as incapable of effective preservation as we have seen, it is justifiable to say that the
only forces which make me run alongside my body's
determination to live and keep pace with it, are my
personal happiness and art. My personal happiness
is staggeringly insecure, for it is conditional on the
continued existence of a group of people, on the preservation of my health, on the maintenance of a
harmony that any calculation of probabilities will
show to be not worth a gambler's money. It is only
on art, which is imperishable because it is collective
and detached from man's perishable body, that I can
rely for unfailing inspiration in this business of living.

So it was far from illogical of me to feel pleasure
when I had slipped into an authentic and animated
relationship with art after a long divorce from it that
day in Paris. I only wonder I did not sing in the
streets; and perhaps I did. There was in me, I
remember, a really tremendous state of pleasure. No
sense of unwilling loyalty to a heavy, brooding preoccupation with personal issues prevented me from
following through the cider-coloured autumn sunshine the dove which bridged the tall side of the Rue
de l'Odéon. As I gave myself to interior agreement
with its movement, I was able to give myself also to
interior agreement with the other movement of the
leaves which a moment before I had seen picked up
by a wind on the paths of the Luxembourg, at first
spinning flatly and slowly as if they had weight, then
swirling quickly in circles with the appropriate

weightlessness of dead leaves, fairy gold (they might have been) at the moment of its withdrawal from currency. Knowledge of these two movements co-existed in my mind, and was joined later by knowledge of the movement of the leaves that fell past the windows of the house on the Ile St. Louis, in golden hesitancy, as if Zeus were stricken with compunction by the sight of Danaë's youth and delayed, though he did not desist. These three movements form a pattern in my mind, a harmony, and they will never go from me because I can preserve them for ever either by apprehending some work of art with nearly the same theme (I think there is music by Ravel which is apposite), or by doing what I can to create a work of art on that theme. I cannot see that art is anything less than a way of making joys perpetual.

VII

I have run after myself like an excited *douanier* and insisted on searching myself because I have observed myself behaving in a suspicious manner. I find that I seem to be a quite sane and respectable person, and to have a perfect right to all the emotional goods that are found on me. But . . . what about this? This blazing jewel that I have at the bottom of my pocket, this crystalline concentration of glory, this deep and serene and intense emotion that I feel before the greatest works of art. You know, what Roger Fry means when he says somewhere, 'That is just how I felt when I first saw Michael Angelo's frescoes in the Sistine Chapel.' I get it myself most powerfully from 'King Lear.' It overflows the confines of the mind and becomes an important physical event. The blood leaves the hands, the feet, the limbs, and flows back to the heart, which for the time seems to have become an immensely high temple whose pillars are several sorts of illumination, returning to the numb flesh diluted with some substance swifter and lighter and more electric than itself. Unlike that other pleasure one feels at less climactic contacts with art it does not call to any action other than complete experience of it. Rather one rests in its lap. Now, what in the world is this emotion? What is the bearing of supremely great works of art on my life which makes me feel so glad?

It might be, of course, that in such works there are references to the conditions of another world which would be more friendly to us than this. There, most often, are these colours, these forms; there sounds sound most often like this music; there experience most often takes this turn. This universe must be real as ours, since it is weakening to brood on what is wholly fictitious (as apart from imaginary, and I have suggested that imagination is a function created by the organism to deal as specifically as the digestion with purely mundane experiences, and consequently could play no part here) and the effect of this contemplation is strengthening. It must therefore lie parallel with this, our paradise from which we are exiled by some cosmic misadventure, and which we can re-enter at times by participating in the experience of those artists who are supposed by some mystical process to have gained the power to reproduce in this universe the conditions of that other. But the overwhelming argument against this theory is that the people who prefer science to art appear to get precisely the same emotion out of contact with achievements, say in the sphere of mathematics or physics, which relate beyond all doubt to the universe of which we are a part and no other. One must look for another explanation of our good fortune in possessing this blazing jewel of emotion, this priceless treasure.

An analogy strikes me. Is it possible that the intense exaltation which comes to our knowledge of the greatest works of art and the milder pleasure that comes of our more everyday dealings with art, are phases of the same emotion, as passion and gentle affection are phases of love between a man and a woman? Is this exaltation the orgasm, as it were, of the artistic instinct, stimulated to its height by a work of art which through its analysis and synthesis of some experience enormously important to humanity (though not necessarily demonstrable as such by the use of the intellect) creates a proportionately powerful excitatory complex, which, in other words, halts in front of some experience which if left in a crude state would probably make one feel that life was too difficult, and transform it into something that helps one to go on living? I believe that is the explanation. It is the feeling of realized potency, of might perpetuating itself. But . . . do I really love life so much that I derive this really glorious pleasure from something that merely helps me to go on living? That is incredible, considering that life has treated me as all the children of man like a dog from the day I was born. It is incredible, that is, if things are what they seem, if there is not a secret hidden somewhere. . . . I can't justify it, I can't answer half the questions I ask myself. I can just gape and wonder and turn over in my hands this marvellous jewel which, there's no question, I certainly do possess. 'There's a whole lot of things I'd like to know about you, my lad!' exclaims the exasperated *douanier*, dashing off to peer into a peasant woman's basket, or touch his hat to an automobile, or somehow to deal with the respectably objective. I want him to come back and bully me, for I too would like to know a lot of things about myself. Not only am I wandering in the universe without visible means of support, I have a sort of amnesia, I do not clearly know who I am . . . what I am. . . . And that I should feel this transcendent joy simply because I have been helped to go on living suggests that I know something I have not yet told my mind, that within me I hold some assurance regarding the value of life, which makes my fate different from what it appears, different, not lamentable, grandiose.

UNCLE BENNETT

ALL our youth they hung about the houses of our minds like Uncles, the Big Four: H. G. Wells, George Bernard Shaw, John Galsworthy and Arnold Bennett. They had the generosity, the charm, the loquacity of visiting uncles. Uncle Wells arrived always a little out of breath, with his arms full of parcels, sometimes rather carelessly tied, but always bursting with all manner of attractive gifts that ranged from the little pot of sweet jelly that is 'Mr. Polly,' to the complete meccano set for the mind that is in The First Men in the Moon. And he brought all the scientific fantasies, and the magic crystals like *Tono-Bungay* and *The New Machiavelli*, in which one could see the forces of the age sweep and surge like smoke about brightly coloured figures that were blinded by them, that saw through them, that were a part of them, that were separate from them and were their enemies, that were separate from them and were their allies, and illustrated as well as it has ever been done the relationship between man and his times.

This impression of wild and surpassing generosity was not in the least one of youth's illusions. One had, in actual fact, the luck to be young just as the most bubbling creative mind that the sun and moon have shone upon since the days of Leonardo da Vinci was showing its form. The only thing against Uncle Wells was that he did so love to shut himself up in the drawing-room and put out all the lights except the lamp with the pink silk shade, and sit down at the piano and have a lovely time warbling in too fruity a tenor, to the accompaniment of chords struck draggingly with the soft pedal held down, songs of equal merit to 'The Rosary.'

You know perfectly well what I mean: the passages where his prose suddenly loses its firmness and begins to shake like blanc-mange. 'It was then I met Queenie. She was a soft white slip of being, with very still dark eyes, and a quality of . . . Furtive scufflings . . . Waste . . . Modern civilization . . . Waste . . . Parasitic, greedy speculators. . . . "Oh, my dear," she said, "my dear . . . darn your socks . . . squaw. . . ." ' But take him all in all, Uncle Wells was as magnificent an uncle as one could hope to have.

So, too, was Uncle Shaw. He brought his mind for the children to look at, his marvellous shining mind. Too thin a mind, Philistines would object; but the very finest French watches are as thin as a couple of half-crowns and yet keep better time than the grosser article. He did for his age what Voltaire and Gibbon did for theirs: he popularized the use of the intellectual processes among the politically effective class. And he did it with such style. There is a pride in his mental movements that reminds one of the bull-ring, of the walk of the matador into the centre of the arena when he is going to fight the bull to the finish. That walk has panache. It has pride: not only individual pride, which is a little thing and not impressive, since the individual can boast of nothing that will not die with its short life, but the pride of a species, which has reason to suppose that if it justified that pride by splendid performance it may live as long as the earth.

In effect he says, 'You are a bull. It is a fine thing to be a bull. Nevertheless . . . it is better to walk on two legs than four. I will show you in a minute!'

For those who have the courage to recognize change, who dare remould the *status quo*, are a mental species that have a long past behind them, as long as history, of which they are indeed the better part; but those who stand by the *status quo* are no older than that *status quo* and die with it. That gives him his panache, which is never, no matter what the mob says, insolence. For the insolent artist betrays himself in his craftsmanship, and there is no more diligent craftsman than Uncle Shaw. How adroitly he gets us, with our innate inertia, to put on ourselves the intellectual toil of swallowing his dialectics.

The measure of his adroitness is to be seen in the way he induced us to accept his plays as realistic. They are about as realistic as Lord Dunsany's. Look at those terrific long speeches which begin with a few crisp imperturbable sentences, break suddenly into a cascade of rich rolling periods working up to the final tremendous epigram! This is no naturalist transcript of modern conversation. It is a crib from the technique of something which presided over Uncle Shaw's youth and which has never been denounced on the score of realism; and that is Italian grand opera. Uncle Shaw knew that whatever the Italians did or did not know about music, they knew a great deal about the preliminary step of charming the human attention with the human voice. Therefore, whenever he wanted to force some important part of his argument on his audience he employed just the same form that the operatic composer did when he wanted to score his strong point; the deliberate, preparatory phrases of the recitative, the melodious memorable convulsions of the aria, the impressive cadenza. It is only in certain of his historical dramas, where he knows his audience is already charmed into receptivity by the associations their imaginations have formed with the subject, and the pageantry he can use on the stage, that he permits himself to write anything like realistic dialogue. There's artfulness for you.

There is, of course, to be set against this, that Uncle very often makes quite bad jokes; his comic relief is often as footling as Shakespeare's. He has nothing like Uncle Wells's happy power of inventing character after character that are all alive and kicking; the reproduction of Britannicus from 'Cæsar and Cleopatra' as William de Stogumber in 'Saint Joan' is symptom of a real deficiency. And when he talks about science he makes a noise like a Los Angeles Yogi. But again, take him all in all, what a magnificent uncle to have.

Uncle Galsworthy, of course, was always quieter about the house. He was really Uncle Phagocyte. For it is the phagocytes who, when the blood is attacked by hostile bacteria, rush to the seat of infection and eat up the invading hosts, and this is the function that Uncle Galsworthy has performed for the English middle class. That class had enjoyed a degree of peace and prosperity which was positively unwholesome in the long fat period between the Crimean and the South African Wars, and it had, therefore, fallen a prey to the infections of materialism and self-righteousness and narrowness and all

the more detestable, decorous, unjailable forms of
hoggishness. Uncle Galsworthy repelled these infections more than one would have thought it possible
for one human being to do. It is true that there are
ways in which he is not nearly so attractive as the
first two Uncles. There is about his work a certain
pallor. But it is the white corpuscles of the blood and
not the red that are engaged in this fight against
infection. That doubtless accounts for Uncle Galsworthy, as it accounted, perhaps, for Henry, Lorelei's
husband in *Gentlemen Prefer Blondes*. But that is a
little thing beside the grace of his pity, and those
pages of his writing that are as lovely as the under-
wing of a butterfly where the message is most delicately written, in fine patterns, in faint and lovely
colours. Take him all in all, he is a very good uncle
to have, too.

And there is Uncle Bennett. . . .

Now, that is just the odd thing. Why is Uncle
Bennett as good an uncle as any of them? Why, one
might ask, does he count as an uncle at all? For it is
not at all easy to chalk up what he has done for us.
The mark of the visiting uncles, we have decided, is
charm and generosity and loquacity. Now Uncle
Bennett has, superficially, very little charm at all.
Very rarely does he attain that flash of phrase which
is to the literary personality what brightness of eye
and lip are to the physical personality. He is often a
flat writer. Not a quiet writer, or a sober writer, or a
restrained writer. Just a flat writer. His loquacity is
neither spontaneous like Uncle Wells's, nor artful
like Uncle Shaw's, nor poignant like Uncle Galsworthy's. It is never urgent. There are innumerable

occasions when one suspects that he writes, not because he has something to say, but because of that abstract desire to write, which is hardly ever the progenitor of good writing. His generosity certainly does not lie in the direction of general ideas, for he rarely refers to any, nor to an extent that must be almost without parallel among the greater novelists in the invention of character.

Hardly any of his figures remain alive in the memory. There is certainly Elsie in *Riceyman Steps*, and Denry in *The Card*, but the one is an exquisitely drawn abstraction of tenderness and the other no more than a comic gesture. Elaborately worked over though the Clayhanger trilogy is, it may be doubted if anybody ever attempted to alleviate the tedium of a journey from, say, Chicago to South Bend, Ind., by leaning back, closing the eyes and exclaiming, 'Let me recall what I can of those delicious creations, Edwin Clayhanger and Hilda Lessways!' Even *The Old Wives' Tale*, which has profoundly impressed every intelligent young person of the last twenty years or so, gives us no characters. And the worst of it all is that his books are so often isolation hospitals full of the most feeble qualities.

All the Uncles have written twaddle in their time. Uncle Wells once sent into the world a large blond novelette with a heaving bosom called *The Passionate Friends*. All of 'Back to Methuselah' after the first act makes me feel so much older than Methuselah that I find myself regarding it as one of those plays about the younger set. Uncle Galsworthy once wrote a book called *Beyond* that was the back of beyond. But Uncle Bennett does it again and again. *The*

*Book of Carlotta, Lilian, Elsie and the Child, Our
Women* — these are mere runnings of the pen. And
the plays — *Judith, The Bright Island*. That last
set a whole London theatre whimpering with
boredom.

Yet the man is great. We must, indeed, count him
as one of the Uncles of the English-speaking world
who have more influence on innumerable young
people than anybody else save their fathers and
mothers; who fix thereby the colour of their times.
He does not give what the others give, but he gives.

And one can see what his gifts are, and how lavish
he is with them, and why he is incapable of giving
what the others do, if one turns to *Lord Raingo*.
That book is a failure and it is a success. It is a
success because one likes it to the extent of carrying it about with one all day, reading and re-reading
little pet half-pages. It is a failure because it does
nothing at all with its subject. It distils no significance from it; it merely makes a bungling statement
of it.

The subject is a romantic legend that went the
rounds during the latter part of the war, which
has rather less verity to it than the tale of the
Russians that were hurried through England in
August, 1914, or the Angels of Mons. The worst of
making war, as of acting for the 'movies,' is the
amount of waiting around on the lot; and waiting
men are likely to pass the time telling lies. This
legend had it that a certain politician who died during
the war had been having a love affair with a young
woman who, just before his sickness fell upon him,
suddenly took a journey to a watering-place and

threw herself over a cliff: and that the old man on his death-bed had been perturbed out of all comfort, murmuring his puzzlement till that moment when he puzzled over nothing any more. There is nothing against it except that the parties involved seem not to have met.

Now this is a subject with which something might have been done. As a matter of fact, I would not have chosen it for any of the Uncles. Uncle Wells would have run to succulence in the first person. 'That Saturday we took a long walk, somewhere out Highgate way. I seem to remember a lunch of bread and cheese and beer at a little inn covered with rambler roses, and some astonishingly good talk about Neolithic man. I told her all about the Piltdown skull and the St. Valière kneecap.' . . . Uncle Shaw would find it difficult to impose on persons in this situation quite that cheerfulness, bright and unbroken like a wall done with washable enamel, which he extracts from his modern characters. And Uncle Galsworthy would have made the young woman succumb to the politician's importunities because of the necessity for buying a surgical boot for her crippled brother.

But at any rate, they would have got something out of it, whereas Uncle Bennett gets nothing at all. The love affair, which must have been in the nature of blandness in the midst of asperities, a relaxation into softness and delight for one of whom it was demanded that he should be braced perpetually against the harsh demands of war and age and power, is so awkwardly presented that when one closes the book one is left with no picture of it save poor old Sam

Raingo clumping up the steps to the aerie where he keeps the lady and being either embarrassed by finding her with her sister, the bus conductor, or desolated by not finding her at all. Almost as little is done with the climax of the story. He gives no explanation of the girl's cruel desertion of her old lover for death except an innate melancholic taint, acted upon by the appearance in the casualty list of a former lover. But he does not convince us beforehand that she had that melancholic taint. It is perfectly true that he tells us so several times, but only by flat statement. ('If she had a fault, it was a tendency toward melancholy. The war made her gloomy and pessimistic. The casualty rolls reduced her to the very depths of blank, prostrate despondency.') . . . But never once does he invent the phrase, the speech, the incident, that would be the right hieroglyphic to stamp on our minds for ever the conviction that this creature, though young and beautiful and passionate enough to make an ageing man feel that his age was an adjustable defect like something a little wrong with the eyesight, had nevertheless looked on the waters of life and seen them dark.

Lord Raingo himself is treated almost as perfunctorily. The physical circumstances of his death are magnificently described, the *va-et-vient* of the modern sick-room, in which the invalid realizes that thanks to the marvellous developments of medicine and nursing he might just as well have lain down to die in the middle of Fifth Avenue so far as peace and quiet are concerned. But the obvious poignancy of his mental situation, the despair which must have

crept over the old man as he realized that the woman
he had chosen to wipe out the fact of death with her
abounding life had betrayed him and gone over to the
side of the enemy, is simply not stated. One gets not
the slightest sense, in between the paragraphs which
are tersely devoted to its manufacture, that he was
saturated with love for this woman and distress at her
fate; without which sense there is no subject at all.

And there is Gwen. Deplorably there is Gwen.
She is the bus conductor sister of the suicidal
mistress, impossibly beautiful, as are many of Mr.
Bennett's less successful female characters, and she
makes insane, explosive interruptions into the story,
repeatedly casting herself on Lord Raingo's death-
bed, or fainting round it, and failing throughout to
establish any sort of organic connection with the
theme. In her, and in the equally irrelevant Mrs.
Blacklow, who wanders through the story, being the
most explicitly expectant mother in fiction, though
having none of the characters to thank for it, is made
manifest the curious hectic incompetence which
comes upon Mr. Bennett so long as *Lord Raingo* is
faithful to its main subject.

Yet the book is full of exquisite things. Once he
steps out of the romantic circle of his principal characters, he has beauty at his finger-ends. There is, for
example, the incident of Wrenkin.

'Wrenkin, aged forty-seven, was the factotum of
the estate. An all-round, efficient, honest, indus-
trious, shabby and disagreeable man! He maintained
the radiators and hot water supply, manufactured
the electric current, kept Raingo's room in order,

grew vegetables and fruit, fought rear-guard actions against weeds, the cook and his mistress, and wangled coal and coke from Harwich. All for £2 a week. He believed himself to be, and not without some justification, the most remarkable man that ever lived. Everybody hated him except his master. These two understood one another and conversed together on the plane of masculine realism.'

At the time of Lord Raingo's illness he has been called up to the army. And when all the family and the doctors and nurses and servants are standing round the death-bed, waiting for the last breath, a grim figure in khaki appears in the doorway. 'He glared gloomily and challengingly around according to his custom.' It happens that just then the electric light is failing. The servants, flustered out of all routine by the presence of death, have left the lights on all over the house, and Wrenkin's deputy has not made enough current.

'Everybody noticed it, but nobody spoke or moved. Everybody thought how fitting, how impressive, how supernatural it was, that as Lord Raingo lay dying the lights of the house should fade. Everybody except Wrenkin. The lights suddenly went up – not much, but a little. Wrenkin had turned off every light on the ground floor. Time passed.

'Then the thudding beat of the dynamo in the engine-house by the garage came into the room through the opened windows. Wrenkin, making the situation tolerable for himself! The lights slowly resumed their proper brilliance.'

Now, that is superb. There is genius in that picture of the queer, gaunt-spirited creature working away in the engine-room, partly in selfishness, to find relief for the aching at his heart, partly out of loyalty to the quality of his friendship with his master, trying to keep this moment, when all might be lost to sentimentality, on the plane of masculine realism. . . .

There are lots of things like that throughout the book; things that have the rich air of not having been looked for, of having happened to the author; or rather, so independent of him do they seem, to his manuscript, of having inscribed themselves on the paper without the intervention of the pen by virtue of their fidelity to life, their propriety to the theme they illustrate. They are little presents given to the book by the unconscious.

A good book cannot be written without them. For only the unconscious knows why the author has chosen his theme and what he really has to say about it, and is, therefore, in a position to give it the really useful and apposite gifts. And if such gifts are withheld, it is a bad omen, since it indicates that the unconscious considers the conscious a fool for choosing such a theme and will hinder him in every way he can. Now, Mr. Bennett's unconscious clearly reveals to us in *Lord Raingo* by its alternate meanness and lavishness, what its preferences are, and why he is one of the most unequal writers who ever attained to eminence. It does not do a hand's turn for him when he is dealing with his romantic theme. It refuses to present him with one felicity. And it leaves him as severely alone in the other part of the novel which deals satirically with the quarrels and intrigues of our statesmen during the war. The thing is competently done, but there is nothing over and above the unsurprising findings of logic.

But once Mr. Bennett deals with subsidiary themes that lead him away from the great ones of the earth to the humble, that lead him from what are considered the high lights of life to its obscurities, then these gifts are showered on him. There is Wrenkin, there is Lord Raingo's old clerk, Swetnam; there are all the little people in the ministry, there are the doctors and nurses, all living, all significant, all inscribing themselves with the right hieroglyphics.

The fact is that Mr. Bennett's unconscious suffers from predilections that if they expressed themselves in the sphere of theology instead of art would be termed essentially Protestant. The movement away from Roman Catholicism to Anglicanism and further still to Nonconformity is caused very largely by a dislike of pomp and picturesqueness, which finds relief in the elimination of vestments and church music; a dislike of the hieratic priestly system, because that lends to a certain class of man a glory that is lacked by others; a dislike of too great a concentration on the sacraments since that discredits the common hours of life, which are not made spectacular by emotion but nevertheless travel slowly and surely toward sacredness.

All these things Mr. Bennett's unconscious feels about the subject-matter of his art. It distrusts pomp and picturesqueness. When he wrote a play on the obviously gorgeous theme of Judith it would not do a thing for him. It hates the elevation of one

man above another. Mr. Bennett can never work
happily on a character which is not socially and
personally mediocre. It wants to skip all the
moments in life that are traditionally splendid and ro-
seate in favour of the moments that are simply pieces
of the general texture of life. Whensoever a Bennett
character embraces a physically pleasing female
his prose crumbles in clichés, in which the words,
bland, superb, delicious, tender, are apt to occur.
It is when an old clerk grumbles at his employer,
a housemaid pokes her head over the banisters, that
Mr. Bennett's unconscious softens, warms, glows in
a transport of generosity, and gives him such inspira-
tions as this sullen, loving vigil of Wrenkin in the
power-house.

And that is why Uncle Bennett ranks as an
Uncle; as one who brings gifts to the minds of the
young, who is fixing the colour of his times. For
there is a great deal in this Protestant art. It is
quite true that if pomp and picturesqueness are cut
away from worship the thoughts of the worshipper
may turn to simpler and deeper issues. It is quite
true that there is a glory about all men, about the
flock as well as its leaders. It is quite true that life
unlit by excitement is nevertheless a light shining
in the darkness of the universe.

That is what Uncle Bennett's art proves to us.
He shows us a commercial traveller and the silly
girl he is going to run away with looking down a
railway embankment at some navvies wielding their
picks. There is nothing glorious there. All parties
concerned are nearly anonymous. Yet because of
the downward looks of the young couple, marvelling

at the mass of the earth and the strength man has to tame it, and the upward looks of the navvies, envying their youth and their freedom and their love, the moment is somehow beautiful, somehow memorable.

He can do more than that. He can show us a man going into a shop to buy shoes as one who performs a wonderful ritual, beautiful because all those participating in it follow grooves so patiently worn down by those who, in following them through the ages, have served certain human necessities, certain human ideals of duty. He can see the tram-car passing through a suburb at twilight as the chariot of fire it veritably is. Like Wordsworth, he has triumphed over the habitual; he has not let it disguise the particle of beauty from him. Though he might never produce one single perfect or even imperfect work of art, or never produce a work of art at all, he remains an artist.

THE CLASSIC ARTIST

THE most sensuous of writers, Willa Cather builds her imagined world almost as solidly as our five senses build the universe around us. This account of the activities of a French priest who was given a diocese in the south-west during the late forties, impresses one first of all by its amazing sensory achievements. She has within herself a sensitivity that constantly presents her with a body of material which would overwhelm most of us, so that we would give up all idea of transmitting it and would sink into a state of passivity; and she has also a quality of mountain-pony sturdiness that makes her push on unfatigued under her load and give an accurate account of every part of it. So it is that one is not quite sure whether it is one of the earlier pages in *Death Comes for the Archbishop* or a desert in central New Mexico, that is heaped up with small conical hills, red as brick-dust, a landscape of which the human aspect is thirst and confusion of the retina at seeing the earth itself veritably presenting such re-duplications of an image as one could conceive only as consequences of a visual disorder. When the young bishop on his mule finds this thirst smouldering up to flame in his throat and his confusion whirling faster and faster into vertigo, he blots out his own pain in meditating on the Passion of our Lord; he does not deny to consciousness that it is in a state of suffering, but leads it inward from the surface of being where it feebly feels itself contending with innumerable purposeless irritations to a place within the heart where suffering is held to

have been proved of greater value than anything else
in the world, the one coin sufficient to buy man's
salvation; this, perhaps the most delicate legerdemain
man has ever practised on his senses, falls into our
comprehension as lightly as a snowflake into the
hand, because of her complete mastery of every
phase of the process. But she becomes committed
to no degree of complication as her special field. A
page later she writes of the moment when the priest
and his horses come on water, in language simple as
if she were writing a book for boys, in language
exquisitely appropriate for the expression of a joy
that must have been intensest in the youth of races.

Great is her accomplishment. That feat of making
a composition out of the juxtaposition of different
states of being, which Velasquez was so fond of
practising, when he showed the tapestry-makers
working in shadow, and some of their fellows
working behind them in shadows honeycombed
with golden motes, and others still further back
working in the white wine of full sunlight, is a
diversion of hers also. She can suggest how in this
land of carnelian hills that become lavender in storm,
of deserts striped with such strangeness as ochre-
yellow waves of petrified sand, of mesas behind which
stand cloud mesas as if here Nature had altered her
accustomed order and the sky took reflections as the
waters do elsewhere, of beauty on which a quality
of prodigiousness is perpetually present like a powerful condiment, the Bishop and his boyhood friend
would find refreshment in going back in memory to
the cobbled streets of Clermont, where ivy that is
cool to the touch and wet about the roots tumbles

over garden walls and horse-chestnuts spread a wide shade which is scarcely needed, and simple families do explicable things and eat good food and love one another. Perfectly conveyed is the difference in palpability between things seen and things remembered; as perfectly as those other differences in palpability which became apparent to the senses of the Archbishop as death approached him. Then the countryside of Auvergne became a place too wet, too cultivated, too human; the air above it seemed to have something of the heaviness of sweat. The air that can only be breathed on land which has not yet been committed to human purposes, the light, dry air of the desert, is more suited to one who is now committed to them as little as it. He has now the excess of experience which comes to old age; since no more action is required from him. There is no particular reason why his attention should be focused on the present, so as he lies in his bed in the study in Santa Fé where he had begun his work forty years before, all the events of his life exist contemporaneously in his head: his childish days in Clermont and on the coast of the Mediterranean, his youth in the seminary at Rome, his travels among the deserts and the mesas, the Mexicans and the Indians. That is well enough but it could not go on. He longs, and one can feel the trouble in the old man's head as he wishes it, for this free wind that has never been weighed down by the effluvia of human effort to blow away his soul out into its sphere of freedom.

The book, it may be seen, though clear as a dewdrop, is not superficial. The author is inspired to her best because she is working on a theme that is peculiarly sympathetic to her. When Father Vaillant goes to administer the sacraments to the faithful on the ranchero of Manuel Lujon he bustles into the kitchen and with scarcely less care than he bestows on preparations for the holy office he rescues the leg of mutton that is destined for his dinner and cooks it himself, so that when he carves it at table a 'delicate stream of pink juice' follows the knife. It is an incident which Miss Cather relates with a great deal of sisterly feeling; and it is, of course, a beautiful symbol of the effective synthesis which inspires the Roman Catholic Church to its highest activities. That Church has never doubted that sense is a synthesis of the senses; and it has never doubted that man must take the universe sensibly. The people, the suffering generations, deprived of material for the enjoyment of the senses, cry out for saints who shall sanctify their own fates by being holy and choosing it as the most suitable medium for their holiness, who court suffering, who deprive their senses of all material enjoyment. But behind them watches the Church to see that they avail themselves of this hungry sainthood only as one does of some powerful opiate, in small doses and not habitually. Not for long were the faithful to be allowed to abuse or miscall the body which has been given them as the instrument with which they must perform their task of living. Those who claimed supersensual ecstasies were — as one may read in the life of St. Teresa — exposed to the investigations of persons who comported themselves like Inspectors of Nuisances. While it is untrue to say that Protestantism invented or even specially stimulated Puritanism – the type of mind which tries to satisfy an innate sense of guilt by the coarser forms of expiation is naturally attracted to whatever the current religion may be and emerges equally under Catholicism or Paganism or Islam or any other formulated faith – it is true to say that Catholicism has always suppressed with extreme rigour such heresies as led to unwholesome abstinences becoming the general practice. The Cathari, for example, were persecuted because although their ascetic teachings might have led to individual sinlessness they would have wiped out the community, and there would have been so many happy villages the fewer. It would almost seem sometimes as if the Church burned heretics because it was afraid that if it did not man would burn his soup.

And soup, as the Roman Catholic Church knows, as Miss Cather knows, is a matter of the first importance. 'When one comes to think of it,' said the Bishop, sitting over a meal prepared by Father Vaillant on one of their early days at Santa Fé, when they were gloomily discussing the possibility of maintaining a French propriety of diet in a country so basely ignorant that it knew nothing of the lettuce, 'soup like this is not the work of one man. It is the result of a constantly refined tradition. There are nearly a thousand years of history in this soup. . . .' Doubtless he would, if pressed, have admitted that while the introduction of good soup and lettuce was not the object of his labours in his diocese, they would at least afford a test of success. It was with no sense of trivial declension from his activities that,

at the end of his life, he chose for the country estate
of his retirement land on which he had seen an
apricot-tree with 'two trunks, each of them thicker
than a man's body,' which was glorious with great
golden fruit of superb flavour, and because of that
indication of suitability planted orchards of pears
and apples, cherries and apricots there from which
he furnishes young trees for his priests to plant
wherever they went, for their own eating and to
encourage the Mexicans to add fruit to their starchy
diet. In all his intermediate activities he has never
really gone far from the earth that grows lettuces
and apricots. There is a chapter relating to the re-
bellious Father Martinez, in which Miss Cather
with a blacksmith's muscle has lifted into a com-
pendious form a prodigious deal of reading about
the problem the Church has had to face in its efforts
to secure priests lion-like enough to maintain the
faith on the raw edges of civilization against the
paganism of lawless men and yet lamblike enough to
remain in loyal subjection to authority seated half
the world away; it too is a demonstration of sense
founded on a fusion of the senses. The Bishop,
although fastidious to almost the point of squeamishness, tolerates this priest who rides at the head of a
cavalcade of Mexicans and Indians like their robber
chief, whose corridor walks are perpetually painted
with a shadow-show of servant maids fleeing before
young men whose origin seems to be indicated by
the tart disputations at the supper-table concerning
the celibacy of the clergy, whose past is stained with
bloodshed arising out of lecherous desire for certain
lands, as hot as the lands themselves. In spite of all

this the Bishop does not deprive him of his parish.
He looks around and marks the theatrical fervour of
the landscape of 'the flaming cactus and the gaudily
decorated altars,' of the gestures with which the
women flung shawls on the pathway before him and
the men snatched his hand to kiss the episcopal
ring; and perceives as in complete keeping with that
world this passionate and devout scoundrel who gives
his virility to the chanting of the Mass as he gave
it to murder, to the enrichment of his church with
vestment and shining vessels as to the complication
of his domesticity with amorousness. It is as if he
tasted a *chili con carne*, judged it just as the Mexicans
who were going to eat it would like it, and out of
regard for the harmonies of life smoothed from his
face all signs of what his French palate thought of
the high seasoning. Though this may be an affair of
importance, it is still an affair of the senses.

But there is more to life than this. St. Teresa was
greater than her investigators. The community that
chose to die might know more in the moment when
it went out to death than the neighbouring unper-
verted community might know when it came into
supper. It is inconceivable that man was born of
woman to suffer more forms of agony than there are
kinds of flowers simply in order that he should make
good soup. That complaint might be made against
Miss Cather herself, for her own absorption in sense
and the senses. She arranges with mastery such
phenomena of life as the human organism can easily
collect through the most ancient and most perfected
mechanisms of body and mind. But must not such
an art, admirable as it is, be counted as inferior to

an art which accepts no such limitations, which deals
with the phenomena of life collected by the human
organism with such difficulty that to the overstrained
consciousness they appear only as vague intimations,
and the effort of obtaining them develops new
mechanisms? Ought not art that tries to make
humanity superhuman be esteemed above art that
leaves humanity exactly as it is? One is reminded
constantly of that issue while one is reading *Death
Comes for the Archbishop* by its similarity in material
to some of the recent work of Mr. D. H. Lawrence.
Both come face to face with the Indian and find
there is no face there but an unclimbable cliff, giving
no foothold, like the side of a mesa; but each takes
it so differently. 'The Bishop,' says Miss Cather, of
a certain conversation by a camp fire, 'seldom ques-
tioned Jacinto about his thoughts or beliefs. He
didn't think it polite, and he believed it to be useless.
There was no way in which he could transfer his
own memories of European civilization into the
Indian mind, and he was quite willing to believe
that behind Jacinto there was a long tradition, a
story of experience, which no language could translate to him. A chill came with the darkness . . .'
and so on. There is no attempt to fit the key into the
lock. That door will not open. But Mr. Lawrence
cries out in his last book of essays, 'The consciousness of one branch of humanity is the annihilation of
the consciousness of another branch. . . . We can
understand the consciousness of the Indian only in
terms of the death of our consciousness.' There is
nothing here to say he will not try it. Indeed, the
querulousness of it suggests a tired, brave man be-

coming aware of an imperative call to further adventures. There may be necessary a re-entrance to the darkness of the womb, another fretful birth. He will do it!

The difference in their daring is powerfully suggested by a certain chapter of this book named 'Stone Lips.' The Bishop and his Indian guide are on the desert when a snowstorm breaks and covers the land with a white blindness. The Indian makes the Bishop leave the mules and clamber over rocks and fallen trees to a cliff in which there is a cave that has an opening sinister enough in itself, with rounded edges like lips. It is large, shows signs of being used for ceremonial purposes, and is clean and swept; but it is icy-cold and full of a slight but loathsome odour. There is a hole in the wall about the size of a watermelon. This the Indian guide fills up with a mixture of stones, wood, earth and snow. Then he builds a fire, and the odour disappears. There is, however, a humming as of bees, which puzzles the Bishop till the guide takes him to a part of the cave where there is a crack in the floor through which sounds the roaring of an underground river. The Bishop drops off to sleep, but wakes up and finds the boy mounting guard over the hole in the wall, listening as though to hear if anything were stirring behind the patch of plaster. The episode owes its accent, of course, to the proximity of the cave to the pueblo of Pecos, which was reputed to keep a giant serpent out in the mountains for use in its religious festivals. Miss Cather passes through this experience responding sensitively and powerfully to its splendid portentousness, but she

223

stays with the Bishop the whole time. Mr. Lawrence,
on the other hand, would have been through the
hole in the wall after the snake. He would have
been through the crack in the floor after the river.
Irritably and with partial failure, but also with
greater success than any previous aspirant, he would
have tried to become the whole caboodle. Does not
such transcendental courage, does not such ambition
to extend consciousness beyond its present limits and
elevate man above himself, entitle his art to be ranked
as more important than that of Miss Cather?

To ask that question is our disposition to-day. It
is the core of contemporary resentment against the
classics. But one must suspect it. It leads to such
odd preferences on the part of the young: for example, to the exaltation of James Joyce over Marcel
Proust, although *A La Recherche du Temps Perdu* is
like a beautiful hand with long fingers reaching out
to pluck a perfect fruit, without error, for the accurate eye knows well it is growing just there on the
branch, while *Ulysses* is the fumbling of a horned hand
in darkness after a doubted jewel. Such a judgment
leaves out of account that though a jewel is more
precious than a fruit, grace also is one of the ultimate
values, a chief accelerator of our journey towards the
stars. It should, like all occasions when we find ourselves rejecting non-toxic pleasantness, make us examine ourselves carefully to see if we are not the
latest victims to the endemic disease of Puritanism,
to this compulsion to satisfy an innate sense of guilt
by the coarser forms of expiation. There is, after
all, no real reason to suppose that there is less
Puritan impulse in humanity than there ever was,

since the origin and control of such infantile fantasies as the sense of guilt has hardly yet begun to
be worked upon; and it would be peculiarly apt at
this moment to express itself in the sphere of art.
The Church no longer takes care of it among the
literate, for during the last century they either ceased
to go to church at all or have transferred it to some
faith which does not pander to those lownesses; but
they found a new and disguised channel for the old
impulse in reformist politics. That again has been
denied them, for the war has damped political en-
thusiasms just as the biological advances of the
nineteenth century damped religious fervour. The
weaker spirits are scared by the evidence that social
change may involve serious hardship and have
scuttled back to Toryism; the stronger spirits who
can bear to envisage hardship are just as paralysed
by their doubt whether there is any economic system
yet invented which is certain to justify by success
the inconveniences of change. There has happened
therefore a curious reversal of the position in regard
to the gratification of the Puritan and counter-
Puritan impulses in the last century. The young
men who were Puritans in politics were anti-Puritans
in literature. They were willing to die for the independence of Poland or the Manchester Fenians; and
they relaxed their tension by voluptuous reading in
Swinburne. Nowadays the corresponding young
men gratify their voluptuousness by an almost complete acquiescence in the political and economic
status quo, an unremorseful acceptance of whatever
benefits it may bring them personally; and they
placate their Puritanism by demanding of literature

225

that never shall it sit down to weave beauty out of the material which humanity has already been able to collect with its limited powers, that perpetually it must be up and marching on through the briars towards some extension of human knowledge and power.

It is characteristically Puritan, this demand that the present should be annihilated. The church-goers of the breed insisted that we should have no pleasures in this world but should devote ourselves to preparation for the next. The political sphere made the same demand in many veiled forms, which one may perceive, in the phrase constantly used in propagandist literature that it is the duty of each generation to sacrifice itself for the sake of future generations. That is, of course, pernicious. It makes man try to live according to another rhythm than that of the heart within him, which has its systole and its diastole. It deftly extracts all meaning out of life, which, if it were but an eternal climbing of steep steps, sanity would refuse to live. And æsthetically it is the very deuce, for in rejecting classical art it rejects the real sanction of the revolutionary art it pretends to defend. When Willa Cather describes in terms acceptable to a Catholic Missionary Society the two young priests stealing away secretly from Clermont to avoid saying good-bye to their devoted families, who would have been too greatly distressed by the loss of their sons, she is not as explicit as Mr. Lawrence would be in his statement that in this separation a creature as little Christian as a snake was trying to slough its skin, that a force as hidden from the sun as an underground river was trying to separate itself from its source. But by proving exhaustively what joy a man can have and what beauty he can make by using such materials and such mechanism he already has, she proves Mr. Lawrence's efforts to add to their number worth while. Since man can work thus with his discoveries, how good it is that there should be discoveries! There is nothing here which denotes rejection of any statement of life fuller than her own. Her work has not that air of claiming to cover all the ground which gives the later novels of Henry James the feeling of pretentiousness and futility which amazingly co-exists with the extremes of subtlety and beauty and which is perhaps due to his attempt to account for all the actions and thoughts of his characters by motives established well in the forefront of consciousness. She is indeed deeply sympathetic to what the order of artist who is different from herself is trying to do, as can be seen in her occasional presentation of incidents that would be beautifully grist to their mill: as in the enchanting story of the El Greco painting of a St. Francis in meditation, which was begged from a Valencian nobleman by a hairy Franciscan priest from New Mexico for his mission church, who forced the gift by his cry, 'You refuse me this picture because it is a good picture. It is too good for God, but it is not too good for you'; and was at the pillaging of the mission church either burned or taken to some pueblo. How we can imagine that part of the spirit of El Greco which was in that picture, crying out while flames made it the bright heart of an opening flower of massacre, or while the smoke of the adobe dwelling discolours and

stripes it like a flagellation, '*It is just as I thought!*'
And how like the anguished accents of Mr. Lawrence's work sounds that imagined cry. Willa Cather
is not unaware of these fissures in the solid ground
of life, but to be aware of them is not her task.
Hers is it to move on the sunlit face of the earth,
with the gracious amplitude of Ceres, bidding the
soil yield richly, that the other kind of artist, who
is like Persephone and must spend half of his days
in the world under the world, may be refreshed on
emergence.

THERE is no end to the pleasant debts one owes
to that Mr. Ford Madox Ford who passes
among us breathing heavily because of deep dives,
of prolonged natations, in perilous seas of faerylands
forlorn, now as novelist, now as poet, now as his-
torian, once — and it was then that many of those
debts were contracted — as editor. Most magazines
have that look of being predestined to be left
which one sees on the faces of the women whose
troubles bring them to the Law Courts. The more
lurid type of popular magazine with its pages that
shine like shoulders after massage and its illustrations of ladies in evening dresses which remind us
that in the sight of God we are all mammals, resembles those young women whose lack of all characteristics save a willingness to entertain as many people
as possible leads ultimately to nobody accepting responsibility for them but the Morals Court. The
chaster type of popular magazine which week after
week publishes admirable but identical issues, resembles the plump but puzzled housewives who tell
the Court of Domestic Relations stories of conjugal
felicity broken suddenly by flight accompanied by
incomprehensible strangled cries concerning monotony. And the more conservative type of monthly,
which specializes in sober essays by the oldest female
inhabitant of Baltimore on the decay of almost everything except, oddly enough, teeth, is too like those
little women with pinched mouths who tell stories
of marital cruelty so bravely borne, so excusably inflicted. In any case, all, all are deserted. There is no

moment of the day when it is not true that thousands
of the more lurid magazines are not whirling on in
trains from which their purchasers have descended,
even as their prototypes are driven off in the patrol
wagon from negligent companions. And the others
rest unread at the back of the bookshelf, like dull
women living unvisited on alimony. Not so was Mr.
Ford Madox Ford's *English Review*.

Each number of that was a sturdy member added
to the family. Had one left it in the train one would
have stopped it, by some of the devices one has seen
on the movies, galloping horses, flags; a cultured
railroad President would have understood and for-
given. And they live well to the forefront of the
bookshelves, those blue volumes made solidly as
boxes. Boxes full of giants. You have only to
part the pages to find Thomas Hardy, Conrad,
Wells, Galsworthy, Cunninghame-Graham, Norman
Douglas, and a man named H. M. Tomlinson.
Some essays of his were published there, I think;
and certainly I received the first news I ever had of
him in an appreciation of him written there by
Mr. Ford Madox Ford himself. It intimated in
general that there had arisen — no, that cannot have
been the word, nor emerged either, for both are too
aggressive for this gentlest of movements — rather
that there had percolated into English literature a
new master of prose, and in particular that he had
written a book of the first order of beauty named
The Sea and the Jungle. Both of those intimations
were true. One had but to read that single book to
see that eternally there was among us, and among all
who shall ever read one language, a hesitant little

man on whose shoulder perched all the strangeness of the steamy parts of the earth in the likeness of a multi-coloured parrot. He was one of those supremely gifted writers who do it all by writing. There was no synthesis performed by the imagination, no marshalling of events into a significant pattern; in spite of the immense suggestion exerted on all writers of that time he was nothing of the novelist. Simply he let events drift by him and as they passed he caught the quality of each in the exact word; and lo! the pattern appeared. That parrot was his, not because of a snare, but because of what came from his lips. It was for the same reason that the birds of Paris used to fly down to the old man who sat on the bench of the Tuileries gardens, crying out the right call. One perceived, as one should anew every time one reads great writing, how wise is the old belief in spells, in the possibility that the arrangement of words in their proper order may force the tangible world into new forms and sequences; how not impossible at all is the Talmudic hope and dread that this power is without limit for the destruction of things and the resurrection of them, that even it might place words together so that the universe should be shattered and into the resultant vacuum there should rush the substance of God.

He had begun his literary career, this unobtrusive person, as a reporter on *The Daily News*, which is a much more unusual beginning for a writer in England than it is in America. There is no living major English author, and very few minor ones who have made their approach to literature from the reporter's desk; and indeed there can be imagined no worse

preparation for the exercise of an art than the
physically exhausting pursuit of what is as likely as
not to be the trivial, and the chronicling of it without
the deliberation which is the first condition of artistic
effort. To think otherwise must be the result of a
Puritanism which feels that writing in discomfort
must necessarily be rewarded by the power to write
well. The years Mr. Tomlinson spent as a reporter
he would count as mostly lost. Certainly they must
have been a perilous time for the good of his soul.
It cannot be pleasant to feel that one is blunting an
exquisitely fine nib by writing with it from morning
to night on all manner of rough surfaces; particularly when one has never proved that it is exquisitely
fine, so that one's feeling may be mere vanity, and
nothing to which one ought to abandon oneself. He
was, however, not embittered. As one may learn
from the secondary moral music that sounds through
his sentences, he has established within himself a
perfect equilibrium. During those years he very
probably did not think much of himself at all.
Simply he sat, say at the press-bench in the police
court, and dreamed of the steamy places of the earth
towards which he desired to sail some day, where a
sun being so strongly light itself, would inspire all
that it shone upon to be as strongly themselves, so
that the green dusk of the jungle is greener and
duskier than anything but the lower depths of the
sea, and the butterflies compress into each wing such
blueness as would suffice for a whole northern sky.
His mind's eye must have tinkered considerably with
the conditions of that sober court, sending shoals of
flying fish between him and the immobile magistrate,

bright tropical birds to exercise their freedom round
the dock. Nothing done by a person of such quality
can ever be wholly wasted, but those years of reporting came as near to it as they could. The only grate-
ful aspect of them appeared when *The Daily News*,
being accustomed to having him on its staff, and
having had his quality revealed to it by *The Sea and
the Jungle*, sent him out as a war correspondent.
One's relief that this should have been contrived may
seem surprising to those unfamiliar with the pattern
of Mr. Tomlinson's career. Surely a writer of such
unique descriptive powers would have been bound
to find himself in the grand-stand at that event? It
is not certain. The jungle receives him, the sea supports him, but the cities of humanity he finds not
so friendly. It is unfortunate for humanity that the
reason for this seems to lie in the equilibrium which
is one of his most obviously gracious qualities.

The writing he did about the war established him,
at least in the eyes of all other writers, as a person of
the first importance. *The Sea and the Jungle* was a
superb book, but it might have been a sole production, the flood that came when an imagination was
liberated along the channel down which it was appropriate that it should flow but which had been
dammed to it all its life long. It might be that the
psychic energy which then displayed itself was the
accumulation of years, that now the channel was open
the flow might be meagre enough. But, as one may
see by turning to the 1914–18 papers which are included in the book of essays named *Old Junk*, he
attained a rare exactitude and non-neurotic quality
in his attitude to the war which betokened him

as having the power not to lose his way among the phenomena of life which is the first essential of the artist. Needless to say, his soldiers do not wear the wide flesh-splitting grin of sexless sensuality that the advertiser and the militarist, both having for their own ends to pretend that people enjoy things which are outside the sphere of enjoyment, paint vigorously but never realistically on the faces of those who drink cocoa or wield the vacuum-cleaner, who bestow and receive the bayonet. But on the other hand they are not the queasy fellows fancied by the radical writers. The trouble about the soldiers in Mr. Siegfried Sassoon's poetry, for example, is that they are the kind of people who in a railroad train have to travel with their backs to the engine. Peace can have but few corners softly padded enough for such sensitives. Why then rage against war? But in Mr. Tomlinson's pages the war is poignant as it actually was: a martyrdom of those framed for cheerfulness but forcibly acquainted with sorrow, which practises the further cruelty of not permitting a clear passage for one's indignation, since men would be far less than they are if they had not the fortitude to organize themselves to suffer this and all danger. He could admit that, even though his eyes had seen such sights as, say, a boy of eighteen lying face down in the mud, having seen mud at the last, and all promises that he should see other and better things in the hereafter being less in the class of securities on which the banks lend money than one would like; and though he more than other men would see the pity of such an early expulsion from life, since he knew what it would have been for him to go out of life without

234

having seen the green dusk of the jungle, those blue butterflies. His essays written then give the true war feeling, the sense of an iron band about the ribs, constricting, not to be loosened by easy pacifist words, crushing the air out of the lungs, but failing to subdue the beating of the heart.

It was plain that he could cope with experiences; and there were other essays in the volume which showed that he could also cope with experience. He has a paper on a moment that came to him when he looked on a certain light upon the land and realized it to be earthshine, felt himself at the source of a stream of light that flowed down to other stars and showed them a star, to be seen only by such crickings of the neck as shows them to us. He rises then to a region of mysticism, where excitements flow from forces that have no proper name, and carry on the work dropped by a lagging logic as music does. The same achievement one felt in *Tidemarks*, a book about travel among eastern islands which is almost too delicately written, so that the eye feels puzzled as the ear does when it is exposed to music composed on a subtler scale than ours, but which passes the test of arousing in the mind when one thinks of it a vivid picture which is nowhere to be found in the text itself. It makes one see a small figure lying in the surf of a shore which it has visited to some danger to itself, while the beauty and strangeness of life break over it in great waves. It adds to the significance of the scene that the writer who is subjecting himself to this experience has lost nothing of the gentle, mousey character of the average man; that one conceives that if he should rest for a little while

after his bathe he would cover his face with a handkerchief knotted at the corners, that when he plods
homeward over the sands it will be with his boots
hanging round his neck by knotted laces.

Now he has written a novel, another turn in the
spiral of perfection, in spite of an iniquitous opening and close. I regret to confess that Mr. Tomlinson's first chapter contains an old man with a
beard who cryptically tells us what the book in particular and life in general is about. Old men with
beards ought to be prohibited in art. The trouble is
that if a type is expressed perfectly in art it is hard
for subsequent writers not to prevent their attempts
to express it from falling into the grooves of that
perfect expression. For example, it is difficult to
invent a clergyman who serves both God and Lady
Charlotte without finding oneself clumsily re-invent-
ing Mr. Collins; and when Edward Lear wrote,
'There was an old man with a beard, Who said it is
just as I feared, Two larks and a wren, Three owls
and a hen, Have all made their nets in my beard,'
he set as ineluctable a prototype. (Consider the senile
pest who circulated through *The Dybbuk*, remarking
that there were milestones on the Dover Road.)
Mr. Tomlinson does even worse than the resuscita-
tion of this sententious old party in his final chapter,
where he represents his hero as having been so
changed by his adventures on sea and land that he
takes a decision which is diametrically opposed to
that he took before he started, which is a metamor-
phosis clear out of his line. He is one of those who
have reached the stage of being, and his attempts to
regress to the state of becoming have the lack of

spontaneity, the sense of the necessity for careful adjustments, that are an inseparable part of condescension, however unconscious that may be. But we all know the inspired speaker who clears his throat and stutters at the beginning and the end of his speech. Who would judge Shelley by the excerpts from a polite letter-writer, Wordsworth for the critical cotton-wool that they thought fit to publish in front of their poems? Such failures are proofs that what is being presented is divided from the common matter of the mind by a chasm so deep that it is difficult offhand to build a bridge or cross it without wavering, giddiness, and doubts whether it is worth doing.

But the book itself practises the same magic. By naming things rightly he creates them. Because of his phrases a ship that in the yards would take months and much sweat to build rides on the water after a page's reading, and introductions without adjectives, followed by the briefest lines of dialogue, people the decks and cabins with men as real as human begetting could make them. When the storm strikes the ship and sets all those men refusing to let their minds stagger as their bodies must, the prose sets out the facts with a Kiplingesque precision and over and above that constantly conveys the plunging rhythm of the sea and the counter-rhythm of the men's determination. There are two chapter endings like thunderclaps when the ship loses its rudder, and when the captain refuses the offer of the liner to take him off, if he will abandon his ship; and when the rhythm and the counter-rhythm meet for the last time, and the waters close over the ship and the

captain, it is as if the book gave out a sound like
deep continuing music. There follows a space in the
boats, when the city clerk, in whose escape from trial
for murder this storm and shipwreck are an incident,
sits and feels as landlubberly a hero-worship for the
sailors as if he himself were still safe on shore and
had not raised himself to their level by doing as they
do – a queer misplaced and fragrant piece of dry
landishness, like the smell of may-blossom that one
may sometimes in spring smell unaccountably far
out in the English Channel. His rescue takes him
to one of the great cities of the East where uneasily
the West sticks to its philosophy with warehouses,
whisky pegs, and hotels where exiled nights are supported under grey mosquito netting, but has the
inner sickness of one who realizes that the reticent-
people around him suspect him of being mad, and
that he must be very careful. That is only a resting-
place for our clerk before he passes into the jungle
and experiences again the rhythm of a great natural
force contending with the counter-rhythm of man's
will. With the exposition of that force which is so
strong that it need not buffet man about to make him
stagger but can make him do it with its silence and
its immobility, the book should end, will end to the
fastidious reader of the sort that does not read the
tags to Shakespeare's plays, nor the last chapters of
Vanity Fair.

One wonders how far this book will be recognized
for what it is. We all have habits nowadays which
render that uncertain. Mr. Tomlinson is not an
author who appears sufficiently regularly or on a
scale of verbosity to impress a public which in this

matter makes no allowance for a certain change that has taken place in the writing of prose during the last half-century or so. When the prose-writer was pre-eminently a producer of narrative, when he expressed his theme by inventing large groups of people and disposing them with a loose grip here and there over a wide map, he was working under no great tension; and by the constant retreats he could make into impersonation by becoming one or other of his characters and expressing himself in their terms, he could constantly achieve the refreshment of running away from himself and forgetting his personal conflict. When his psychic energy flowed down such a broad and easy channel it was reasonable for the reader to suspect it, if it did not flow fast and free, of that lack of abundance which is fatal to any artistic performance. But the case of a poet is entirely different. The works of no poet cover so much of the bookshelf as the *Waverley Novels*, or the writings of Charles Dickens or Henry James. It could not be otherwise, for the psychic energy of the poet has an infinitely harder task to achieve. He is not going to express his theme only by describing the position of certain objects in time and space in terms acceptable to logic. He is going to express it also by suggestions arising out of the use of images that would not be judged strictly relevant by logic; and he is going to amplify his expression still further by suggestions arising out of the use of rhyme and rhythm in ways which are as entirely beyond the purview of logic, as utterly outside the field of intellect, as music. He is therefore living with the utmost intensity possible to him on two planes at once. He cannot take refuge in impersonation, even if he is a dramatic poet. The putting of poetry into the mouths of the characters forbids it. The demand that all the characters should speak in the terms of whatever synthesis of the intellectual and super-intellectual planes the writer has achieved, that it should not seem artistically absurd and inappropriate that they should do so, is an admission that they are but projections of the writer himself. The writer who does that is in the position of a psycho-analysed person who has made the realization that all persons he dreams of are disguised versions of himself. Though the writer's admission may not be conscious, it gives him a solemnity, a sense of being pinned to his business, a sense that run into what shape he may he shall not escape the problems he has found in his own heart. The poet then has a harder, less mitigated task. One cannot therefore expect him to produce so much work. The reader has learned this thoroughly; but has not learned to extend his tolerance to poets who no longer find it necessary to employ the forms of verse, but are able to express their synthesis in modern enfranchised prose. Mr. Tomlinson's writing is of lyric intensity. This is, to all intents and purposes, a book of poems. There are those who write a magazine story every week. There are none who write an 'Ode to the West Wind' every month.

There is another reason why Mr. Tomlinson may perhaps slip by us, as he slips out of the ordinary cities of men into the jungle or out to the ship in the fairway. You will hear people saying, 'Tomlinson? Oh, he's an imitator of Conrad, isn't he?' There is

no resemblance whatsoever, save what springs from
a common marine preoccupation. One might as well
allege that the Bible was compiled by an imitator of
Conrad, on the strength of the phrase, 'The sea and
all that in them is.' This must be a ruse of the common mind. It must fancy that some benefit will
accrue to it if it can prove that Mr. Tomlinson is
not an individual genius but an inferior copyist of
Joseph Conrad. The explanation lies perhaps in
the non-neurotic quality of Mr. Tomlinson. We are,
speaking generally, hot and bothered. Therefore we
like our geniuses to be hot and bothered. Though
Joseph Conrad was a great man, nobody was ever
more hot and bothered than he was. Change was his
idol. He longed to change himself from a Pole to
an Englishman; from an intellectual to a man of
action. In his writing he exercised his love of
change; he would think a sentence in Polish, change
it in his mind to French, change it on paper to
English. And he loved the effect of what he wrote
to be a mutation of his life to its opposites: to meta-
morphose himself from the fluent, responsive little
man one met when one met him to the great, slow
patient presence, brooding over the affairs of men
like a dark cloud of grave wisdom, whom we encounter in his work. In fact, when he wrote he was
resolving some conflict within himself. As most of
us are doing the same thing, this and his greatness
gratify us inordinately. We feel he is a certificate
that on the stage we ourselves have reached it is
possible to do tremendous facts, that perhaps there
is no real necessity for us to travel further. But Mr.
Tomlinson gives us no such satisfaction, no such

hope. Quite plainly he has gone beyond us. He has resolved his conflicts. There is serenity within him, not war. The motive of the neurotic writer is to establish order within himself in the light of an empirical vision of harmony. The motive of the non-neurotic writer, as Mr. Tomlinson shows, is to reconcile by understanding and appreciation the disorder of life with the order he knows by experience as an established fact within himself. Perhaps this makes us a little envious of him. With this peace within him he has, it may clearly be seen, such a happy time. Nobody wants to admit that those who have been able to go further than they have fared much better. At any rate, our attitude does him no harm. That we prefer to wanton with novels and magazines like desertable females rather than to marry our attention to his subtle writing will not embitter him. He will go on his way as undismayed by the vast indifference of the public as he has been by any other vastness, contemplating with unresentful interest the contemporary under-estimation of him, as he might some strange knotted liana of the jungle.

WHY does one at times passionately prefer the writers of last century to the writers of this? Perhaps it is because one is liable when one opens the works of one's contemporaries to find passages like this:

'Returning to that life (of a burlesque road show) after an interval of a year or two in order to revisit your friends or your old haunts must be among the most peculiar experiences possible to human beings, for it must give your own decaying sensibilities a kind of jealous immortality to see your place filled so rapidly and easily by some one who might well be yourself, re-born into flesh and health. Everything would be altered, while remaining, in all its essentials, exactly the same. The same hotel buildings, only with a freshly darkening coat of paint and perhaps new carpets and sofa covers, and with the band playing another set of tunes that, though new and unfamiliar, were with difficulty to be distinguished from the old. Clerks and people in shops have their positions filled as easily out of the plethora of human beings once they are gone, but it is no part of their lives to pretend that even a simulated gaiety is required from them in the hours of work.

'Toward these pathetic tones of gaiety any one who had actually worked himself or herself into a permanence on the theater boards could not possibly help feeling both a compassion and a deep degree of interest, like that we feel on discovering some trait typical of Europeans among the natives of the Congo or the Amazon, which emotion has its sort of return boomerang of sentiment in the platitude about our all being brothers and sisters. So must doctors of true medical science regard the witch doctors of the Zulus.

'A kind of repressed and constipated hysteria in need of a perpetual laxative must be one of the motives that drive people into what are really, in those kinds of cases, but different conditions of the same profession, for you cannot be forced to go upon the stage any more than you can be driven by necessity into an immediately successful livelihood from the streets. There is a nicely-graded road into the fully-fledged conditions of both of these ways of life, and along this people cannot be propelled who have not some innate yearning toward the more dangerous degrees of comfort. I suppose that nearly all these women are the children of mothers who have suffered the same constraints of necessity and predisposition.'

That is bad writing of the same sort as Mr. Theodore Dreiser's, which can be understood better if it is read quickly than if it is read slowly. The more careful reader is apt to catch his mental coat-tails on such briars as that sentence beginning 'A kind of repressed and constipated hysteria' and get no further for a quarter of an hour. This is all very sad, for the passage is an extract from Mr. Sacheverell Sitwell's *All Summer in a Day*, which is in many respects a delightful book and one that should shine in the public eye, since neither the importance of the Sitwells as a group nor of Mr. Sacheverell Sitwell as an individual can well be exaggerated.

The three Sitwells, Edith, Osbert and Sacheverell, are among the few illuminants England possesses which are strong enough to light up post-war England. They are the legatees of perhaps the most glorious group that English life has ever produced, the Whig aristocracy of the eighteenth century. The society that received Voltaire on his visit to England embraced their ancestors and from it they have inherited their graceful intellectual carriage, a boundless curiosity concerning the things of the mind and the quality of taste. That quality requires a synthesis of all the attributes that have raised man from the brute: for to identify the nature of a work of art, to discover of what conflict it is an attempted resolution, is not possible unless one owns the diligence to study history and the memory to record one's studies. That one may see how far the artist followed the fashion, and how far he wrote of what was in him, and how far the problems that interested him were of time or of eternity, and to determine how far the work is a resolution of that particular conflict and how much or how little the artist has resorted to such weak means of sublimation as sentimental interpretation or suppression of the facts, one must be as sensitive as a bird dog and be able to fight against one's own conflicts like a successful Laocoon in order to achieve an attitude of detachment. That synthesis is part of the remarkable endowment of the Sitwells. Moreover, each of them is inhabited by a bland demon, as the German metaphysicians used to call that which gets into a man and makes him creative, not so forcibly that it turns them away from criticism, but valid enough to give them the right to speak with

245

the authority of artists. They have indeed by merely
moving through society very excitingly, being themselves, done as much for culture in London as anybody since Mr. Ford Madox Ford severed his connection with the *English Review*. Edith Sitwell writes
poetry as gay as a flower garden; its confused joy-
ousness half heard through jazz music, as it is in
the performance she and her brothers give called
'Façade,' is to me a deal pleasanter than much of
the confused passionateness one hears at the opera
through the music of Wagner or Strauss, and surely
just as legitimate. Osbert Sitwell gives us lovely verse
and the amusing grotesqueness of *Triple Fugue*
and *Before the Bombardment* and scholarly notes on
his travels such as very few critics of the last generation would have been equipped to write. And
Sacheverell Sitwell has written a great deal of
beautiful poetry, complicated by reason of an over-
weight of content and not short-weight of execu-
tion, and a book called *Southern Baroque Art*, in
which this bland demon rears a structure of argument and sensation that has real and precious
idiosyncrasy.

Yet here is a Sitwell indulging in a page blowsy for
lack of that exactitude which makes Mr. Thomas
Hardy delight us, when we open the pages of this
new collected edition of his poems and read such a
poem as 'The Oxen.' Since one's first reading of it
that has stood alone in one's mind, a thing as simple
in its favour and its prettiness as a view down a cottage path between the hollyhock rows, a thing that
is the map of a mental continent. It is about the
legend which tells that at midnight on Christmas Eve

all the cattle in their stalls go down on their knees in
worship of the Saviour.

> 'So fair a fancy few would weave
>   In these years! Yet I feel,
> If some one said on Christmas Eve,
>   "Come, see the oxen kneel
> In the lonely barton by yonder coomb
>   Our childhood used to know,"
> I should go with him in the gloom,
>   Hoping it might be so.'

The wistfulness of the cadences, that enormously
significant word 'hoping' in the last line, lays before
one the mood when life repents of the turn toward
thought that it took in the eighteenth century, of the
burden of analysis that has lain so heavily on it ever
since. There is very little in Mr. Aldous Huxley's
and Mr. T. S. Eliot's complaints of disillusionment
which is not implied in that sixteen-line-long poem.

Exactitude, certainly, is here: restraint, cunning
compression. There is a dramatic poem, 'One Ralph
Blossom Soliloquizes,' which is a masterpiece of
impersonation contrived in twenty-six lines. In it a
rake imagines what certain seven women whom he
had brought to public shame would say to him when
they met in hell, and by the couple of lines he puts
into their mouths reveals the complete character of
each one of them; and by his own attitude, his combination of an extreme appreciation of their qualities
and an essential coldness toward them, such as a
jeweller might feel for his stock, he reveals what it is
to be a rake. Every line brings up the theme over the

247

horizon of the mind like a rising sun. And there are here all the lyrics that, in a few lines framed with the mosaic metrical skill which comes of familiarity with Latin verse, put the philosophy of one who is too much in love with reality to lie and pretend that that which is harsh is smooth. 'The Mother Mourns,' 'To Life,' 'The Lacking Sense' and 'The Bedridden Peasant' have the iridescence of tear-bottles, the fine grave form of the funeral urns that they recall.

But, unfortunately, there is more here than exactitude. The collected poems of Thomas Hardy do not, of course, include his finest poetry: for that is in *The Dynasts*. One may doubt, indeed, whether the gathering of his shorter verse in one volume does him quite such good service as such a collection usually does for a poet. For one thing one would rather read *Wessex Poems* and *Poems of the Past and Present* in the form in which they have previously appeared, with Mr. Hardy's own illustrations. Those drawings are very interesting. Because Mr. Hardy learned his technique as an architectural draughtsman he knows no use for perspective, and the world he draws is as flat as the print on the wall; but every shape he depicts is drawn with such intensity that it is as lively as life. So they are at once remote and actual, perplexing and satisfying. But quite apart from any matter of illustrations, it is a pity to read Mr. Hardy's shorter poems in one volume, for the reason that when one gets them all together one is apt to be overwhelmed by one of their characteristics. One is apt to be discouraged by the frequency with which Mr. Hardy has persuaded himself that a macabre subject is a poem in itself: that, if there be enough of death and the tomb in one's theme, it needs no translation into art, the bold statement of it being sufficient.

Really, the thing is prodigious. One of Mr. Hardy's ancestors must have married a weeping willow. There are pages and pages in his collected poems which are simply plain narratives in ballad form of how an unenjoyable time was had by all. 'The Supplanter' is typical. It tells how a man who goes to lay a wreath on his bride's grave arrives just when the cemetery-keeper is giving a small dance for his daughter's twentieth birthday, and gets involved. It turns out to be quite a party: he spoils his wreath by dancing on it and seduces the daughter; and there is great play a year after over the bride's grave with the cemetery-keeper's daughter producing the child of this festivity, and the man showing much irascible repentance. It is the grisliest setting for love betrayed or gratified. One seems, since one is not exalted by any revelation coming out of the treatment, to be listening to the merriment of some lewd morticians. 'It seems that there were two registered at the Vale of Rest Marble Mausoleum.' Nearly half the poems in the volume fall into this same category. 'Satires of Circumstance,' indeed, get a kind of style from their repetitiveness, from the multiplication of their terse diagrams of misery, from the abundance of their terse shorthand notes of woe, just as the drawings of almost any medieval Dance of Death series have an impressiveness given to them over and above their individual merits by the cumulative effect of their reiterated subjects. But that does not really obscure the fact that they, too, resort to sublimations of the conflict behind the poem which one would call false, were it not that it seems a pity to brand them with the same epithet one applies to such compounding with public favour as sentimentality. But, any way, it is odd, unharmonious, unsatisfying: strangely so for the author of three books that are as satisfying as *The Mayor of Casterbridge*, *The Trumpet Major* and *Under the Greenwood Tree*.

This aspect of Thomas Hardy's work is, of course, not peculiar to his poetry. It is characteristic of any of his volumes of short stories, of *Life's Little Ironies*, for example, or *A Group of Noble Dames*, which are too often mere recitals of odd ways of getting into the churchyard. In other words, it is peculiar to his shorter work. And that, perhaps, gives us a clue to the course of this taint of eccentric morbidity. Thomas Hardy is a man of culture. He is, as a matter of fact, a much more cultured man than Henry James was, for he had a more systematic education and attained to something of scholarship in Greek and Latin, and had the further discipline of his training as an architect; and he had the advantage for which Henry James so yearned, of having been born into a social order so long established that a code of manners had been worked out which enjoined on all persons the sort of behaviour which had been found to be most conducive to general harmony. But, oddly enough, he was always very artless. Though he was instinctively an artist, he could not formulate to himself what art was or understand how other artists got to work. It was similar to the way in which Samuel Butler was more interested in science than in anything else, but never came to any conscious comprehension of the scientific spirit, so that he was always attributing the strangest motives to Huxley and Darwin. Once Thomas Hardy became engaged on a long and important book his lack of comprehension of what art was about mattered nothing; for in meditating on the adventures throughout any prolonged train of events he fell, as artists do, into the equivalent of a trance state, during which his subconscious pushed up into the conscious such events and phrases as are appropriate symbols for the matter that had to be expressed. But in briefer composition the mechanism did not set to work as quickly; and there obtruded on him his habitual perplexity as to what art could possibly be about, which he would try to allay by conforming to the two reasons for which country-folk tell each other stories. That they do first for the sake of entertainment, and secondly for the sake of wisdom, to add to the map of life's contours. He, therefore, sat back and tried to remember true stories that belonged to the type of truth.

Now, it happens that if one tries to remember like that, if one stays still in the present and lets the events rush to one out of the past, it is the fractures of one's normal life that appear first. One remembers what was not customary. The customary condition of Thomas Hardy's mind was an abundant appreciation of life. There comes into such a scene as that when Sergeant Troy shows his sword drill to Bathsheba Everdene, the most complicate system of joys circling within joys, like the stars dancing among themselves in the heavens: a joy in the earth itself, in bodies, in beauty, in strength, in sex, in the play of the body that pulls the mind and itself near to sex and

then away again; in the play of the mind that, in not
quite the same rhythm, pulls the body and itself near
to sex and then away again; joy in the peacock strut
of the male, joy in that aspect of the woman which
may be symbolized by a moist, pouting, dark rose
lower lip. That was what his subconscious pleasur-
ably saw in life; but because it was so habitual, it does
not leap to the recalling memory. He does not remember the warmth which his sound blood, which
has kept him going for most of a hundred years,
sends through his veins. Rather he remembers the
time when the blood seemed shocked out of his body
by the chill air that rises from an open grave. Hence
these many records of mere calamity, of charnel
accidents, which are merely the defects of a great
quality, shadows such as must be cast by a strong
light, nothing to be counted against him.

But Mr. Sitwell's book lies beside us to remind us
that there has recently come into literature a force
which will in future prevent any such novelists as
come under its influence from any such misinterpre-
tations of their own pasts. It is a force that is only
novel so far as it is applied to prose, for it is the
inspiration of nearly all lyric poetry, and a great deal
of the rest. It is the force of memory practised as an
art. Those who seek remembrance this way do not
stay still in the present and let the accidents of the
past fight to them by shock tactics. They project
themselves into the past as before they have pro-
jected themselves into an invented world, and re-
create the experiences they already have had by passing through them imaginatively, just as in a plain
matter of fiction they pass imagination through the

experiences they never have had. This gives their account of them an extreme psychic importance. These experiences already have brought certain things to the subconscious mind and changed it; the conscious goes back and revisits the mind in its first state and compares it to the mind in its second state, and by reason of that comparison and the processes involved in it changes it again to a third state; the internal conflict which is the root of the artist's desire to create is intensified and concentrated, since many of the small dog-fights that take place round the central battle are seen for what they are and suppressed; and the general sense of harmony with which the artist hopes to reconcile his conflict must be immensely increased by the pleasure he must get in moulding this material, so specially malleable with familiarity, into beauty. It is for this reason, perhaps, that poetry has hitherto always had a greater prestige than fiction, which has heretofore been so much less personal, so much less a matter of direct memory.

The release of the force of memory in fiction is, with certain few and momentary exceptions, a novelty belonging to this age. It is curious that, although subsequent developments of it have proved that it is supremely suited to unseal the tragic springs of life, its first exponent should have been a great comedian. For one could not deny that title to George Moore, since the ultimate result of his reminiscent work is happy laughter. (How joyously, for example, one remembers *Euphorion in Texas*, in which a Texan lady visits Mr. Moore in the hope that his attentions might enable her to found a line of artists in that state, when one picks up a little book called *The*

Creative Arts in Texas, which capably tells us that there are now in that State forty-seven poets, five playwrights, eleven novelists, eleven short story writers, twenty-three essayists, eight historians, six collectors, twenty-three composers, nine sculptors, and fifty-one painters. One must congratulate Mr. Moore on unusual greatness of an unusual kind.) The unique personality of Mr. Moore prevented the method from being recognized for what it was, or as anything but a phase of his extraordinary being. The next person who tried it was Dorothy Richardson, and though she created interest by the power inherent in her method, she killed it by the relative insignificance of her internal conflict. And then the perfect transplantation of the poetic mood to prose was effected by Marcel Proust.

The greatness of Proust! One cannot exaggerate it. Like the greatest, he draws one out of the house of one's life into his house. Shakespeare performed such abductions mercilessly. Making one's father less real than King Lear, his old lips turning back like a wolf's from his toothless gums while his dying flesh cursed live mating flesh and he talks of the small gilded fly; and the wench that broke one's heart less real than Cleopatra, proving curiously that all love is not divine. The memory, the poet's memory, experiencing and re-experiencing, has such power over one's mere personal life, that one has merely lived. Even so, one finds oneself seated in the great salon of Marcel Proust's mind, witnessing events which are more clarified than those of life, which clarify life. There is that affair of the phrase from the sonata by Vinteuil. Through all Swann's odious humiliations he could be consoled by those sounds. They had been moulded into a shape that just fitted the hole that had been cut in his heart. Yet he never learned that the sonata had been written by the snuffy old M. Vinteuil. Nor if he had known would it have availed anything. He could not have established any relationship with old M. Vinteuil, divided as they were by several abysses. Human comprehension, the thing one longs for above all else, is not so easily to be achieved. That there are phrases of music which adorn a situation like a garland set on the brow of a statue; that is enough. At any rate, that must be enough, since there is no more. What is real, if this is not real? Did that not actually happen in the world in which one lives? Or rather, does one not actually live in the world where that happened?

Under that spell Mr. Sacheverell Sitwell has fallen; and he has re-created very beautifully an after-noon of childhood, a night of youth. The writer of to-day who can profit by the immense researches into consciousness that have been made since Henry James began to write is now amazingly fortunate in his awareness of himself, in his knowledge of his own nature, which is his own instrument and at least half of his material. Yet at the same time one perceives from certain pages of poor writing that the freedom from any factual constraints in the new form, the absence of any necessity to keep dates with one-self such as was imposed on the writer of the old-fashioned novel, with a plot to work out, or the old-fashioned essay with a point to prove, are something of temptations to inexactitude.

And there we are where we began. The point in

which Mr. Sitwell irritates us by his inferiority to Mr. Hardy proves to be the result of his use of that same force, the lack of which makes Mr. Hardy jeopardize his superiority by faults to which Mr. Sitwell would not be subject, his ignorance of his own nature, his tendency to present the abnormal phases of his being as if they were the normal. One perceives that adding to the technique of art is not like throwing out a new wing in the town hall. Rather is it like some great movement under the waters on the face of the earth, that opens a channel here, that afar off lifts up a reef, according to the great terrestrial rhythms.

THE place of honour in the volume of critical essays which Mr. Drake has selected from the American periodicals of 1926 called 'American Criticism, 1926,' very certainly belongs to Mary Colum. Her portrait of Stuart Sherman is a thing of clear colours and a few significant lines, which would give pleasure even if it were not true, but it is also as accurate as an Admiralty map. One can check up on it by turning to the end of the book, to Stuart Sherman's evaluation of Masefield, just as in a studio one looks from the canvas on the easel to the sitter. All is there, just as she says – the integrity of his absorption in his subject, his Puritan bias, his not at all discreditable willingness to subdue his sense of artistry when he had snuffed up the intimation, for which he had so marvellously sharp a scent, that a book was alive. It is the business of the critic, as of the portrait painter, to synthesize a million glances at his subject that will tell the on-looker at one glance the truth about him, as ultimate as he can get it.

But all this must be done for some other purpose, it occurs to one when one reads this volume, than for the reader's mere information. There is something more vital afoot than that. One does not learn that so much from one's appreciation of fine criti-cism, for all good work, whether creative or critical, tends to light up the same mood of exhilaration. But one gets a clear intimation of it from one's emotional reaction to poor criticism. A bad short story or novel or poem leaves one comparatively calm, because it does not exist, unless it gets a fake prestige through being mistaken for good work. It is essentially negative, it is something that has not come through. But over bad criticism one has a sense of real calamity. That sense comes to one twice in this volume, first in an essay by Miss Agnes Repplier, entitled 'The Fortunate Poets.' It is gracefully enough about nothing in particular, but in the course of it Miss Repplier gets around quite a bit among contemporary writers and falls to pondering on why Mr. Yeats and not Mr. Thomas Hardy received the Nobel Prize in 1923. We in England are past pondering on this matter. We were greatly relieved when George Bernard Shaw received it the other day; to judge from the previous awards it might just as easily have gone to the Duke of Marlborough or Ricciotti Garibaldi. But in her discussion of this strange state of affairs Miss Repplier remarks: 'If the prize had been an English one Mr. Hardy's attitude toward what he called "the dark madness of the war" might possibly have disqualified him. Like Viscount Morley, he felt, or at least he expressed, nothing but resentment at England's struggle for safety. It seemed to be part of his resentment at an imperfect but not altogether worthless civilization, which we cannot afford to let go until we are sure we have laid hands on something better.'

Now, it would surely not be possible for three sentences to be more compact of error than these three, more drearily fraught with the suggestion of a lifetime spent in giving the whole of the time and half the attention to literature. It is not true that

Thomas Hardy felt nothing but resentment against the war. He deplored it as part of the identity of man's destiny and woe. He wrote many beautiful and sympathetic poems about the armies. Having the intensely practical mind of a craftsman, who is the son of a long line of craftsmen who have been disciplined into a racial common sense by dealing through the ages with obstinate material substances— by ploughing earth, by carving wood, by baking bread – he is the last person to practise any such flimsy intellectual type of pacifism as Miss Repplier implies. He never condemned those who started the war, for the sublimely simple reason that he could not see what else they could have done. Moreover, I do not know that one could have trusted Thomas Hardy to turn pacifist, even if his logic had taken him to it. It happens that he comes of a part of England which, recently enough for him in his distant childhood to have been thrilled by first-hand tales of it, had good cause to realize that, though it was an island, it was not so outlandish after all. It is significant that all along the southern coast, of which he wrote, by which he lived, there are coves where local tradition says Napoleon once landed from a rowboat and strutted on the cliffs to learn how this soil he meant to conquer felt underfoot. And it is perfectly possible that of one of these coves tradition speaks the truth. The greatness of Thomas Hardy was very largely due to the intensity with which he has learned such lessons as were taught him by the soil where he was born. He would, therefore, be specially unlikely to overlook the practical difficulties of pacifism on the part of a country liable to invasion.

'Like Viscount Morley,' is one of those phrases that stick in the fastidious mind as a fish-bone in a throat. How could Thomas Hardy be *like* Viscount Morley in this or any other respect? That doctrinaire Radical, who had many admirable qualities, but who was about as full of the ripe wisdom of earth as an umbrella frame, was a pacifist for the same reason that he was one of the worst prose writers that ever lived. He could not see why he could not force his intention of peace on the world in spite of the contrary movement of history. Just as he never could see why he could not force his meaning on the reader in a certain mould of words in spite of the contrary disposition of the English language.

Thus we arrive, shaken as if we had been travelling on a springless cart, at the final sentence, which is as reelingly off the perpendicular of accuracy as all the rest. 'It seemed to be part of his resentment against an imperfect but not altogether worthless civilization, which we cannot afford to let go until we are sure we have laid hands on something better.' This sentence is initially obnoxious simply as writing. There is no switch in the middle to inform us that the description of civilization does not belong to Mr. Hardy's cerebrations, but is a piece of school ma'amish crispness on the part of Miss Repplier. But its major offence is its ignorance of the sufficiently patent facts that there never was a great writer who more completely swallowed civilization, hook, line and sinker, than Thomas Hardy. Life he resents, sure enough, the limitations placed on the will of man by his own nature and the physical frame of existence. The boundless opportunities afforded to pain enrage him. But of civilization, of the methods which man takes to establish himself in life and, so far as possible, to circumvent it, he is curiously un-critical. *Tess of the D'Urbervilles* and *Jude the Obscure* scandalized their age not because they threatened social revolution, but because they were tragic. So far as they had propagandist intention they advocated trifling extensions of sexual and religious tolerance and educational facilities which had been demanded often and long before and have been carried into effect fairly painlessly since. What shocked his readers was his statement which he made with such intensity that it cut through the solid mass of Victorian optimism as if it were cheese, that there are people who, when they die, are God's creditors, who have not been paid what was due, and who probably never will be. But neither there nor in any other of his works is there a single line which suggests that the present economic structure of society could pos-sibly be improved; and the remoteness of revolution from his social conceptions may be judged from the fact that when, just after the war, he sat down and pondered what England really needed, he decided it was a revival of the Anglican Church.

Now, it is undoubtedly the case that these sen-tences of Miss Repplier's infuriate the reason far more than three sentences of fiction would do, even if those matched them in fatuity. This acerbity is not peculiar to the occasion. One can reawaken it from the same volume by turning to Miss Anne Douglas Sedgwick's paper which she calls, with that trick, much practised by Henry James's disciples, of pick-ing up a common phrase and using it with a wise, kind, playful air, surely very offensive, 'The Heart of the Matter.' Miss Sedgwick herself is a writer of great merit who persistently stultifies her talent by naïvely admiring the cheapest effects of other authors and imitating them with a deadly intensity and power. This led her at one time to commit a large number of stories which climbed up slowly and with an air of extreme sensitiveness to renunciatory tags of the sort that were to Henry James far worse than drink. Indeed Henry James and Mrs. Wharton and Miss Sedgwick were responsible for an entire school of fiction writers who invariably ended their stories with an elliptical remark on the part of their principal figure: ' "Oh, but you see," he said humbly, "I never really did," ' and rounded them off with a brief passage ecstatically ascribing to him reduced circumstances and spiritual radiance. These are the glycerine tears of fiction. Miss Sedgwick rationalizes this inclination in her paper by selecting with gusto similar passages from various modern writers.

Now, these false identifications of Miss Sedgwick's contemporaries immediately engender the same sense of calamity which came on one in reading Miss Repplier's ideas concerning Thomas Hardy. And it becomes more and more acute as she pays various brief visits of misapprehension on the great, which are rendered much more irritating by her air of confidence and graciousness. One would think she was putting flowers in their studies. Of Henry James she says, 'Reality alarmed as much as it fascinated him, and he only approached it when he saw it safely clothed in the complexities and preoccupations of super-civilization. Enchanting, absorbing as he is, lovable and often deeply moving, we do not feel that sense of tears for a single one of his situations or figures — unless it is the wistful little figure of "The Pupil".' The jaw drops. If it had not, one would have inquired, 'Four Meetings?' 'Washington Square?'

Miss Sedgwick then passes on to Marcel Proust, whom she discusses in that same manner which one has found so deplorable in Mrs. Wharton when she dealt with the same subject, as if she were a cultured and fastidious society woman in doubt as to whether to engage a chef because, though his cooking is excellent, his references concerning character are not quite satisfactory. The situation is, in fact, different. The man was a god. Miss Sedgwick coughs in church in this essay by a curious allegation that he was heartless, though obviously 'Le Temps Retrouvé' is an epic of the heart. The power which the 'I' of the tale had, which made his friends forget his sickliness and fretfulness, was his power to love. The books are an account of his quest first of a society, then of a relationship, where he would know nothing but harmony and the gracious practice of the affections, such as he had known with his adorable grandmother. But what can one expect of a writer who astonishingly describes Jane Austen as 'tearless'? Is it really possible that anybody could read *Sense and Sensibility* or *Persuasion* without seeing behind them a face graven with weeping? 'It is dangerous to feel much unless one is great enough to feel much; and wise and charming as she is, her glance would be the pinprick to many an inflated emotion, though to many real ones she would be blind.'

Really, it is time this comic patronage of Jane

263

Austen ceased. To believe her limited in range because she was harmonious in method is as sensible as to imagine that when the Atlantic Ocean is as smooth as a mill-pond it shrinks to the size of a mill-pond. There are those who are deluded by the decorousness of her manner, by the fact that her virgins are so virginal that they are unaware of their virginity, into thinking that she is ignorant of passion. But look through the lattice-work of her neat sentences, joined together with the bright nails of craftsmanship, painted with the gay varnish of wit, and you will see women haggard with desire or triumphant with love, whose delicate reactions to men make the heroines of all our later novelists seem merely to turn signs, 'Stop' or 'Go' toward the advancing male. And the still sillier reproach, that Jane Austen has no sense of the fundamental things in life, springs from a misapprehension of her place in time. She came at the end of the eighteenth century, when the class to which she belongs was perhaps more intelligent than it has ever been before or since, when it had dipped more deeply than comfortable folk have ever done into philosophical inquiry. Her determination not to be confused by emotion, and to examine each phenomenon of the day briskly and on its merits, was never a sign of limitation. It was a sign that she lived in the same world as Hume and Gibbon. Her cool silence on the wherefore of the why is a million times more evidential of an interest in the fundamental things of life than ' "Brother, brother, how shall I know God?" sobbed Alyosha, who by this time was exceedingly drunk,' or any such sentence from those Russians.

Now, why is Miss Anne Douglas Sedgwick annoying us so much more by all this than Mr. A. S. M. Hutchinson would do by an equivalent number of pages which would criticize life with such vast malappropriateness as she has criticized the great? It will help, perhaps, if we try to recognize the particular kind of emotion we are feeling, and ask ourselves if we ever feel the same emotion on other occasions. We will find, I think, that we do; and that the occasion is when some one, a clumsy servant or visitor, breaks some treasured family possession. A sweep of the wrist, that Bristol decanter, that Nailsea vase is gone for ever. Something beautiful that has lasted a long time is at an end. The man who made it, the hundreds of people who have tenderly appreciated it and guarded it, are insulted by its fracture.

There, in that identity of feeling, one gets a clue. Criticism is a process that ought to be continuous. Every man is in a state of conflict, owing to his attempt to reconcile himself and his relationship with life to his conception of harmony. This conflict makes his soul a battlefield, where the forces that wish this reconciliation fight those that do not and reject the alternative solutions they offer. Works of art are attempts to fight out this conflict in the imaginative world. They are great works of art if the forces involved are immensely numerous, and if the artist can truthfully report the conflict as he knows it. It is the business of the critic to give a detached report on the conflict. The artist cannot tell you exactly what happened, any more than the soldiers in a battle can tell you exactly what has happened.

There is need for an outside observer who will stand
clear and look down on the proceedings as from a
height. He is able to see the new angles of the
spiritual situations because, as all human beings are
unique, his conflict will not be the same as the artist's.
But because he has, if he has sufficiently vital need
to make his criticism of value, a conflict of his own,
his view also will have its limitations; which, however, can be corrected by some other critic who will
come along and read both the work and the criticism
and in the light of both and his own state of mind
can provide yet another interpretation of the conflict.

We have an example of criticism at this stage
in this volume, where that delightfully scrupulous
critic, Alyse Gregory, turns her intelligence on Mr.
Van Wyck Brooks's story of Henry James. But the
chain of criticism can be interminably long. We have
Professor Gilbert Murray here in this country to-day
holding a golden chain whose other end is held by
Euripides and Sophocles, and certainly he will not
be the last man to hold it. Mr. T. S. Eliot disputes
with him, the writers of *The Criterion*, given a
standard by his high standard, will keep the disputa-
tion in mind, it will reappear some day in their
writings, others bred in another school will bring
them to argument, and so on. . . .

Such are the elements that make for continuity in
literature; that make the wisdom of the artist live
longer than the grasses of the field which are cut
down in the fall of the year. But criticism such as
Miss Repplier and Miss Sedgwick have indulged in
in the present volume defeat this movement towards
immortality. They are ungracious to the gracious

past. They are ruptures of tradition. They take the end of the chain with which patient critics have linked the common mind to the harmony of Henry James and Thomas Hardy and Jane Austen and they let it fall into the darkness. Worse still, they circulate rumours which would prevent any intelligent person from picking it up again. It is admirable to contemplate such essays in this volume as Mr. Edmund Wilson's admirable 'Literary Vaudeville,' where he soundly estimates the importance of contemporary American writers, computing the importance of their conflicts and rejecting those of them who sublimate them too easily; and to reflect that we have such sober critics, so truly reverent of art, to counter those like Miss Repplier and Miss Sedgwick, who will sacrifice the heritage of our past to a smart phrase, and pull down the reputations of our great men in a glib and facile epigram.

SINCLAIR LEWIS INTRODUCES
ELMER GANTRY

THIS sequence of sermons and seductions – two forms of human activity which Mr. Lewis, contrary to the opinion of mankind from pole to pole, represents as on a common plane of tedium – is probably one of the most disappointing books that a man of genius has ever produced. It is full of wilful abnegations of fine qualities. Why should Mr. Lewis, who used to tread the sward of our language as daintily as a cat, use the word 'amour'? Not 'an amour,' which is good eighteenth-century English, but 'amour.' 'When Elmer as a freshman just arrived from the pool halls and frame high school of Paris, Kansas, had begun to learn the decorum of amour. . . .' In 1917 he ceased, we are told, 'to educate his wife in his ideals of amour.' A loathsome usage. It makes one see a pimpled male child smoking a cheap cigar outside a place marked 'Eats,' sustaining his soul against the drabness of Main Street by turning over in his mind a nickelodeon conception of Europe. So need not Mr. Lewis be, unless he chooses.

Mr. Lewis has also thrown away his sound engineering capacity for handling incident, such as he showed, for example, in contriving the death of Leora in *Martin Arrowsmith*. In the course of this novel it becomes necessary for him in a manner of speaking to incinerate Aimée Semple McPherson, and a poor job he makes of it. Elmer Gantry meets and preaches and is entwined with a woman evangelist named Sharon Falconer, who is a sufficiently curious and interesting conception. She is a play-

acting hussy, little Katie Jonas of the Utica brickyards, who flows above reality on the tides of her own
ecstasy, being God's right hand in a flowing white
robe among lilies and roses in a shell-shaped pulpit
in a mission tent, being a member of 'an old Virginian family' in correct sports clothes in 'her old
home' (acquired from an authentic Virginian family
bearing the name of Sprugg by a series of financial
transactions ultimately unsatisfactory to the Spruggs),
being a pure and holy woman in circumstances that
would make most of us withdraw the claim, because
of her conviction that whatever happens to her is
sanctified: A new expression of Madame Guyon in
terms of Lulu Belle. She has all the charm of the
fantasy builder, who combines the fascination of the
talented liar capable at any moment of arranging the
phenomena of reality into a wilder pattern than that
into which life has cast them; and she has also the
lovability of the perfectly sincere person who believes
every word she is saying and will be as hideously dis-
appointed as anybody if it is brought home to her
that it is not true. She would be a remarkable creation if, oddly enough, she had not absorbed her
creator. When she stages a preposterous scene for
her first amorous encounter with Elmer, in a shrine
which had apparently been prised out of the Paramount Picture Theatre, with chanted prayers in the
Los Angeles free-liturgical style, one has an uneasy
feeling that Mr. Lewis himself is as impressed as
Elmer Gantry was; that, for a minute, he has sunk
from his own high level to that where little Katie
Jonas of the Utica brickyard put it over on him.

It seems good to Mr. Lewis that Sharon should

die a violent death, that Gantry may be bereft and
free to find his way to the orthodox pastorate where
we leave him; though these surely are the aniline
dyes of the fancy rather than the sunset colours of the
imagination. Surely the way of life would have been
that she would have passed into a fantasy where he
was not, and looked at him with a lack of knowledge
of him which would have been as integral and true
to itself as her lying, as her sincerity, as her purity,
as her voluptuousness. But Mr. Lewis insists on
grilling her to a cinder in a pier hall that goes on fire
during a big meeting, and his preparations for this
climax are unbelievably, disgracefully crude. Preliminary hints concerning the layout of the hall,
explanations during the crisis of exactly where the
flames broke out so that the platform party would not
get away, remind one of the maps people used to make
during the war on the dinner-table with forks and
spoons and glasses. One has the same conviction that
there are times when clarity ought to be sacrificed to
the preservation of even a superficial harmony.

Now, Mr. Lewis is a very considerable person.
He has mimetic genius to an extent that has hardly
ever been transcended. *Babbitt* as a book was plan-
less; its end arrived apparently because its author had
come to the end of the writing-pad, or rather, one
might suspect from its length, to the end of all writ-
ing-pads then on the market. But George Babbitt
was a triumph of impersonation. It was a bit of
character-exhibition comparable to Mr. Micawber;
and if it be recalled to Mr. Lewis's disadvantage that
Dickens invented a host of characters as vivid, it can
also be recalled that never did Dickens make so com-

plete an inventory of a human being as Mr. Lewis
does in George Babbitt. We know the poor fatuous
being in his standing up and his lying down. And
so, too, we know Elmer Gantry, this snorting, cring-
ing creature, this offspring of the hippopotamus and
the skunk, between whose coarse lips the texts sound
as if he were munching sappy vegetation, under
whose coarse hands sex becomes a series of gross acts
of the body ending in grosser acts of the spirit, such
as deceit and cruelty. There are one or two conver-
sations in the book — the scene where he refuses to
marry a frightened girl who pretends she is going to
have his child, the scene where he rushes like a
charging pachyderm on his moneyed and insipid
bride — when one can hear in one's ears the alternate
whine and snarl of the creature, its blind bellow, its
canoodling softer tones. How exquisite, too, is his
response to Mr. North, the vice-crusader, when that
gentleman at last comes across with the long-sought
invitation to speak on behalf of the National Association for the Purification of Art and the Press. 'Do
you suppose you could address the Detroit Y.M.C.A.
on October 4?' 'Well, it's my wife's birthday, and
we've always made rather a holiday of it — we're
proud of being an old-fashioned homey family — but
I know Cleo wouldn't want that to stand in the way
of my doing anything I can to further the Kingdom.'
How exquisite also are his notes for a sermon:

Love:
a rainbow
AM and PM star
from cradle to tomb

inspires art etc. music voice of love
slam atheists etc. who do not appreciate love.

Since Mr. Lewis has not lost this power of impersonation, since he has on certain pages exercised it even more successfully than he has ever done before, there must be some flaw in the central conception of the book which explains why the effect of the whole is tedious, and why he falls into these tricks of flat writing and lethargic handling of incidents. The sense of tedium must be the result of one's feeling that all these sermons and seductions are leading nowhere. The incompetence must be the result of the author's feeling that the enterprise on which he has embarked is not worth while. The trouble is that the book is not merely the life of a particular individual named Elmer Gantry, it is a satire on organized religion; and Mr. Lewis has neglected a very necessary condition which the satirist must fulfill before he starts working.

What that condition is has probably never been more neatly illustrated than by Yvonne Printemps in the vaudeville prelude of 'L'Illusioniste.' She comes forth as the singer and dancer who practises under the *nom de guerre* of – is it Miss Hopkins or Miss Tompkins? It is ten years since I saw the play and I can remember only its essence. It is at any rate an English *nom de guerre*, for she is a second-rater and needs every adventitious aid she can find, and an English singer has an aroma of romance; since all the peoples of the world suspect that their neighbours have been endowed with an intenser life than themselves, and in peace are more alluring, as in war they are more hateful. Assuming this meagre personality, Yvonne Printemps gives a performance that is a satire on nearly all bad singing and dancing; on nearly all bad art of every kind. She cannot let her personality speak for itself. She has to point her youth and prettiness by assuming a baby beauty expression which is superimposed on the real expression into which her innate characteristics and her embarrassment at the present situation have moulded her young flesh, so that the result is confused and ineffective. She lifts up her little voice and it is strangled to a weak pretty pipe in her throat, because she has no clear idea of what sounds she wishes to produce. She importunes the audience, 'Listen! Listen! I am being tender! Listen! Listen! In a minute I am going to be even more tender!' Even so her dancing creates no definite effect because she has not previously imagined a pattern woven through the air which she must follow, and her movements are retarded and qualified by this doubt of her enterprise.

Yvonne Printemps is able to do all this because she knows how not to do all this. She is an artist. She paints her personality not by assuming airs and graces, but by eliminating everything that is irrelevant to its effective characteristics. She has so clear a conception of what she wants to do before she does it that her voice and her movements flow in an unimpeded stream of grace toward their goal. Having known from the beginning that she was going to encounter certain crises in her theme, she is able to treat them with absolute justice, not dragging them on before their turn, not intervening between them and the audience by explanatory over-emphasis. It is because she has habitually practised perfection that she is able to anatomize imperfection and imitate it.

That is the first necessary condition which the satirist must fulfil. He must fully possess, at least in the world of the imagination, the quality the lack of which he is deriding in others.

Mr. Lewis does not fulfil that necessary condition of the satirist. He has not entered into imaginative possession of those qualities the lack of which he derides in others. He pillories Elmer Gantry and those who follow him because they are obviously misusing the force that makes men want to speak and to hear speech of religion; but he has no vision of the use they ought to be making of it. The passages in the book which present to one what Mr. Lewis regards as the proper attitude to religion are disconcertingly jejune — are disconcertingly on the same mental plane as Elmer Gantry. There is a St. Francis of Assisi type of good man who worries not at all about theology because of the comfort he can draw for himself and for others from God the Father. But he is perfunctorily described. One seems to hear a flushed and disorderly introduction, 'Wancha to meet Father Pengilly. One of the best friens I have.' . . . Mr. Lewis's enthusiasm over him is as glib and rootless and meaningless as the getting together of the salesmen of the Pequot Farm Implement Company, which he so masterfully records ('My name's Ad Locust — Jesus, think of it! The folks named me Adney. Can you beat that? Ain't that one hell of a name for a fellow that likes to get out with the boys

and have a good time! But you can just call me Ad')
and from which he so properly recoils.

There is – and this is far more painful – a sincere
seeker after truth named Frank Shallard, a minister
who is troubled by doubts, who against all his
worldly interests gives up his ministry because he is
not satisfied of the validity of the Christian religion.
But he turns out to be an albino Babbitt; and those
doubts are represented as taking place on a mental
plane lower than is conceivable.

Listen, for example, to his remarks on Jesus:

'. . . I'm appalled to say I don't find Jesus an
especially admirable character!

'He is picturesque. He tells splendid stories. He's
a good fellow, fond of low company . . . But He's
vain. He praises himself outrageously, He's fond of
astonishing people by little magical tricks which
we've been taught to revere as "miracles." He is furi-
ous as a child in a tantrum when people don't recognize Him as a great leader. He loses His temper.
He blasts the poor barren fig-tree when it doesn't
feed Him . . . Far from the Christian religion – or
any other religion – being a blessing to humanity,
it's produced such confusion in all thinking, such
second-hand viewing of actualities, that only now are
we beginning to ask what and why we are and what
we can do with life!

'Just what are the teachings of Christ? Does He
come to bring peace or more war? He says both.
Did He approve earthly monarchies or rebel against
them? He says both. Did He ever – think of it, God
Himself, taking on human form to help the earth –

did He ever suggest sanitation, which would have saved millions from plagues? . . .

'What *did* He teach? One place in the Sermon on the Mount He advises – let me get my Bible – here it is: "Let your light so shine before men that they may see your good works and glorify your Father which is in heaven," and then five minutes later, "Take heed that ye do not your alms before men, to be seen of them, otherwise ye have no reward of your Father which is in heaven." That's an absolute contradiction. Oh, I know you can reconcile them. . . . That's the whole aim of ministerial training. . . .'

Now, is this not reverse English for Babbittry? Remember, Mr. Lewis is not exhibiting this stuff for our pity; he is not tearfully demonstrating that the texture of life in the American hinterland is so miserably poor that even the best of it is far less than good; he is holding it up for our admiration. Actually he admires this clodhopping comment on that tale of a Son of God who comes down and partakes of life and death along with man, which is so near to some fantasy that lies at the heart of all created men that, no matter whether we believe in its actual truth and whether it comforts us or not, we know it as something as much a part of us as our flesh and blood, as something intensely relevant to being. He can tolerate re-entrance into that mood of scorn for the past which makes *A Yankee at the Court of King Arthur* one of the most painful books in the world. Mark Twain looked at medieval Europe and said in astonishment: 'My, weren't they dumb?' because he was so uninstructed that he believed the philosophical assumptions of his age had always existed for the intelligent to lay hold of when they wanted, and was unaware that they had been slowly and courageously snatched out of chaos by the past he was despising. Even so, Mr. Lewis talks of the Church as something apart from human thought and a brake on it, whereas the Church happened to be a channel, and for centuries the main channel of human thought. 'It's produced such confusion in all thinking' . . . Zip! Bam! Zowie! It was St. Thomas Aquinas who went that time. As for that suggestion that Christ should have halted on the way to the Cross to recommend the American bathroom, no doubt performing a really useful miracle by placing the requisite metallurgical resources at the disposal of the population of Palestine slightly ahead of time, it ought to go into the Americana section of the *American Mercury*.

Is it not curiously below Mr. Lewis's form? Is not that comparison between the two tests strange in one who wrote such a fervent plea that George F. Babbitt should let the light of his real character shine before men instead of darkening it by insincere standardized speech and behaviour, and who should know better than to regard an ordinary rule of good manners as contradiction to that plea?

The trouble is that Mr. Lewis is possessed by an idea that in order to combat Babbittry it is necessary to enter into argument with Babbitt; to disprove what he says; to reverse his opinions. This is a profound error which if persisted in would sterilize all radicalism. Babbitt receives pernicious ideas because he is arguing on a plane of thought where it is pretended that life is simpler and coarser than it is, so

278

that our conclusions reached there can be valid in reality. Merely to contradict him is to take up another position in a futile world of fantasy. It is no effective repartee to prohibition to get drunk on Scotch. That is merely to match one crudity with another. But to educate one's perceptions in the direction of ecstasy by taking exactly the right amount of Napoleon brandy, that is an assertion of all that prohibition denies. In the practical world one may have to fight Babbitt when he does something foolish and tyrannous, and it may be the duty of the artist to turn journalist for a second or two and explain to the general public exactly what the silly old fool has been up to. But in the world of art, in the world of intellect, the artist must first raise himself above Babbitt by practising a finer and more complicated mode of thought and feeling. That Mr. Lewis has failed to do. Just as he ends by consorting with little Katie Jonas of the brickyards as an equal, so he approaches Elmer Gantry on his own level. The result of that is that this book will not start any great movement towards enhanced sensitiveness of life, which might make people reject fake religion. It will start a purely factual controversy as to whether parsons do in any large numbers get drunk and toy with their stenographers, which is really a matter of very little importance. Because hypocrisy stinks in the nostrils one is likely to rate it as a more powerful agent for destruction than it is. It is the creatures, with longings so largely and vaguely evil, that they cannot disappoint them by realizing them in the terms afforded by this wholesome world who make the dangerous opposition; as all those must realize who have heard the most famous vice-crusader preach and marked how he got more lustful pleasure out of saying the word 'brothel' than any sinner ever got by going to one.

Why has Mr. Lewis produced a book that in spite of its humour, its research, its bravery, has not succeeded in being the satire he has the wit to plan? It is because he has not left himself enough energy to make that ultimate vigorous contraction of the muscles of the soul which is necessary for a work of genius. He has dissipated his forces in going about making the effect of a hand grenade, in throwing up his hat and cheering at floridities of existence that anybody over fourteen ought to take calmly. He has committed himself to pettiness by imitating the futile school of radicalism which finds no game too small and will on occasion waste powder and shot on a silly old woman in Iowa who announces her intention of reading the Bible for the three-hundredth time in her life, as if Voltaire would have got anywhere if he had spent his emotions on the pietistic errors of washer-women in Brittany. If he would sit still so that life could make any deep impression on him, if he would attach himself to the human tradition by occasionally reading a book which would set him a standard of profundity, he could give his genius a chance.

SHERWOOD ANDERSON, POET

WHEN one decides, as any reasonable person must decide, that so far as writers of fiction under fifty years of age are concerned, the United States makes an immensely better showing than England, Sherwood Anderson undoubtedly plays a great part in that calculation. It is beyond any question that *Winesburg, Ohio,* and *The Triumph of the Egg* are two of the most interesting books of short stories ever written. The story that gives its name to the second volume is a beautiful grotesque which, like a great deal of Chinese art, like the more whimsical Greek bronzes, like much Maya sculpture, like the Buddha himself, achieves through its grotesquerie a serene effect that art directed and censored by idealist considerations can rarely attain. The statue of a Greek athlete says nothing more than that the part of life which is obviously beautiful is obviously beautiful; and that everything in the spectator which is more concerned with other parts of life rises up in conflict against his appreciation of it. But the Buddha, whose face is like a cup filled to the brim with wine and good living, who is the height of spirituality and the deepest pit of grossness, occupies all conceivable concerns of the spectator and satisfied them according to the workmanship of the particular manifestation. The great Buddhas of the world stimulate practically all the emotions that humanity can feel on beholding itself in the mirror to their highest pitch of intensity; and since they are all being satisfied to their full bent, there is no more conflict between them than if none of them had been stimulated at all. There is, there fore, simultaneous excitement and serenity, which is perhaps the most agreeable sensation permitted to man. And that Mr. Anderson gave to his readers in *The Triumph of the Egg* by the ambivalence of his feeling for the father, his affection for him, his dislike for him, his contempt for him, his respect for him, his patience with him, his capacity for being endlessly entertained by him. Just as he gave it in *A Story Teller's Story*, that beautiful book, by his co-equal love and hate of himself, of his father, of America.

But I refuse to accompany Mr. Sherwood Anderson on all his adventures. *Dark Laughter* made me feel that negroes must be a lot more easily amused than I am. *Many Marriages* made me feel that he had borrowed the technique of Mr. George White[1] to very little purpose. His characters were unable to become Scandals. They never seemed to attain the dignity of complete nudity; their complexes clung to them like dark woollen socks. And *Poor White*, for all its magnificent beginning, was spoiled for me by subsequent passages describing how the hero, unable to face the duty of consummating his marriage, although he liked his bride, wandered about the arable land in the neighbourhood all night until her father and brothers came and fetched him, all looking positively deformed with taciturnity, like the men they choose to play Abraham Lincoln in the 'movies.' This makes me guffaw. So do all Mr. Anderson's massively reluctant lovers, the kind who watch each

---

[1] An American theatrical manager who produces an entertainment called 'The Scandals' in which he treats the female form with considerable gusto.

other for seventeen years from opposite windows in a Chicago tenement and then meet one night in a hallway. You know the sort of thing. 'She stood with her back to the wall, her elbows close to her side. She did not seem to see him. But she seemed to be waiting for something. They stood there for fifty-five minutes. Then the man walked to the door and went out into the street. He never told anybody about it.' Not a bit like George Moore.

I wish I could follow Mr. Anderson in his excursions along this line. In vain I have remonstrated with myself. 'You are regarding this incident as if you were a travelling salesman in the club car exchanging anecdotes with his kind. The sort of thing you would really enjoy, my dear, is that story about the two who registered at the hotel in Springfield, Mass., which Josie, the cabhorse, so eloquently told the cabdriver in "White Wings".' . . . But I am not really ashamed, because I strongly suspect that in this matter the travelling salesman would be right. Nearly everybody laughs at the old story of the man who, on being rebuked for pouring the salad over his head, said, 'My God, I thought it was spinach'; and that is an exact parallel to the story of the husband who spent his wedding night in the fields. It is evident that the husband had some curious misconception of sex just as the other man had of spinach; and that his author's breach of the etiquette of rural marriage should bring this to light in front of his bride's father and brothers is a companion piece to the mistaken identification of the salad which suddenly betrays the spinach fantasy to a circle of guests. The thought of the misconceptions would in both cases be

bound to make us laugh, for they suggest that both
men held a vision of the universe unshackled by the
logic of life, and that relieves our tension, because we
are all sick to death of those shackles, and that relief
shakes laughter out of us, which is reinforced and
made more explosive by our thought of those others
before us — the bride's relatives and the dinner guests
— to whom accident betrayed these misconceptions.
No, the fault does not lie with those of us who find
that our sense of humour is apt to rise and shatter the
steady mood of appreciation in which one would like
to read Mr. Anderson's works. It is an unfortunate
fact that the particular fantasy form into which most
of Mr. Anderson's imaginings flow when they concern sex is one that almost inevitably sets in motion
the psychological motion that produces laughter.

But there is little of that in Mr. Anderson's latest
book, *Tar, a Mid-West Childhood*, though there are
other things at which a reader might balk. It has, for
one thing, that curious falsification of character in the
direction of flatness which belongs to books about
children written by most adults. If one casts one's
mind back to one's childhood and does not flinch, one
has to admit that one then possessed all the emotional
characteristics that are called adult in a far more
marked degree than one ever had them later. Mr.
Booth Tarkington pointed out in *Penrod* how im-
measurably more acute a boy's sense of taste is than
any man's, so that a dose of medicine can be a
hideous torture; and that difference may be taken as
an index of a generally superior sensitiveness. One
could not possibly love a man and carry on life if one
loved him with the tremendous, blinding passion

that one felt for the little boy who lived next door. Adult Europeans during the Great War probably knew in their international reactions some faint shadow of the throbbing hatred that one habitually felt at school for the little girl with the blond pigtails, and the sewing-teacher. And all the intervening notes in the emotional scale, save where they function only in relation to adult interests, are of a correspondingly higher intensity. But we cannot bear to admit this, since it means that we who are mature and no more than mature, nevertheless, have already begun to suffer a decline. Decomposition of the soul has begun to set in long before death, just as, so the white streaks in the X-ray photographs tell us, it invades the body so soon as that is well into its teens. So we frequently ascribe to childhood an insipidity of nature, a temperance of heart, which is actually an attribute of old age. Thus comes into being the mawkish common run of children's books, which, being lies, die quickly. Those which survive do not repudiate this intensity of youth. It is accepted in Mrs. Molesworth's *Jackanapes*, in which the boy riding his first pony has all the gallantry he can ever have had when he was a disciplined soldier; in *The Jungle Books*, which show a child walking unafraid among the beasts of the jungle; in *Water Babies*, which shows a little chimney-sweep as brave as Hercules; in *Tom Sawyer* and *Huckleberry Finn*, youths of more than adult enterprise; in *Alice in Wonderland* and *The Wind in the Willows*, which are extravagant fantasies not too extravagant to embody infantile imaginings about life.

There is in *Tar* just a trifle of this depreciation of

the essential quality of childhood, and the lack of interest in children, which is its root. Mr. Anderson inquires surprisingly whether there can be such a thing as a vulgar child, and pronounces it inconceivable. Yet there could surely be nothing more evident than that there are innumerable children who come out of the everywhere into here wearing a made-up tie. Not to have perceived that is to enroll oneself among those who say, 'I love children,' or, 'I hate children,' which is as absurd as to say, 'I love people,' or, 'I hate people.' Whoever could make such a remark betrays that he is unable to observe the individualities of children, because he is dominated by some abstract conception of childhood. Of a certainty Mr. Anderson was not among such when he wrote that superb short story about the boy on the race track, *I Want to Know Why*. But unquestionably the small boy Tar is painted in pale sepia tints to square with the common ideal of the mediocrity of the young; and the representation is still further weakened by indulgences of Mr. Anderson's curious tendency to drag the *tempo* of life, by breaking up movements that in normal humanity are easy and sweeping into delayed, puttering motions, by inserting inarticulateness like a plum in the mouths of his characters. This is an irritating trick of his, because it does not belong to his artistic vision of life. It is an intrusion on his work of his attempt to settle a moral problem of his own. One of his characteristics is a glorious facility, which he possibly gets from his Latin blood. One sees it again and again in his work when he gets going. There is a passage in *A Story Teller's Story*, in which he flings a vivid expression of a certain aspect of America across four pages just as Michaelangelo filled a panel of the roof of the Sistine Chapel with his image of the creation of Adam, with an air of having spent no time or effort on it, having just called it into being by a whole turn of the will, a half-turn of the wrist. But this facility is a gift that Mr. Anderson quite unfairly dislikes, because he insists on identifying it with the braggart, hail-fellow-well-met, yarn-spinning tiresomeness of the father he describes in *A Story Teller's Story* and in *Tar*, though if there is any connection between them the second is merely an expression of the first so embryonic as to be useless and certainly not to be taken as evidence against it. But Mr. Anderson has his prejudice. Therefore, he rejects harmony of being. He is infatuated with human machinery that groans and creaks.

But there are two passages in *Tar* which far outweigh all its faults, which make it a book to be read and kept. There is a chapter describing how this father, Dick Moorhead, came home drunk when the children were at supper. His children sit round the table with bowed heads, very quiet, uncomfortable, frightened. They have been brought up decently by their mother. Dick has never come home like this before. He tries to serve them with the baked potatoes in the dish in front of him. But his fork misses the potato and strikes the dish. The mother gets up and takes the dish from him and serves the children herself. Dick, uneasy, guilty, starts talking, not to the family around him, for he feels they are rejecting him, but to the stove. His shame at his failure in life makes him cry out to the stove innumerable names of persons who owed him money when he ran a harness shop some years before, and had never paid him. Tar, who had been every ill, who is sitting up at the table for the first time after many days, falls into a kind of waking dream, fits faces to all those names, which appear and disappear in the darkness behind the stove. Amazing world, where a man can.do something to hold sway as if he were a tree and not a man, and talk to a stove as he would usually talk to his family, and change from a protective, authoritative father into a fighting and pitiful stranger. No wonder the walls waver, the faces dance and dissolve in the shadow, the little boy slips from his chair into the darkness, slips so that his mother will pick him up and carry him away in the darkness of her arms. That is an exquisite chapter. It makes one think of some of the best of Hans Christian Andersen, of *What the Moon Saw*.

The other chapter is about Tar and his sister Margaret. Margaret was feeling very nervous. As a matter of fact, Mrs. Moorhead was very sick and was going to die soon, and maybe they all knew about it, although they didn't admit it to each other. And, anyway, the Moorhead house wouldn't be a very good place for a girl to grow up in. She would get discouraged. Tar was a newsboy then; he went down to the trains and got the papers and delivered them at the houses of all the people who had ordered them. One night a bridge got washed out and the trains were late. Tar went down to the station for the 4.30 train to no purpose, and he tried again at 6 and 9. Then he meant to give it up and go to bed, but Margaret got all worked up and excited about

it. So they went back at 10, and again at 11, and
then they just stayed at the station and waited, though
the telegraph operator told them they were crazy
kids. The train came in at 1.30 and then they took
the papers and went all over town slipping them
under the people's doors, though the electric lights
were turned off and it was pouring with rain. And
they dared come home by the short cut through the
cemetery. . . .

It is a superb account of the intangible adventures
of youth and the mysterious satisfaction they give.

Certainly Mr. Sherwood Anderson is an unequal
writer and *Tar* is disfigured with flatness and sham
naïveté, but that does not, of course, affect my conviction that he has genius. Unequal writing is less
of a condemnation of an author than it ever was before, for the conditions in which modern writers
choose their mediums ensure that they shall constantly
be setting themselves difficulties which they cannot
always surmount. The people who wanted to write
about a man's private adventures, those that go on
within his own breast, used always to write verse.
But now they are impatient of using metre and
rhyme. They like to sport among the subtler
rhythms of prose. It would be interesting to know
how far that state of affairs has been produced by the
tremendous intensive training of the ear that has
been carried on during the last century by modern
music, whether the change in our faculties that makes
us accept Wagner's chords as normal didn't make us
reject the iambic pentameter as commonplace. Anyway, the transition has had the disadvantage that it
made the poet turn to the novel, which had had its

standards set when it was used by people with logical minds to tell a story; and unfortunately he very seldom has the courage to reject those standards altogether and to set up new ones.

Why could not Mr. Sherwood Anderson have written those passages by themselves, just for the glorious pattern of sight and sound and feeling that they are? The reason is that he is afraid somebody will ask, 'But what happened next? Isn't it rather pointless the way you've left it?' Certainly they would have had the right to ask that if what they were reading was a chapter about Tom Jones in a book whose aim was to be a history of Tom Jones. But they would be wrong if they asked that question after the last line of 'We'll go no more a-roving' or 'The Ode to the Nightingale.' Since something has been revealed by the poet which is true in eternity it is frivolous to ask him what happened to it in time.

That Mr. Anderson is wrong to listen to such inquiries has been proved by the fact that his art has always shown itself at its worst in his novels, at its best in short stories and the go-as-you-please rhapsodic form of *A Story Teller's Story*. When he follows his bent he may seem to be violating the traditions of fiction, but he is being loyal to the tradition of poetry, which after all is older and of greater importance: just as Mr. Sherwood Anderson, fussy and humourless and hell-bent on disharmony, as he often is, is nevertheless more important than half a dozen of the glibber novelists of the day, because of his vein of authentic inspiration.

'LET's see that there plank. . . . Anybody can see that this plank never was fit in building a boat. It is of that worthless red oak, just as the defendant says. It is knotty, cross-grained and rotten, and so full of wormholes that it's a wonder the boat was floated at all. Why, I could stick my finger through it! You can't fool me on those damned Kentucky boats! I was in command of one of the things once, and lost it by striking a yellow-bellied catfish! It must have been a catfish that I hit, because there wasn't anything else near, not a rock or a snag or a floating piece of wood; not even the cork out of a jug. Therefore I made up my mind that a catfish had flipped his tail up through the bottom. Now, Mr. Winchester, any man who will risk his goods in a Kentucky-built boat deserves to lose them. And this court finds for the defendant.'

That is magnificent English, resonant with the majesty of horse sense. That stern son of the voice of God, as Wordsworth so beautifully put it. So Fielding might have spoken if his Anglo-Saxon nature had been given just that accent which comes from the tensity of frontier life; and that, of course, is the secret of the fascination that pioneering America exerts over the English mind. The substance of being was the same – the determination to learn the nature of reality so that one is nobody's fool, and to build out of that knowledge as solid a home in the universe as may be. But the rhythm in which that being expressed itself is entirely new. Because of the necessity of spinning round on one's heel to see whether that was an Indian behind the tree-trunk, because of the necessity of pulling one's self round by some debauch of drinking or praying or gambling when some storm or famine had left one naked and helpless on the untamed plains, life marched to a quick and vehement measure. This Justice Richardson, trying a case on the banks of the Ohio River round about 1802, expressed himself with the brio of a high-booted, Czardas-dancing Magyar baron; but one may be sure his upper lip was long with loyalty to horse sense. The mind basks in this brief revelation of him, and pauses to note a possible explanation of why it is so difficult to write a convincing novel about rural life. This speech owes its power to the fact that it is weighted with sound knowledge of material substances which it must have taken a lifetime to acquire. Justice Richardson knew all there is to know about boats; about the function of a plank in a boat bottom; about Kentucky red oak; about catfish, rocks, snags and the Ohio River generally. It is significant that Thomas Hardy, who is one of the few novelists of rural life who can put into his characters' mouths speeches that have this characteristic note of authority, was the son of a village carpenter.

So one goes through this last book of Herbert Quick's, *Mississippi Steamboatin'*, which has been finished by Edward Quick. It is full of entrancing detail, from the description of that early ship-building which no sea-dock can surpass in romance — cedar canoes laden with bear's oil and wild honey, bullboats made of brown hide and willow frame,

hides sewn with sinew, seams sealed with buffalo fat
and ashes, keelboats manned by splendid toughs, who
let the best fighter among them wear a red feather in
his cap as sign of it, who thought nothing of landing
in a small river town and locking the burgesses in
their own jail while they made a good night of it, who
had no fear of other men. When the boat that carried
Louis Philippe and his two royal brothers on their
way from Pittsburgh to New Orleans got grounded,
the half-naked crew cried splendidly into the cabin:
'You kings down there! Show yourselves and do a
man's work and help us three-spots pull off this bar!'
One could eat this, as they say, with a spoon.

The pages glow, so much did Herbert Quick
love his material. His stuff is so lively that one's
imagination is constantly finding in it points of
departure for quite long journeys. One ponders
over the riddle of the existence of Mr. Thomas
Cushing, who 'before becoming a pilot was a well-
thought-of opera singer in New York.' Now, how
in the world did that happen? Was he by chance a
man with a perfectly literal mind and a double
character? Did a conductor he respected say to him
one day in a pet, 'You'd make a better Mississippi
pilot than an opera singer,' and did he, feeling a
little hurt but anxious to be reasonable and not be
silly about taking advice, immediately travel to
the Mississippi and start finding out? And were his
lost years deeply troubled because he never could
meet anybody with sufficient technical knowledge
in both arts to decide which he did best? And did
he die tortured by the impossibility of settling the
matter one way or the other? In my mind he has

done so. One sees his poor white face on his pillow, his blond whiskers neatly combed and trimmed, his bed-linen not greatly disarranged, for he was a mild and self-controlled man to the last, bewilderment drawing a deep line between his brows. He would have liked to know.

Mr. Thomas Cushing is from now on as real to me as anybody of whom I have ever read; and so too is Mr. H. A. Kidd, editor of the *New Orleans Crescent*. He was blown up in a way never before known, owing to his peculiar style. He was sitting on deck with another editor and he noticed a jet of steam and hot water coming out of the main pipe. 'I had never noticed anything of the kind before, and thought the occurrence very extraordinary. Just as I was about remarking this to Mr. Bigny I was suddenly lifted high in the air, how high it is impossible for me to say. I have a distinct recollection of passing rather irregularly through the air, enveloped, as it seemed to me, in a dense cloud, through which no object was discernible.' Watch him go. Sailing slowly up in the air, sailing slowly down to the water. His top-hat and Prince Albert undisturbed through it all. Gifted with what must be one of the most cunctatory styles in literary history, beside which Henry James's last manner seems to have the throbbing breathlessness of jazz, he describes for us a large number of persons being blown sky-high among the wreckage of an exploded steamer, being dropped into the waters of New Orleans harbour and being hauled on board another boat by rope lines, all at the pace at which King George and Queen Mary

ascend the steps to their thrones at the state opening of Parliament. The whole thing must have
taken at least twelve hours, on the most conservative
estimate.

When one has reluctantly finished this book, one
asks oneself a question. How is it that if Herbert
Quick loved his material so much that its pages
constantly come alive; that there walk out of not
too poignantly planned paragraphs living characters
like Justice Richardson of the long upper lip; Mr.
Cushing, of the blond whiskers and the eternal
doubt; and Mr. Kidd, of the unperturbed Prince
Albert; how is it that he was not an artist? For he
was never that. *The Hawkeye* and *Vandemark's
Folly* are both fully as enchanting as *Mississippi
Steamboatin'*, but they are not works of art. They
are indubitably uncreated. All that may be done
by forces here on earth is done, but the miracle
that comes only by the grace of heaven is not
accomplished.

Now usually when one perceives that a writer
has been given the power to bring work to life
and has intellectual structure, and yet cannot produce a work of art, one is tempted to ascribe it to
his lack of absorption in his material. He is not
writing about those characters of his because he is
interested in them, but for some secondary reason.
Either he is writing about them because he wants
to make his mind felt, and the novel is the way
intelligent young people do that nowadays; or he has
been brought up by admiring parents and professors
to write the Great American Novel; or he has made
some cardinal error in mapping the course of his

artistic life. But that isn't what was the matter with Herbert Quick. For the quality of delighted absorption in his subject is the very merit which makes his pages so endearing. There must be some other explanation.

One gets a hint of what that explanation may be if one turns to Miss Frances Newman's first novel, named with so sad an example of the higher wise cracking, *The Hard-Boiled Virgin*. (Though it is not really wise to read these two books together. They leave one with a confused impression that it is much pleasanter to go down the Mississippi in a steamboat than it is to be a virgin; which is a false antithesis.) Miss Newman has an amusing, Louise Fazenda-like literary personality, exerted in the fields of the indecorous. She hurls the sexual facts of life around like custard pies, marriage is pulled from under her like a chair. Her success as a clown draws attention again to one of the most curious miscalculations of the old nineteenth-century radicals. When they upheld the rights of literature to deal candidly with life they believed that they were liberating the tragic spirit; but it has turned out to be the comic spirit that has chiefly availed itself of the liberation. They hoped for more novels like *Jude the Obscure*. They have got *Gentlemen Prefer Blondes* and *The Hard-Boiled Virgin*.

It is true that Miss Newman is sometimes so ugly in her humour that one regrets any social change that facilitated it; there is a facetious account of a young girl's discovery that her brother had died of a venereal disease which has the romping moronic quality of a tabloid front page. But in the main,

The Hard-Boiled Virgin is a social satire which Miss Newman's very high degree of literary accomplishment helps her to polish to brilliance. One perceives her dexterity in the way she employs Matthew Arnold's trick of using a phrase again and again and again, till it accumulates significance like a snowball. Just as in one of his passages on the defects of modern urban civilization he builds a potent image of squalor simply by constantly harking back to a sentence out of a police-court report, 'Wragg is in custody,' so Miss Newman uses the phrase 'members of the Piedmont Driving Club' till it rings in one's ears like a knell for all the unfortunate Southern belles who have had to listen patiently while Southern gentlemen express 'confidence in all the faiths of their fathers concerning God and Women and Negroes and cotton,' because a woman must marry or had better be dead. As a study of the extreme discomforts and humiliations inflicted on women in any society where they are treated as the protected sex it can be put beside Mr. George Moore's study of similar conditions in Anglo-Irish society, *A Drama in Muslin*.

Nevertheless, it is not a work of art. The miracle does not happen. Yet Miss Newman, like Mr. Quick, writes with supreme gusto. Like him she knows the most delightful absorption in her material. But these so different writers are alike in that they are simple as children in the way they enjoy saying their piece. It occurs to one that there, perhaps, lies the secret of their failure to achieve art. They are both of them too simple. A work of art may be simple, though that is not necessary. There is

no logical reason why the camel of great art should
pass through the needle of mob intelligence; to consider the matter from the purely utilitarian point
of view, an artist might do humanity more good
than any other has ever done by work so complex
that only the six cleverest men in his country could
understand it, provided it was powerful enough to
affect them. In any case, the poems of John Donne
exist to prove that a poem can be as complicated
as a telephone exchange switchboard and yet indubitably great. But whatever a work of art may be,
the artist certainly cannot dare to be simple. He
must have a nature as complicated and as violent,
as totally unsuggestive of the word innocence, as
a modern war.

If one looks back at the Victorian novelists one
sees that in each case their art was lifted out of their
nature by the force of internal conflicts just as
islands are lifted out of the waters by subaqueous
earthquakes. Charles Dickens wrote because he was
a snob, who, when he was the world's darling, could
blush if he was reminded that a kind old gentleman had given him a half-crown tip twenty years
before. He found he could escape from the loathed
circumstances of his being by exercising his faculty
of impersonation; by pouring his vitality into the
creation of character after character, with which
for the time being he could identify himself. That
was the secret of his virtue as an artist; just as
the secret of his vice was his determination to use
every device of overloading his books with diffuse,
incomprehensible, mutually destructive plots so that
his imagined world never would crystallize into

coherence, lest it should reveal itself as governed by the same laws as the real coherent world, and he should be born again into obscurity and contempt.

Thackeray also used impersonation for escape from a world he found intolerable for different reasons. It was his nature to inquire without fear into the nature of things; but just how much he feared what Victorian society would do if he gave his nature liberty, may be judged from the paper in which he bickers at Dean Swift in a voice raucous with envy of a man with a similar temperament who had had the luck to be born in a century that was admiring of satire. He was also vexed by his married life. His wife had been taken from him by an illness of a tragic sort which necessitated a separation, and he was obliged to live a celibate life, which he could correct only by temperate friendships with his wife's friends or furtive loves with women grossly his inferior. So he scattered his soul among the Crawleys and the Newcomes and the Esmonds, allowing his work to assume a nearer approach to coherence than Dickens could because his youthful nerves had not been frayed to cowardice by a sense of social inferiority. And Anthony Trollope was in a more acidulated state of fury than any of them, for he hated his spirited, roving, financially unstable mother with that unsurpassable hatred that a man deficient in virility feels for a woman who is the better man. He fled from his loathing of his being and its origin into an endless round of impersonations all having their being in that world of respectability from which he felt his angularly raffish mother had debarred him.

These were not men, they were battlefields. And over them, like the sky, arched their sense of harmony, their sense of the beauty and rest against which their misery and their struggles were an offence, to which their misery and their struggles were the only approaches they could make, of which their misery and their struggles were an integral part. Over the battlefield that was Anthony Trollope there was not enough sky. He was so absorbed in the conflict arising out of his hatred for his mother that he had no energy left for sensitiveness to the flux of life in general. That is why, though he wrote better than Dickens and Thackeray, though the passages concerning the parson suspected of theft in *The Last Chronicles of Barsetshire* beat Flaubert and Maupassant at their own game, he does not rank as such a considerable artist. It is necessary to have both things, the battlefield and the sky.

It occurs to one that the trouble with Mr. Quick is that he had not enough battlefield, the trouble with Miss Newman is that she has not enough sky. One imagines that Mr. Quick had a clear and happy nature, which could make its adaptations to life fairly easily. All that he needed was the picturesqueness of American pioneering history, probably as a compensation for the tedium of this automobile age, and he got it. He opened his books, he visited his chosen terrain, and there it was. The process was finished almost before it was begun. There was no necessity for the sweating adjustments of creation. Miss Newman, on the other hand, is as absorbed as Anthony Trollope in her conflict. It delights her to contemplate an absurd society in the act of rejecting one whose superiority has led her long ago to reject them with a finality and a contempt of which they are comically unaware, and to go a step farther and to make Katherine Faraday, when she does lose her virginity, find the physical facts of the relationship between men and women as tedious as the social system centring round the Piedmont Driving Club, and thus again put herself in the proud position of one who cannot be rejected because she has rejected. She will be completely satisfied if she can adroitly and amusingly enlarge on that theme. There is for her also no necessity for the sweating adjustments of creation. She has got what she wanted. But she has got, alas! — except for that superfluous possession, that dreadful tabloid quality, the eruptions of which make one at times furiously resent Mr. Cabell's linking of her name with that of Elinor Wylie in the publisher's blurb — very little else.

As the name of the author suggests, Mr. Van Loon's *America* is a work of the Dutch School. Every page reminds us of the cleanliness and the brightness and the neatness of Holland. The innumerable facts are piled up as tidily as the red cheeses in the market-place of Alkmaar; phases of history lie as clearly defined as the fields of different sorts of bulbs on the plains; the scenes and the characters appear before us in the gay colours, clear as children's eyes, that show under the temperate sunshine of that not too northern sky. There are no heights here, no moments of inspiration; but there is the very best use that can be made of the flat-lands. And there is abundant evidence of that fastidiousness which makes for spotless little cities with cobbled streets as clear as the untrodden clouds, for houses where mice die for want in midst of plenty and the furniture shines as if it were made of mirror and had grown dark only because of the super-position of reflections through the centuries.

This, of course, is the quality that gives distinction to Mr. Van Loon's cartoons, which far more than these popular histories are what make one hold him high. In each of them he sees some insincerity that has crept into contemporary life, decides that if he is to live there the place must be kept clean, and out this thing must go. So he takes up his broom and sweeps it out into the gutter. His movements are not light, they are not very graceful, but they are immensely effective. That particular piece of ordure has gone. One's world is cleaner. One feels towards him, therefore, a gratitude of a curiously personal nature, as if he performed some basically essential service to the community and was as truly useful as the iceman. Other writers may excite more lively emotions, but they come in on a lower level of indispensability; say, for most of them, along with the piano-tuner.

This quality of blunt and energetic fastidiousness is active enough in Mr. Van Loon's book on America to tackle the main insincerity of history, which is to disclaim nervously the economic motive. For some reason a nation feels as shy about admitting that it ever went forth to war for the sake of more wealth as a man would about admitting that he had accepted an invitation just for the sake of the food. This is one of humanity's most profound imbecilities, as perhaps the only justification for asking one's fellow-men to endure the horrors of war would be the knowledge that if they did not fight they would starve. And it gets short shrift in Mr. Van Loon's discussion of the forces leading to the European competition for settlements in the New World, of the War of Independence, of the War of 1812, of the Civil War. There is no muckraking here; there is none of that automatic response to all human activities in the words, 'Aw, it's all bunk,' which is perhaps the most pernicious and certainly the least helpful way of talking bunk. Simply he recognizes the primal necessities of mankind, and when he is showing you round the house he opens the door and says with a proper emphasis, 'This is the kitchen.'

Nevertheless, at times a certain insincerity succeeds in getting past Mr. Van Loon's broom. It is the very powerful insincerity of over-simplification, and oddly enough though Mr. Van Loon was born and brought up in Europe, it manifests itself more in its handling of European affairs than it does when he writes of America. What is the use, for example, of writing that, 'Most unfortunately for them (the Indians) the discovery of Columbus came at the very moment when the Spaniards, after about six hundred years of uninterrupted warfare, had just driven the last of the Mohammedan caliphs out of their own country. Spain was still full of that strange crusading spirit which is ready to commit the most hideous crimes in the name of the most exalted of religions'? What is the use of repeating without explanation that the Spanish commander who put to the sword the entire Huguenot community founded in Florida by Admiral de Coligny said that he did it, 'not because they were French, but because they were Protestants'?

It is of course true that the Spanish were cruel beyond belief in their persecution of heretics within the confines of the kingdom and overseas. John Addington Symonds, in an interesting passage in his *History of the Renaissance in Italy*, puts them down as preeminently the cruellest nation in medieval or Renaissance Europe; which was going some. But it is also true that this cruelty was an inevitable result of their history. Islam had conquered Spain and had maintained itself there through centuries and during that time had produced a very profound culture. But it was not in the least Christian bigotry which laboured to expel the Moors and destroy that culture. The weakness which led to their defeat made them deserve to be defeated. The caliphs were beaten because they had never attained unity among themselves and broke their front by savage struggles among themselves. They kept Spain in a bloodstained state of inter-tribal warfare in which no one, least of all the common man, labouring on his patch of land, could know security. Horsemen coming down the road might mean that his head stayed on his shoulders just another five minutes, or that he and his family wandered from a smoking farmstead to a delayed death on the hills. It was to rid themselves of this barbarian insecurity, to be sure of their bread and their breath, that the Spaniards drove out the Moors.

Since Rome was, in indisputable fact, the centre of what they saw in the real world around them corresponding to the ideal of social order which had inspired them to revolt, it is not surprising that they should attach a certain importance to the Roman religion. It is also not surprising that their minds established a correspondence between the fact that the caliphs were heretics and they had misgoverned. And in that, it must be said, they were probably right. Islam certainly did not mitigate the wars of its followers by any counsels of mercy, and may well have inhibited the development of such parts of their mind as might develop such ideals as social order. For the strong point of Christianity is that it has always aroused in its believers a keen sense of personal guilt, which in its turn has aroused in them a desire to gain salvation by expiatory works of body and mind. The Christian therefore explores all avenues of advancement, even such as lead to worlds of abstraction and altruism not too congenial to the gross spirit of man, but a necessary habitation if any theory of social order is to be enforced. Islam, however, tells its followers that they are fine fellows, just as they are, and if they only obey the Army regulations are sure to be saved. The Islamite has naturally enough taken him at his word and is content to be the type of fine fellow to which Mohammed addressed this assurance, to live in the same concrete world, simply furnished with such tangibilities as sound and sun, war and women.

So when the Spaniards persecuted heretics they may have been crude, but they were not being unreasonable or unpractical. They were at least wiser than the people of to-day who pretend that it does not matter what a man believes, as who should say that the flavour and digestibility of a pudding will have nothing to do with its ingredients. It would probably be an excellent thing for the future of the United States if every time a manufacturer confessed to a success magazine that his favourite writer was Frank Crane, the populace cried out among itself, 'Disaster will fall upon our community if all these means of production are in the hands of a man who can swallow such bunk, who is happy in contact with mental processes so antithetical to those which we know to be productive of culture and civilization,' and conducted an auto-da-fé at the nearest filling station. Nor were the Spaniards altogether unreasonable in their lack of discrimination against heresies, in their persecution of Jews and Protestants as well as Mohammedans. Considering the general level of intelligence at the time, as the only established social order they had seen when they were fighting it out with the Moslem was the product of Roman Catholicism, that was the only faith it was safe to tolerate.

The thing, of course, went grotesquely worse and worse. The consequence of six centuries of warfare is that military men assume a position of too great importance in the country, which is always a mistake, not because they are men of blood, but because they lead too exemplary lives of industry and devotion to duty. The business of the statesman is to form sound general ideas, and that cannot be done by people who specialize early in an exacting profession. The same reason makes business men's pronouncements on political matters hardly ever worthy of attention. Furthermore, such a situation created the need of a strong unifying dynasty, and it is hard to have that without some time sooner or later producing a king who takes his job seriously and treats the more or less urgent need that brought him into being as a sacred mission that he can make himself a half-god by fulfilling.

Then, under the stimulus of that semi-religious imperialism, the killing habit, which has been established as a matter of physical necessity, becomes a grandiose delight. It begins to satisfy the need of the soul which, if life is to continue, must go hungry. There is in every one of us an unending see-saw between the will to live and the will to die. We can make a false sublimation of the will to die if we kill others, if we feed death with them in our stead. This dark and idiotic impulse is for ever with us; it stands beside us whenever we have to handle the means of punishment, assuring us that not only are we serving our immediate end, but buying a more profound salvation, and that it can be done again. That is why there has never been a period in history when there have been necessary killings which has not been instantly followed by a period when there have been unnecessary killings. This force is not easily to be suppressed, once unnatural death has been invoked.

There was surely an attempt on the part of the Spanish to control it, in the way the examination of the heretics was left to the Church. There was a shuddering repulsion of the soul at its own black content in the relinquishment of the prey to the mediator, 'You are the representative of justice and of mercy. I will not kill him unless you say I should.' But too often that plea for cancellation of the business in hand was only a brief barrier between the soul and its service of death and unreason, because this unformulable force is too strong for any formulated faith, and can speak its decision through lips and heart sincerely dedicated to life and holiness. This drama was not of man's choosing; it should not be used for an easy reproach against man.

This oppression which came thus early on the spirit of Spain, which has left it through the succeeding centuries too sick, too weak to speak save when genius fills it like a deep breath and it speaks with a voice which is like no other, is a warning that it matters not what natural endowment a race may have if it prostitutes itself to the service of death, whether in the name of religion, law and order, or whatever might quite possibly be treated in a sum-mary way by an artist of the Dutch School because of its remoteness from his cheerful scope.

But Mr. Van Loon indulges in just as thoroughgoing an over-simplification of the issue when he deals with the relatively trivial questions of the attitude of the English towards the United States in the War of Independence and the Civil War. Just as he treats the Spanish persecution of heretics as if it were due to an isolated factor of cruelty, so he treats the English provocations towards America as if they were due to an equally isolated factor of insolent stupidity. This is not to say that he loses for one moment his scrupulous fairness, for he represents the revolt and the resistance to it without sentimentality as the inevitable economic protests that they were. But he also represents the ineptitudes of Grenville and North as if they proceeded from a pure inability to count, comprehend, or indeed do anything but be rude; and as if they were in power because England liked that sort of thing.

Yet surely it is of the greatest importance to make clear that the blithering incompetence of English statesmen during the War of Independence was a consequence, and the final death-blow in the English mind, of the aristocratic system of government. There has never been an aristocracy formed in more apparently ideal conditions than the English governing class, which came into being under the Tudors with the economic resources of the expanding empire to give them wealth to buy leisure, and the powerful intellectual stimulus of the Reformation to make them use it in creative activity. Yet it deteriorated. It is not given to man to make efforts to deserve power when he is born to the certain enjoyment of power; it is not given to him to feel the need of raising himself above criticism if no censure can remove him from his position. The principle of avoiding the unnecessary expenditure of energy has enabled the species to survive in a world full of stimuli; but it prevents the survival of the aristocrat. The War of Independence was one of the most important proofs England received that this particular governmental experiment she had been trying was a failure; and so far from liking the manner in which those who failed conducted themselves, they made as memorable a legislative manifestation of resentment against it as the world has ever seen. For the trouble England went to in the succeeding century to establish the machinery of democracy was not merely a libertarian cantrip, it was just as much a practical and remedial measure as mending the roof when the rain comes in.

In Mr. Van Loon's treatment of the English attitude to the Civil War he over-simplifies as much on an even more profound but just as important an issue. He represents the undoubted fact that a great many people in England, comprising perhaps a majority of the governing class, were on the side of the South as also proceeding from an isolated factor of insolent stupidity. He cites: 'The tactful speech of William Ewart Gladstone (the eminent theologian) wherein this official member of Her Majesty's Government suggested that England recognize "the nation which that great statesman, Jefferson Davis, has so successfully founded on the other side of the ocean."' Now, one is walking in a wild garden, not laid out by the plumb-line of logic, when one explores the mind of William Ewart Gladstone, who was temperamentally as like William Jennings Bryan as makes no matter, an inflamed fundamentalist who would unhesitatingly have become an atheist if any of the Divine Persons had contradicted his cosmogony of Genesis, and a startling disproof of Mr. Van Loon's theory that America differentiates itself from the nations by its subjection to oratory. To such usages one wants a clue. And one gets a clue when one remembers that Mr. Gladstone came from a family of West Indian planters whose fortune had been founded on slavery, and who, though they had given up their slaves with a good grace, had undoubtedly suffered grave personal inconvenience by doing so. Certain disagreeable considerations as to the consequences of principles when acted upon, particularly along economic lines, were therefore much alive in him, and indeed in the whole possessive class at the time. The establishment of the machinery of democracy had had to be justified by argument in the course of which certain broad propositions had had to be laid down: and there was a strong movement on the part of conscientious members of the governing classes who thought they had a moral duty to be consistent, and on the part of the urbanized labouring population which the industrial revolution had created, to apply these propositions not only politically but economically and socially, so that Jack should be as good as his master.

Now, it was not settled then whether a civilization can exist except as on a basis of slave labour.

In point of historic fact no great civilization ever has. So the upper and middle classes of England were perfectly right in regarding themselves as engaged in an extremely hazardous experiment. Indeed, even to-day we could not answer them with assurances that would wholly satisfy them that their fears had been without foundation. It would certainly have been easier, from a materialist point of view, to conduct the Great War if one could have filled the munition factories with slaves instead of unshackled and organized labour; it would have been easier, too, to conduct the economic reconstruction of Europe. And the desire that many people in the United States have to keep immigrants so far as possible out of full enjoyment of citizenship is a recognition of these facts. Another element which made England feel peculiarly unhappy was that she was by a long way the pioneer in that kind of social reform. She was the dog on which it was being tried. In such a moment no wonder the South, happily enjoying the extremest form of the renounced arrangement of labour, seemed a morsel of the Lost Paradise which ought to be preserved at any cost. Moreover there was just then a strong feeling against coloured people, owing to the Indian Mutiny. It is true that a Hindu is not a Negro; but on the other hand a black brother is a black brother, and any confusion that leads to the feeling that we whites are the elect and uniquely deserving of good treatment is apt to be retained without criticism.

Now the reason that this over-simplification in Mr. Van Loon's work is more than a sin of omission is that it bolsters up the perfectly preposterous attitude with which he ends his book. In the last two chapters he informs his readers that Europe has been a failure, and, for the discreditable reason that it 'made the accumulation of Inanimate Matter the highest of all civic virtues,' is now in a state of 'chaos. Chaos, complete and absolute.' It appears that the end of the war left America with the discovery that 'evidently something was wrong with the world. By an accursed turn of luck, or by the grace of a merciful God, the American people were called upon to set it right. We can take our choice. But upon our answer depends a great deal more than the future of our own people.

One's eyebrows shoot up into one's hair as one reads that 'our nation, our country, the fortunate strip of land which we call our own, by a strange turn of fate has been called upon to be the guardian of the human race.' Surely N. B. this is a goke, as Artemus Ward used to say.

But it is quite without irony that Mr. Van Loon attempts to induce a Messiah complex in the younger generation. It is true that he does not do it in any spirit of militant Babbittry, that he is emphatic for the scrapping of all standards based on material success; but nevertheless his suggestion is explicitly that somehow or other the world is to be saved. How the world, on hearing that she is once more to be saved, must shudder and wish that she could get some one to double for her in these really dangerous acts!

This is very dangerous false doctrine. To begin with, it is time that people began to ask themselves what exactly they mean when they talk this nonsense about the failure of Europe. By the test of what success can it be said to have failed? Where is the continent that can regard as inferior in achievement the soil which has produced Plato, Aristotle, Aeschylus, Sophocles, Euripides, Virgil, Horace, St. Thomas Aquinas, Spinoza, Kant, Hegel, Dante, Shakespeare, Cervantes, Goethe, Beethoven, Mozart, Wagner, among other local talent? Where is the continent which has the right to look at the beautiful cities of Rome, Paris and Venice and Florence and Innsbruck and Salzburg and Toledo and Seville and Arles and Nîmes and say, 'We have built better than that'? Where is the continent which has the right to look on the parliamentarianism of England, on the industrial organization of Germany, on the perfected commonwealth of Denmark, on the gracious social life of France, and say, 'We have done better'? It is not marked on the map, that superior continent. Is there some other reason for judging Europe a failure? Is it because there was a great war, and she suffered horribly? That is a point of view which would be justifiable only if the war had been evitable.

But to regard peace as something which Europe might have had and wantonly chose not to have is naïvely to ignore every important aspect of the phase of the world's being which is called Europe for short. The work it has done in building up civilization and culture, that is to say in dragging life out of the night where it is suffered into the daylight where it is understood, was bound to be accompanied by strong passions: because only strong passions can supply the dynamic force which enables man to proceed to these activities in despite of the inertia which

makes him leave things as they are. Such emotional
disturbances are bound to unleash the primitive
fantasies at the back of the mind; and peace could
only be the result of these unleashings if in the
human organism the will to live had an overwhelming ascendancy over the will to die. There is no
reason to suppose that this ascendancy exists; indeed,
it would obviously be a calamity if it did, since it
would make the performance of the biological duty
to die infinitely more painful to the individual.

This tendency of the drama not to produce peace
was of course heightened by the special difficulties of
the problems it had to solve. The supreme importance and complication of that problem which centres
round Rome, for example—the problem of how far
one can attain stability of living without stopping
the natural flux of life—was bound to engender panic
and violence in those who puzzled their heads over
it. There was also the overwhelming difficulty that
in this world where it is hard to understand those
within arm's length, even those within our arms, it
is nearly impossible to understand those within our
arms, it is nearly impossible to understand those
who are beyond our sight, who are not explained to
us by ties of birth or the contact of the flesh. For
England to have understood the American revolutionaries, for the American revolutionaries to have
understood England, would have presupposed a
diffusion of imagination among the populations
which would have made them nations of artists:
which is an impossible dream. International relationships are, therefore, preordained to be clumsy
gestures based on imperfect knowledge, and since

peace is determined by international relationships, this is to say that until man had attained an amazing pitch of virtuosity in distinguishing his instinctive follies from his instinctive wisdom and in circumventing them, frequent war was preordained.

If we say that Europe is a failure because out of these battles against the immensest forces with imperfect instruments there came war, then we are applying the name of failure to an essential character of human life. We had better call it effort; and not delude a continent with the hope that if it be full of goodwill it can immediately divest its own life of this character; or cheat it of the just reason for pride it will have in the pattern that character will trace upon its pages.

I n the course of a poem by John Davidson called 'A Ballad of Hell' the damned souls are represented as 'amazed to find that they could cheer.' Something of their amazement, at the jerky fulfilling of a neglected function, I feel to-day. I am amazed to find that I can blush. My sensations, interesting as they are in themselves, I shall probably deal with elsewhere under the title of 'A Forgotten Sport'; my point now is their surprising origin. For they are caused by a volume named *Charles Rex*, by a writer named Miss Ethel M. Dell, who has received every sort of acclamation save only the morning stars singing together; and I doubt if one worries about the lack of super-terrestrial recognition when one can sell nearly half a million copies of a single novel. It is, moreover, a volume that I was predisposed to regard with affection, because of this paragraph on its first page: –

'Saltash turned and surveyed the skyline over the yacht's sail with obvious discontent on his ugly face. His eyes were odd, one black, one gray, giving a curiously unstable appearance to a countenance which otherwise might have claimed to possess some strength. His brows were black and deeply marked. He had a trick of moving them in conjunction with his thoughts, so that his face was seldom in absolute repose. It was said that there was a strain of royal blood in Saltash, and in the days before he had succeeded to the title, when he was merely Charles Burchester, he had borne the nickname of "the merry

monarch". Certain wild deeds in a youth that had
not been beyond reproach had seemed to warrant
this, but of later years a friend has bestowed a more
gracious title upon him, and to all who could claim
intimacy with him he had become "Charles Rex".
The name fitted him like a garment. A certain arrogance, a certain royalty of bearing, both utterly unconscious and wholly unfeigned, characterized him.
Whatever he did — and his actions were often far
from praiseworthy — this careless distinction of mien
always marked him. He received an almost involuntary respect wherever he went.'

It is pleasant to say that Charles Rex keeps up his
form to the end. He habitually said 'egad' and used
'terrible foreign oaths' and broke into French,
though that concussion rarely extends to anything
more than the word *mais*; he 'dismissed the waiter
with a jerk of his eyebrows'; and when dining at
home said to the butler, 'I'm going to smoke on the
ramparts' where his acres lay below him . . . took
the cigar from his mouth and spoke ironically,
grimly, 'There is your kingdom, Charles Rex!' he
said. And in every line that is written about him
one hears the thudding, thundering hooves of a certain steed at full gallop; of the true Tosh-horse. For
even as one cannot walk on one's own trudging,
diligent feet if one desires to attain to the height of
poetry, but must mount Pegasus, so one cannot reach
the goal of best selling by earnest pedestrianism, but
must ride thither on the Tosh-horse. No one can
write a best-seller by taking thought. The slightest
touch of insincerity blurs its appeal. The writer who

keeps his tongue in his cheek, who knows that he is
writing for fools and that, therefore, he had better
write like a fool, may make a respectable living out
of serials and novelettes; but he will never make the
vast, the blaring, half a million success. That comes
of blended sincerity and vitality. It is true that in the
past a very great success could be attained by writers
who had not this latter qualification. It could not be
maintained that either Annie S. Swan or Joseph
Hocking had more vitality than a horse-drawn tram-
car; but they caught a public nearly extinct nowadays, but enormously numerous all over England at
the time they began to write, which had not yet cast
off the Puritan restrictions imposed by the Non-
conformist wave of the late eighteenth and early
nineteenth centuries. This public wanted to read
fiction, but felt uneasy in doing so unless it had an
appearance of religious and moral propaganda.

But the rest of the best-sellers have, like the toad,
a jewel in the head: this jewel of demoniac vitality.
Marie Corelli had a mind like any milliner's apprentice; but she was something much more than a
milliner's apprentice. When one turns over her pages
one comes on delicious sentences – such as the description of the bad man who made a reputation as a
wit by dint of stealing a few salacious witticisms
from Molière and Baudelaire – which make one see
that here was some one who was sure, in rather a
different sense from Stevenson's, that since the world
is so full of a number of things we ought all to be as
happy as kings. Her incurably commonplace mind
was incapable of inaccurately surveying life, but
some wild lust for beauty in her made her take a wild

inventory of the world's contents and try to do what
it could with them. What a gallant try this Molière-
Baudelaire sentence is to do something with some
hearsay story of vice wearing at times an iridescence,
and of French authors writing wicked books! She
rode the Tosh-horse at full gallop; and so, too, did
Sir Hall Caine. Nothing in the history of literature
is more pathetic than the career of this man who,
thrown in his youth into the society of the Pre-
Raphaelites, realized that they had brought into being a lovely and exciting world of the imagination,
and for the rest of his life tried to bring such a world
into being himself by writing immense novels about
illegitimate half-brothers called by the same Christian
name, who, owing to an exact resemblance, serve
each other's sentences in Portland, while all the
female characters become nuns. The best-sellers of
a later day are milder, less interesting stuff; but
theirs, too, is that same source of power. It was impossible to meet Charles Garvice without realizing
that here was a dynamic good man; and his abundant
eupeptic benevolence forced itself through to the
printed word and gave a real warmth to the scenes
where the kindly earl, anxious to make his son's
mill-girl bride feel at home, took the entrée dish
from the butler and helped her with his own hand.
Heaven knows how in the tepid pages of *The Rosary*
its million readers detected the power that lived in
Mrs. Florence Barclay, that made her physically
radiant as a young girl when she was a woman of
sixty and permitted her to enjoy complete confidence
that she was directly inspired by the Holy Ghost;
but it must have leaked through by some channel.

(In trying to understand the appeal of best-sellers, it is well to remember that whistles can be made sounding certain notes which are clearly audible to dogs and other of the lower animals, though man is incapable of hearing them.) Even Mr. A. S. M. Hutchinson, grey and unexuberant as his pages may seem, has this same secret. Throughout *This Freedom* he keeps up the same high level of innocence and idiocy; at the end, as at the beginning, he leans o'er the gold bar of Heaven and the straws in his hair are seven. But of this modern company Miss Dell is a queen. She rides the Tosh-horse hell-for-leather. Positively at the most thrilling moments (of which I prefer the moment when the new Lady Saltash, exceptionally light on her feet owing to early training as a circus-rider, springs out upon the ledge of the family ramparts because she wearies of the way that Lord Saltash has neglected to consummate their marriage, and only steps back when he explains that he has pursued this policy because of spiritual awakening caused by a remark the poor girl had thoughtlessly made to the effect that he had made her believe in God) one feels as if one might be ridden down.

But I blush, and I wonder. This is the story of a middle-aged voluptuary who, when he is cruising about the Mediterranean, comes on an Italian hotel proprietor beating a page-boy, and interrupts the sport. That night he finds the boy concealed as a stowaway on the yacht, and immediately realizes — though he keeps silence — that here is a girl in disguise. For five chapters the story titillates us (us includes, one amazedly estimates, the mass of the population of Surbiton, Bournemouth, and Cheltenham) with a description of the peculiar intercourse that takes place between them in these circumstances. There is a specially pleasing incident when they are playing cards and the girl-boy cheats, and Lord Saltash beats her with a riding-switch. We afterwards learn that she had cheated on purpose that she might have this delicious revelation of the gentleman's quality. There is a collision at sea; the girl's disguise necessarily comes to an end. Lord Saltash sends her to a woman friend to be educated for polite society. Thereafter the story becomes a record of the interest felt by various persons in the question of whether this girl is or is not a virgin. Her fiancé comes to the conclusion that she is not, owing to the fact that a visitor recognizes her as having been a page-boy at the Italian hotel, and precipitately casts her off; although a life of immorality which involves posing as a page-boy in an Italian hotel must have been something so rich and strange that few of us could forbear to pause and inquire. She then marries Lord Saltash, and great play is made with the fact that the marriage is not consummated. The book ends with the approach to the consummation. These figures are dummies; but they are very completely finished dummies.

God forbid that any book should be banned. The practice is as indefensible as infanticide. But one begins to remember what books have been banned during the last few years. Mr. D. H. Lawrence's sincere and not for one second disgusting *The Rainbow*; Mr. Neil Lyons's beautifully felt *Cottage Pie*; *Brute Gods*, that astringent product of Mr. Louis

Wilkinson's unique talent. How true it is that there are those who may not look at a horse over a hedge; and there are those who may lead it out through the gate. There are now at least two sights which must fill the heart of any serious English writer with wistfulness. One is when he looks back over the gulf of time and sees Anatole France being entertained by the Royal Literary Society and utilizing the opportunity to kiss Sir Edmund Gosse. For he may be fairly certain that had he written the *Histoire Comique* and the *Mannequin d'Osier* and *L'Anneau d'Améthyste* he would not have had the opportunity to kiss Sir Edmund Gosse. Far from it. Rather would he have the opportunity to try to see the good side of the Lord Mayor of London or some stipendiary magistrate with simple and stupid views of public morality and the decency imposed upon the printed word. The other sight is when he gazes across the esplanade of any watering-place and looks at the old ladies reading their Ethel Dells. Truly we are a strange nation.

THIS summer I am living on the French Riviera, which does not mean what you might think it must. One alights at a station at which only the slowest trains ever stop, and walks through a little village which has the disorder of a studio, whose inhabitants move about with the slouching and dishevelled aspect of artists at work, and have a right to look so, since they are practising an art in merely living; for they eat better meals than equivalent people anywhere else in the world, they sleep in softer beds with better linen, they design their days like pictures, balancing as in a skilful composition the human need for leisure against the human power and necessity to pay for leisure by work. Leaving behind its rubbish heaps that are like the twisted paint-tubes by the easel, one takes a coast road which winds among rocks that are rose-red, and red with the discretion of the rose, so that they do not quarrel with the blue sea at their base any more than the rose quarrels with the green leaf lower on the stem. Landwards there are hills, low but emphatic as mountains in form, covered with heathy growths which under grey northern skies would be a patchwork of warm colour, but is like pale tweed under this intense white light, which beats down colour as if it were conscious that itself is a synthesis of all colours and is proud of it. Here and there are pinewoods, growing more sparsely than they do in Germany and in Scotland, as if this most rationalist of countries was going to stand no nonsense of the Erl-King or the Lady of the Lake type. And here and there are tiered and galleried quarries of porphyry, grey-blue like old-fashioned blotting-paper.

Presently one comes on a fold in the countryside where the land does not stand up in forms immutable and uncultivable as cast-iron mouldings, where it assumes the softness of a cloak dropped from the shoulders. Here the water, such as there is here in the south in summer, seeps down from the hard hills. Here it is possible to grow trees, to have a garden. The road begins to run between villas. Over the first wall on the landward side looks an oleander, bending forth in the pose of a wife who has run to the end of the garden to see if her dear husband is nearing home; but the quality of its bright pink handsomeness is such that one is surprised by its domesticity, imagines a prelude to it of a different sort, and finds oneself remarking with a sage air that marriages of that kind often turn out well enough. There is a prodigious gate in this wall, a complication of trellis-work which must have been made by a man who thought a cutlet-frill was beautiful; but pushing it back one finds oneself under the strong, sober guardianship of palm-trees. Six stand on either side of the path. By night the trunks of them look like the naked bodies of Nubian slaves.

By day they look like armoured pillars in some Eastern palace; an arrow might fly through the interstices between the bronze-coloured plates, and some brown agility step forth from a sliding panel to work some subtle mutilation on the kill. Their long sharp-edged leaves remind one of swords, of fans; they imply a tyrant to be fanned, to slay for, to be slain, they imply a land too hot for a man to live in unless he can make other people wait on him, where for that favourable position there is a ding-dong battle waged with weapons twice the height of a man and tortures leading the imagination of man twice as far as it is wise to go, where one may train great black slaves to noiseless waiting on one's wants by any means, by scaring them with wounds and setting red ants to people those wounds, but where they learn their lesson so well that at the last they come quite noiselessly between one and the door into the secret passage which one had had dug against the risk of overthrowal.

I never open that gate and step into the blackness which they maintain beneath them like a trust, letting through only slivers of sunlight or moonlight shaped like scimitars and glittering like metal, because of the profundity of the surrounding shadow, without being glad that they made the initial error which makes me not need to fear them, at the dawn of creation when all life had to choose whether to be animal and mobile or vegetable and immobile. There was some trouble saved us then by certain renunciations. If the synthesis of forces which is the red rose had chosen to be animal, if it had pushed its way along the strains into humanity, to what powerful a compulsion of love would our poor hearts have been exposed! And if the synthesis of forces which is the palm-tree had expressed itself in terms of the animal, had it stayed beast there would have been so much of the wild less easily conquerable, had it become man, there would have been a considerable increase of occasions when the weak found argument useless. It would not have qualified itself by melting into the common flood of humanity. The rose would have done that, one is certain; there would have been those in whom the strain was nearly pure, whose lives would have consisted of romances exquisite and numerous as petals, and as easily detachable from the parent stem; but there would also have been those not beautiful, not gifted, but fortunate in their hearts, in whom a slight trace of it had the wistful but powerful fragrance of the last drop in the scent-bottle. But the palm-soul would have kept itself apart, would have made itself a separate people, a race. Followers of the Prophet, without a doubt. Islam might not have been so politically impotent, so merely a rattling of lances across the map, had this choice been made.

Behind them one sees, as one walks up to the house, the dusty shadow, pierced only by lean tree-trunks, which is a southern garden. These palm-mercenaries charge for the shade they cast by drinking the earth dry for yards around, so that there can be no flowers or grass. But these are not wanted here. One requires flowers in northern climates because one wants to set colour against the prevalent grey-ness, green grass to contrast with neutral mould, but here darkness alone can balance the prevalent light, and since the characteristic of the soil in these parts is that it is broken by heat into gritty particles, the impalpability of shadow is the most pleasing contrast to it. The aridity is quite by design. There is indeed nothing at all accidental about this place. There are no palm-trees, there is a clearing which permits the fullest pouring of sunshine down on the preposterous flight of concrete steps which rises from the avenue to the house, taking forms which no steps can lawfully assume, exhibiting bevelled edges which belong properly only to dressing-table sets and whirls inappropriate to any substance except whipped cream.

That staircase is not only illuminated, it is illuminating. For immediately on seeing it one perceives in that unnumbered dimension which is the imagination the figure of the architect who designed it and who chose the incredible gate. So solid does it appear that almost it obscures some of the trails of bougainvillea that surround the glass doors with snippets of pale magenta paper: a tall and slender personage carrying himself with a deliberate stoop because the early nineteenth century Romantics' convention of a connection between phthisis and the arts has never been repudiated in provincial France, wearing a moustache which trails like a delicate fern, a flowing tie which says he is an artist, a wildness of the pupil of the eye which says the same thing as the tie, and is as purely an arranged external device. There is just a suggestion of repressed but dominant horse-sense about him — say, in that retracted but abundant paunch which shows that he loves good food — to distinguish him from the handsome shabby goose who recites his lame verses in the cafés; there is just that to account for his being employed by the architect, to account for his building fantastic and comfortable houses.

According to the laws of this most mysterious dimension, one perceives at one and the same time this solid figure which is not there, and the main events of his fatuous but not contemptible life. He

discovered himself an artist because of his mother's
and grandmother's fond exclamations on his sensitivity. He studied his art in the nineties and was
immensely excited by *l'Art Nouveau*, that curious
movement towards distortion of form which tried to
give all objects of common use from houses down to
hairpins aspects of the totally irrelevant, piercing a
turret with gaping ellipses like the mouths of marine
animals, giving a staircase a balustrade as strange as
the skeleton of a dinosaur, going down to the sea to
find decorations for objects peculiarly of the land,
back to the past to find shapes for objects peculiarly
of the present. He and his wife ventured on the long
journey to Paris which at that time must have lasted
the full twenty-four hours for those who could not
afford seats in the *rapide*, because they wanted to see
the Exposition of 1900. When the train was sliding
into the Gare de Lyons he sharply bade his wife
wipe her face with her handkerchief, which in those
days was the only way a good woman could deal with
shininess of the skin, since powder was still an un-
holy thing. And he was a little forgetful of her,
walked sometimes rather too fast for her short step,
as he moved dazed and speechless with emotion
about this extraordinary Exposition, which in its
exhibits and the buildings that housed them must
have been like a fantasy created by the gentleman
whose genius for the vigorous use of inappropriate
material led him, in the Victorian comic song, to cut
his throat with a lump of cheese. He turned his head
away from her when in the mornings he lay in bed
and day-dreamed of what might have happened if
his talent had not been hampered by obscure parent-

age and lack of fortune and an early marriage, of how he might have worn a red ribbon in his buttonhole and been kissed on both cheeks by great men with immense beards before a public that rose in applauding tiers to the furthest back seat conceivable by even such a mind when dreaming of an applauding public, of how duchesses bearing a close personal resemblance to greyhounds would have begged him to design houses for them, and more than that.

But quite often he was very glad that his wife was with him, particularly when they went into restaurants, and people seemed to be looking at his suit, which was being reflected in far too many mirrors at once. It was misery to be a provincial. But after all it was in the provinces that the true distinction of France was to be found. She agreed with him about that when he woke her about two in the morning to tell her; she consented to go home a day earlier than they had intended, although they had never had that afternoon he had promised her of just sitting in the Bois and watching the people drive by. And she stood by him always in the succeeding years when with the air of being a martyr to his art he engaged in ceaseless struggles with such of his clients as were gifted with some sense of the decorum of form and wanted things to look as if they were used for the purposes for which in fact they are. He was not without recognition of her goodness. If anything troubles him while he lies dying, which will happen in about ten years from now, after he has had a marvellous time being a beautiful old man and a genius who was too elevated to be accepted by his age, it will be that he was not thinking entirely of his wife when he designed the bedrooms of this villa where when one wakens one sees the tossing of green branches in the Empire mirrors over the mantelpieces, the high balconies where one drinks the morning coffee with the mimosa shaking fragrance at one with the golden feather-dusters of its bloom. The commissioning client in this case was a well-known playwright, and while designing it the architect had been much visited by dreams inspired by the classic view of the playwright's opportunities and privileges, of wasp-waisted tragediennes slowly closing immense ostrich fans and relaxing into a slow-motion surrender, of comediennes approaching the same considerations in a blither spirit, of taking the low road where the tragediennes take the high road and getting to heaven before them. This will probably have been his only infidelity.

Each of these romantically conceived bedrooms has its romantically conceived balcony; and there each of us lives till lunch-time. At eight o'clock in the morning one crawls out from under the white veil of the mosquito netting, on which infatuated flying beetles have hung all night; one puts on a dressing-gown and slippers and goes on to the balcony for one's coffee. There is never enough milk with it. That, oddly enough, is because the cook's father was a stone-mason. He came from Carrara to work in the porphyry quarries here and was killed a few days after his arrival. Jasmine, who was then four years old, had to go with her mother begging from door to door in a country where doors open not too easily to either aliens or beggars and hardly at all

334

to those who combine these characters. The consequence is that of the foods with which she was
acquainted at this time she is more than parsimonious.
Waste of them is associated in her mind with such
calamities that an enduring fear has been established.
I have to be firm to get a saucer of milk for the cat,
she short-rations us on bread, on macaroni, on cab-
bage. But I can have all the langoustes I care to pay
for, profusions of red mullet, of chicken, of caviare,
of Montrachet and Mersault of the best years. Her
fear has another grotesque and piteous effect on my
household economy, for when there are only the five
of us who live here at a meal there is ample of the
permitted food provided, but when there are guests I
have to go into the kitchen to make sure there is
enough. In those early days when the crust had to
be shared it was terrible, terrible. When I am ordering the meal her mouth smiles widely, showing teeth
that seem white as almonds in her brown face; volup-
tuously because she is imagining the taste of the food
she is going to cook: gaily because she likes the
excitement of new people coming, of going out into
the lane and looking at the make of their automobiles
and calculating their cost, peering round the corner
of the door at the women's dresses and enjoying the
pleasures of just judgment; proudly because she
knows the end of it will be deserved praise for her.
But her hot, black, brave eyes pucker up as if she
were frightened.

Over this little matter of milk for the morning
coffee she has her way, for nobody complains, because
of the sense of well-being we have on these high
shelves. Here the particular dead rat which this

puppy-like architect brings in in his mouth, expecting to be patted and called a good dog, is Pompeian classicism. There are white and terra-cotta stucco pillars, and stone seats, to sit on which one should wear a toga and must have a cushion, and balustrades of wrought iron, on which there climbs wisteria. That, however, is not so pleasing, since at this late season of the year it too powerfully suggests the standard design on which is laid down the life of the woman artist. In the spring it gave all its energy to the making of as much blossom as the trunk would carry, pendants of pale mauve flowers which look like an assemblage of butterflies as if they had been attracted by their fragrance instead of creating it, lovely, abundant, narcissistic. As the year drew on the flowers fell and it began to make leaves instead, the leaves which are the real business of trees. Now there are enough of these, they run everywhere, the extended growth of the plant is guaranteed, and as if it felt it again had leisure it puts out a second crop of flowers. They are a deeper and more beautiful purple, they have as exquisite and less volatile a scent; but half the buds never open, they are as different in texture from the early blossom as potpourri is from rose-leaves. There is above all an air of effort, for which no enrichment of quality could ever compensate. One thinks of the later work of Alice Meynell in its contrast to the first poems of her youth. But one does not see so much of the wisteria, one sets one's knees against it as one leans over the balustrade during the contemplative space after breakfast and before work, which here is prolonged to the furthest limits of conscience, and looks down on this garden that we keep entirely to ourselves, that we do not share with strangers any more than Orientals do, who lock their pleasances in the central courtyards of their homes.

For this garden which below seemed arid and to grow no crop but shadow, has its parterres and its verdancies as much as any garden, but on a different plane. It wears them not on its soil, but in its upper air. Here as down below the palm-trees are masters. Before all else one sees the orange date-clusters at the base of the hard-edged leaves; it might be that dark arms ringed with bracelets of red gold, sign of a tribe, raise their swords with hilts touching, sign of an oath. Round them and in among them are the mimosas, that are in all ways delicate, that have fluttering leaves like long fingers of narrow hands on little wrists explaining some fine meaning, that have small, trembling, sunshine-coloured flowers that look as if they would melt in the mouth if one should eat them, that shake with the bobbing movement which the dancing girl makes from the waist when her male partner lifts her high in the air. When the wind blows, and the palm trees brandish themselves, and the mimosas dip and rise, it is as when the negroes and the queens dance together in the ballet of Scheherazade. There are dark bushes set here and there to make one think of rest. There are acacias, a graceful species amusingly devitalized by sentimentality, this kind drooping its leaves with the grace of a young widow bowed in controllable grief, this one obscuring them with a smooth silver as of placid tears. They please, like the minor French novelists of the eighteenth century, by suggesting a universe in which nothing cuts deep. And round the garden as a palisade are the larches and firs, not shapely in form but offering many sorts of this blessed colour green, which is to the eye what water is to the mouth. White roses clamber out of the too absolute darkness beneath and hang in the more reasonable shadow on their arms in mats of flowers like the banners of an innocent army. Morning glories climb the fence and try to hypnotize the house with their blue stares; common as dirt they are, with their albino-eye pink centres, with their form as vulgar as a gramophone horn, with their nought-and-cross system of veining, but blue, bluer than the Mediterranean which runs like a second wall behind the tree-trunks, a further boundary to our delight; low-bred, imbecile, irresistible beauties.

All these things, and the scent which swings on the breeze from the mimosa tree to the balcony like a slim young trapeze acrobat, are one's own. This garden cannot be seen from any other villa; and no other villa has one like it. People can come to the house and can walk through the base of it without knowing that it is there. They need never know of it unless one likes them and takes them up on to the balconies to see it. Because of the secret garden in the architect's heart one has at last a secret garden. There is possibly nothing more necessary. To have a place full of delights and nothing but delights, which one does not have to explain and defend to people who have ideas unsympathetic to one, it is to economize the forces which keep one from ending like the wisteria, from committing the unpardonable sin of doing things with difficulty.

Not till lunch-time does one go downstairs; and there the spirit of the architect leaves one. He was not interested in the dining-room. He could not dream about it, because he really would have felt very strange sitting down to meals with anybody but his wife. But in the large high room to which in the end his collapsed fantasy declined, one's interest is taken over by the spirit of the dramatist whose house this is, who lets it furnished. The room is always dark. One opens the windows to let in the air, to admit the scent, so amusingly too sweet, so positively affable, which accumulates in a formless mass like a sand-heap round the oleanders; and one closes the shutters, all but one little slat which shows the cool blue-green fingers of the unsunned lower branches of the mimosas. As one's eyes get accustomed to the gloom there emerges the most amazing surrounding incongruity of furniture. Upstairs in the bedrooms all the furniture is good: old Provençal beds and cupboards and chests of drawers, cut in chestnut-wood warmly coloured as autumn, with sound workmanship though with a lack of appreciation of grace in form that is natural enough in a nation which does not set sufficient store on youth, which takes no notice of women under thirty, which with an insane logic gives them as much time to build up reputations of beauties as it gives men to build up their businesses. There are some of these noble solidities down here, but there are also horrors so dreadful that the architect would have adored them. There is a chaise-longue with a back shaped like a couch, painted with aluminium paint; there are chintzes on which crawl the many-coloured fruits of marriages between

339

flowers and centipedes, and statuettes everywhere, of
terra-cotta ladies wriggling bare shoulders and saying
they cannot do a thing with their hair the day after
they have washed it, of Joan of Arc sitting listening
with that exasperated air of a young French woman
in charge of an office, as if she did wish the voices
wouldn't shout, and would speak at more regular
hours; and of children giving each other flowers with
such an insincere yet unctuous air that one suspects
a mutual agreement to go out and torture the cat the
minute the sitting is over.

It is an inconsistency which was completely explained when one found in a reference book that the
dramatist had married twice. What was not so easily
explained was the finding in one of those old wooden
wall-cupboards in which the Provençals kept their
salt and their matches, things no bigger than holy-
water stoups and naïvely carved, of a finely worked
female garment, of a kind that is well to wear but
which it is possible to go home without. But of
course there was widowerhood. When the servant
found it on the morning after the party she did not
like to take it to her master; she did not take it for
herself, because she was honest and left alone what
belonged to other people, also because she was virtuous and did not like touching anything to do with a
girl of that sort, also because she was robust and it
would not have fitted her. One wonders when the
loser noticed the loss, and if she was sufficiently
economist to put it down in her little notebook under
the proper head of dilapidations. He should have
married her. The pattern of the lace is very discreet,
she would have been loyal to the first, the correct

furniture. The second wife's clothes may always
have come home to roost, but for all that she was no
comfort to a man; she loved things, and the wrong
things at that. It is probably she who will not let the
old man sell the house, although he needs the money,
for his pieces no longer hold the stage.

One perceives, on the evidence of this furniture,
the marriages, the garment, why that would be so.
His was the converse of the architect's case. That
other, whom almost anybody would call a donkey,
who was totally unable to learn what nearly all the
rest of mankind masters easily, had yet the prime
necessity of the artist, for he had idiosyncrasy; that is
to say, there was the nucleus of a creative vortex in
his mind, a spot where his individual vision of reality
had become dynamic, was swirling around the general
matter of his mental being so that it was precipitat-
ing in significant forms. But this dramatist, whom
nobody in the world could call a donkey, was unable
to do anything except learn what the rest of mankind
has mastered. He has no idiosyncrasy, because he
had no individual vision of reality to become dynamic,
being one of those abject souls who do not aspire to
one, who are agitated by the lower problem of giving
the right reflexes to reality, who are all the time looking round nervously to see if they are giving the
same ones as other people whom they modestly conceive to be their betters. It was his ambition to write
plays because in the happy laughter of a theatre audience one can get the most immediate and numerically
impressive guarantee that there is nothing in one's
mind which is not familiar to the mass of persons
living at the time.

His passion for the average showed in his wives. When he was a young man he had not the hardihood to marry a young girl, in case they should make the mistakes of youth together, for youth and its folly are in the nature of special cases, since the majority of human beings alive at any one time are middle-aged and sensible. So he married a woman older than himself. To make quite sure that his vitality, in which he took no pride since it was not the common lot, was counterbalanced, he chose one whose light was dimmed by temperament as well as years. Her desire to furnish her house with pedantically chosen furniture not so suitable to a modern home as to evoke visions of ancient Provence, with these old salt and taper cupboards, the wooden bird-cages in which they used to keep the bread, the tables on which they kneaded it, showed her to be of the same type which gratifies an instinctive recession by reading only quiet memoirs, diaries whose sole interest is that they are dated long ago. He was thereby laying up for himself a bereavement that came too early, which was sad. And it was sad too that in his second marriage also he had to placate his respect for the average. For he married this young and coarse woman because he was getting old, and because he feared that his age was giving him an involuntary etherealism; and still it remained true that the majority of human beings are middle-aged and sensible. This respect brought him no compensating rewards in his work. For it takes such enormous energy to master the innumerable superficial reactions of the crowd in any particular decade that one has none left to adapt oneself to the changes which take place in the next. So his pieces are no longer played; it is we who are living in his villa.

For all its implications it is a good room to sit in, to smell the oleander, to look at the mimosa, to eat *bœuf à la mode* embedded in a jelly which is a mixture of magnificences like a sunset; and to call Jasmine into later, to congratulate her and ask for the recipe. Her face is at once animated and heavy with undischarged genius as she says, 'It's nothing, it's quite easy to make, the only thing is that it takes about five hours and it has to be watched very carefully.' Then her eye wanders past one, her hand darts out like a sting, and she cries out, 'The forest fire! Look, it has started again!' One turns about in one's chair and sees that the pool of sunshine between the two doors is the colour of a ginger cat. True enough, that means that somewhere some sublime valley is being laid waste as by war, and that for the rest of the day the sunward side of the sky will be a half-sphere of tortoise-shell, and the sea bruise green. Jasmine goes on, 'It must be the same fire that started last night. It's burned all the village where we get our honey.' She says it with an accent of terrible joy, of simultaneous consummation of fear and desire. One perceives that again and again she has destroyed her life when it was forming into shapes of happiness because of her loyalty to her early misery, her conviction that that has the sanction of ultimate reality, and that beside it all other things are trivial. 'It must be spreading, it must be spreading fast. What shall we do? We will have to get the fishermen to row us out to sea.' Her eyes shine. So Turner wanted the world to go up in fire. She continues to look out into the discoloured sunlight with a smiling fixity, until her fingers begin to work. In the meantime she must do something perfect. She says, 'Don't go out to tea. I'm going to make you a cake. With potato flour, that's lightest.'

Opening
doors to
the World
of books

**Book
Tokens**

Book Tokens
can be
bought and
exchanged
at most
bookshops